Duplicate Death

Author of over fifty books, Georgette Heyer is one of the best-known and best-loved of all historical novelists, making the Regency period her own. Her first novel, *The Black Moth*, published in 1921, was written at the age of fifteen to amuse her convalescent brother; her last was *My Lord John*. Although most famous for her historical fiction, she also wrote twelve mystery novels. Georgette Heyer died in 1974 at the age of seventy-one.

Praise for Georgette Heyer

'We . . . had better start ranking Heyer alongside such incomparable whodunit authors as Christie, Marsh, Tey and Allingham' – *San Francisco Chronicle*

'Georgette Heyer is second to none in her ability to make detective stories entertaining' – *Sunday Times*

D1463645

Available in Arrow Books by Georgette Heyer

The Historical Novels

The Black Moth	Simon the Coldheart
These Old Shades	Beauvallet
Powder and Patch	The Masqueraders
Devil's Cub	The Conqueror
An Infamous Army	The Convenient Marriage
The Talisman Ring	Regency Buck
Royal Escape	The Corinthian
Faro's Daughter	The Spanish Bride
The Reluctant Widow	Friday's Child
The Foundling	Arabella
The Quiet Gentleman	The Grand Sophy
The Toll-Gate	Cotillion
Sprig Muslin	Bath Tangle
Sylvester	April Lady
The Unknown Ajax	Venetia
A Civil Contract	Pistols for Two
False Colours	The Nonesuch
Black Sheep	Frederica
Charity Girl	Cousin Kate
My Lord John	Lady of Quality

The Mystery Novels

Footsteps in the Dark	Why Shoot a Butler?
The Unfinished Clue	Death in the Stocks
Behold, Here's Poison	They Found Him Dead
A Blunt Instrument	No Wind of Blame
Envious Casca	Penhallow
Duplicate Death	Detection Unlimited

GEORGETTE HEYER

Duplicate Death

arrow books

Published in the United Kingdom by Arrow Books in 2006

1 3 5 7 9 10 8 6 4 2

Copyright © Georgette Rougier, 1951

Georgette Heyer has asserted her right under the Copyright, Designs
and Patents Act, 1988 to be identified as the author of this work

First published in the United Kingdom in 1951 by William Heinemann Ltd

Arrow Books
The Random House Group Limited
20 Vauxhall Bridge Road, London SW1V 2SA

www.randomhouse.co.uk

Addresses for companies within The Random House Group Lmited can be found
at: www.randomhouse.co.uk/offices.htm

The Random House Group Limited Reg. No. 954009

A CIP catalogue record for this book
is available from the British Library

ISBN 9780099550358

The Random House Group Limited supports The Forest
Stewardship Council (FSC), the leading international forest
certification organisation. All our titles that are printed on
Greenpeace approved FSC certified paper carry the FSC logo.
Our paper procurement policy can be found at
www.rbooks.co.uk/environment.

Typeset by SX Composing DTP, Rayleigh, Essex
Printed in the UK by CPI Bookmarque, Croydon, CR0 4TD

This book having been written in response to the representations of certain members of the Bench and Bar is therefore dedicated to them with the Author's humble duty.

One

There were several promising-looking letters in the pile laid on Mrs James Kane's virgin breakfast-plate on Monday morning, but, having sorted all the envelopes with the air of one expectant of discovering treasure-trove, she extracted two addressed to her in hands indicative either of illiteracy or of extreme youth. One was tastefully inscribed in red ink; the other appeared to have been written with a crossed nib trailing a hair. Both were addressed to Mr and Mrs James Kane, but the incorporation of her husband's style with her Own Mrs Kane very properly ignored. Both missives would undoubtedly open with the formula: *Dear Mummy and Daddy*, but any share in their contents to which Mr James Kane could lay claim would be indicated by the words: '*Tell Daddy*'. Such information as was conveyed under this heading would be of a sporting nature. Urgent needs, ranging from money for the defraying of unforeseen and inescapable expenses to the instant forwarding of possessions only to be found after several days of intensive and exhausting search, would be addressed, with rare prescience, to Mummy.

So it had been since the grim day of Master Silas James Kane's departure, at the age of eight, to his preparatory school in the West; so it was on this Monday morning in February, although Master Silas Kane was beginning to take more than an aloof interest in such trials of knowledge as the Common Entrance Examination; and his junior, Master Adrian Timothy Kane, had been for several terms pleasurably employed in upholding the tradition set for him at St Cyprian's of throwing himself wholeheartedly into all the more violent athletic pursuits, baiting unpopular masters, and doing as little work as was compatible with physical comfort. Had she been asked to do so, Mrs James Kane could have supplied the enquirer with a very fair paraphrase of either of her elder sons' letters, but this circumstance in no way detracted from the avidity with which she searched through Monday's post, or the satisfaction with which she perused the two documents that made Monday a red-letter day.

Neither contributed much to her knowledge of her offspring's mental or physical well-being. An anxious question addressed to Master Adrian on the subject of an unidentified pain which might, or might not, turn out to be a grumbling appendix had been left unanswered, together with an urgent command to Master Silas to *Find out from Mr Kentmere when half-term will be so that Daddy and I can make arrangements to come down*. Both young gentlemen would have been much distressed by a failure on the part of their parents to put in an appearance at this function, but thus early in the term their minds were preoccupied with more pressing matters, chief amongst which was the need to replace the bath-sponge of one Bolton-Bagby,

2

'*which*', wrote Master Adrian Kane, '*got chucked out of the window of Big Dorm.*'

Mr James Kane, regaled with this passage, grinned, and said: 'Young devil! What's Silas got to say?'

Mrs James Kane, in loving accents, read aloud the letter from her first-born. It opened with a pious hope that his parents were enjoying good health; adjured her to tell Daddy that '*we had a match against St Stephen's, we won 15-nil, they were punk*'; requested the instant despatch of an envelope containing such examples of the stamp-engraver's art as were known to him as 'my swops'; and informed his mother that owing to the thievish habits of some person or persons unknown a new pair of fives-gloves was urgently required. A disarming bracket added the words: *if you can manage it*; and a postscript conveyed kindly words of encouragement to his sister Susan, and his infant-brother William.

'So *they're* all right!' said Mrs Kane, restoring both these interesting communications to their envelopes.

Mr Kane did not ask her on what grounds she based this pronouncement. Since his post had contained a demand from the Commissioners of Inland Revenue which anyone less well-acquainted with this body of persons might have supposed to have been an infelicitous essay in broad humour, his son's request for new fives-gloves fell on hostile ears. He delivered himself of a strongly-worded condemnation of his wife's foolish practice of bringing up her children in the belief that their father was a millionaire. When she grew tired of listening to him, Mrs Kane said simply: 'All right, I'll tell him he can't have them.'

Mr James Kane was a gentleman of even temper, but

at these wifely words he cast upon his helpmate a glance of loathing, and said that he supposed he would have to see to it himself. He then passed his cup to her for more coffee, adding bitterly that Silas grew more like his half-uncle Timothy every day.

'Talking of Timothy,' said Mrs Kane, returning to the perusal of a letter covering several sheets of paper, 'I've got a long letter from your mother.'

'Oh?' said Mr Kane, sufficiently interested to suspend the opening of the newspaper. 'Does she say how Adrian is?'

'No, she doesn't mention him – oh yes, she does! "*Tell Jim I am relying on him to help me to spare Adrian any unnecessary anxiety. He is frailer than I like, and this wretched weather is doing him no good.*"'

Mr Kane held his stepfather in considerable affection, but his response to this lacked enthusiasm. 'If Timothy's up to mischief again, and Mother thinks I'm going to remonstrate with him, there's nothing doing!' he said.

'Darling Jim, you know perfectly well you'll have to, if he really is entangled with some frightful creature. I must say, it does sound pretty dire!'

'My dear girl, I've already heard all about the dizzy blonde from Mother!' said Mr Kane, opening *The Times*. 'Mother doesn't like her style, or her background, or anything about her, and I daresay she's quite right. But why she has to go into a flap every time Timothy makes a mild pass at some good-looking wench is something I shall never fathom.' He folded the paper to his satisfaction, and began to fill a pipe before settling down to a happy ten minutes with Our Golf Correspondent. 'You're just as bad,' he added severely. 'You both of you

4

behave as though Timothy were a kid in his first year at Cambridge. Well, I don't hold any brief for young Timothy, but I should call him a pretty hard-boiled specimen, myself. What's more, he's twenty-seven, and if he can't protect himself from designing blondes now he never will.'

'Anyone would think, to hear you, that you didn't care what became of him!' remarked Mrs Kane. 'Besides, it isn't the blonde: it's another girl.'

'Fast worker!' observed Mr Kane.

Mrs Kane paid no heed to this, but went on reading her mother-in-law's letter, a frown slowly gathering between her brows. She looked up at the end, and said seriously: 'Jim, really this isn't funny! He's going to marry her!'

'Timothy?' said Mr Kane incredulously. 'Rot!'

'He told your mother so himself.'

'But who is she?'

'That's just it. Your mother says she can't discover *who* she is. She doesn't seem to have a single relative, or any sort of a background. Her name,' said Mrs Kane, consulting Lady Harte's letter, 'is Beulah Birtley. Your mother says that she hopes she isn't a snob – yes, all right, there's no need to make that noise! It isn't being snobbish to want to know what sort of people your son's wife springs from! – Anyway, she says she wouldn't mind if only she knew *something* about the girl, or even liked her.'

'Has Mother actually met her?'

'Yes, at Timothy's chambers. She says she can't imagine what Timothy sees in her, because she isn't in the least his type, hasn't any manners, and is obviously up to no good. In fact, she says Adventuress is written all over her.'

5

'Good lord!' said Mr Kane. 'But, look here, this is cockeyed! Not a month ago Mother was having the shudders over the blonde beauty, and telling us what hell Timothy would have with Mrs Haddington, or whatever her name was, for a mother-in-law. When did he pick up this new number?'

'At the Haddingtons'. She's Mrs Haddington's secretary. Your mother says that she found her definitely hostile, and she's convinced that there's something thoroughly shady about her. She says she hasn't said a word about it to Sir Adrian, because the girl is just the type he would dislike, and she won't have him worried. Apparently the engagement isn't official yet. Here, you can read her letter for yourself!'

Mr Kane laid aside *The Times*, and read through five close-written pages with what his wife considered maddening deliberation. He then folded the letter and handed it back to her.

'Well?' she said impatiently.

'I can't say it sounds good,' he replied. 'However, you've only got Mother's word for all this, and if you've seen the damsel she thinks worthy of Timothy I can only say I haven't.'

'No, but don't you think it's odd for a girl meeting her future mother-in-law not even to mention her own parents?'

'May have been shy.'

'Nonsense! There's something fishy about her, Jim, and you know it!'

'I don't know any such thing, and if I did, what the hell do you think I can do about it? I'm not Timothy's keeper!'

'No, but you're years older than he is, and you know how he's always adored you, and looked up to you!'

'My good girl,' said Mr Kane revolted. 'I may have been a hero to Timothy when he was a kid – not that he ever gave much sign of venerating me – but that's years ago!'

'Of course I didn't mean he still looks on you as a sort of demigod, but he's awfully fond of you, Jim!'

'He'd need to be if he was going to put up with me barging into his affairs,' said Mr Kane grimly.

'Jim, you must try to do something! You can't pretend you want Timothy to make a muck of his life! It's no use saying he's hard-boiled, and old enough to take care of himself: being a Commando doesn't make a boy worldly-wise! If you don't care, I do! Obviously he's making a fool of himself, but I shall never forget how angelic he was to me all through that ghastly Dunkirk time, and how he gave up two whole days of his leave to come and see me in that disgusting place I took the children to when you were in Italy. He tried to teach Silas to catch a ball, too, which was quite futile, because the poor sweet was far too young!' She added in a besotted tone: 'He *did* look such a pet!'

'Now, look here!'

'Not Timothy: Silas, of course! Anyway, you can't just do nothing, Jim! You ought to try and find out something about this girl. Couldn't you go up to London, and *see* them?'

'I am going to London next week, and the chances are I shall look in on Timothy, but as for doing any private sleuthing – I suppose next you'll be wanting me to set a detective agency on to the unfortunate wench!'

7

'Well, if you thought there really was something fishy about her – !' said Mrs Kane dubiously.

At this moment, and before Mr James Kane could put his indignation into words, they were interrupted by the entrance of Miss Susan Kane, Master William Kane, and the despot who ruled over the entire Kane family.

'Good-morning, Daddy and Mummy!' said this lady, apparently speaking for all. 'Here we are, come to kiss Daddy and Mummy good-morning!'

So saying, she dumped Master William Kane upon his mother's lap, for she was not one to grudge parents a share in their children, and smiled indulgently upon Miss Kane's demand for a *canard*. She then swept up the hearth, straightened a chair, and said in a voice of unabated cheerfulness: 'I'm afraid we've got some bad news for you this morning, Mummy, for I said to Winnie as soon as I heard, there's no sense in worrying Mrs Kane before she's had her breakfast, I said, and we all know Daddy likes to have his breakfast in peace, don't we?' Here she caught sight of *The Times*, which Mr Kane had allowed to slip to the floor, picked it up, refolded it, and laid it down well out of his reach.

Mr Kane, engaged in the matutinal duty of trying to teach his ecstatic daughter to balance a lump of sugar on her nose, paused to cast a sneaking glance across the table at his wife. Mrs Kane smiled in what she hoped was a soothing way, well-knowing that at the earliest opportunity she would be informed that she might take her choice between That Woman and her loving spouse. In moments of acute stress, Mr Kane had been known to threaten to take matters into his own hands, saying that he failed to see why he should be treated in his own house

8

as if he were a cross between an imbecile and a two-year-old. He added that if the infernal woman called him Daddy once more he would not be responsible for the consequences. Fortunately for the smooth-running of the house he was either too much in awe of Nanny to put his threats into execution, or too well-aware of the irreplaceable nature of her services. For Nanny, a tower of smiling strength in time of war, rose to fresh heights when the horrors of peace sapped what little vitality was left in her employers. The Kanes, returning to take up their interrupted residence in one wing of a mansion inherited by Mr James Kane from his grandmother, prohibited by excessive taxation from giving employment to the eight or nine persons necessary for the upkeep of the house and its grounds, found in the highly-trained and starched ruler of their nurseries a Treasure whose brassy cheerfulness rose triumphant above every domestic crisis. If the cook left, having heard that she could earn three times her present wages in London without being obliged to prepare more than two dinners in the week, London employers being easily terrorised into eating most of their meals at expensive restaurants, Nanny would laugh in a jolly way, say that what could not be cured must be endured, and if Mummy would give an eye to the children she would see what could be done. If Winnie, who was the house-maid, and mentally defective, but not (said Nanny bracingly) so as you would notice, became incapable through the agony caused by one of the teeth which she obstinately refused to have drawn, Nanny would sit up all night, ministering to the sufferer. Unresponsive to new ideas, Nanny, having listened with at least half an ear to the progressive doctrine of

9

Maximum Wages for Minimum Work, dismissed it by saying That was as might be, but Talk wouldn't get the silver cleaned. It spoke volumes for her personality that the exponent of this noble doctrine only expressed her contempt for such retrograde ideas by a sniff, and a flounce, and then applied herself to the burnishing of spoons and forks.

This extremely trying paragon now said, with the air of one recounting a humorous anecdote: 'Yes, Mummy, That Florrie hasn't come this morning, which doesn't surprise me in the least, her being paid by the week like she is, and it being Monday and all. No loss, is what I say, for really, if I was to tell you some of the things she did, but the least said the soonest mended, and no good crying over spilt milk! So I thought I would just pop Bill in his pram presently and walk down to the village to see if Mrs Formby would oblige till you get suited, Mummy, though why Oblige is more than I can tell, considering what you pay her, but what I say is, it won't do if Cook, was to get Upset, and Susan will like to go down to the village, won't you, ducky? Oh, dear, dear, look at those sticky handy-pandys, and every drop of hot water to be boiled on account of Jackson forgetting to stoke the boiler before he went off home last night! Really, one doesn't hardly like to say what the world is coming to! Yes, Mummy, Mrs Formby it must be, but if I was you I would put an advertisement in the *Glasgow Herald*, because, say what you like, those Scotch girls are *clean*, which is more than we can say about some others, whose names we won't mention, not in present company, will we, my ducks?'

Unable to bear any more of this excellent creature's

discourse, Mr James Kane rose from the table, with the slight awkwardness peculiar to those who had left the better parts of their left legs to be decently interred in enemy soil. What Mr James Kane secretly thought of his loss he had divulged to none, his only recorded utterance on the subject being a pious thanksgiving to Providence that he had an artificial leg to raise him, in the eyes of his progeny, above the spurious claims to distinction of their Uncle Timothy. But Mrs James Kane, to whom the sight of Daddy Putting on his Leg was not a Treat of the first order, could never see this slight awkwardness without suffering a contraction of the heart, and she now said, quickly, and quite irrationally: 'Never mind about Timothy! *Must* you go to town next week?'

Mr James Kane, perfectly appreciating the cause of this sudden *volte face*, grinned affectionately at her, limped round the table to bestow a chaste salute upon her cheek, said, *Goop*! in a fond voice, and departed to pursue his avocation in the neighbouring metropolis. From which Mrs Kane gathered that the loss of a limb was troubling him neither mentally nor physically, that he had every intention of visiting London in the immediate future, and that he would use his best endeavours to dissuade his young half-brother from contracting an undesirable alliance. She was thus able to devote her mind to the domestic problem confronting her, for whatever Jim might say he possessed great influence over Timothy, and would no doubt contrive at least to avert disaster.

In these comfortable conclusions Mrs James Kane might have been proved to have been right if Lady Harte had enlisted her help rather earlier, or had Mr Kane put forward his journey to London. In the event, Mr James

Kane reached London in time only to take part in proceedings of which, as he vulgarly informed his wife, he had already, during the course of a singularly blameless life, had a bellyful.

Two

'Have an éclair!' suggested young Mr Harte encouragingly. 'Probably made with egg-substitute, certainly filled with synthetic cream, guaranteed rather to atrophy than to increase the figure.'

His companion, who had been sitting in brooding silence for several minutes, looked up, smiled, and shook her head. 'No, thanks. I'm not afraid of getting fat.'

'Well, that's something,' said Timothy. 'What a repellent joint this is!'

'What do you mean?' she asked quickly.

'That which repels. A table which is not only too small, but which stands on unequal legs; rout chairs, than which there is nothing less conducive to habits of easy social intercourse; a general atmosphere of mob-cappery; and –'

'Not that. Why is it something that I'm not afraid of getting fat?'

'Oh, merely that it's the only thing I've discovered, to date, which you're not afraid of!'

For a moment her rather stormy grey eyes lifted to his in a wide, startled look; then they were lowered, and she said in a hard voice: 'Don't be absurd!'

'Of course, I don't mean that there is nothing else you're not afraid of,' said Timothy conversationally. 'Only that I haven't yet discovered what these things are. Have some more tea!'

'I'm not going to marry you,' said Beulah abruptly.

'Announcements like that,' said Mr Harte, not noticeably abashed, 'should never be made in crowded tea-shops. Besides, it isn't true.'

'It is true! I can't possibly marry you! I ought to have seen that at the start!'

'Why? Have you got a husband who's an RC and won't give you a divorce, or any little thing like that?' enquired Timothy, interested.

'No, of course not!'

'Oh, well, then we needn't worry!'

'That's what you think!' said Beulah crudely. 'Look here, I – the thing is – There are things in my life you don't know anything about!'

'Good God, I should hope there were!' retorted Timothy. 'I've only known you a month!'

'And some of them you wouldn't like!'

'I daresay. Come to think of it, I can tell you of one thing in your young life I don't like right now, and that's Mr Daniel Seaton-Carew.'

She flushed. 'He's not a thing in my life: you needn't worry!'

'That's fine. Dissuade him from putting his arm round you, and calling you his little protégée.'

Her colour was still heightened; she kept her eyes on her plate. 'It's only his way. He's old enough to be my father!'

'Yes, that's what makes it all the more objectionable,' said Timothy.

She bit her lip, but said in a sulky voice: 'Anyway, it's got nothing to do with you.'

'It has everything to do with me. You have plighted your troth to me, my girl.'

'It's no use. I can't marry you.'

'Then I shall sue you for breach of promise. Why, by the way, have you had this sudden change of heart?'

'It isn't possible. I must have been crazy! I can't think why you want to marry me!'

'Good lord, didn't I tell you? I love you!'

She muttered: 'Yes, you told me. That's what I – what I don't understand! Why should you?'

'Oh, I shouldn't worry over that, if I were you!' said Timothy kindly. 'Of course, if you insist, I'll enumerate the various things which attract me to you, but they really haven't got much to do with it. To be thoroughly vulgar, we just clicked. Or didn't we?'

Her face quivered; she gave a rather convulsive nod. 'Yes, but –'

'There you are, then. You know, for an intelligent girl, you say some remarkably stupid things. You'd be properly stymied if I asked you what you saw in me to fall in love with, wouldn't you?'

A flicker of humour shone in her eyes. 'No, I shouldn't,' she replied. 'Anyone can see what I fell for at a glance! Exactly what about fifty other girls have fallen for!'

'You are exaggerating,' said Mr Harte, preserving his sang-froid. 'Not much, of course, but slightly. Forty-three is the correct number, and that includes my niece. I'm afraid she may not take very kindly to our marriage, by the way. She says she is going to marry me herself, but of course that's impossible. If we had only lived in medieval times I could have got a dispensation, I expect. As it is –'

'You are a fool!' interrupted Miss Birtley, laughing in spite of herself. 'Nor do I think that your niece is the only member of your family who wouldn't take kindly to our marriage.'

'You never know. It's within the bounds of possibility that your family may not take kindly to me.'

'I have no family,' she said harshly.

'What, none at all?'

'I have an uncle, and his wife. I don't have anything to do with them.'

'What a bit of luck for me!' said Mr Harte. 'I was rather funking being shown to a clutter of aunts and cousins. My half-brother says it's hell. He had to go through the mill. Said his hands and feet seemed too large suddenly, and whenever he thought out a classy line to utter it turned out to be the one thing he oughtn't to have said.'

'Like me with your mother.'

'Not in the least like that. I distinctly recall that you said how-do-you-do to Mamma, and I seem to remember that you made one unprompted and, I am bound to say, innocuous remark about the evils of progress as exemplified by pneumatic-drills. The rest of your conversation was monosyllabic.'

There was an awful pause. 'Well, there you are!' said Miss Birtley defiantly. 'I *have* no conversation!'

'I have no wish to appear boastful,' returned young Mr Harte, 'but from my earliest days it has been said of me by all who know me best that I talk enough for two, or even more.'

'Your mother,' said Miss Birtley, giving him a straight

look, 'wrote me down as an adventuress, and that is exactly what I am! So now you know! My aim is to marry a man of good social standing, independent means, and a background. That's why I encouraged you to propose to me.'

'Is it really?' said Mr Harte. 'Then why on earth did you waste your time on me, instead of gunning for our newest and most socialistic peer?'

Miss Birtley's air of slightly belligerent gravity was momentarily impaired. 'Are you talking about Lance Guisborough? Well, if he ever cleaned his nails, or got his hair cut –'

'My good girl,' said Mr Harte severely, 'if you are going to let little things like that weigh with you, you will never get anywhere! Tut-tut, I thought better of you! What were you thinking about to waste your time entrapping me into matrimony when there was a whole, live baron waiting to be picked up? Or have you been misinformed? I shall, at what I trust may be some far distant date, inherit a baronetcy; but when you talk of independent means, you are speaking outside the book. Lawyers and clients being what they are, I am at this present very happy to appear in the dingiest of police-courts for the modest fee of three-and-one, or even less; my well-groomed air of affluence being due to the generosity of my Papa, who makes me a handsome allowance. This is what comes of judging by appearances. I don't say that Guisborough is a rich man, but you should remember that a bird in the hand is worth two in the bush; and many a promising Communist has been persuaded by a good woman's influence to cut his hair, and abstain from wearing fancy ties.'

'Oh, Timothy, *do* shut up!' begged Beulah. 'Besides, he's one of Cynthia Haddington's admirers!'

'Well, considering the number of times you've cast it in my teeth that I too was one of her admirers, I can't see what that's got to do with it.'

'So you were!' said Beulah, with a touch of spirit. 'If you hadn't been pursuing her, we should never have met!'

Mr Harte sighed. 'If dancing three times with a girl to whom one had been presented at a private party, subsequently accepting an invitation to a ball given by her mother, and following this up with a civil call to return thanks, constitutes pursuit, I plead guilty,' he said.

'At all events,' said Beulah somewhat viciously, 'Mrs Haddington regards you as the best of the eligibles! And if she knew I was having tea with you now she would probably give me the sack!'

'In that case, you trot straight back to Charles Street, ducky, and tell her!' recommended Mr Harte. 'Pausing only to pay the bill here, I will burst off to procure a special licence so that we can be married tomorrow. You shall beguile some long winter's evening for me by recounting to me the circumstances which induced you to take a job as dog's body to that well-preserved corncrake.'

'If you want to know,' responded Miss Birtley, 'Dan Seaton-Carew got me the job! *Now* how do you feel about marrying me?'

'Shaken but staunch. Seriously, how *did* that woman muscle on to the fringe of decent society?'

'I don't know, but I *think* she was sort of sponsored by Lady Nest Poulton,' said Beulah. 'They're very thick, that I *do* know.'

'What times we do live in, to be sure! Poor old Greystoke has had to sell his place, of course, but I shouldn't have thought an Ellerbeck would have stooped quite as low.'

'That *must* be a thoroughly unfair remark!' said Beulah. 'I know nothing about Lord Greystoke's circumstances, but everyone knows that Lady Nest's husband is rolling!'

'Just what I was thinking,' agreed Timothy. 'So what's the tie-up?'

'Why should there be a tie-up?'

'Because, my sweet, feather-headed nit-wit though she may be, and indeed is, the Lady Nest doesn't make a bosom-friend of a brassy-haired widow on the up-and-up without having some strong inducement so to do.'

'And they say women are spiteful!' exclaimed Beulah scornfully. 'Do you also imagine there's a tie-up between her and Dan Seaton-Carew? She's a friend of his as well.'

'Good God!' said Timothy. 'I wonder if there's any insanity in the Ellerbecks?'

'Seaton-Carew is considered to be rather an attractive type.'

'What does he attract? Pond-life?'

'Apparently, Lady Nest Poulton – if you call her a form of pond-life.'

'No, but an unsteady type. Sort of woman who used to go to Limehouse for a thrill in the wicked twenties. That may be it, of course – though I should rather describe your Charles Street set-up as a menagerie.'

'Really, Timothy!' she expostulated. 'Lots of perfectly respectable people come to the house!'

'I will grant you a sprinkling of fairly harmless types, who probably feel that if Lady Nest knows Mrs Haddington she must be all right –'

'You don't suppose that Colonel Cartmel or Sir Roderick Vickerstown would be influenced by that, do you?'

'No, my love, I don't. It is well-known that both these aged crocodiles will lend the *cachet* of their presence to almost any house where the food and the wines are first-class. Does your respected employer buy exclusively on the black market?'

'If I knew I shouldn't tell you. After all, she does employ me!'

'So she does. What, by the way, is your precise status in the house? Yes, I know she calls you her secretary, but you appear to me to spend half your time chasing round London with a shopping-list.'

'Well, I do do her secretarial work, only, of course, there isn't a great deal of it, so I shop for her as well, and see that things are all right when she gives a party, and – oh, anything that crops up!'

'And what,' enquired Mr Harte politely, 'are your hours?'

'I don't have regular hours. I'm supposed to leave at six but Mrs Haddington likes me to be on tap.'

'Does she, indeed? You must be pulling down a colossal screw!'

Beulah gave a rather bitter little laugh. 'Unfortunately I don't belong to a Union! I get three pounds ten a week – and quite a number of meals. If another female is wanted, with the family; if not, on a tray in the library. Which I prefer!'

She glanced up, and found that Mr Harte's very blue eyes were fixed on her face in an uncomfortably searching look.

'Why do you stick it?' he asked. 'Your employer, to put it frankly, is a bitch; she treats you like mud; and you're at her beck and call, from morning till midnight. What's the big idea?'

'It suits me,' she said evasively. 'Jobs aren't so easily come by these days.' She said, too swiftly changing the subject: 'Are you coming to the Bridge-party?'

'Yes, are you?'

'I shall be there, of course. Not playing.'

'That goes without saying. Who's going to be there? The usual gang?'

'I think so. Eleven tables, plus one or two people who are coming either as scorers, or just to watch. Lady Nest is bringing her husband, which will make it a red-letter evening. Generally he never comes near Charles Street.'

'And who shall blame him? I needn't ask if the dashing Dan Seaton-Carew will be present?'

'Of course he will be. Look here, Timothy, are you – do you imagine you've any cause to be jealous of him? Because, if so, get rid of the idea! I thought at first that there was some kind of a liaison between him and Mrs Haddington, but I seem to have been wrong: it's Cynthia he's after.'

'Satyrs and Nymphs. What a repulsive thought! Let us hope it is but a fleeting fancy. I shouldn't think he was a marrying man: his tastes are too – er – catholic. However, if he's spreading his charm over the Shining Beauty, that would no doubt account for the display of temperament young Sydney Butterwick treated the company to on the night we were bidden to Charles Street to listen to the Stalham String Quartet.'

'You are disgusting!' said Beulah.

'It wasn't I who was disgusting,' Timothy replied. 'Not that disgusting is the word I should have chosen to have described any of it. I'm all for light relief, I am, besides being very broad-minded.'

'Broad-minded!'

'Yes, but not broad-minded enough to stomach the Charles Street ménage as a setting for the girl I'm going to marry.'

'You do think I'm an innocent flower, don't you?'

'Yes, and that in spite of all your endeavours to convince me that you have been a hardened woman of the world for years.'

She shrugged. 'It's not my fault if you persist in cherishing illusions. I told you that you knew nothing about me.'

'Oh, not quite as little as that!' said Timothy cheerfully. 'I know, for instance, that at some time or another you've taken a nasty knock which has led you to suppose that the world is against you. Also that you have quarrelled with your relations; and that beneath your not-entirely convincing air of having been hard-boiled early in life you are more than a little scared.'

'Scared? Why should I be scared?' she asked sharply.

'That,' he replied, 'I do not know, and do not propose to ask you. I am quite content to wait for the day when your woman's instinct tells you that I am a fit and proper person to confide in.'

She rose abruptly to her feet, gathering up her gloves and her handbag, and saying: 'I must go. I'd no idea it was so late. Don't come with me! I – I'd rather you didn't!'

Three

The house in Charles Street which was rented by Mrs Haddington differed externally hardly at all from its neighbours, but was distinguished internally, according to young Mr Harte, by an absence of individual taste which made it instantly remarkable. Nothing in the furnishing of its lofty rooms suggested occupation. From the careful arrangement of expensive flowers in the various bowls to the selection of illustrated periodicals, neatly laid out on a low table before the drawing-room fire, the house reminded the visitor of nothing so much as an advertisement of some high-class furnishing emporium. Sofas and chairs of the most luxurious order were upholstered in the same material which masked the tall windows, and were provided with cushions which, embellished with large tassels, were exactly placed, and incessantly plumped up, either by her butler, or by Mrs Haddington herself.

The entrance hall and the staircase were carpeted with eau-de-nil pile. A Regency sidetable stood under a mirror framed in gilt, and was flanked by two Sheraton chairs whose seats were upholstered in the exact shade of green to match the carpet. A door on the right of this broad passage opened into the dining-room – mahogany and wine-red brocade – and beyond the discreet door which gave access to the basement-stairs was one leading into an apartment built out at the back of the house and furnished as a library. Two tall windows, fitted with interior shutters, and draped with curtains of studious brown velvet, looked out at right-angles to the dining-room on to a yard transformed into a paved garden with a sundial and several flower-beds, which displayed, at the appropriate seasons, either daffodils, or geraniums. Standard authors in handsome bindings lined the walls; a massive knee-hole desk, bearing a blotter covered in tooled leather, a mahogany knife-box converted to accommodate writing-paper and envelopes, and a silver ink-stand, stood between the two windows; and all the chairs were covered with oxhide leather. Above this apartment, and having access on to the half-landing between the ground and first-floors, was a similar room, dedicated to the mistress of the establishment, and known to everyone except Miss Birtley (who persisted in calling it Mrs Haddington's sitting-room) as the Boudoir. It was of the same proportions as the room beneath, but decorated in quite another style. Diaphanous folds of nylon veiled the two windows by day, and opulently gathered ones of lilac brocade, drawn across the shallow embrasures, shut out the night. A low table of burr walnut, bearing an alabaster cigarette-box and an ash-tray *en suite*, stood beside a day-bed furnished with cushions of lilac and rose silk. There were two arm-chairs, upholstered in lilac satin; several others, described by their creators as incidental, filling gaps against the panelled walls; a carpet of purple pile; and, in the corner between the door and the first of the two windows, a spindle-legged table bearing on it a telephone (cream enamel) and a reading-lamp, shaded in rose silk. Thoughtfully placed beside this table was a low, cabriole-legged chair, its lozenge back and sprung seat uphol-stered in the same delicate shade of lilac brocade which hung beside the windows. The floral decoration of the room was provided by an alabaster bowl on a torchére pedestal, filled in summer with roses or carnations, and, in winter, by honesty and sea-lavender.

The first floor of the house was wholly occupied by the drawing-room (Empire), which was an L-shaped apartment, originally two rooms connected by an archway. Above this were the respective bedrooms of Mrs and Miss Haddington, with their bathrooms; and above this again, for two floors, was a vast terra incognita inhabited by Mrs Haddington's staff.

Miss Beulah Birtley, whose errand on this February afternoon had been to discover whether there existed in London a firm willing to supply fresh caviare at a cut price for a party of fifty-odd persons, returned to Charles Street to discover her employer in the drawing-room, sustaining a visit from her sole and unmarried sister, Miss Violet Pickhill.

There was a slight physical resemblance between the two ladies, both being lean, long-limbed, and of an aquiline cast of countenance; but it would have been hard to have found a more ill-assorted pair. Mrs Haddington was as well-groomed as she was well-dressed; and her thinness, coupled as it was with considerable height, inspired dressmakers to congratulate her on her wonderful figure. Her beautifully waved hair showed no grey streaks, being of a uniform copper, and if it occasionally seemed to be rather darker towards the roots this was a blemish which could be, and was, very easily rectified. Her eyes were of too cold a blue for beauty, but her features were good, and if there was a hint of ruthlessness about her tinted lips this was generally disguised by the social smile which had become so mechanical that she frequently assumed it when addressing persons, such as her secretary, whom it was quite unnecessary for her to charm.

Miss Pickhill, some years her senior, had no artificial graces. She was shorter and thinner than her sister, and both her complexion and her hair were her own. The one was non-existent, and the other had faded from gold to dusty straw, here and there streaked with grey. She wore clothes of good material but tasteless design, lived in a gaunt house in one of the roads leading off Putney Hill, which she had inherited from her father, and interested herself in Parish matters, the Girl Guides, the Women's Conservative Association, and various other worthy enterprises. No one could fathom what attracted her to the house in Charles Street, for she plainly disapproved of everything she saw there, and received no encouragement to continue her visits. The truth was that she was not at all attracted, but had been brought up to know where her duty lay. She said that it was her duty to keep an eye on her sister. She also considered it to be her duty to utter the most blighting criticisms on Mrs Haddington's manners, appearance, morals, and ambitions; and to prophesy a rapid descent to the gutter for her niece, who had been brought up, she said, to think of nothing but painting her face and running after young men.

She was engaged on this fruitful topic when Beulah returned from having tea with young Mr Harte, and had just informed Mrs Haddington (whom she persisted in calling Lily in the teeth of every injunction to alter this commonplace name to Lilias) that she would live to rue the day when she sent her daughter to be educated at a school in Switzerland, instead of rearing her to be a useful member of society, when Beulah walked into the drawing-room.

Mrs Haddington betrayed no pleasure at the sight of her secretary. 'Well?' she said sharply. 'What is it?'

'I'm sorry to interrupt you,' said Beulah, laying a scrap of silk on the arm of her chair, 'but this is the nearest I can get to the stuff you gave me to match.'

'Well, it won't do,' said Mrs Haddington, contemptuously flicking the scrap with one pointed, blood-red fingernail. 'Really, I should have thought you could have seen that for yourself!'

'I did, but I thought I'd better bring you a sample of it. And caviare is the same price everywhere.'

'I sometimes wonder what I pay you for!' remarked Mrs Haddington.

Beulah flushed, and folded her lips.

'Exactly what I have always said!' remarked Miss Pickhill. 'What a healthy woman of your age, Lily, wants with a secretary, or whatever Miss Birtley calls herself, to run her errands for her is more than I can fathom. Caviare, indeed! More of your grand parties, I suppose! Enough to make poor Father turn in his grave!'

'That will do!' Mrs Haddington said, dismissing Beulah.

'Will you want me any more today?' Beulah asked.

Mrs Haddington hesitated. She was taking a party to the theatre, and dining afterwards at London's newest and smartest restaurant, so that there really was nothing at all for her secretary to do. 'No, you can go,' she said at last. 'And please don't be late in the morning!'

'I never am,' replied Beulah. 'Good-night!'

'A very impudent manner that girl has,' said Miss Pickhill, as the door closed behind Beulah. 'Not but what you bring it on yourself, with your slave-driving ways. I suppose *she'll* be leaving next!'

'Oh, no, she won't!' replied Mrs Haddington, with a slight laugh.

'Yes, that's what you say, but nowadays girls won't put up with the way you treat them, and so I warn you!'

'You needn't worry: I know too much about Miss Beulah Birtley for her to leave me in a hurry. Now, if you don't mind, it's time I went up to change. I have a theatre-party.'

Miss Pickhill said severely: 'Theatres and balls! You don't seem to me to think of anything else. Where you get the money from to pay for all this wicked extravagance is more than I can tell! It's no use saying Hubert left you very well-off: he didn't leave you with a fortune; and, what's more, if he had it would be taken away from you by the Government. Sometimes I lie awake for hours worrying about the way you live, Lily, and expecting to read in the paper any minute that you've been had up for cheating the Income Tax, or running a gaming-house.'

'Running a gaming-house! Really, Violet – !'

'I wouldn't put it beyond you,' said Miss Pickhill darkly. 'You can fool all these grand friends of yours, I daresay, but you can't fool me! There's very little you'd stop at, Lily. You've always been the same: out for what you can get, and never mind how! I shall never forget how you threw poor Charlie Thirsk over because Hubert came along with twice his income. Well, I'm sure I don't wish to speak ill of the dead, but I never did like that man, and no more did Father. He always said there was something not quite straight about him, and as for the people he went about with – Well, there's only one word to describe them, and that's flashy! Like that Mr Seaton-Carew I'm always running into here!'

'There's a remedy for that,' retorted Mrs Haddington. 'Don't come here!'

'Oh, I know very well I'm not wanted!' said Miss Pickhill, in no way abashed. 'But blood's thicker than water, and I know my duty, Lily!'

With these words she offered her cheek to her sister, a courtesy which Mrs Haddington acknowledged by touching it with her own, said that there was no need to ring for the butler, since she was quite capable of seeing herself out, and went away. Mrs Haddington was just about to go up to her bedroom when the door opened again, and her daughter strolled into the room.

Cynthia Haddington was nineteen years old, and a girl of quite outstanding beauty. She was dazzlingly fair, with large, china-blue eyes, and hair of shining gold. A slender figure, exquisite tailoring, and the discreet use of mascara on brows and lashes brought her appearance to perfection. An expensive finishing-school, while adding very little to her mental attainments, had taught her to move with more grace than was often to be seen amongst her contemporaries; she was a good dancer; she skated well; played a moderate game of tennis; and had a good enough seat on a horse to show to advantage on the Row, if not in the hunting-field. Her disposition was uneven; nor did she give the impression of being one who enjoyed robust health. During her first season she had flagged rather frequently; but she seemed to be growing accustomed to late hours and town-life, and was beginning to develop astonishing recuperative powers. When she was doing what she liked, she was gay and good-humoured, but when anything happened to thwart her plans she was inclined to fall into what her mother called a nerve-storm and everyone else called tantrums. Those who disliked her said that she was wholly devoid of intellect, but this was unjust. Whenever she had a few minutes to spare between her various engagements she would turn over the pages of society journals, even reading the captions under the pictures; and she never entered her bedroom without turning on the radio.

She came in now, looking tired, but extremely smart in navy-blue, with a tiny hat on her head, and very high heels to her shoes, and uttered in the slightly adenoidal voice acquired through constant study of the delivery in vogue amongst her favourite announcers: 'Oh, Mummy, too sickening! I walked into Aunt Violet on the doorstep! I do think she's *too* lethal! Why do you *let* her absolutely infest the house?'

'Because I can't stop her,' replied Mrs Haddington. Her eyes ran over the charming figure before her, and softened. 'That frock suits you. I wasn't sure, at the time, but it's just right. Where have you been, darling?'

'Oh, I went to a flick with Lance, and then tea,' responded Cynthia, sinking into a chair and casting off her hat. 'It was rather ghastly, really, with captions and things, because of being in Italian, and an absolute *purge*, Mummy, which Lance thought was *too* terrific!'

'Oh!' said Mrs Haddington. 'Lance. . . . Well, that's all right, I suppose. I can't say I really like that young man, and in some ways I'd rather hear that you were running round with Timothy Harte.'

'I think Timothy's marvellous!' agreed her daughter, with simple enthusiasm. 'I mean, he's much better-looking than Lance, and I go frightfully big for that kind of blue eye that goes with dark hair, don't you? In some ways, I wish it was him that was a peer, and not Lance.'

Mrs Haddington saw nothing to deprecate in this naive speech; she agreed with it in the main, but said that peers were not everything. 'I don't like the way Guisborough lives, or the ridiculous ideas he has. If he hadn't come into the title –' She paused. 'Well, of course, he *is* Lord Guisborough, but he wasn't brought up to be!' she said. 'From all I can discover, his mother was quite a common sort of person, besides – But never mind that!'

'D'you mean being Lance's father's mistress before he married her?' enquired Cynthia. 'I know all about that. Trixie's frightfully proud of it, because she believes in doing away with marriage-ties, on account of being a Communist.'

'I can believe anything of Beatrice Guisborough, but doing away with marriage-ties has nothing whatsoever to do with Communism that I ever heard of!'

'Oh, hasn't it? P'raps I got it wrong, then. Only I do know she wishes her father hadn't married her mother, because if he hadn't Lance wouldn't be Lord Guisborough, and she simply hates that. She won't be an Honourable herself, and she's always trying to get Lance to go on being plain Mr Guisborough. Actually, I don't think Lance wants to, poor sweet. In fact, *I* think he's rather thrilled about being a Lord.'

'Then I wish he would learn to behave like one!' said Mrs Haddington tartly.

'Yes, I do too,' agreed Cynthia.

'In some ways, I should prefer young Harte for you.'

'Yes, but he won't ever be a Lord, Mummy,' Cynthia pointed out.

'No, but he'll be a baronet. He comes of a very good family; he's well-off; and he's got the sort of background I want for you, my pet. I'm not too sure about Guisborough. The people he mixes with, and the political opinions he holds, and the fact that he wasn't brought up in the right surroundings – well, sometimes I wonder whether he'll ever have the entrée – title or no title! His father seems to have been a waster, and of course he more or less dropped out when he made that disastrous marriage.'

'How on *earth* did you find out all this?' demanded Cynthia.

'I made it my business to find out,' said Mrs Haddington shortly. 'I'm not going to let you make a mistake that might ruin your life. You're all I've got, and all I care for, Cynthia, and I'm determined you shall have the best!'

Her daughter yawned. 'Actually, I shall marry anyone I like,' she said. 'In some ways, I think I should rather like it to be Lance, because there's simply *nothing* he wouldn't do to please me, besides being Lord Guisborough. Of course, he isn't utterly devastating, like – oh, like anyone! Anyway, I haven't made up my mind, and the whole thing is *too* boring!'

Mrs Haddington looked searchingly down into the flower-like face, just now set into lines of weariness and discontent. 'You're tired,' she said. 'You ought to go straight to bed, only that we're going to this first night.'

'I shall be all right,' Cynthia murmured, her eyelids drooping.

'You shouldn't have let Guisborough take you to the cinema this afternoon.'

'Oh, Mummy, don't be so silly! What on earth else was there to do? Sit at home, and read a book?'

Mrs Haddington appeared to feel the force of this argument, for she said nothing for a moment or two. The delicate chime of an ormolu clock on the mantleshelf made her raise her eyes quickly to it, and exclaim: 'We must hurry, or we shall be late! Cynthia – tell me, my darling! – you haven't been meeting Dan unknown to me, have you?'

Cynthia's eyes flew open at that. 'Dan? Whatever do you mean?'

Mrs Haddington sat down on the arm of her daughter's chair, and tenderly smoothed the helmet of spun gold about her pretty head. 'Listen, my pet! I know Dan's attractive, but he's not the man for you. He's an – an old friend of mine, but if I thought that you –'

'*Darling* Mummy, *do* be your age!' begged Cynthia. 'I haven't the *slightest* desire to cut you out with Dan!'

Mrs Haddington saw no need to reprove her offspring for this speech. She merely said: 'Then that's all right. But you mustn't think I don't know that he's been doing his utmost to get you to fall for him. And, of course, men of his age –'

'*Too* Victorian!' interrupted Cynthia. 'Really, Mummy! Oh, God, is it actually six o'clock? I must fly!'

34

She wrenched her slim body out of the chair, and bent to pick up the discarded hat. Mrs Haddington said: 'You'll have time for a hot bath: it'll freshen you up.'

'I shall be all right,' Cynthia repeated. 'Who's coming with us?'

'Roddy Vickerstown, the Kenelm Guisboroughs, and Freddy Atherstone.'

'Christ!' observed Cynthia.

'Well, I know, darling, but the Kenelm Guisboroughs know *everybody*, and I'm particularly anxious to get you invited to Mrs Atherstone's dance. It'll be one of those *intime* affairs –'

'It sounds lousy,' said Cynthia. 'And Kenelm Guisborough is so dull he makes me practically basin-sick, besides having that dim wife, and hating Lance's guts for being the heir! I suppose it'll be some ghastly play, too, with a Message, or something that makes you want to *cry* with boredom!'

Mrs Haddington regarded her in some perturbation. 'Darling, if you're really too tired, I'll ring Nest up, and ask her if she can possibly –'

'Oh, Mummy, do stop *fussing*!' Cynthia said impatiently. 'I shall be all right when I've had a bath!'

Mrs Haddington looked doubtful, but when she next saw her daughter she perceived that the hot bath had had unexpectedly recuperative powers. A vision in delicate shades of floating yellow chiffon, Cynthia ran down the stairs three-quarters of an hour later, and burst upon the assembled theatre-party, partaking of sandwiches and cocktails in the library, with apologies for her tardiness on her smiling lips, and such a brilliant glow in her eyes as caused Mr Freddy Atherstone, hovering on

35

the brink of matrimony with another, to experience a serious cardiac qualm. Only Mrs Haddington, staring for an unwinking moment, seemed to derive no pleasure from her daughter's radiant beauty; and although Mrs Kenelm Guisborough afterwards informed her husband that Lilias had looked at Cynthia in the most extraordinary way, the revealing moment passed so swiftly that Mr Kenelm Guisborough was able to assert that he had noticed nothing, and that his wife was always imagining things.

Four

By the time that Mrs Haddington's duplicate Bridge-party assembled, at nine o'clock on a Tuesday evening, several persons' tempers were exacerbated, and Miss Beulah Birtley had been obliged to swallow an aspirin to quell an incipient headache.

The day began badly with the inevitable discovery by one of the invited guests that circumstances over which he had no control would prevent his honouring his engagement. Having assured the delinquent, in her sweetest voice, that it didn't matter at all, Mrs Haddington slammed down the telephone, and ordered her maid, who had just brought up her breakfast-tray, to send Miss Birtley to her at once, and to tell her to bring the address-book with her. Upon its being pointed out to her that Miss Birtley was not due to arrive in Charles Street for another quarter of an hour, she delivered herself of some rather venomous remarks about the inefficiency and laziness of every member of her staff, which did nothing to endear her to the representative before her. Indeed, this prim-lipped virgin lost no time in requesting her employer, in accents of painful gentility, to accept her notice.

'Don't be a fool! Why should *you* want to leave?' demanded Mrs Haddington.

Miss Mapperley said that she would rather not say; and at once, and in curious contradiction of her statement, began to enumerate the many and varied reasons which made her disinclined to remain under Mrs Haddington's roof. Chief among these seemed to be her dislike of being expected to wait on two people. She said that she had never been one to complain but that maiding Miss Cynthia was one person's work, and work, moreover, for which she had not originally been engaged.

As Mrs Haddington had been determined to set her henchwoman to work that day on the task of altering the frock she had bought for Cynthia to wear that very evening, and which a conscienceless *couturier* had delivered on the previous afternoon in a far from perfect condition, these fell words made it apparent that some at least of the day's plans would have to be re-edited. She was not the woman to bandy words with one who would all too probably walk out of the house on slight provocation, so she merely dismissed Miss Mapperley from her room and vented her wrath presently on her secretary.

The fact that Beulah did not arrive in Charles Street until ten o'clock furnished her with an excellent excuse for verbally blistering the girl. That she had herself ordered Beulah to go first to Covent Garden market that morning, to buy flowers for the party, she at once acknowledged and dismissed by saying acidly that she would have supposed Beulah to have had time to have gone there twice over.

'Don't stand there making excuses, but go downstairs and fetch me my address book! I'm a man short tonight! And when you've done that you'll have to go to Fulham and get hold of Miss Spennymoor, and tell her I want her to come here today to alter Miss Haddington's frock. Why the wretched woman isn't on the telephone is more than I can fathom! She doesn't deserve to be employed at all when she makes things as difficult as she can. You can do the flowers when you get back.'

By the time Beulah returned from her errand to the little dressmaker in Fulham, Mrs Haddington had been driven into the last ditch, and forced to fall back, for her substitute guest, on the one person she had vowed never to invite again. Rather than include herself amongst the players, an arrangement which she considered detrimental to the smooth running of the party, since a hostess's eye (she said) should be everywhere, she had unbent towards Mr Sydney Butterwick, who was providentially free that evening. By rearranging the tables, so that he and Dan Seaton-Carew should play in different rooms for as long as was possible, she hoped that he might be deterred from giving expression to the jealousy he suffered every time Mr Seaton-Carew bestowed his favours elsewhere. Mrs Haddington was even broader-minded than young Mr Harte, but she had the greatest dislike of shrill-voiced, nail-biting scenes being enacted at her more select parties.

The intelligence, brought by Beulah, that Miss Spennymoor would, as she herself phrased it, do her best to fit Mrs Haddington in during the course of the afternoon, brought a slight alleviation of the morning's ills, but this was soon dissipated by an unnerving message from the chef that no lobsters had as yet reached London, and that as none of the fishmongers whom he had personally rung up could give him any assurance that the dilatory crustaceans would arrive in time to appear at the party, he would be glad to know with what alternative delicacy Madame would desire him to fill one hundred patties. Hardly had Mrs Haddington dealt with this difficulty than her attention was claimed by Thrimby, her extremely supercilious butler. Since she paid him very handsome wages, and always supported him in any quarrel he might have with the other members of the staff, he had been in her service for longer than any of his colleagues, having been engaged when she first moved into the house in Charles Street eighteen months earlier. He was always very polite, for this was something which he owed to himself, but he deeply despised her, and frequently regaled such of the upper servants as he honoured with his patronage with odious comparisons drawn between her and his previous employers. The economies which Mrs Haddington practised behind the scenes, and, too often, at her servants' expense, never failed to mortify him, for Such Ways, he said, were not what he had been accustomed to. He was in the present instance offended by his mistress's refusal to employ outside labour to assist him in his duties that evening, and had already conveyed by a stiff bow, and perceptibly raised eyebrows, his opinion of those who were content to see at least half their guests waited on by a secretary and parlour-maid. This affront to his dignity made him disinclined to be co-operative, and led him to lay before Mrs Haddington a number of difficulties and obstructions which, in any other household, he would quietly have overcome. He was also annoyed with Beulah, whom he disliked at the best of times, because she had dumped an armful of foliage in the basin in the cloakroom, left several shallow wooden boxes containing hot-house flowers in the hall, and adjured him not to touch any of them; so he wound up his speech to Mrs Haddington by asking her, in a voice of patient long-suffering, whether Miss Birtley would finish the flowers before luncheon. He added that if she intended to arrange the bowls in the cloakroom it seemed a pity that he should not have been warned of this earlier, since this apartment had already been swept and garnished, and would now have to be done again.

This gave Mrs Haddington an opportunity to say that the flowers ought to have been arranged hours earlier, which made Beulah lose her temper, and retort that so they would have been had she not been sent off on an errand to Fulham. She then stalked off, determined to scatter as many leaves, stalks, and scrapings of bark as possible all over the cloakroom floor, and peace reigned until Cynthia Haddington, no early riser, erupted from her bedroom with a loud and insistent demand that everyone should immediately abandon his or her task to search for her favourite powder-compact, which she had mislaid. This appalling loss seemed likely to embitter her whole life, and at once rendered the house hideous. Her temper, never at its best in the morning, grew steadily worse; and after exasperating everyone by insisting that all the unlikeliest places should be searched, reiterating passionately that she *knew* she had had it when she went to bed the previous evening, she nearly provoked a domestic crisis by asserting her belief that someone had stolen the compact.

Mrs Haddington, who had not till then accorded the disaster more than a perfunctory interest, rather hastily intervened, telling her daughter not to talk nonsense, and reminding her that she had at least four other compacts at her disposal.

'But this was my *favourite* one!' Cynthia said. 'I can't *bear* it if it's lost! It's the round one, covered with petitpoint, with –'

'Yes, darling,' interrupted Mrs Haddington, with careful restraint. 'We all know what it looks like. It's the one Dan gave you for Christmas, isn't it? I expect it'll turn up. Just don't fuss!'

But this advice fell on deaf ears. Cynthia went on drifting from room to room, leaving chaos in her wake, and maintaining a maddening flow of complaints and conjectures, until she was forced temporarily to abandon her search by the realisation that since it was now one o'clock, at which hour she was pledged to join a luncheon-party at Claridge's, she would obviously be rather late unless she left the house at once.

Mrs Haddington had also a luncheon-engagement, but found time, before departing to keep it, to condemn Miss Birtley's arrangement of the flowers, characterising the bowls as messy.

'Well, I know they aren't good,' said Beulah, sighing. 'It's a bit difficult, with so little choice, and carnations will flop so!'

'Anyone with a grain of sense,' said Mrs Haddington, 'would have used tangled wire to hold them. It seems to me I have to think of everything! They must all be done again – and do please use your intelligence!'

'I haven't any, so would you also think what kind of wire, and where I can find it?' snapped Beulah.

Mrs Haddington's eyes narrowed. 'My good girl, if you speak to me like that you will have considerable cause to regret it,' she said. 'Ask Thrimby for some picture-wire, and if he has none you have plenty of time to go out and buy some!'

She then walked away; and Beulah, knowing that Thrimby would derive a subtle pleasure from disclaiming all knowledge of the presence of picture-wire in the house, once more sallied forth on an uninspiring errand.

The rearrangement of the flowers, accompanied as it was by a good deal of walking up and downstairs with the various bowls and vases, left Miss Birtley feeling decidedly limp; nor was the tangling of rather thick and ropy picture-wire unattended by difficulties. A guilty suspicion crossed her mind that picture-wire was not really what was wanted, but by dint of much labour and ingenuity she did succeed in using it to some advantage. The bowls were replaced, the floor of the cloakroom once more swept, the spare wire neatly coiled, and left on the shelf against a future need; and Beulah was just wondering whether she dared snatch half an hour's respite, when the front-door bell rang, and, a few minutes later, Thrimby came to inform her that the dressmaker had arrived, and would like to know what she could be getting on with until the return of Miss Cynthia from her luncheon-party.

Well aware that her employer would acidly resent any idleness on Miss Spennymoor's part while she was under her roof, Beulah climbed the stairs again, this time to Cynthia's bedroom. This apartment, which was at the back of the house, on the second floor, was a triumph of the decorator's art, and might well have been called a Symphony in Satin. Satin, of a ravishing shade of peach, covered the window, all the chairs, the kidney-shaped dressing-table, and had even been used for the padded head and foot boards of the bed. Several rather grubby dolls were propped up in dejected attitudes on various pieces of furniture, one being used to cover the pink-enamel telephone by the bed. The room was in its usual state of disorder, the combined efforts of one personal maid and two housemaids being insufficient to keep pace with Cynthia's habit of having discarded clothing on the floor, and littering the dressing-table with powder, hair-combings, and dirty face-tissues. According this uninviting table no more than one disgusted glance, Beulah pulled open a drawer in a large chest, and extracted from it a tangle of stockings. It was safe to assume that they all stood in need of repair, so she bundled them under her arm, and mounted yet another flight of stairs to a small room set apart for Miss Spennymoor's visits. This boasted a chair, a table, a sewing-machine, an electric iron, two ironing-boards, and an antiquated gas-stove which made up in fumes and hissing what it lacked in heating-power.

Miss Spennymoor, who was known to her many patronesses as 'a little woman who comes to me', was a small and spare spinster, who eked out a precarious livelihood by trotting cheerfully all over London to sew in other people's houses. She called herself a dressmaker, but this was a slight misnomer, only the most unexacting customers employing her in this rôle. She was an excellent needle-woman, but, as she herself was the first to acknowledge, an indifferent cutter. But her mending was faultless, and not merely could she alter garments to fit their wearers: she would never have dreamed of telling her clients that the task set her would take at least three weeks to perform. Above all – and this was a virtue much extolled by her patronesses – she charged very little for her services. 'For,' as she frequently pointed out, 'I generally get my dinner, which has to be taken into account, and is a great saving. Of course, sometimes I'm unlucky, some of my ladies not having what I should call a proper meal midday, but one has to take the rough with the smooth, dear, and often there's a cup of tea in the morning, which I must say I do appreciate, not that it is a thing I would ever *expect*, if you understand me.'

Miss Spennymoor's life might have been thought to have been as drab as it was lonely, but she would have been greatly surprised at such a mistaken judgment. Not only were the lives of her clients a constant source of interest to her, but her own life had not been without its romance. As a much younger woman, she had been a theatrical dresser, and although she had never risen in this profession above the dressing-room inhabited by the ladies of the chorus, this period in her career was one which she looked back upon with pride and pleasure, and her album, with its faded portraits of forgotten beauties, was a solace that never failed her.

She received the stockings from Beulah with her usual cheerfulness, for she would have thought it quite as shocking as Mrs Haddington that she should be idle. 'Well, it wouldn't be right, would it?' she said. 'For she pays me for my time, and it's only to be expected I should be working while I'm here. It was lucky you caught me this morning, Miss Birtley, for I was just about to pop on my things and go to one of my ladies that lives in Hampstead. Oh, dear, what a nasty hole in the toe of this lovely stocking! More like a potato than a hole: it *does* seem a shame, and quite new, I should say. I never think a darned stocking is the same, do you, dear? I'll lay it by until my regular day next week, for I daresay Miss Cynthia will come in, and I wouldn't like to leave it with the needle stuck in it, as I should have to, because it wouldn't hardly be reasonable to expect Miss Cynthia to wait. Very much surprised she would be if I was to suggest such a thing, which, of course, I shouldn't dream of doing, not for a moment! I'll just be getting on with this little hole in the heel. Is it a big job Mrs Haddington wants me to do for Miss Cynthia?'

'I don't think so. Apparently, André sent home the frock she means to wear tonight with a crease across the back.'

'Tut-tut, that's very bad!' said Miss Spennymoor, shaking her grey head. 'A firm like that, too! Really, one would hardly credit it, but since the War I don't know how it is but no one seems to care how they do their work as long as they're paid for it. And what they charge! Is it a grand party tonight, dear?'

'Much as usual, I think,' Beulah replied, perching on the edge of the table, and lighting a cigarette. 'No good offering you one of these, is it?'

'No, dear, thank you. I don't know how it is, but I never seemed to take to it. It isn't my scruples, because I'm very broad-minded, although I'm sure my poor old father would practically have turned me out of the house if he'd have seen me smoking. He was very particular, was my father. He wouldn't have what you might call a risky story told, not in his hearing he wouldn't; and the way he took on when short skirts first came in you wouldn't believe. Yes, he was a very good man, except for the drink, and there I'm bound to say he was a wee bit of a trial to my mother, because as sure as fate she'd have to go and look for him in the public houses as soon as ever he got his wages, and often he wasn't at all willing to go home with her, not at all. But I often say it takes all sorts to make a world, and he was very highly respected, on account of his principles. Is it a dance tonight, dear?'

'No, just a Bridge-party.'

'I'm bound to say I've never played Bridge, though I used to be very fond of a rubber of whist. I daresay there will be a lot of celebrities?' Miss Spennymoor said hopefully.

'Yes, quite a lot,' said Beulah, knowing that the little dressmaker used this term to describe any titled person. She perceived that more was expected of her, and added: 'Lady Floddan – do you know her?'

Miss Spennymoor shook her head. 'I don't think she ever got her name in the papers, dear,' she said simply.

Realising that she had failed to give satisfaction, Beulah tried again. 'Well – Sir Roderick Vickerstown!'

'Now him I *do* know!' said Miss Spennymoor, pleased. 'He was at the races, though which races I don't precisely remember, not at the moment, with the Marquis of Chetwynd and Lady Caroline Ramsbury, smoking a cigar.'

'It sounds very probable. Lady Nest Poulton,' offered Beulah.

47

'Ah, now, what a lovely girl *she* was!' sighed Miss Spennymoor. 'She used to be in all the papers. One of the Season's débutantes; that was before she was one of the Leaders of the Younger Set, of course. Sweetly pretty, and such dresses! I remember when she got married she had a wedding-dress of cloth of gold, which created a regular sensation, because it was quite an innovation, as they say, at that time. Anyone else?'

'I don't think so. Except Lord Guisborough.'

'Yes, I thought he'd be coming, for I hear he's very sweet on Miss Cynthia, but he's not what I would call a celebrity, dear, if you know what I mean. You see, I knew his mother – oh, ever so well I knew her!'

Since this was by no means the first time Beulah had been the recipient of this confidence, her reply was a trifle mechanical. 'Really?'

'First line,' said Miss Spennymoor cryptically. 'Oh, she was a one! Daring! You wouldn't believe! Never till my dying day shall I forget the night she went off to some party with no more money in her bag than would pay for her taxi-fare (for keep twopence together she could not!) and the dress she wore as one of the Guests at the Grand-Duke's Reception. Now, what *was* the name of that show? It'll come back to me. Of course, I should have got into trouble if it had ever been found out, not that I knew anything about it, for she did it when my back was turned, I need hardly say. What a lad! All the other girls used to laugh at her for taking up with Hilary Guisborough the way she did. Hilary! Well, I couldn't help laughing myself: what a name for anyone to have! The funny thing was she was the last girl you'd have thought would have been so soft, but there it was, and, as

I've often said, he who laughs last laughs best, for he married her. No one ever thought he would, but he said he wasn't going to have people calling his kids bastards, if you'll pardon the expression, which shows that he was a real gentleman, doesn't it? Not that it did her much good, because what must that Hilary of hers go and do but catch cold and die of a pneumonia when the twins were no more than six years old, if as much. Not that he was ever much use, reely, in spite of his grand relations, but half a loaf is better than no bread, when all's said and done, and there she was, left with two children on her hands, and nothing but a lot of bills to pay. Still, she kept up her spirits, and always enjoyed a joke. I sometimes think what a laugh she'd have if she knew her Lance had come into the title!'

She indulged in a little laughter herself at this reflection, but her mirth was cut short by the entrance of Mrs Haddington, who walked into the room, raising her eyebrows at her secretary, and saying: 'So this is where you are!'

'Do you want me, Mrs Haddington?' asked Beulah.

'Kindly go downstairs and see that the markers are all ready, and the pencils properly sharpened. Miss Spennymoor, please come to my daughter's room! I should have thought you could both have found something better to do than to sit gossiping here.'

'Yes, Mrs Haddington!' said Miss Spennymoor meekly. 'Not but what it was quite my fault, and not at all Miss Birtley's, which it is only right I should say, because I was telling her how I used to know Lord Guisborough's poor mother, and one thing leading to another –'

'Lord Guisborough's mother?' repeated Mrs Haddington. 'Indeed!'

This icy interjection not unnaturally covered the little dressmaker with confusion. She scuffled her thimble and her scissors into her work-bag, and picked it up, saying in a crushed voice: 'Quite ready now, Mrs Haddington!'

'Then please come downstairs!' said Mrs Haddington.

Five

At eight o'clock, fortified by the tablet of aspirin she had swallowed on her hurried return to her lodging in Earl's Court earlier in the evening to fling herself into her one dinner-dress, Beulah joined the small party assembled in the drawing-room. Originally, the only invited guest had been Dan Seaton-Carew, but Cynthia, encountering Lord Guisborough and Mr Harte at her luncheon-party, had, with reckless hospitality, begged both to dine in Charles Street before the rest of the Bridge-guests arrived. Since Beatrice Guisborough, who shared a studio with her brother, had not been present, she was easily able to forget the propriety of including her in her invitation; and as Lord Guisborough was contemptuous of all social conventions, and, in any event, never considered the convenience of anyone but himself, he had no hesitation in accepting the invitation, and leaving Beatrice to join the Bridge-party under her own escort.

Mrs Haddington, informed midway through the afternoon of this alteration of her plans, had almost lost her temper with her idolised daughter, even going so far as to say that it was really rather thoughtless of her. Her chef entirely lost his, and was only deterred from walking out of Mrs Haddington's life then and there by the reflection that the incident, judiciously handled, would provide him with an unanswerable pretext for demanding an increase in his already handsome salary.

'My pet, if you had invited *one* of them, it would have been quite all right,' said Mrs Haddington, in the fond voice none but her daughter was privileged to hear. 'But now our numbers are wrong!'

'Oh, Mummy, what on earth does it matter? Besides, they always were!'

'Nonsense, I don't count Dan as a regular *guest*! I suppose I shall have to tell that Birtley girl she can dine with us.'

She then remembered that the library, where Beulah usually partook of meals served to her on a tray, was swept, garnished, and furnished with card-tables; reflected that the servants would infallibly be affronted by any suggestion that they should serve two separate meals that evening, and became more cheerful. Beulah received a curt intimation that she was expected to dine with her employer with outward apathy. Her spirits were not raised by the contemplation of her image in the mirror set within the panel of her wardrobe door. The discreet dinner-dress, bought for just such an occasion as the present one, had, for its *provenance*, the Inexpensive Department of a London store distinguished more for its reasonable prices than for its exclusiveness of design, and had been worn rather too often. Not even the addition of a pendant of antique and charming design, bequeathed to her by her Italian mother, could redeem it, she considered. A dab of Indian ink had concealed a cut on one of her satin sandals; but her thick brown locks, springing attractively from a broad, low brow, would have been the better for re-setting. 'Oh, blast, who cares, anyway?' demanded Beulah of her scowling reflection, and dragged a comb through her hair once more.

She was guilty of the extravagance of hiring a taxi to convey her from Nevern Place to Charles Street, and alighted from it just as Mr Seaton-Carew was about to press the bell beside the front door of the house. He waited for her to join him, saying, in the half-caressing, half-bantering tone he was apt to adopt when addressing pretty young women: 'Well, and how is my little protégée?'

'Thank you, I am perfectly well, and you would oblige me if you would stop calling me your little protégée!' Beulah replied.

He laughed gently, and gave her arm a squeeze above the elbow. 'What a farouche child it is!' he remarked. 'Ungrateful, aren't you? Eh? Who got you this job, I should like to know? And what thanks has he ever had for doing it? Now, you tell me that, you impossible young termagant!'

'If you had got it for me without telling Mrs Haddington every detail of my past career, I might have been grateful – even to the extent of letting you paw me about!' retorted Beulah fiercely, detaching his hand from her arm.

Again he laughed, and this time playfully pinched her chin. 'Does Lilias put it across you? What a shame! But I really couldn't foist you on to her without letting her know the worst, could I?'

Beulah sought angrily in her purse for her latch-key, realised that she had left it in her shopping-bag, set her

53

finger on the bell, and pressed it viciously. 'I told you the truth, and you pretended to believe me!'

'Of course I did! That's one of the rules of the game, my silly sweet.'

'And, what is more, you *did* believe me!' Beulah flashed. 'I know enough now to be sure that you'd have found quite another use for me if you hadn't! You saw I wasn't in the least the sort you were looking for, but it occurred to you that you could supply your dear old *friend* with a slave who wouldn't leave her the first time she was poisonously rude if you sent me to her – complete with my dossier!'

He still seemed to be genuinely amused. 'Poor little savage! Do you hate me for it?'

'No more than I hate cockroaches!'

At this moment, Thrimby opened the door. Mr Seaton-Carew stood back with an exaggerated gesture of civility to allow Beulah to precede him into the house. His eyes mocked her; he said, as he handed Thrimby his hat: 'What do you do to cockroaches, my dear? Put your foot on them?'

'When I get the chance!'

'What a cruel little girl! I'm afraid you won't, you know!'

She turned, at the foot of the stairs, to look back at him. 'Don't be too sure of that, Mr Seaton-Carew! Add determined to cruel, and you'll be very nearly right!'

'Your overcoat, sir?' said Thrimby, in a voice that clearly expressed his opinion of this interchange.

Beulah postponed her entrance to the drawing-room until the last moment, and did not join the party until after the separate arrivals of Lord Guisborough and Mr

Harte. She found her employer very stately in black velvet and diamonds, with a large black lace fan, mounted on ebony sticks, which she carried in one hand. This was in imitation of a certain much admired Duchess, and was a plagiarism which Mr Harte had instantly recognised and appreciated. He caught Beulah's eye as she entered the room, and directed it to the gloves and the fan. Since Beulah had not been informed of the identities of the two extra guests Mr Harte's presence came as a glad surprise to her. Her rather forbidding expression was lightened by an involuntary smile, and a faint flush. These indications of her pleasure were not lost on her employer, who observed them with a steely light in her eyes. But Mrs Haddington never committed the solecism of being rude to her secretary in public, and she said, with her mechanical smile: 'Ah, here you are, Miss Birtley! You know my secretary, don't you, Lance?'

The latest flower of the peerage was seated beside Cynthia on a deep sofa, engrossed in expounding the high principles infusing every Russian bosom, but he turned his head at these words, waved a vague hand, and said graciously: 'Oh, hallo!'

'And Mr Harte I feel sure you have met before, Miss Birtley,' said Mrs Haddington.

'How do you do? May I mix you a drink?' Timothy said, shaking hands with his unofficially betrothed, and moving towards the tray laid upon a side-table.

Beulah refused it, and Mrs Haddington, who saw no reason why she should provide a member of her staff with cocktails as well as an expensive meal, said lightly: 'I'm afraid you won't be able to persuade her, Mr Harte. Miss Birtley doesn't drink.'

55

'What an exemplary character!' remarked Seaton-Carew, amusement in his sleepy eyes.

'Dinner is served, madam,' announced Thrimby, from the doorway.

A buffet had already been set up in the back half of the dining-room, and the mahogany table, much reduced in length, had been thrust wholly into the front half. Mrs Haddington, with a graceful apology for what she described as a picnic-meal, requested Lord Guisborough to take the head of the board, seated herself at the foot, with Timothy on her right, and Seaton-Carew on her left, and directed her daughter to the vacant chair between his lordship and Mr Harte. This left the place beside Seaton-Carew to Beulah, and since Lord Guisborough continued to address himself exclusively to Cynthia, and Timothy, handicapped by an upbringing, politely set himself to entertain his hostess, she was obliged to maintain an unwilling exchange of small talk with him.

Of this he had an easy and inexhaustible flow. He was a middle-aged man who had wonderfully preserved his figure, and his air of youth. He was handsome, in a slightly florid style, and possessed a marked amount of rather animal magnetism. His manner, which was a nice blend of indulgent amusement and affectionate flattery, strongly attracted a certain type of woman, and various young men whose careers had not hitherto earned them any very distinguishing attention either from their contemporaries or from their seniors. He lived in a service-flat in Jermyn Street, and was apparently a gentleman of leisure. His position in Mrs Haddington's house was undefined, but it was generally supposed that the past veiled a greater degree of intimacy than now prevailed between them. As Miss Mapperley so shrewdly phrased it: 'Anyone knows what to think when someone asks a gentleman to go and fetch her something out of her bedroom.' Miss Mapperley added with relish: 'But if My Lady thinks he's still got a fancy for her she'll very soon smile on the other side of her face, for it's her precious Cynthia *he's* after, as anybody could see with half an eye. Disgusting, I call it!'

Lord Guisborough, who, while rapidly disposing of half a dozen oysters, was angrily condemning a state of Capitalism which had neglected to make oysters the staple diet of the Masses, had long since decided that Mr Seaton-Carew was a parasite who, in a more golden age, would have perished under a guillotine, and paid little heed to him, beyond casting one or two fiery glances in his direction, and contradicting three of his statements. These in no way discomposed Dan Seaton-Carew, but seemed rather to amuse him. He had very little interest in impoverished peers; and as it was common knowledge that the late Lord Guisborough, upon the death of his last surviving son, had divided all his unentailed property between his daughter and his more favoured nephew Kenelm, he had never made any attempt to captivate the heir. Lord Guisborough was a bony young man, with a cavernous eye and hollow cheeks, who had been employed for some years on the staff of a firm of left-wing publishers. He was not without ability, but he lacked ballast. An older and a shrewder colleague had once described him as being over-engined for his beam. He was capable of bearing an intelligent part in discussion for just as long as the subject had no bearing on the

Kremlin, but the smallest reference to Soviet Russia acted upon his brain like a powerful drug, slaying in an instant his critical faculty, and inspiring him with a fanaticism that dismissed as Capitalist Propaganda all the more displeasing activities of an Asiatic race which from time to time came to light. He had taken no active part in the War, at first because he had conscientiously objected to it; and later, when the enforced participation of Russia in the hostilities had altered his outlook, because he was engaged on Educational Work of paramount importance. This consisted of a series of lectures, which he was perfectly well qualified to deliver, having completed his education at the London School of Economics.

In general, he was by no means popular with the more ruthless sex, most of whom, in defiance of all attempts to enlighten their minds, continued to let instinct govern their impulses, and maintained an obstinate preference for stalwart males who showed every sign of being able and willing to defend their own. Some of these ladies who had spent the war-years doing rescue work in blitzed areas, could scarcely look at him without wishing to hand him a white feather. Mr Harte, who possessed an elegant leather case containing a row of miniature medals which made his mother's heart swell with pride, was more tolerant. He said that Lord Guisborough's war-time activities were not due to common funk, but to a form of beany intellectualism, and bore him not the slightest ill-will for his failure to share in the heat and burden of the day. But he did think that his remarks on the subject of oysters lacked civility to his hostess, and were deserving of punishment, so he remarked, in what he knew his victim would consider an Oxford drawl, that it was extremely doubtful that the masses would appreciate the addition of these bivalves to their diet.

'When oysters were more plentiful,' he said affably, 'it was one of the articles of indenture for apprentices that they should not be fed on them more than a strictly limited number of times in the week. Which doesn't lead one to suppose that they were very popular, does it?'

Since his lordship was unable to refute this piece of recondite knowledge, he could think of no adequate retort, and therefore said nothing. So, having successfully put him in his place, Timothy continued in an easy, conversational tone: 'Rather odd, the way different foods go in and out of fashion. My mother tells me that when she was a girl, for instance, scallops, which we think very well of, were considered to be too cheap and common to figure on any menu.'

'I had the pleasure of meeting your mother at dear Mary Petersfield's party,' said Mrs Haddington. 'I should so much like to know her better: what an interesting woman she is! How much I enjoyed her book describing her adventures on the Congo border!'

Timothy, who shared with his half-brother, Mr James Kane, an ineradicable conviction that the Second World War had been inaugurated by providence to put an end to their beloved but very trying parent's passion for exploring remote quarters of the globe, bowed, and murmured one of the conventional acknowledgements with which the more astute relatives of an author take care to equip themselves.

'Is Norma Harte your mother?' demanded Guisborough abruptly. 'I can't say I've read any of her books, but I've heard of her. She knows Equatorial Africa pretty well, doesn't she? What are her views on the native question? Or hasn't she any?'

Timothy had not read his mother's books either, but he was not going to put up with this sort of thing. He replied with deceptive readiness: 'Oh, rather! I believe she's very sound. In fact, if you're thinking of a safari you couldn't do better than to consult her. She'll tell you which tribes make the best carriers, and what you want to look out for in your headman, and what are the main pitfalls: Christianised boys, boys who try to talk English to you, and sit down in your chairs – that sort of thing!'

'That,' said Guisborough, reddening angrily, 'is not what I meant! I was referring – though possibly this might not interest Lady Harte! – to –'

'Oh, do shut up about Africa and natives!' interrupted Cynthia. 'I do think all that sort of thing is *too* boring!'

Mrs Haddington, although she could not but be glad of the intervention, uttered a reproving exclamation, looking rather anxiously at her daughter as she did so. Cynthia was in one of her petulant moods, rejecting most of the dishes offered to her, fidgeting with the cutlery, and taking no pains at all to be polite to her mother's guests.

'Tired, baby?' asked Seaton-Carew, smiling at her across the table. 'I suppose you've been on the go since breakfast-time, as usual?'

'I'm afraid she has,' said Mrs Haddington. 'I think I shall have to have the telephone dismantled! It never stops ringing from morning till night, and always it's someone wanting my frivolous daughter, isn't it, Miss Birtley?'

'Always,' responded Beulah obediently.

'Oh, Mummy, what lies you do tell!' said Cynthia, hunching a pettish shoulder.

'That reminds me,' said Seaton-Carew, with what even Mr Harte acknowledged to be praiseworthy swiftness, 'I've been cursing the telephone all day myself. Been expecting an important call, which hasn't come through. I've told the Exchange to put any calls for me through to this number, Lilias. I knew you wouldn't mind.'

In this he was mistaken. Mrs Haddington might be grateful to him for trying to cover up her daughter's lapse, but she could scarcely be expected to contemplate with pleasure the prospect of seeing the smooth running of her Bridge-party disturbed by the interruption of a telephone-call. Her response, though civil, was so lacking in cordiality that even Lord Guisborough became conscious of an atmosphere of constraint. However, Timothy was inspired to ask Cynthia if she had seen the latest gangster-film, showing at the Orpheum, a gambit which dispelled her ill-humour, and induced her to launch forth into an animated and enthusiastic discussion on this and several other films of the same order. The rest of dinner passed without untoward incident. Mrs Haddington rose from the table, playfully apologising for not being able to allow her male guests more than ten minutes with the port, and inviting them to join her in her boudoir for coffee. She then led the way out of the room, and while Cynthia went up to her bedroom to put more powder on her face and to exaggerate the already beautiful curve of her upper lip, she reminded Beulah what her various duties would be during the rest of the evening. Obedient to her command, Seaton-Carew brought his fellow-guests up to the boudoir in good time; and Thrimby, leaving a couple of flurried subordinates to clear away the remains of dinner and transform the dining-room into a refreshment buffet, followed him with the coffee-tray, which he majestically offered to everyone in turn. Cynthia reappeared just as he was leaving the room, and nearly caused Seaton-Carew to spill his coffee by seizing his free hand and saying: 'Oh, Dan darling, I've something frightfully important I want to tell you! *Do* come up to the drawing-room!'

'Not now, my pet,' said Mrs Haddington firmly. 'You can talk to Dan some other time.'

'But, Mummy, you don't *understand*! I particularly want to say something to him *now*!'

'Darling, you're forgetting! You must stay and entertain Lance, and Mr Harte. Besides, I want to have a word with Dan myself.'

'We'll go into a huddle together later on, Cynny,' said Seaton-Carew soothingly.

Cynthia pouted, and protested, but before her voice had developed more than a hint of a whining note her harassed parent had inexorably swept Mr Seaton-Carew off to the library, to discuss with him, she said, certain minor details of the approaching contest.

'I do think people are sickening,' Cynthia remarked. 'Where's my coffee? Oh, thanks, Timothy, you are an angel! Did you pour it out for me?'

She then gravitated, as though drawn by a magnet, to the radio-cabinet in one corner of the room, switched it on, and began to twiddle the dials. Lord Guisborough followed her, and Timothy seized the opportunity to say to Beulah, in an undervoice; 'Aren't we having fun? Have you had a bloody day? You look worn-out.'

'That's not very polite. I expected better things of that charming Mr Harte who has such lovely manners.'

'Less of it, my girl!' said Timothy.

At this moment a reverent voice announced that they were listening to the Third Preeogramme, and were about to be regaled with a composition by Meeozart. 'This little-kneeown work,' continued the voice, in the kindly tone of one addressing a class of backward students, 'was compeeosed by Meeozart at the age of eighteen. It was originally –'

'O God!' ejaculated Cynthia, swinging the dial round.

This seemed, on the whole, to be fair comment. 'Well said!' approved Timothy. 'I bar having my enjoyment of a concert marred by a patronising voice that tells me a lot of arid facts I am capable of looking up for myself, should I by any chance wish to acquaint myself with them.'

'Wireless programmes are not primarily intended for the privileged few who have had the opportunity and the leisure to acquire *your* culture!' said Guisborough offensively.

'Wireless programmes are neither primarily nor secondarily intended for cultured persons,' replied Timothy, quite unruffled. 'Too often they appear to be intended either for the entirely witless, or for those desirous of acquiring without effort a little easy knowledge. I remember that someone once gave a fifteen minute talk on the Battle of Waterloo. A sobering thought.'

'Well, at least that's better than incessant and uninspiring glorification of the Little Man,' said Beulah.

'I suppose,' said Guisborough contemptuously, 'that

you are one of those who fondly imagine that history is made by the so-called Great Man?'

'Yes,' replied Beulah. 'I am.'

'Good heavens, woman, you mustn't say things like that!' exclaimed Timothy, shocked. 'Next you will say that the race is to the swift!'

Guisborough flushed angrily, but the retort he was seen to make was providentially drowned by the cacophony of sound produced by Cynthia's efforts to discover a programme that appealed to her. While she rapidly travelled from one station to the next, conversation was impossible, and by the time she had switched the current off in disgust, Mrs Haddington had come back into the room with the curt announcement that the first of the guests was arriving. She too was somewhat flushed, and it was apparent to the most casual observer that her interview with Dan Seaton-Carew had not been attended by complete harmony. Her lips were compressed, and her nostrils slightly distended; and it was some moments before she was again able to assume her social smile. She drove her guests upstairs to the drawing-room, told Beulah rather harshly to see to it that the coffee-cups were removed from the boudoir, and swept out to receive Mr Sydney Butterwick.

Six

By the time Mr Sydney Butterwick had been relieved of his hat and coat, and sped on his way up the stairs to where Thrimby waited to announce his name, other guests were arriving. Mrs Haddington had stationed herself just within the doorway to the front half of the drawing-room. This, since the room was L-shaped, faced the stairs, and stood at right-angles to the door leading into the back half of the room. Eight card-tables were set out in the drawing-room, the remaining three being relegated to the library on the ground floor.

Sydney Butterwick was a pretty youth, with fair, curly locks, a too-sensitive mouth, and an asthmatic constitution which had wrecked his early ambition to excel at games, and had later made him unacceptable to the authorities for military service. Very few people knew how deeply a canker of frustration had bitten into his soul, most of his acquaintances considering that he was that most fortunate of created beings: a rich man's son, with a flourishing business to step into. But Sydney, realising at an age when life could be blighted by a broken ambition, that lack of physical stamina set his First Fifteen colours and the

Drysdale Cup beyond his reach, could not be content to play Rugby football or squash for the mere pleasure these games afforded him. He abandoned sport for headier amusements; drifted at school into a precious set, thence into company even more dangerous for a youth of his unbalanced temperament; and, by the time he had attained his majority, had forgotten earlier and healthier ambitions, and reserved his enthusiasm for Surrealism, the Ballet, racing motor-cars, and several exotic pursuits denied to young men of more limited means. He was neurotic, passionate, and easily influenced, spoilt by parents and circumstance, and morbidly self-conscious. He would respond like a shy girl to flattery, but he was quick to imagine slights, and could fly in an instant from the extreme of affection to the opposite pole of wounded hatred. As a child he had revelled in being the focal point of his mother's life; and he had never outgrown his desire of being petted, and admired. This led him to dislike girls, with whom he felt himself to stand in a relationship alien to his temperament, and to be happiest in the company either of elderly women who mothered him, or of such men as Dan Seaton-Carew.

There was no motherliness in Mrs Haddington's manner towards him. She accorded him no more than a chilly smile, and two fingers to shake, her eyes going beyond him to the portly figure of that noted sportsman and *bon viveur*, Sir Roderick Vickerstown, who was heavily ascending the stairs in his wake. This immediately clouded Sydney's pleasure. He mistook his hostess's indifference for dislike, and was at once hurt and ill-at-ease. That he had no liking for her, and no particular desire to be invited to her house, weighed with him not at all: he could not be happy if he was not approved of. He lingered beside her for a moment, fidgeting with his tie, fancied that he could detect hostility in Sir Roderick's choleric blue eye, and flung away to join Timothy and Guisborough, who were standing before the fire in the front drawing-room.

Guisborough, never one to disguise his sentiments, responded to his greetings with an ungracious nod; but Timothy was more civil, and even, since he was just about to light a cigarette, offered his case to him. Sydney was momentarily soothed, but as he stretched out his hand to take a cigarette, he most unfortunately caught sight of Dan Seaton-Carew, talking to Cynthia at the far end of the drawing-room.

That damsel, not to be baulked in her determination to get Seaton-Carew to herself, had dragged him into the back drawing-room, and appeared to be pouring some confidence into his ear. In her artless fashion, she had acquired a grip on the lapel of his coat. His attitude might have been described as fatherly by the charitably-minded. He stroked her shining head in a soothing way, and seemed to be uttering such words as a man might use to reassure an unreasonably troubled child.

Sydney uttered an exclamation, and hurried into the back drawing-room. 'Dan!' he said eagerly.

'Bloody little pansy!' remarked Lord Guisborough, drawn into brief fellowship with Mr Harte.

'Dan!' Sydney repeated. 'I wondered if you'd be here! I've been trying to get hold of you all day!' He glanced at Cynthia, jealousy in his face, and said curtly: 'How do you do? Dan, I rang you up five times, but your man said you were out!'

Seaton-Carew, like many before him, had grown tired of the exigencies of intimacy with his young friend. Moreover, he disliked having his *tête-à-têtes* interrupted. He said, rather brutally: 'Yes, that's what I told him to say. What the hell's the matter anyway?'

Sydney flushed vividly, and stammered: 'I haven't seen anything of you for days! I was afraid you were ill, or something!'

'Well, I'm not. Do, for God's sake, stop barging in where you ought to be able to see you're not wanted!'

The flush died, leaving Sydney's face very white. 'I see!' he said, in a low, shaking voice. 'That's how it is, is it? When Cynthia's around you've no use for me!'

'Oh, shut up!' Seaton-Carew said roughly. 'I've had enough of your scenes! Either behave like a reasonable being or get out! Making a damned exhibition of yourself – I'm fed up with it!'

'You mean you're fed up with me!'

'All right, I mean that!' Seaton-Carew said, exasperated.

Cynthia gave a nervous giggle, glancing towards the front drawing-room, where people were beginning to assemble. 'For goodness' sake!' she whispered. 'Mummy will have a *fit!*'

For a perilous moment it looked as though Sydney might so far forget himself as to strike Seaton-Carew. He stood staring at him, his eyes burning in his white face, and his fists clenching involuntarily. His chest heaved with something like a sob; he began to say something, in a trembling, almost inaudible voice, and was mercifully interrupted.

'Cynthia darling! How sweet you look! Oh, Dan! How lovely!'

Lady Nest Poulton, a little wisp of a woman, with great eyes in a heart-shaped, haggard face, came up to the group in a cloud of chiffon; and Sydney, recollecting his surroundings, turned rather blindly away.

'Charming frock! Dreadful young man!' murmured Lady Nest, with her fleeting, appealing smile. 'You know Godfrey, don't you? Yes, of course you do!' She hesitated for the fraction of a second, and added: 'And Mr Seaton-Carew, Godfrey, whom you've met.'

Her husband, a stockily-built man, with a square, impassive countenance, favoured Seaton-Carew with an unsmiling stare, bowed infinitesimally, and turned from him to speak to Cynthia. The smile wavered pathetically on Lady Nest's face; for a moment she looked nervous, her eyes shifting from him to Seaton-Carew, and away again; then she gave her empty tinkle of laughter, and flitted off to exchange over-affectionate greetings with a raddled brunette in petunia satin.

Sydney Butterwick, plunging away from the group like a stampeded mustang, startled several persons by his mien, which they afterwards described as distraught. He seemed to be making for the door, but fortunately for the smooth conduct of the Bridge-party he encountered a fellow balletomane, who hailed him with delight, exclaiming: 'Sydney! I saw you last night. What did you think? *Will* she be a *ballerina assoluta*? *Did* you count her *fouettés*? Though I thought she was *definitely* at her best in the *pas de quatre*.'

These words had the happy effect of checking Sydney in mid-career. He responded automatically to them, and in an impassioned discussion on *arabesques*, *élévations*, *enchaînements*, *ballerinas*, and *danseurs nobles*, managed to recover himself. His eyes, and his twitching fingers, showed him to be still very much upset, but by the time his ecstatic acquaintance had deserted him for a middle-aged diplomat who could well remember the stars of the Maryinsky Theatre, he had apparently recollected the impropriety of incontinently rushing from the house; and went up to Sir Roderick Vickerstown instead, to discover from him who was to be his partner.

Sir Roderick, and that fashionable consultant, Dr Theodore Westruther, had consented to be the scorers and general managers of the party, dual roles which bade fair to reduce both gentlemen to a state of nervous prostration. The difficulties attendant upon persuading a chattering crowd of guests to postpone the exchange of confidences, and to take their places at the various tables were enormous; and when twelve persons had at last been singled out from the crowd and driven downstairs to the library, and those who were to remain in the drawing-room shepherded to their tables, it was still some time before play could begin. Earnest players, itching to inspect the hands stuck into the slots of the duplicate-boards, in vain suggested that Bridge and not conversation was the order of the evening. A babel of voices made play impossible, for besides the inveterate recounters of anecdotes, there was a strong faction of persons bent on making known the systems which governed their play; a still stronger one of those who were willing to play any convention, but who required to be reminded of the rules governing all but their particular choice; several nervous people who had never played duplicate Bridge before and had to have the procedure explained to them; one or two ladies of terrifying aspect, who warned their partners in menacing accents that they expected to be taken out of a No Trump call; and a small clique of fanatics who filled in the time before play started by describing in a very boring way the interesting hands they had held recently, and the skill with which they had made their contracts.

However, the united and patient efforts of the two scorers, Mrs Haddington and Miss Birtley, at last prevailed, and a sudden silence fell.

Timothy, who had been paired with Cynthia, resigned himself to an unsuccessful evening, for a very few minutes sufficed to convince him that her Bridge was of a dashing variety that took little account of part scores. She had a certain aptitude for the game, and since her social education had included a course of lessons from an expert, she was familiar with most of the conventions. But the gambling instinct was alarmingly strong in her; and an inability to concentrate her mind for any sustained period led her largely to ignore her partner's discards, and frequently to forget that an important card still lurked in one of her opponents' hands.

Timothy, who was dummy during the first hand, had leisure, while Cynthia struggled to make her contract, to look round the room, and study the assembled company. For the most part, his fellow-guests seemed to be an innocuous set of persons, hovering on the fringes of Society; but there were one or two people, like Lady Nest Poulton and Sir Roderick Vickerstown, and the Kenelm Guisboroughs, who had been born into a world the rest aspired to adorn. There were also some unplaceable specimens, such as Seaton-Carew, who fell into no easily definable class.

71

The Kenelm Guisboroughs were seated at the next table to Timothy's, playing, in this first hand, against Lord Guisborough, and Mrs Criddon, a stout matron wearing a profusion of diamonds and an air of stern concentration. Possibly Mrs Haddington had felt that the sooner the cousins met, and were parted, the better it would be: certainly an atmosphere of dangerous restraint hung over their table. No greater contrast could have been imagined than that which existed between the cousins. Lord Guisborough, wearing a soft shirt, a tie askew, and with a lock of unruly hair drooping over one eyebrow, slouched in his chair, and, having told his partner she could play any convention she liked, declared on some undisclosed system of his own, and played his cards with a careless acumen and an air of boredom which made nearly every man in the room wish to kick him. Kenelm, on the other hand, who, in spite of springing from a younger branch of the family, was some years his cousin's senior, looked like a Guardsman, which he was not, and might have served as a model of good, if rather pompous, form. He had a round and florid face, with a tooth-brush moustache, and slightly protuberant eyes, and whenever his noble relative succeeded in enraging him, which was often, his colour rose, his moustache bristled, and he looked very much as though he would burst. His wife, Irene, was a bloodless blonde, who habitually spoke in a complaining voice, and maintained a running fire of criticism of her husband's bidding and subsequent play. Lord Guisborough she largely ignored.

Beulah was not in the drawing-room during the first hand, but she came in as the cards were being restored to the boards, and the various couples changed their tables, and began mechanically to empty ashtrays, and remove glasses. Supper would presently be served in the dining-room, but Mrs Haddington was well aware of the beneficial results of keeping her guests supplied with stimulating liquid refreshment, and had instructed Beulah to lose no time in asking if she might not get some harassed player a drink. This was, in fact, no more than a daughter of the house might have been expected to do, but nevertheless it annoyed Timothy to watch his beloved waiting on everyone, and looking more and more weary as the evening progressed. He tried several times to catch her eye, but she refused to look at him; once he saw Seaton-Carew address some remark to her which brought a flash into her eyes, and caused her to move away from that table at once; and although this was better than seeing her submit to that dashing gentleman's familiarities, it did nothing to add to Timothy's enjoyment of the party. He began to think rather badly of a state of civilisation that made it impossible for him to pick a quarrel with Seaton-Carew upon frivolous grounds, and then inform him that his friends would wait upon him in the morning; and to derive what satisfaction he could from the realisation that no more inimical partner could have been selected for Mr Seaton-Carew than Miss Beatrice Guisborough, who visibly despised him, and audibly condemned his card-play. The knowledge that Seaton-Carew would have liked to have had Cynthia for his partner, and was extremely bored, was poor comfort, however: Mr Harte was glad to see him and Miss Guisborough vanish from the room, and sorry to be obliged, a quarter of an hour later, to follow them to one of the tables set out in the library.

Beulah was well aware that Mr Harte had tried to catch her eye, and equally well aware that he had observed her brief encounter with Seaton-Carew. She hoped that he would make no attempt to single her out during the supper-interval, and made up her mind to keep as much out of his way as was possible. She was conscious of being kept under observation by Mrs Haddington, whose double-edged remark earlier in the evening had not been lost on her.

She was on her way upstairs, bearing a whisky-and-soda for Colonel Cartmel, when the intermittent ringing of the telephone-bell informed her that Mr Seaton-Carew's call had at last come through. In expectation of it, she had informed him that it would be best for him to take it in Mrs Haddington's sitting-room, and she now set down the little silver tray she carried, and went into this apartment. She emerged a moment later to see her employer upon the landing outside the drawing-room.

'If that is for me, I hope you told whoever it is that I can't possibly come to the telephone now!' said Mrs Haddington.

'It isn't. It's a long-distance call for Mr Seaton-Carew,' replied Beulah.

Mrs Haddington uttered an impatient exclamation. 'I'd forgotten. Really, I do think – Well, it can't be helped! He's in the library: you'd better go down and tell him at once. He can take it in my boudoir.'

'I've already told him so,' said Beulah, departing on her errand.

'And just keep your eye on things for a minute or two!'

added Mrs Haddington, carefully gathering up her long skirt, preparatory to ascending the flight that led to her bedroom. 'I'm going to powder my face.' She became aware of Sydney Butterwick at her elbow, and stared at him. 'Dear me! Is anything wrong, Mr Butterwick?'

'No – oh, no!' he said, stammering a little. 'I just thought I'd get myself a drink – we've finished at our table!'

'Of course!' she said, with a graciousness he found even more quelling than her asperity. 'You know your way to the dining-room, don't you?'

At the table he had deserted, in the front drawing-room, Lady Nest sighed: 'I can't imagine what induces him even to *try* to play Bridge. Darling Jennifer, too cruel to have saddled you with him! My heart bleeds for you! Why do you suppose he took you out of your heart call?'

'God knows!' responded Miss Cheadle, a raw-boned lady with the indefinable look of a horsewoman. 'Feel a bit sorry for the boy: got something on his mind.'

'I don't want to depress you, Jenny,' remarked Mr Charles Ashbourne, 'but, according to Roddy, you've been fobbed off with a stop-gap. Jack Doveridge stood Lilias up at the last moment.'

'Oh, well!' said Miss Cheadle largemindedly. 'That's all right: somebody had to have him!'

At this moment, two redoubtable ladies at a table in the middle of the room created a diversion by arguing with steadily mounting choler on the correct play of the hand which one of them had just (according to the other) mismanaged. It was a cardinal rule that these devoted friends should be kept apart at any Bridge-party, for each had a voice like the screech of a macaw, and neither had the smallest control over her temper. It was of course impossible to keep them apart throughout a duplicate-contest, but it had been hoped that since one was North and the other West no cause for dissension would arise. Unfortunately, North saw fit to criticise West's play, which, considering she and her partner had benefited by it to the tune of five hundred points above the line, was unhandsome of her. An altercation arose which showed every sign of developing into a brawl; and Mrs Haddington came back into the room to find play at all tables at a standstill. It said much for her tact that she was speedily able to soothe both ruffled ladies; and still more for her admirable command over herself that she did not betray her annoyance by so much as the flicker of an eyelid. Only Beulah, entering the room a moment later, knew that she was at all put out. Mrs Haddington, smiling with determination, said to her in an acid undertone: 'I thought I told you to keep an eye on things for me!'

Play was resumed, but another hitch soon occurred, which was explained by Dr Westruther, who came up from the library to say that they were held up there by Seaton-Carew's absence. 'Called away to the telephone in the middle of a hand,' he said. 'They're waiting to finish it.'

'*Still* telephoning?' said Mrs Haddington. 'Nonsense! He can't be. Or, if he is, he oughtn't to be!' she added, with a perfunctory laugh. 'It's really very naughty and inconsiderate of him, and I shall scold him severely! Roddy, do go and remind him that he's holding everyone up! In my boudoir: you know where it is!'

'I'll soon have him out of it,' said Sir Roderick, who

disliked him, and had already confided to Dr Westruther that the fellow was a bounder.

He then stumped out of the room, colliding in the doorway with Sydney Butterwick. He glared, his sapient eye taking in the fact that this weakheaded young man had been fortifying himself a little too liberally. 'Now then, now then, look where you're goin', young fellow!' he growled, and went off down the stairs to the boudoir.

A minute later he came back into the drawing-room, breathing rather hard, and looking very much shaken. He seemed to find some difficulty in speaking, and it was seen that his hand was trembling. Everyone stared at him; and Lady Nest, perceiving his pallor, jumped up from her chair, exclaiming: 'Roddy, are you feeling ill?'

He gulped, and made a gesture waving her aside. 'Westruther!' he said. 'Job for you! Go down there! That fellow – Seaton-Carew!'

'What is it?' Mrs Haddington demanded sharply. 'Roddy, what's the matter? Where's Dan?'

Sir Roderick tottered to a chair, and sat down. 'He's dead,' he said bluntly. 'Turned me up a bit. Nasty shock. No, no, Lilias, you stay where you are! Job for Westruther, not you. The fellow's been strangled!'

Seven

THE insistent clamour which had been intruding for some time into Chief Inspector Hemingway's dreams at last woke him. He swore, raised himself on one elbow, and groped for the lamp beside his bed. A moment later a voice said in his ear: 'Chief Inspector Hemingway?'

It was a brisk, official voice: the Chief Inspector recognised it as one that belonged to his superior, and life-long friend, Superintendent Hinckley, of the Criminal Investigation Department. He said, with great correctness: 'Yes, sir.'

'Sound sleeper, aren't you? Easy conscience, I expect. There's a job waiting for you.'

'Now, look here, Bob!' said the Chief Inspector, abandoning the official manner. 'If you're having a joke with me –'

At the other end of the wire, Superintendent Hinckley grinned unseen. '*I'm* not lying in my nice, warm bed! I'm on duty, and I'll thank you to remember it, my lad!'

Chief Inspector Hemingway, around whose exposed shoulders an icy draught was blowing, replied to this sally in terms which caused his superior to inform him severely that he wanted to hear no more of his lip. 'Wake up!' he said. 'This is a job after your own heart.'

'At this time of night?' said Hemingway indignantly. 'Don't tell me another Pole has gone and got himself knifed by one of his pals, because I'm not as young as I was, and if I've got to go off at this hour and listen to a lot of highly excitable foreigners, all jabbering different lies at me, I'm chucking the Force right now!'

'It isn't anything like that,' replied the Superintendent. 'Didn't I tell you it was after your own heart? Some bloke's been strangled in a house in Charles Street. Very classy joint: what you call good décor!'

In spite of himself, Hemingway was interested. 'You don't say! What's it all about? Robbery with violence?'

'No, nothing of that sort, as far as I can make out. In fact, no one knows rightly *what* it's all about. It happened in the middle of a Bridge-party, that I *can* tell you!'

'Ah!' said the Chief Inspector. 'Daresay the chap led his partner a heart after he'd signalled he wanted a club. Well, I've got no sympathy for him!'

'Look here!' interrupted the Superintendent, in whom this suggestion awoke galling memories. 'If I have much more from you, Stanley, you'll know it! Get up and dress! I'm putting you in charge!'

'What's C Division done?' demanded Hemingway, swinging his legs out of bed, and groping with his bare feet for his slippers. 'Don't they do night-duty these days?'

'You'll find Inspector Pershore waiting for you at the house,' said the Superintendent, with some relish.

'Oh, I will, will I? Well, isn't that a bit of luck for me? Of course it would have to be him, wouldn't it? He'll tell me all about it, I expect, and give me a few hints and tips as well, if I speak nicely to him! Hold on, while I shut this damned window, Bob!' He laid down the receiver, pushed the sash up, shrugged himself into a dressing-gown, and sat down again on the edge of the bed. 'All right: go ahead! Who's the murdered chap?'

'Man called Seaton-Carew.'

'Anything known about him?'

'Nothing known about any of them.'

The Chief Inspector groaned. 'Any line on it at all?'

'Might be, might not. Doesn't sound like a cinch, from the first report. There were forty-nine people in the house at the time –'

'*What?*'

'Fifty-five, counting the servants,' said the Super-intendent.

'And I suppose any one of them could have bumped this chap off! You know, Bob, I believe I've got an attack of 'flu coming on, or maybe it's scarlet fever!'

The Superintendent laughed. 'That's all right: it isn't as bad as that! Pershore has established that most of them couldn't have had anything to do with it. Not counting the servants, there seem to be seven people who might have had the opportunity.'

'Is that all! It's too easy, Bob!'

'According to Pershore, it's easier still. He says it's a clear case against one person – young fellow, name of Butterwick.'

'Well, if that's what he says, I've only got six people to interrogate – not counting the servants,' said the Chief Inspector unkindly. 'In fact, he may as well send young Butterwick off home to bed at once. I'd better get round there before he gets us all into trouble jugging a lot of innocent people. Let me have Sandy Grant, will you, Bob? Setting aside he knows my ways, once you get used to his silly habit of never giving you a straight yes or no, I'd sooner have him with me than any of the rest of them.'

'I've already detailed him, and Sergeant Snettisham, to you.'

'That's fine, but you don't have to go dragging Snettisham out of his bed at this hour: he's a married man, and I shan't need him tonight. Besides, I've got some consideration for other people, even if there are some that haven't.'

'All right, all right! I'll send a car round to pick you up.'

'You're spoiling me!' said Hemingway, and rang off.

It was shortly before two in the morning that the police car drew up behind two others, and an ominous ambulance, outside Mrs Haddington's house in Charles Street. Chief Inspector Hemingway, followed by the wiry, redheaded Inspector Grant of the CID, got out, and were admitted into the house by a uniformed constable, who saluted, and said that Inspector Pershore was awaiting them in the dining-room. Inspector Pershore came out of this room to greet them. He was a large, hard-faced man, with a consequential manner that had never yet failed to annoy the Chief Inspector. He took himself and his duties very seriously; and if Hemingway disliked him it was only fair to say that this dislike was cordially reciprocated. The higher Hemingway rose in the Department, the more important the cases that were entrusted to him, the less could Inspector Pershore understand the rules governing such promotion. He could not be brought to believe that anyone as incorrigibly flippant as the Chief Inspector could be what he called an efficient officer. He had been heard to express his astonishment at what the Chief Inspector's superiors put up with, and would certainly have been staggered to learn that no less a personage than the Assistant Commissioner had once said: 'Put Hemingway on to it! He'll threaten to resign – but he'll bring home the bacon!'

'Good-evening, Chief Inspector!' said Pershore punctiliously. 'Superintendent Hinckley informed me that he would be despatching you to the scene of the crime. I trust –'

'Well, there's no need for you to start talking like a newspaper report!' said Hemingway irritably. 'What he told you was that he'd be sending me along, because nobody ever heard him talk in that silly style – not outside the witness-box, that is!' He put his hat down on the table under the gilded mirror, and struggled out of his overcoat. A glance round the eau-de-nil hall out of his bright, birdlike eyes made him nod approvingly. 'Very classy!' he said. 'Where can we go where we shan't be interrupted?'

'I have made the dining-room my headquarters, Chief Inspector. The staff has not yet cleared away the refreshments intended for the party that was earlier assembled –'

'You couldn't have hit on a better place,' said Hemingway, walking into the dining-room, and warming his hands before the electric radiator. 'I daresay we shall need some refreshment before we're through. Now, what's all this about, Pershore?'

Pershore, clearing his throat rather pompously, glanced at his voluminous notes, and replied: 'I should say, Chief Inspector, that it is a clear case. At first sight, it may seem impossible that the crime could have been committed under the circumstances in which it was done; but, pursuant upon my interrogation of several of the persons present in the house, I reached the conclusion that this is a case that presents few difficulties –'

'What you want to do is to hire a hall, and give a series of lectures on police work,' interposed Hemingway. 'You'll probably make a lot of money: people will pay to listen to anything! I wouldn't, of course, but that's because I have to listen to you, and even the Department wouldn't expect me to pay for doing what I can't help. Now, you stop trying to annoy me, and tell me what's been happening here without any trimmings!'

The Inspector glared at him, but the exigencies of discipline prevented him from uttering a retort. He said stiffly: 'The house is rented by a Mrs Lilias Haddington, of whom nothing is known. She resides here with her daughter, Miss Cynthia Haddington, and a staff of six persons. There is also a young woman who is her secretary. She was on the premises at the time, but does not reside here. The murdered man was a Mr Daniel Seaton-Carew, address Haughton House, Jermyn Street. I understand him to have been a close friend of Mrs Haddington. He was one of forty-four persons invited to take part in some sort of a Bridge-game, and had previously dined here in company with Mrs and Miss Haddington, Miss Birtley, who is the secretary, Lord Guisborough, and a Mr Harte. There were two other guests, acting as scorers, one of whom is Dr Theodore

Westruther, who was the first to inspect the body. The murdered man was called to the telephone, which is situated in the room known as the boudoir shortly after eleven pm; and some minutes later, nobody being able to state with certainty how many, Mrs Haddington saying about ten, and Miss Birtley putting it rather higher, and no one else admitting to any knowledge of the exact hour at which Mr Seaton-Carew was called to the telephone, which is, of course, possible, if they hadn't happened to look at the clock –'

'Take a breath!' advised Hemingway.

The Inspector found that he had lost the thread of his narrative, and was forced to refer to his notes.

'The murdered man was called to the telephone,' Hemingway prompted.

'Some minutes later,' resumed Pershore coldly, 'Mrs Haddington requested Sir Roderick Vickerstown to go down to the boudoir, and remind Mr Seaton-Carew that they were all waiting for him. Sir Roderick complied with this request, and discovered the body of the murdered man as you will see for yourself, Chief Inspector. I come now to the persons whose movements during the period when the murder may be assumed to have been committed are unaccounted for.'

'No, you don't. First things first is my motto! I'll see the body before I get any more confused than what I am already. Take me to the boudoir you talk of!'

'Of course, it is just as you wish, Chief Inspector. I will lead the way,' said Pershore, suiting the action to the word. 'Sergeant Bromley arrived shortly before yourself, and is engaged in photographing any finger-prints in the room which may have a bearing on the crime, but nothing, I need hardly say, has been touched since I was called in, and arrived at 11.53 pm'

Since it would have been extremely improper for anything to have been touched before the arrival of a representative of Scotland Yard, this unnecessary assurance exasperated the Chief Inspector. He cast a fulminating look at Inspector Pershore's back, but was interrupted before he could utter the words trembling on his tongue.

'Whisht, now, whisht!' said Inspector Alexander Grant soothingly.

'I don't say you're not right,' retorted Hemingway, 'but if you're telling me to shut up, which I think you are, I'll put in an adverse report about you, my lad!'

The Inspector smiled in the way that gave him an odd resemblance to one of the shy stags of his own Highlands, and said no more. They had by this time mounted the stairs to the half-landing. Inspector Pershore opened the door into Mrs Haddington's sitting-room, and stood aside for Hemingway to enter.

There were several people in the room. All that remained of Dan Seaton-Carew was seated in the chair beside the telephone-table in the angle between the door and the first of the two long, curtained windows, his face most horribly distorted, and with two strands of picture-wire protruding at the back of his neck. His head had fallen forward on his breast; both his arms hung slackly beside him; one leg was stuck stiffly out before him, its foot under the fragile table which held the telephone; the other bent, so that its foot was against the leg of the chair.

The Chief Inspector observed him without blenching,

glanced round the room, and said cheerfully: ''Evening! No, I mean, good-morning! How's the kid, Tom?'

The photographer grinned at him. 'Going on fine, sir, thank you. Out of quarantine this week.'

'That's good.' Hemingway turned from him, and surveyed the still figure in the chair. 'Well, well!' he said, scrutinising every detail. 'The things people will get up to!'

He spoke in an absent tone, and all but one of his subordinates waited in respectful silence, well-aware that whatever inanities he might utter, his quick brain was anything but inane.

'The murder, as you will see, Chief Inspector,' said Pershore, 'was committed by means of a length of ordinary picture-wire, twisted about the neck of the victim by means of a tourniquet, supplied by some instrument unknown. As I see it, the murderer held one end of the wire, and this instrument, or implement, in one hand, say, right, quickly passed the other round the neck of the victim, standing behind him, of course, caught this end under the thumb of the left hand, so that the implement was held, as it were, between the two strands of the wire, and gave the said implement a couple of twists, or maybe more, thus producing death by asphyxiation within –'

'Och, hasn't he eyes in his head?' interrupted Grant. 'Will you not hold your peace, you silly man?'

'– a matter of seconds!' ended Pershore, swelling with indignation. 'You'll observe, Chief Inspector, that the wire is twisted hard up against the neck of the murdered man, and again just below where the strands part, showing that between these two places some implement has been inserted, and later withdrawn.'

86

'Found?' asked Hemingway, who did not appear to be paying much attention.

'It has not so far been discovered, Chief Inspector,' owned Pershore.

Hemingway's glance flickered round the room. 'Nothing here likely to be suitable. Might be almost anything, and won't do us any good if we did find it. I fancy I see this bird leaving his prints on it! Gone over the wire, Tom? You won't get anything off it, of course, but we've got to try everything.' He nodded to the photographer. 'Now then, I want a shot of the whole of this corner of the room first, taking it from about where you are.'

For the next few minutes, he was fully occupied with the photographer; and when this worthy, having taken all the photographs which were demanded, began to pack up his impedimenta, he stood still for a moment or two, still studying the unpleasant scene.

'The ambulance, Chief Inspector, is waiting to remove the body, if you have finished,' said Pershore.

'Is this exactly how he was found?' Hemingway asked. 'Nothing been moved?'

'According to the evidence given by Sir Roderick Vickerstown and Dr Westruther, which I have no reason to doubt, neither of them touched the body at all. I questioned the doctor very particularly, thinking he might have tried to resuscitate the murdered man, but he states that he saw at a glance that life was extinct; and he did not disturb the body. Later, the Divisional Surgeon, of course –'

'Yes, I'm not worrying about him. Nothing in the room been touched?'

'Nothing, barring the telephone-receiver, which I found hanging on the end of the wire, having apparently been dropped by the murdered man. It was replaced,' said Inspector Pershore grandly, 'under my supervision, and has since been photographed for finger-prints.'

'All right. Have the body taken away,' said Hemingway. 'Did Dr Yoxall say – No, never mind! I'll see him myself.'

The Inspector relayed the order to remove the body, saw that Hemingway had pulled the heavy brocade curtain away from the window behind the telephone-chair, and said: 'There's no doubt the murderer was concealed behind that curtain, Chief Inspector.'

'There's a lot of doubt,' responded Hemingway tartly. 'And if you go on calling me Chief Inspector every time you open your mouth, you and me will fall out. It's getting on my nerves. I don't say the murderer wasn't concealed: he may have been; but from the look of things it seems highly probably he wasn't concealed at all.'

'You mean, Chief – you mean that the victim was not expecting the murderer to attack him?' said Pershore slowly.

'Well, I don't myself expect to be murdered when I sit down to a game of Bridge with a party of friends. It may have happened just like you think, but to my mind, the chair's too close to the window for anyone to hide himself behind the curtain without attracting his victim's attention when he came out. If there wasn't a rustle, anyone sitting there, at an angle to the window, would be bound to see the curtain move, out of the corner of his eye. In which case, he'd have had time to have put up a bit of a struggle, at the very least. No sign of any struggle here, not a vestige. A nice, neat job, that's what I call it.'

'It is a cruel, wicked murder!' said Inspector Grant severely.

'You only say that because you don't like strangling cases. All murders are wicked. I've seen a lot more cruel than this one, and so have you.' He watched the shrouded body of Seaton-Carew carried out of the room on a stretcher, and said: 'That's better: now we can get on! What I want to know now, Pershore –'

'The suspected persons are being detained –'

'What I want to know now,' repeated Hemingway, 'is why this character, who lives in Jermyn Street, gets rung up in somebody else's house. In fact, is it established that he was rung up?'

'Naturally that point had occurred to me, Chief Inspector. It appears that the murdered man himself arranged to have the call put through to this house, and mentioned the matter when at dinner, in the hearing of the five other people seated at the table. The butler states that he was not in the dining-room at the time, and knew nothing about the arrangement. I've got no reason to disbelieve him so far,' said Pershore darkly, 'but he's not a good witness.'

'I daresay you didn't handle him right: there's a knack in examining butlers. So, on the face of it, only five people knew this call was coming through? Quite enough to be going on with too. Who answered the 'phone? The butler?'

'Miss Birtley states that she answered it, in this room. It was a Personal Call for the murdered man, from Doncaster.'

'Have it traced, Sandy.'

'At the time when it came through, the murdered man was playing at one of the tables in the library, which is the room directly underneath this one. There were eight other tables in the drawing-room, which occupies the whole of the first floor; and barring Mrs Haddington, and one of the guests, whom I will come to in due course, no one left that room during the period in question. We checked up carefully on that, and there doesn't seem to be any doubt about it, for they were all playing this Bridge-game, and nobody could have left the room without the three other people at his table remembering it. The names and addresses were taken, of course, but I saw no reason to detain anyone but this Sydney Butterwick I was speaking about.'

'Quite right. Go on!'

The Inspector once more consulted his notes. 'Miss Birtley's story is that when she came out of this room, with the intention of summoning Mr Seaton-Carew to the telephone, Mrs Haddington had come out of the drawing-room on to the landing above this. Mrs Haddington, according to Miss Birtley, showed annoyance when she heard the call was for Mr Seaton-Carew, but told Miss Birtley to go and fetch him up to take it. In this, Mrs Haddington concurs. She then told Miss Birtley to keep an eye on things while she went up to her room, which is on the second floor. Miss Birtley then went down to the library, where the murdered man was playing –'

'Look, I thought you'd shaken off that habit!' objected Hemingway. 'Stick to the man's name! If you're going to talk about the murdered man playing Bridge you'll give me the creeps!'

'Very well, Chief Inspector. What I was about to say when interrupted was, where the – Mr Seaton-Carew was playing Bridge at one of the tables. At the same table were Miss Guisborough, who was his partner, and is twin sister to Lord Guisborough, also in the library at the time; Mr Godfrey Poulton; and a foreign lady, calling herself Baroness –' He drew a breath, and enunciated painstakingly: 'Baroness Rozhdesvenskiy!'

'How much?'

The Inspector displayed his printed note. 'I got her to spell it, and the way I said it is the way she did.'

'It may be, but if you take my advice you won't say it any more, or you'll have people thinking you've got something the matter with you. As far as I'm concerned, she's the Baroness. Don't tell me! She's a Russian, and talked you silly! Let's get back to Miss Birtley's story!'

'Miss Birtley states that a moment or two after Mr Seaton-Carew left the library, during which time she emptied a couple of ashtrays, and replaced them, she went up to the drawing-room, picking up on the way a tray containing a whisky-and-soda, which she had put down on the chair outside this door when she originally answered the call. This she carried to a Colonel Cartmel, in the drawing-room, setting it down on a small table at his elbow. The Colonel more or less corroborated this, saying that he did not remember Miss Birtley doing it, but found the glass there when next he looked round. He was playing the hand at the time, and Miss Birtley did not speak to him. The other people at the table seem to think they remember seeing Miss Birtley put the glass down, but they are what I should call vague about it. Miss Birtley states that she lingered for a minute or two in the drawing-room, saw that one of the cigarette-boxes was nearly empty, and went downstairs to fetch up a fresh supply from a cupboard in the dining-room. In the dining-room, she states that she found Mr Butterwick, drinking a whisky-and-soda, supplied to him by the butler. She did not exchange any words with him, but got out the cigarettes, and went back to the drawing-room. That,' said Inspector Pershore, 'is her story.'

'And why have you got it in for her?' asked Hemingway, who had been watching him closely.

'I hope I have not got it in for anyone, Chief Inspector, but I should describe Miss Birtley as a very unsatisfactory witness. What is more, I have reason to think that she was concealing part of the truth from me. She was hostile, for one thing. Very unwilling to answer my questions, and very anxious to make me believe she hadn't had time to have murdered Mr Seaton-Carew – which it's my belief she had, only one person corroborating her story that she lingered for a minute or two in the library when Seaton-Carew had left it. And I didn't set much store by that, because it was as plain as a pikestaff he'd have corroborated anything she chose to say! The rest of the people in the library say they don't remember, that she was in and out a good many times during the evening. Also, I had occasion to ask her if she noticed whether Mr Butterwick seemed at all agitated. She said she didn't notice anything about him that was unusual, but the butler says nobody could have failed to have noticed it, because he looked very queer and jumpy, didn't seem to pay much attention to what was said to him, and drank off a couple of doubles before you could say Jack Robinson.'

'Before we come to him,' said Hemingway, 'what's Mrs Haddington's evidence?'

'Mrs Haddington states that after Miss Birtley had set off downstairs to fetch Seaton-Carew to the telephone, she was just going up to her room when she found that Mr Butterwick had come out of the drawing-room, and was standing behind her. He said he was going down to the dining-room to get himself a drink, play having finished at his table. She then went on up to her bedroom, and cannot state whether he went straight downstairs or not. She remained in her room for a few minutes only – uncorroborated, except that one or two people in the drawing-room say she wasn't gone for long – and then returned to the drawing-room, which she did not again leave until after the murder had been discovered. Mr Butterwick tells the same story. He says he left Mrs Haddington going upstairs, and himself went running down to the dining-room. He did not meet either Seaton-Carew or Miss Birtley and that, Chief Inspector, is where I think he's lying. He also states that he didn't hear any of the conversation between Mrs Haddington and Miss Birtley about this telephone-call, and that's another lie, or I'm much mistaken. He stayed in the dining-room, and came back into the drawing-room just as Sir Roderick Vickerstown was leaving it to find out what was keeping Seaton-Carew. Corroborated by Sir Roderick. The butler doesn't know when he left the dining-room, because he himself had gone down to his pantry while Mr Butterwick was still there.'

'I see. And has this Butterwick any reason for killing Seaton-Carew?'

'To my mind, he's got more reason than anyone else,' said Pershore. 'By what I've gathered, and from the looks of him I don't find it hard to believe, he used to be very thick with Seaton-Carew, and always flying into tantrums if ever Seaton-Carew paid too much attention to anyone else.'

'Oh, a homosexual, is he? Of course, I would have to strike a case with one of them in it!'

The Inspector looked down his nose. 'That is how he seems to me, and it's what I've been given to understand. But the butler, and Mrs Haddington's personal maid, both state that Seaton-Carew was after Miss Cynthia Haddington, which was not at all what Mrs Haddington wished, for he was as old as she was, and, what's more, he was very intimate with her. But that,' he added austerely, 'is uncorroborated gossip.'

'Nice goings-on!' commented Hemingway. 'Where are we getting to? Did Mrs Haddington strangle Seaton-Carew because he was making up to her daughter, or did Butterwick do it for the same reason?'

'Well,' said Pershore, 'it's only fair to state that both the butler and the parlourmaid say that after dinner tonight Mrs Haddington and Seaton-Carew were alone together in the library, and it sounded as if they were having some kind of a dispute – to put it no higher. And Miss Haddington says that when Butterwick arrived he found her talking to Seaton-Carew in the back drawing-room, and created a scene. She says he flew into a rage, and she was afraid he was going to do something silly, he was so upset. Lady Nest Poulton more or less agrees with that, though she didn't hear the actual words that passed between him and Seaton-Carew. She just says he seemed to be upset, but it wasn't anything out of the way with him. A Miss Cheadle, who was his partner, says that she thought he had something on his mind, but she knew nothing about the quarrel with Seaton-Carew.'

'Oh!' said Hemingway. 'Did Miss Birtley have a row with this Seaton-Carew as well?'

'According to the servants, Miss Birtley has always disliked him, and made no bones about showing it. He and she arrived at the house together tonight, and when the butler opened the door to them it was plain Miss Birtley was very angry with Seaton-Carew. He was laughing, and taunting her, by what the butler could make out, and she said something of a threatening nature about being determined as well as cruel, and he'd better not be too sure of something.'

'Yes, that's the sort of evidence that makes me wish I'd gone in for lorry-driving, or something easy. Any more people who had a silly quarrel with this popular number?'

'No, not exactly,' replied Pershore. 'But it seems that Lord Guisborough couldn't stand him – in fact, he as good as told me so. He's in love with Miss Haddington too, but he's accounted for: he was playing Bridge at one of the tables in the library, and he never left the room till the murder had been discovered. None of them did, at his table.'

'What a shame!' said Hemingway. 'Quite my fancy, he was. I've never arrested a lord yet, and he seems to have got just as much motive as anyone else I've heard of so far. What about the rest of the gang in the library?'

'Two only left the room while Seaton-Carew was absent. Mr Poulton, who was playing at his table, went out to get a breather – they all agree it was a bit stuffy in the room by that time. He states that he strolled along the hall to the front-door, and stood for a moment or two at the top of the steps. Then he went back to the library, visiting the cloakroom on the way. No corroboration.'

'Any motive either?'

'Not,' said the Inspector, 'that I have been able to discover.'

'That's fine: we'd better fasten on him,' said Hemingway.

'Fasten on him?' repeated the Inspector, staring.

'Well, I'd rather have no motive at all than the lot I've been listening to. Who else left the library?'

'Mr Harte. He was playing with Miss Haddington, against Mr and Mrs Kenelm Guisborough, who are by way of being Lord Guisborough's cousins. Some minutes after Mr Poulton had gone out, Mr Harte became dummy, and he too left the room. He met Mr Poulton coming out of the cloakroom.'

'And what did he do?'

'According to his story, he too went into the cloakroom. Mr Harte has no apparent motive – so perhaps you'd prefer to fasten on him, Chief Inspector!' said Pershore, with heavy sarcasm.

'You know, every time you say that name it rings a bell with me,' said Hemingway, frowning. 'But for the life of me I can't place it. Harte – Harte – I know I've met it before!'

'He is a nice-looking young gentleman,' offered Pershore. 'In the late twenties, I should say. He's a barrister, so perhaps that's how you come to know of him.'

Hemingway shook his head. 'No, that's not it. Oh, well! Perhaps I'll remember when I see him.'

'He is being detained in the drawing-room, along with Miss Birtley, Mr Butterwick, Mr Poulton, and Dr Westruther. Dr. Westruther, being a scorer, was in the library when Seaton-Carew left it, and went up to the drawing-room to inform them there of the cause of the delay in the game before the discovery of the murder. Dr Westruther states that he had not met Seaton-Carew previous to this evening.'

'Well, what do you want to go detaining him for?' demanded Hemingway. 'A nice temper he'll be in by this time!'

'Properly speaking, I did not detain him. He remained of his own choice, or perhaps Mrs Haddington asked him to, Miss Haddington being a good deal upset – quite hysterical, she was, at first, but he got her calmed down.'

'Thank God for that, at all events! What I'd better do is to see these people, and get rid of those who don't belong here, or we shall have them pitching complaints in about the way they were kept up all night for no reason. What about the servants? Are they sitting up too?'

'Only the butler and the parlourmaid. None of the others was unaccounted for at the time, being in the servants' hall, and the kitchen.'

'Sandy, go and talk to them, and pack them off to bed! One last thing before I give your suspects the once-over, Pershore! Anyone know where that bit of picture-wire that was used for the job came from?'

'The wire, Chief Inspector, is part of a coil bought this morning – that is to say, yesterday morning – by Miss Birtley, at Mrs Haddington's instigation. Some of it she used to make what I understand to be a kind of flower-holder; and the rest she left on a shelf in the cloakroom.'

'In full view of any of the gentlemen who went into the cloakroom, I suppose?'

'Yes,' said the Inspector, considering it. 'Anyone washing his hands, or maybe straightening his tie in the mirror, would be pretty well bound to see it, if she left it where she says she did.'

'It gets easier and easier, doesn't it?' said Hemingway.

'It doesn't strike me that way. And not one of them did see it. Or, if they did, they won't own to it,' said the Inspector.

Eight

A group of six people was assembled in the front half of the drawing-room, from which the card tables had been removed. The velvet curtains had been drawn across the archway leading into the back drawing-room, and the fire was burning brightly in the grate. The room presented a comfortable, if slightly over-opulent, appearance, but nothing could have looked less comfortable than five of the six persons disposed round the fire. In one corner of a sofa, Mrs Haddington sat bolt upright, staring into the flames, her thin, ringed hands tightly clasping her fan. She had risen magnificently to the occasion, when first the body of her old friend had been discovered, her social instincts prevailing over more primitive emotions; but the effort of carrying off an entirely unprecedented situation, coupled with the rapid collapse of her daughter into strong hysterics, had levied a toll on her vitality. She looked haggard, every muscle on the stretch, as though it was only by a supreme exercise of will-power that she refrained from breaking-down. Beside her, occasionally glancing at his wrist-watch, and imperfectly stifling a yawn, sat Dr Westruther, wondering why he had allowed his nobility to lead him to announce that he would remain on the premises until the arrival of 'the man from Scotland Yard'. He had not, of course, supposed that this would be so long delayed.

Opposite the sofa, in a deep armchair with wings, Mr Godfrey Poulton sat, contemptuously flicking over the pages of a weekly periodical, yawning quite openly, and presenting the appearance of one who ought to have been in bed several hours earlier. A little withdrawn from the fire, and seated limply in a chair, her eyes shaded by her hand, was Miss Birtley. Her other hand ceaselessly kneaded her handkerchief. Completing the circle, were Mr Sydney Butterwick, and Mr Timothy Harte. Mr Butterwick's first reactions to the tragedy had rivalled Cynthia's in intensity and dramatic expression. From these transports of unbridled and slightly spirituous emotion, he had passed into a mood of such distressing despair, that Mr Harte, the only unaffected member of the party, had exerted himself, partly from pity and partly from dislike of watching adult males weeping bitterly, to divert his mind. The task had been a difficult one, but Timothy had persevered, to such good effect that by the time Chief Inspector Hemingway walked into the room Sydney had been coaxed into his paramount hobby, and was passionately assuring Timothy that *Giselle* was the only real test of a classical dancer's art.

Inspector Pershore ushered Hemingway into the room, announcing that the Chief Inspector wanted to have a word with its occupants.

'Good-evening!' Hemingway said cheerfully, his tone a welcome contrast to the accents of officialdom assumed by his subordinate. 'I'm afraid you've been kept waiting a long time, and I'm sorry about that.'

'Good God!' said Mr Harte, staring at him between narrowed eyelids. 'You're the Sergeant!'

It seemed, from Inspector Pershore's alarming demeanour, that he only awaited a sign from the Chief Inspector to take Mr Harte instantly into custody; but Hemingway, regarding Mr Harte with interest and surprise, gave no such sign. 'Well, I was once, but I've been promoted,' he replied. 'Did you happen to know me when I was a Sergeant, sir?'

'Of course I did!' said Timothy, rising, and going towards him, with his hand held out. 'You probably don't remember me, but don't you remember the Kane case?'

A blinding light flooded the Chief Inspector's brain. 'Harte!' he exclaimed. 'I said it rang a bell! Well, well, well, if it isn't Terrible –' He broke off, for once in his life confused.

'Terrible Timothy,' supplied Mr Harte. 'I expect I was, too. How are you? I should have known you anywhere!'

'I'm bound to say I shouldn't have known you, sir,' said Hemingway, warmly shaking him by the hand. 'If you don't mind my saying so, a nice nuisance you were in those days! And how's that brother of yours? I hope no one's been trying to bump him off since I saw him last?'

'Only Jerry. He lost a leg at Monte Cassino, but otherwise he's flourishing. Got four kids, too.'

'You don't say! Well, time certainly does fly! When I think that it seems only yesterday you were a nipper yourself, sir, driving me mad trying to help me solve that case – well, it doesn't seem possible!'

'I do seem fated to be embroiled in murders, don't I?' agreed Timothy. 'Only this time I'm suspect, you know!'

'Yes,' said Hemingway severely, 'and from what I remember of you, sir, that'ud just about suit your book, that would! Of course, I was handicapped on the Kane case, you being only a kid, but things are different now, and I give you fair warning, if you start getting funny with me I shall know what to do. Because the more I look at you, the more I see you haven't changed so very much after all!'

This interchange, though revolting to Inspector Pershore, insensibly brought about a relaxation of tension amongst the rest of the company. It was felt that if young Mr Harte stood upon such friendly terms with the man from Scotland Yard the mantle of his popularity might well be stretched to cover some at least of his fellow-suspects. Spirits rose, only to be depressed again by the Chief Inspector's next words. Still speaking in a tone of the warmest approbation, he said: 'I'll have to come and hear all about what you've been up to since I saw you last, sir. Now, Inspector Pershore's got your address, so that I shall know where to find you, if I should happen to want to ask you any questions about this little affair; and it won't do for me to keep you hanging about here any longer tonight. The Inspector tells me you gave him your evidence very nicely: he's got it all down, so I won't waste your time asking you a whole lot of questions you've answered already.'

Timothy grinned at him appreciatively. 'Did you find me easy to get rid of when I was fourteen, Chief Inspector?' he asked.

'No, sir, I did not, but I warned you things were different now! I can get rid of you fast enough.'

'Oh, no, you can't!' retorted Timothy. 'I'm Miss Birtley's legal adviser!'

This cool announcement had the effect of jerking Beulah's head up, and of causing Mrs Haddington to look sharply first at her, and then at Timothy.

Beulah said in a disjointed way: 'No, no! I don't need – I don't want – I'd much prefer that you didn't!'

'Yes, you would think up a crack like that, wouldn't you, sir?' said Hemingway. 'All right, you stay! You won't worry me. And since you're here you may as well make yourself useful, and tell me who everyone is, so that the Inspector here needn't wait about any longer.'

Inspector Pershore, who appeared to be more sensitive to suggestion than Mr Harte, said: 'If you have no further need of me, sir –'

'No, that's all, thank you, Inspector. I shall be seeing you later, I daresay,' replied Hemingway affably.

The Inspector then withdrew, and Timothy made the remaining five persons present known to Hemingway. He favoured each in turn with his keen, bright look, but singled out Dr Westruther, saying: 'You'll be wanting to get off home, doctor, and I'm not going to keep you. I think Inspector Pershore asked you everything, and I know where to get hold of you, if any point should arise that you might be able to help us over. I understand you were with Dr Yoxall when he inspected the body, and there wasn't any disagreement between you?'

'There could hardly have been any in this case,' said the doctor. 'Death must have occurred within a matter of seconds.'

'Just so, sir! And Mr Poulton is anxious to get home

too, so I think it would be best if I asked him a few questions first. Now, sir, if you'll be so good!'

Godfrey Poulton, rising in a leisurely way from his chair, said: 'Certainly, Chief Inspector,' in his deep, rather cold voice, and followed Hemingway from the room.

'No objection to coming in here, I trust, sir,' said Hemingway, opening the door into the boudoir. 'It seems to be the only room that isn't full of playing-cards or prawn-patties.'

'I have no objection, since I assume that –' Mr Poulton paused, allowing his eye to fall upon the chair by the telephone. 'Precisely,' he said.

'Oh, no, that's all right!' Hemingway said, understanding his cryptic utterance. 'I don't think I shall be keeping you for many minutes either, sir.' He saw that Poulton was looking at his second-in-command, and said: 'Inspector Grant. Sit down, sir! I understand you left the library at some time during Mr Seaton-Carew's absence from it. I think I have all that in Inspector Pershore's notes. Was the deceased a friend of yours?'

Poulton shrugged. 'Hardly that. I suppose I've met him half a dozen times.'

The Chief Inspector, before entering the drawing-room, had read Pershore's voluminous notes, and he had an excellent memory for relative detail. 'Did he visit your house, sir?'

'I daresay,' Poulton replied, his heavy-lidded eyes dwelling indifferently on the Chief Inspector's face. 'My wife entertains a great deal, but I am a very busy man, and I am not invariably present at her parties.'

'Quite so, sir. Mr Seaton-Carew was Lady Nest's

friend rather than yours?'

'It would be more accurate to say that he was an acquaintance of hers. My wife originally met him through her friendship with Mrs Haddington.'

'Were you on good terms with him, sir?'

Again Poulton shrugged. 'Certainly – though that's a somewhat exaggerated way of describing it. If you mean, had I quarrelled with him – No. If, on the other hand, you mean, did I like the man? Again, no.'

'It's a funny thing about this Seaton-Carew,' remarked Hemingway, 'that he seems to have been a popular sort of a character, and yet he got himself murdered.'

'Very funny,' agreed Poulton. 'Perhaps you are confusing popularity with usefulness. Unattached men, Chief Inspector, are greatly in demand amongst hostesses.'

'Ah, very likely!' said Hemingway. 'Well, it doesn't seem as though you can help me much, sir, so I won't keep you any longer.'

Inspector Grant rose, and opened the door.

'Thank you,' said Poulton. 'I shall be glad to get to bed. I have a heavy day ahead of me. Good-night!'

The Inspector closed the door behind him, and glanced across at his superior. 'You did not press him, sir.'

'No, I'm never one to waste my time. If you were to have given Mr Godfrey Poulton the choice between having a sewer-rat loose in his house or the late Seaton-Carew, it's my belief he'd have chosen the rat. Make a note of Lady Nest: we'll see what she has to say. I'd better interview this Butterwick now. Fetch him down, Sandy!'

The Inspector lingered. 'Would that one have had the time to have committed the murder, you think?'

'Any of them would have had time and to spare. In fact, this is one case where the time-factor isn't going to bother us – or help us either, for that matter! As far as I can make out, it was anything from ten to twenty minutes between Seaton-Carew's being called to the 'phone and Sir Roderick's finding him dead. How long do you reckon it would take *you* to nip up half a flight of stairs, twist a wire round a bloke's neck, and nip down again?'

'It is in my mind,' said the Inspector, 'that it would have been a strange thing for him to have gone into a room where he knew a man to be speaking on the telephone.'

'You mean you think it would have put Seaton-Carew on his guard. It might, and it mightn't. Of course, if Seaton-Carew had reason to think Poulton wanted to do him in, I agree that you'd expect to find some sign of a struggle. Supposing he hadn't? Supposing this Poulton-bird walked in, just said, "Excuse me!" as though he'd just come to fetch something?'

'*Och, mo thruaighe!*' exclaimed the Inspector. 'What would he have come there to fetch, tell me that?'

'By the time Seaton-Carew had thought that one up,' retorted Hemingway, 'the wire was round his throat! Mind, I don't say it happened like that, but even if it didn't there's no need for you to make those noises, which I take to be highly insubordinate. Go and fetch that pansy down to me!'

Mr Sydney Butterwick, ushered into the boudoir a few minutes later, flinched perceptibly, but seemed to have himself fairly well in hand. His face still bore traces of the emotions which had ravaged it, but he was able to smile, albeit a little nervously, at Hemingway, and to assure him that if he could possibly be of assistance to the police they could count upon his cooperation.

'I was devoted to Dan!' he said. 'Utterly devoted to him! I suppose anyone will tell you that. In some ways, you know, he was rather a marvellous person. Slow extravert, of course, and I'm definitely a quick extravert, but with a certain amount of overlap, if you know what I mean. I suppose you might call me an intuitive extravert. I'd better tell you at once that I wasn't in the least blind about Dan! In fact, I recognised and accepted him for what he was. In some ways, I do absolutely agree that he was just a handsome brute, and I shan't deny for one moment that I used to quarrel with him quite terribly. As a matter of fact he upset me rather poignantly tonight, and it's the most ghastly thought that the last time I saw him I was furious with him! Well, not so much furious as wounded. Of course, I know I take things to heart too much: my type always does – I don't know if you've read Jung?'

Inspector Grant's gaze shifted to the Chief Inspector's face. The Chief Inspector had two hobbies: one was the Drama; and the other, which he pursued to the awe, amusement, and exasperation of his colleagues, was Psychology. He had listened amiably to Mr Butterwick's flow of words, but at this challenge he lost patience. 'Yes, and Wendt, Münsterburg, Freud, and Rosanoff as well!' he replied tartly. 'That's how I know you don't belong to the Autistic Type. I haven't had time yet to decide whether you're Anti-Social, or Cyclothymic, but I daresay I'll make up my mind about that presently.'

This unexpected rejoinder threw Sydney off his

balance. He said, with a titter: 'How marvellous to meet a policeman interested in psychology! I think I'm definitely the Anti-Social, or Hysteric Type. I mean, I haven't a single illusion about myself. It's fatal not to face up to oneself, isn't it? For instance, although I adore Michael Angelo I do realise that that's probably an expression of empathy-wish, in the same way that –'

'Sit down, sir!' said Hemingway.

Sydney obeyed him, passing a hand over his waving fair locks, and then mechanically straightening his tie. 'Do ask me any questions you like!' he invited. 'I shall answer them absolutely honestly!'

'That's very sensible of you, sir,' said the Chief Inspector dryly. 'Suppose you were to tell me, as a start, what was the cause of your quarrel with Mr Seaton-Carew last night?'

'He had hurt me,' replied Sydney simply.

'How did he manage to do that?'

'I hadn't seen him for three days, and he wouldn't speak to me on the telephone. That was the sort of thing he used to do, when he was in that mood. Teasing me, you know, but not really meaning to hurt. He told me once that I took life too hard, and I suppose it was true, but –'

'You thought he was sick of you, didn't you?' interrupted Hemingway ruthlessly.

'Oh – ! Not really!'

Hemingway glanced at the notes under his hand. 'You said to him, *I suppose that means you're fed up with me!* and he replied, *All right, I am!* Is that correct, sir?'

The colour rushed up to the roots of Sydney's hair. He exclaimed in a trembling voice: 'How do I know what I said? I suppose you got that out of that little bitch of a Haddington girl!'

'Do you, sir? Why?'

'I've no doubt Cynthia Haddington imagines that just because he took a little notice of her Dan was in love with her!' said Sydney, trembling slightly, and quite ignoring the Chief Inspector's question. 'Well, he wasn't! He wasn't! And if she's stuffed you up with some tale of my being jealous of her, it just makes me want to laugh! That's all!'

Anything further removed from laughter than Mr Butterwick's aspect would have been hard to have found; but Hemingway, while making a mental note of this fact, forbore to pursue the matter. He merely requested Sydney to describe to him what had been his movements from the moment of his leaving his table to get himself a drink to the moment of his re-entry into the drawing-room.

'Oh, of course, if it interests you –' said Sydney, shrugging his shoulders.

'*A Chruitheir!*' uttered Inspector Grant under his breath.

'There's really nothing to tell,' said Sydney. 'We had finished playing that particular hand at my table, and I seized the opportunity to go down to the dining-room, that's all. I didn't see anyone, except the butler, if that's what you want to know.'

'Didn't see anyone, sir? I understand that you had some conversation with Mrs Haddington, at the top of the stairs.'

'Oh, that! I thought you meant, did I see Dan, or anyone else, who might have killed him. Yes, I believe I did exchange a word or two with Mrs Haddington, but I don't remember what was said. Quite unimportant, in any case.'

'Was anyone else on the landing, or the stairs, when you came out of the drawing-room, sir?'

'I really don't remember. I don't think so.'

'What was Mrs Haddington doing on the landing?'

'Good God, how should I know? She was going up to the second floor – in fact, she started to go up when I went down.'

'Miss Birtley, I take it, had gone down before you followed her?'

'Yes – that is, I suppose she must have, because, to tell you the truth, I don't recall seeing her. I daresay she may have been there: I wouldn't notice. And, of course, since it all happened mere trivialities have passed from my mind.'

'Did you hear the telephone-bell ringing, sir?'

'No, but I probably wouldn't, because it's got a muffled bell, and only makes a sort of burring noise.'

'Is that so? How do you happen to know that, sir?'

Sydney stared at him for a moment. The smile wavered on his lips. 'Oh – oh, this isn't my first visit to the house!'

'I see. And you didn't hear it tonight, didn't know the call was for Mr Seaton-Carew, and didn't hear anything that passed between Mrs Haddington and Miss Birtley? I want to get this quite straight, sir, so that Inspector Grant can take it down accurately, and we shan't have to make a lot of corrections later.'

Sydney glanced at the impassive Inspector, and from him to Hemingway. Once more he smoothed his hair.

'No, I don't know what they said. I mean, now you bring it to my mind I do seem to remember vaguely that Miss Birtley was there, but that's definitely all. If you're thinking that I knew she'd gone to fetch Dan up to take the call, and that it was I who murdered him in that ghastly way – well, you're not only wrong, but it's utterly absurd! If you must know, I was terribly upset by the whole affair – anyone will tell you that! It was the most appalling shock: in fact, for a moment I damned nearly fainted!' He glanced at Inspector Grant, seated with a notebook in one hand, and a pencil in the other, and burst out angrily: 'It's no use asking me to sign a statement, because I won't! I'm too terribly shattered to know what happened this evening!'

'Well, you haven't made a statement yet, have you, sir?' said Hemingway. 'All you've done is to answer a few questions, and hand me a few lies, which it's only fair to tell you I don't believe.'

'You've no right to say that!' Sydney declared, a trifle shrilly. 'You've no shadow of right to talk to me like that!'

'Well, if that's what you think, sir, all you have to do is to lodge a complaint against me with the Department,' replied Hemingway. 'You'll have to convince them that you didn't hand me a lot of silly lies, of course – and, come to think of it, you might just as well convince me of that, and save us both a heap of unpleasantness. And if you'd stop thinking you'll be pinched for murder if you admit you knew Mr Seaton-Carew was telephoning in this room, we'd get on much faster. There isn't any question but that Mrs Haddington and Miss Birtley both knew it, but I can't arrest the three of you, nor I don't want to!'

'O God!' Sydney ejaculated, and, to the patent horror

of Inspector Grant, dropped his head in his hands, and broke into sobs.

'Och, what a *truaghan*!' muttered Grant. '*Ist, Ist, nach ist thu?*'

'Now, don't you start to annoy me!' his superior admonished him. 'Come, now, sir, there's no need for you to take on like that!'

'I know you think I murdered him!' Sydney said, in a choked voice. 'All right, think it! Arrest me! What do you think I care, now Dan's dead? Oh, Dan, oh, Dan, I didn't mean it!'

This extremely embarrassing scene caused the Inspector so much discomfort that he could only be glad to hear Hemingway recommending Mr Butterwick to go home, and to bed. He ushered him out of the room, and came back himself, mopping his brow. 'Indeed, sir, I was glad to see you get rid of that one!' he remarked. 'Though I would not say Pershore was wrong when he thought it possible he was the man we are after. To my mind, he would be likely to weep the eyes out of his head if he had killed his friend.'

'Very likely. And to my mind it was a case of drink taken; and waste my time on maudlin drunks, without a bit of solid evidence to go on, I will not!'

'He was not drunk precisely,' said the Inspector, with native caution. 'I should say, however, that he had had a dram this night.'

'Half a dozen, more like. I'll see Mrs Haddington next.'

Mrs Haddington walked calmly into the room five minutes later. She looked quite as well-groomed and as well made-up as when she had stood within the drawing-room to receive her guests, many hours earlier; but she had removed her diamonds, and her gloves. She inclined her head in a stately fashion to Hemingway, and disposed herself in a chair beside the fireplace. 'What is it that you wish to ask me – er – Chief Inspector, I believe?'

'I want first to ask you, madam, where you were when the telephone rang this evening. In fact, I should like you to tell me just what your recollection is of what happened then, and up till the moment that Sir Roderick Vickerstown found Mr Seaton-Carew dead in this room.'

She replied without hesitation: 'When the telephone rang, I was standing just inside the front drawing-room. I went out on to the landing, meaning to tell whoever answered the call that I could not speak on the telephone at that moment.'

'You thought the call was for you?'

'I did think so,' she admitted. 'That, however, was forgetfulness: I knew that Mr Seaton-Carew expected to be rung up, for he had mentioned it to me at dinner. I was not best pleased, though it seems heartless to say that now. Telephone conversations in the middle of a Bridge-evening hold up the game, and are extremely annoying for everyone else. Miss Birtley answered the call, and I told her to fetch Mr Seaton-Carew up from the library, where he was playing, to do his talking where he would not be disturbed – and where he would not disturb others. I can't tell you when he came up to this room, because by that time I had myself gone upstairs to my bedroom. Nor can I tell you how long I was absent from the drawing-room: not, I think, many minutes. When I came down again, there was no one either on the landing, or on the staircase, and the door into this room was shut. I assumed that Mr Seaton-Carew was still telephoning, and went back into the drawing-room. There was a slight dispute going on at one of the tables, which occupied my attention. I recall that I was very much displeased with my secretary – Miss Birtley – for not keeping an eye on the smooth running of things while I was absent from the room, as I had asked her to do. She was not even in the room, but only entered it some minutes after I did. Then Dr Westruther came up from the library, to say that everyone was waiting for Mr Seaton-Carew to return, and I asked Sir Roderick to come down to this room, and – well, put an end to all this telephoning.'

'I think you expressed surprise, didn't you, madam, that Mr Seaton-Carew should still be speaking on the 'phone?'

'Did I? Quite likely: I remember thinking that he had had ample time to have made two calls.'

'Can you form any estimate of the time that had elapsed between your going up to your room, and Sir Roderick's coming here to look for Mr Seaton-Carew?'

'Really, I would rather not commit myself,' she said. 'I wasn't paying any particular heed to the time, you see. It might have been ten minutes – I think not less – or it might have been longer. I have no idea.'

'I see. And did anyone, other than yourself and Miss Birtley, know of this call?''

'Everyone who dined here knew that the call was expected. I assume that those people who were in the library must all have known that he was fetched to answer the telephone. Mr Butterwick also knew: he was standing at my elbow when I told Miss Birtley to fetch Mr Seaton-Carew.'

'You are quite sure of that, Mrs Haddington?'

She stared at him. 'Perfectly.'

'You don't think that there is any doubt that he heard your conversation with Miss Birtley?'

'Not the slightest. He is not deaf.'

'That wasn't quite my meaning. You don't think it possible that he came out on to the landing after you had finished speaking to Miss Birtley?'

'Certainly not. At one moment I was speaking to Miss Birtley; at the next I became aware of young Butterwick hovering just behind me.'

'Thank you, that's very clear. Now, I understand that the wire found twisted round Mr Seaton-Carew's neck has been identified as part of a length bought yesterday afternoon by Miss Birtley, and left by her on the shelf in the cloakroom.'

'So I have been told. I never saw the wire myself.'

'You didn't go into the cloakroom?'

'I had no occasion to do so. I am aware that Miss Birtley has stated that she left what she did not use of the wire on the shelf. I can only say that if this is true she had no business to do so: the shelf in the cloakroom is not the place for odds and ends. Furthermore,' she added, 'it seems to me a very peculiar circumstance that not one of my guests saw the wire in the cloakroom.'

'Have you any reason for thinking, madam, that Miss Birtley did not leave the wire there?'

She shrugged. 'I should not, myself, place any very great reliance on what Miss Birtley said,' she replied.

'How long has Miss Birtley been in your employment?'

'About five months.'

'I take it that she doesn't give entire satisfaction,' said Hemingway. 'Would you mind telling me if her references were all in order?'

'I'm afraid I can't help you over that. I engaged her on the recommendation of Mr Seaton-Carew.'

'Is that so, madam? Was Miss Birtley a friend of his?'

'Mr Seaton-Carew had – most kindly – interested himself on her behalf. A form of charity rather than of friendship. I should have said that Miss Birtley cordially disliked Mr Seaton-Carew. It would be better, perhaps, if you questioned Miss Birtley her self. I am very reluctant to say anything more about her than that she is in my employment, and that while she has been with me I have had no reason to complain of her conduct. Now, if that is all – ?'

'Not quite, madam. How long have you known Mr Seaton-Carew?'

She had made as if to rise from her chair, but she relaxed again. 'For very many years. He was a close friend of my husband's – almost one of the family. Since my husband's death, twelve years ago, he has advised me on business matters. His death has been a terrible shock to me: I can scarcely realise it yet. I find it very painful to be obliged to discuss it.'

'I'm sure you must,' agreed Hemingway sympathetically. 'I understand he dined with you tonight?'

'Yes, he did.'

'Was there any sort of disagreement between you, madam?'

She looked at him, her tinted lips thinning. 'I see. You have been listening to servants' gossip, I think, Chief

Inspector. It is quite true that I had occasion to be most annoyed with Mr Seaton-Carew, and equally true that I took him sharply to task, after dinner, and before my Bridge-guests arrived.'

'I'm afraid I shall have to ask you what was the cause of this quarrel, madam.'

'There was no quarrel. Mr Seaton-Carew never quarrelled with anyone. He was not a man who took things seriously. He was sometimes, in fact, far too flippant, which made him very irritating. This was by no means the first time he had succeeded in making me lose my temper, I can assure you!'

'Very understandable, madam. And the reason?'

'If you must know, I told him that I would not allow him to philander with my daughter! My daughter is an extremely lovely girl, but quite inexperienced, and Mr Seaton-Carew's manner towards her was putting ridiculous ideas into her head. He was a very attractive and handsome man, and I expect you know as well as I do how flattered a young girl can be when a man of his age makes a pet of her. He meant nothing, of course, but a child of nineteen couldn't be expected to realise that. I told him that this foolish flirtation must stop, or I should be obliged to stop inviting him to my house. He tried to make a joke of it, and I lost my temper. That is all. Is there anything else I can tell you?'

'Just one thing, madam. Is Mr Butterwick a frequent visitor to your house?'

She was perceptibly amused. 'Sydney Butterwick! He most certainly is not! I think I first met him at a party given by Mrs Chetwynd. He came to a ball I gave for my daughter at Claridge's, and I remember, to my cost, that

I invited him to a musical soirée at this house about a month ago. The quite ridiculous and revolting scene he created on that occasion because he imagined that Mr Seaton-Carew was paying too much attention to someone other than himself, made me say I would never again invite him. Nor should I have, but that I was let down yesterday by one of my other guests, and had to fill a gap at a moment's notice!'

'And on the occasion of this musical evening, Mrs Haddington, do you recall whether the telephone rang?'

She raised her brows. 'Good heavens, no! If it did, my butler would have answered the call, and said that I was engaged. I should not, in any event, have heard the bell, because it is muffled. It rings in the hall, and in the butler's pantry, and the call can be taken from any of the instruments I had installed in the house.'

'Thank you, madam, I shan't keep you any longer tonight,' said Hemingway.

Inspector Grant closed the door behind trailing folds of black velvet, and turned to survey his chief with a troubled look in his eyes. 'It is in my mind,' he remarked, 'that she is a bad woman – a verra bad woman! Look you, it is a *clach* she has in her body, not a heart!'

'I wouldn't wonder!' retorted Hemingway. 'Talk English, Sandy, can't you? '

'And all she said to you about that *caileag* was spite!' pursued the Inspector, disregarding this admonition.

'If,' said Hemingway patiently, 'the *halleuk*, or whatever it was you said, means Miss Beulah Birtley, I'm not at all surprised. What *does* surprise me is that she gave the girl a job in the first place. Because she's not my idea of a philanthropist, not by a long chalk!'

'What is this?' demanded Grant.

'Well,' replied the Chief Inspector, 'apart from Terrible Timothy, Miss Beulah Birtley is the only one of this push I ever saw before. And I saw her a matter of eighteen months ago, at the London Sessions. She got sent down for nine months, I think, for robbing her employer. Forgery, I think it was, but it wasn't my case, and I might be mistaken about that. Fetch her down to have a nice heart-to-heart with me, will you?'

Nine

Mrs Haddington, sweeping into the drawing-room, found that young Mr Harte was still seated by the fire, engaging Miss Birtley in desultory conversation. Mrs Haddington favoured him with her mechanical smile, but addressed herself to her secretary. 'I imagine the Chief Inspector will wish to interrogate you, Miss Birtley. I suppose you had better spend the rest of the night here – unless you could get hold of a taxi to take you home. At my expense, of course, but heaven knows what the time is, and whether there are any taxis still on the streets I have really no idea.'

'Don't worry!' Timothy said, rising to his feet. 'I've got my car outside, and I'll run Miss Birtley home when the Inquisitors have finished with her.'

'I wish you wouldn't bother!' Beulah said.

'No bother at all, dear Miss Birtley: a pleasure!' Timothy responded promptly.

'Really, I think it is extremely kind of you!' Mrs Haddington said, slightly raising her plucked eyebrows. 'If you will forgive me, I shall go up to bed.'

'Please don't sit up on my account!' Timothy begged. 'You must be dropping on your feet!'

'I am very tired,' she acknowledged. She turned her head, as the door opened, and said: 'Ah, you want my secretary, I expect!'

'If you please, madam,' said Inspector Grant.

Beulah rose jerkily. 'I'm quite ready. I – I wish you wouldn't wait, Timothy!'

'You've said that before,' he pointed out. 'My own conviction is that you ought to be supported by your legal adviser during this interview.'

'No, no, really I'd rather not! *Please!*'

'The Chief Inspector, sir, would like to see Miss Birtley alone, I think,' said Inspector Grant.

'What the Chief Inspector would like leaves me very cold,' retorted Timothy.

'Timothy, I would much prefer to be alone!'

'That,' said Timothy, 'is quite another matter. Go with God, my child!'

Upon entering the boudoir, Beulah could not forbear casting one shrinking glance towards the chair beside the telephone-table. It was, of course, empty, and she seemed to breathe more easily. Hemingway, who had equipped himself, at the start of his interrogations, with one of the small tables with which the room was generously provided, rose from behind it, and invited her to take the seat he had placed opposite to his own. He then requested her, in an official tone, to furnish him with her full name.

She said, in her brusque way: 'Beulah Birtley. I've already told the police that once tonight.'

'I know you have,' replied Hemingway. 'What I'm asking you for is your *full* name.' Across the little table, their eyes met, hers challenging, his mildly enquiring. 'I remember Beulah,' said Hemingway conversationally.

'But there was another Christian name, foreign, I think; and Birtley wasn't the surname."

'I don't know what you're talking about!'

'Yes, you do,' Hemingway said. 'I've got a good memory for faces, and yours isn't one I'd forget easily.'

'You are mistaken. You may think you know me, but I've never seen you before in my life!'

'No, you wouldn't have noticed me: I wasn't concerned in your case. But I happened to be in Court that day. So now let's get down to brass tacks, shall we? It doesn't do you any good to tell me lies, and it's very wearing for me. Name?'

She looked for a moment as though she did not mean to answer, but in the end she said sullenly: 'Francesca Beulah Birtley Meriden.'

'I thought there was a foreign name in it,' commented Hemingway, writing it down. 'You got nine months, didn't you? Embezzlement?'

'Also forgery.'

'How old are you?' he asked, glancing shrewdly at her.

'Twenty-four.'

'Parents?'

'Both dead.'

'Any other relatives?'

'I have an uncle – though he would prefer me not to say so. I've neither seen him nor heard from him since my imprisonment. He's probably forgotten my existence by now: he's very good at forgetting unpleasantness.' She shot him a darkling look. 'What has all this got to do with what happened here tonight? I suppose you think that because I was convicted of theft and forgery you can pin this murder on to me?'

'Not without a bit of evidence I can't. Though it'd be just like the wicked police to fake up a lot of evidence against you, wouldn't it? Let's cut that bit! You'd be surprised the number of times I've listened to it before. How long had you known Seaton-Carew?'

'Since I came out of prison.'

'Oh? How did you get to know him?'

She hesitated.

'Come on!' Hemingway said. 'What was he up to? Giving a helping hand to lame ducks? Or did you meet him socially?'

'No, I didn't. Someone told me to go to him. Said he'd find me a job.'

'Who was that?'

'A woman.'

'Probation officer, by any chance?'

'No. A fellow convict!'

'Now, that's very interesting,' said Hemingway. 'Don't bother to tell me you didn't go to the Probation officer, or report yourself at any police station, because I can guess that, and it isn't what I want to talk about, anyway. What made this woman think Seaton-Carew would find you a job?'

She gave a short laugh. 'I don't know. At least, I didn't know at the time. There were still quite a lot of flies on me six months ago! I don't really know now – but it wasn't because he was a philanthropist! She apparently thought he would find a use for me. He did: he sent me to Mrs Haddington. That was very nice for all of us. He got her gratitude; she got a secretary who wouldn't give notice, however poisonous she was; and I got a fixed wage.'

'Well, that sounds like philanthropy, doesn't it? What was Seaton-Carew's job in life?'

'I have no idea.'

'Now, look here!' said Hemingway. 'You've thrown out a few hints that he was up to no good, so presumably you have got an idea! Suppose you were to stop behaving as though you thought you were Little Red Ridinghood and I was the Wolf! If I were, I should start getting nasty about your failure to report yourself while on licence, whereas I'm not saying anything about that at all. At the same time, you're on a sticky wicket, and the best thing you can do is to come clean.'

'I thought it wouldn't be long before we reached threats!' Beulah said, her lip curling.

Hemingway sighed. 'Have sense!' he begged. 'So far, the only member of this outfit who's got a record is you. You haven't got an alibi; you bought the wire which was used to strangle him. If you can add that lot up to a different total than what I come to you're a darned sight smarter than I think! Which isn't saying much,' he added caustically.

Her eyes narrowed. 'Look!' she said, between closed teeth. 'Once upon a time Little Red Ridinghood thought the police were her guardian angels, and that all she had to do was always to tell them the truth. Then she discovered her error, and, being several darned sights smarter than you think, she didn't fall into it again! I'm not spilling my heart out to you, Chief Inspector! The only thing I'm going to tell you is that I didn't murder Seaton-Carew – though I rather wish I'd thought of it – and if you can pin it on to me, good luck to you! I don't care a damn! I know what kind of a merry hell one can live through if one is a released convict, and I'd a lot rather be dead! I haven't the slightest doubt that you'll tell the world my record, so you may as well make a clean sweep, and arrest me for murder while you're about it!'

'Yes, but, you know, I'm handicapped,' objected Hemingway. 'We do have to be so careful in the Force. Telling the world about your record would be clean against regulations.'

She looked up quickly, but only said: 'Well, I don't care. I don't know anything about Dan Seaton-Carew.'

'All right, we'll leave it at that,' said Hemingway. 'Tell me something you do know! When you took that call, what did you do with the receiver?'

'What did I *do* with it? Put it on the table, of course!'

'Just show me, as near as you can, will you?'

She looked frowningly at him, as though suspicious of a trap. After a moment, she rose, and went to the table, lifting the receiver from the rest with her left hand, and laying it on the table.

'No nearer to the edge than that?'

'I don't think so. I'm not sure, but I think this is how I left it.'

'Thanks; you can put it back now. Who was on the landing outside the drawing-room when you took the call for Seaton-Carew last night?'

'My employer.'

'No one else?'

She frowned. 'No. Not at once. Mr Butterwick came out of the room, but he wasn't there at first.'

'Did he come out in time to hear your conversation with Mrs Haddington?'

'I don't know. I wasn't paying much heed to him.'

'Did you see him again while Seaton-Carew was in this room?'

'I saw him in the dining-room, but I didn't speak to him.'

'Did you notice whether he was what you might call normal, or a bit upset?'

'No. I didn't.'

'You're a great help, aren't you?' said Hemingway.

'I've got no wish to help the police.'

'Go away before I lose my temper with you!' recommended Hemingway.

He succeeded in surprising her. She looked astonished and blurted out: 'Is that all? Don't you want to know what I did with the spare coil of wire?'

'You left it on the shelf in the cloakroom, where no one, not even Mrs Haddington, happened to catch sight of it.'

'So likely that anyone would admit to having seen it! And if Mrs Haddington didn't, it must have been the only thing that did escape her eye in the house! She saw that one of the unfortunate servants had put out the wrong kind of towel in the cloakroom fast enough!'

'Oh, she saw that, did she? Careful housewife?'

'Extremely so! Capable of drawing her finger along the tops of things to be sure there's no dust there!' said Beulah, with a short laugh. 'Anything more?'

'Not at present. You go home, Miss Birtley, and think things over a bit! Then perhaps we'll get on much better when next we meet.'

Inspector Grant rose quietly, and opened the door. Beulah hesitated, looking from him to Hemingway, and then went quickly from the room.

The Inspector closed the door with deliberation. His chief, regarding him with the eye of experience, said: 'All right, I can see you're bursting with something! Let's have it!'

'A verra dour witness,' said the Inspector.

'Well, if that's all – !'

The Inspector's slow, shy smile lit his eyes. 'Och, I saw nothing you did not see yourself! You will not thank me for pointing out to you that Mrs Haddington stated that she had not entered the cloakroom; nor that she has it in her, that lassie, to murder a man.'

'She's got it in her all right, but I'm damned if I see the motive. Look up her case, will you, Sandy?'

'I will, of course. It's verra interesting: no one had a motive.'

'Someone had. Our trouble is that we don't know the first thing about any of them – barring that girl. All we've got is a bunch of classy people, all moving in the best circles, all to be handled carefully, and only one of them known to the police.' He scratched his chin meditatively. 'You can just see a chap like Mr Godfrey Poulton putting up a beef to the Assistant Commissioner about the rude way he's been handled, can't you? And they've all of them got such nice manners they won't talk about each other! To think I should ever be glad to run up against Terrible Timothy in a case! It all goes to show, doesn't it?'

'That would be Mr Harte?'

'It would.'

'I do not think he would strangle a man.'

'I'm dead sure he wouldn't – at least, I would have been before the War, but now I come to think of it he's just the sort of young devil to have got himself into a Commando, and the parlour-tricks they taught those lads were enough to make your hair stand on end! All the same, Terrible Timothy isn't even an Also Ran in my humble opinion. Which is why, Sandy, I am going to call on him in these chambers of his, and get him to give me the low-down on these people! He was very keen on helping me when he was fourteen: well, now he *can* help me!' He rose, and added: 'And what his father and mother would say, if they knew of the highly undesirable bit of goods he's got his eye on, is nobody's business!' He shut his notebook, and restored it to his pocket. 'We'll go and see what the backroom boys have discovered in the way of finger-prints. It won't help us, but we may as well go by the book. After that, we'll give Mr Seaton-Carew's flat the once-over, and see what we can get out of that. No use my hauling some housemaid out of bed to get the story of the wrong towel out of her: that'll keep.'

'What, Chief Inspector, did you make of Mrs Haddington?'

'I'm no judge of snakes, but she seemed to me a good specimen! I didn't like her, I didn't like her story, and I don't like her any the better for the latest disclosure. Come on!'

The finger-print experts had only one thing to show the Chief Inspector that interested him. As he had supposed, no prints could be obtained from the wire twisted round Seaton-Carew's neck; the prints on various objects in the room included only those which would naturally be found there. The telephone-receiver showed several rather blurred prints, a clear impression of Miss Birtley's fingers, and not a trace of the murdered man's.

'Which is a very significant circumstance,' said Hemingway. 'It's no use asking me why it's important, because so far I don't know. I know it is, because I've got *flair*. That's French, and it's what made me a Chief Inspector, whatever anyone may tell you.'

'It means,' said Inspector Grant, 'that the murdered man never touched the receiver.'

'How long did it take you to work that one out?' demanded Hemingway offensively.

The Inspector continued, unmoved: 'And it means that either the instrument was knocked from the table in a struggle, or that someone lifted it, and dropped it. For why?'

'You can rule out the struggle: there wasn't one. If that had been how that receiver came to be hanging down to the floor, the whole table would have been kicked over, and it wasn't. It looks as if someone deliberately lifted it off the table, and let it hang.' He laid down the photograph he had been studying. 'Why? Fair-sized chap, Seaton-Carew, wasn't he? Whoever planned to do him in wanted to be sure of getting him in what you might call a convenient position. If you were called away in the middle of a game of Bridge to take a telephone-call, what would you do?'

'I do not play Bridge.'

'Well, shinty, or whatever your unnatural game is called! You'd pick up the receiver, *standing*! You might even be facing quite the wrong way for the assassin. But if you found the receiver hanging down beside the table, the way it was, what would be the easiest way for you to pick it up? To sit down in the chair, placed so handy, of course! That would bring your neck well within the reach of a shorter person. And don't tell me that every one of the suspected persons, barring Terrible Timothy, was shorter than Seaton-Carew, because I've seen that for myself! I told you this wasn't going to do us any good. What's the time? Seven o'clock? Let's make a night of it, and have some breakfast! After that, we'll go round to this Jermyn Street address, and startle Mr Seaton-Carew's man.'

Before they set forth on this mission, the Inspector was obliged to present his disgusted chief with the information that the call from Doncaster had come from a public call-box.

'Which isn't at all the sort of thing I want to be told at this hour of the morning,' remarked Hemingway, pouring himself out another cup of very strong tea. 'Not that I'm surprised. The only thing that would surprise me about this case would be if I was to get a real lead.'

'Whisht now, it is early yet!' said the Inspector soothingly.

'It isn't too early for me to recognise a thick fog when I see one!' retorted Hemingway. 'To think I told Bob I was glad it wasn't another Pole getting funny with a knife! Now, that was easy!'

'Ay,' agreed Grant. 'There were so many motives you said there was no seeing the wood for the trees, I mind well. And three of the suspects with records as long as from here to the Border. Ah, well!'

'I don't know how it is,' said Hemingway, 'but whenever I get an assistant detailed to me he can't ever find anything better to do than to remember a lot of things I've said which it would do him more good to forget. I had a young fellow once with just that same habit, before the War it was, and do you know what happened to him? He had to leave the Force!'

'If it's Wake you're meaning,' said Grant patiently, 'I know well he left the Force, for he married a widow with a snug business, and already they have three, or it may be four, bairns.'

'Well, let that be a lesson to you!' said Hemingway. 'Stop trying to annoy me, and come to Jermyn Street!'

The morning papers were on sale by this time; as the police-car paused, in a traffic hold-up, before a news-agent's shop, flaring headlines caught the Chief Inspector's eye. One of the more popular journals sought to attract custom by the caption, written in arresting capitals: Murder at a Bridge-Party! Inspector Grant slid quickly out of the car, procured a copy of this enter-prising news-sheet, and jumped back into the car as it moved forward.

'That,' said Hemingway grimly, 'must have been sent in before two o'clock this morning – if not earlier! Nice times we live in!'

Scanning the somewhat meagre information contained in the paragraphs beneath the headlines, Grant said: 'I doubt this is the butler.'

'Well, I don't!' said his superior. 'There isn't any doubt at all about it! Come to think of it, butlers must make a pretty penny on the side. I wonder what they gave him for this tit-bit?'

'I do not know,' said Grant conscientiously. 'But it is in my mind that he would not have done this if he had been in the service of his last employer. Mind, I do not, myself, set any great store by a Sassenach, but I would say that Lord Minsterley was a gentleman-born, and would be respected by his servants! It is as I told you: they have no respect for Mrs Haddington. There was a telephone in the butler's pantry. Content you, he sent the news before ever we arrived at that house.'

'Why you should suppose that should content me I don't know, but never mind!' said Hemingway. 'It only means the crime reporters will be badgering us a bit sooner than we looked for.'

Mr Seaton-Carew's flat, in a block of bachelors' chambers, was on the third floor. An electric lift bore the two police officers to this floor; and the door of the flat was opened to them by a willowy manservant, who, if he did not appear to be startled by their arrival, was certainly nervous. He said that he had been advised earlier of his master's death; and made haste to usher them into the sitting-room.

The flat was not extensive, consisting merely of two bedrooms, a dining-room, a sitting-room, and what were known as 'the usual offices'. It was furnished in an expensive but undistinguished style, its amenities including mirrored panels in the bedroom, and the tiny hall; a plate-glass dining-table; numerous deep chairs covered in oxhide, and lavishly provided with velvet cushions; a glass-fronted bookcase, containing sets of standard authors in tooled calf bindings, which bore all the appearance of having been bought to form part of the room's decoration; an opulent radio-cabinet; several pictures in slightly exotic taste; and such repellent adjuncts as a standard lamp, upheld by a naked bronze female, an alabaster ashtray, surmounted by a silver aeroplane, and a cocktail-cabinet, furnished with an interior light, a bewildering array of bottles, and a complete set of glasses, all of which were embellished with erotic designs.

'In fact,' said Hemingway, 'the sort of décor that puts very funny ideas into one's head.'

A cursory inspection of the flat yielded no clue to Seaton-Carew's profession. It was strangely impersonal, nor did a rapid survey of his pass-sheets, discovered in a drawer of the desk, provide Hemingway with an explanation of his obvious wealth. His investments seemed to be few and orthodox, but on the credit side were numerous sums briefly described as Cash.

'Up to no good,' said the cynical Hemingway. 'Or perhaps he was only bilking the Inland Revenue,' he added charitably. 'This place tells us nothing at all, Sandy.'

The Inspector, who had gazed with an affronted eye upon the pictures adorning the walls of Mr Seaton-Carew's bedroom, and who had been noticeably affected by the sybaritic aspect of his bathroom, replied austerely that it told him a great deal.

'That's only prejudice,' said Hemingway. 'The trouble with you is that you're not broadminded. Ever noticed that all pansies have exactly the same kind of man-servant? Funny thing: you can spot 'em at a glance! We'll go and have a nice heart to heart with this specimen!'

But it was soon made manifest that Mr Francis Caister had not been admitted into his master's confidence. Smoothing his thick, curly locks with one unquiet hand, he said that he had been in Seaton-Carew's employment for eighteen months, and that it had been a very pleasant situation, Mr Seaton-Carew being a gentleman as was often out to meals. He did not think that his master had been in business. If he might, he would describe him as a gentleman of leisure. Questioned, he was a little vague on the subject of Seaton-Carew's visitors: he had had so many. He recalled Mr Butterwick, however, and said, with a genteel cough, that that was a young gentleman as took things to heart, as one might say. Quite hysterical sometimes, he had been, particularly if he found another young gentleman, or, as it might be, a lady visiting Mr Seaton-Carew.

'Did Mr Seaton-Carew entertain many ladies?' asked Hemingway.

'Well,' replied Caister coyly, 'not what one would properly term ladies. But,' he added, with a touch of vicarious pride, 'he used to visit in very nice houses.'

'Had he any relatives?'

Mr Caister was unable to answer this: he had never seen any; nor could he oblige the Chief Inspector with the name of Seaton-Carew's solicitor. A search through the desk in the sitting-room yielded little result: Mr Seaton-Carew had apparently made a habit of destroying his correspondence, nor did he keep an address-book. A cheque-book, however, furnished Hemingway with the name and address of his Bank. Leaving Inspector Grant to visit the Manager of the Branch patronised by Seaton-Carew, Hemingway went off to ring up Mr Timothy Harte, at his chambers in Dr Johnson's Buildings. Mr Harte, not being engaged in Court that morning, most obligingly said that he would be happy to entertain an old acquaintance there and then, but suggested (since he shared a small room with another budding barrister) that the rendezvous should be at his home address, in Paper Buildings. Thither the

Chief Inspector wended his way.

He was admitted to Timothy's chambers by a middle-aged man, who had Old Soldier written clearly all over him, and ushered into a comfortable room overlooking the garden, which smelt of tobacco and leather, and was lined with bookshelves. Most of these carried ranks of depressing Law Reports, and other legal tomes, some of which, having been acquired at second or third hand, had a slightly mildewed appearance. An aged Persian rug covered most of the floor, and a large knee-hole desk stood in the window. Young Mr Harte, in the black coat and striped trousers of his calling, was seated at this, smoking a pipe, and glancing through a set of papers, modestly priced on the covering sheet at 2 *guas*. He threw these aside when Hemingway came into the room, and got up. 'Come in, Chief Inspector! Welcome to my humble abode!' he said. 'Chuck those things off that chair, and sit down! Sorry about the general muddle: that's the way I like it!'

'Well, I'm bound to say I like it better than the last set of gentleman's apartments I was in, sir!' responded Hemingway, shaking hands.

'You do? Whose were they?'

'Mr Seaton-Carew's.'

'Fancy that now!' said Timothy. 'I should have thought he would have done himself very artily.'

'He did,' said Hemingway, removing *The Times*, a paperbacked novel, a box of matches, two bundles of papers tied up with red tape, and a black cat from a deep chair, and seating himself in it. 'Quite upset Inspector Grant. But then, he's a Scot! I'm more broadminded myself. No, thanks, sir, if it's all the same to you, I'll light my pipe. I thought I'd just look in to have a crack with you about old times.'

'Having the morning on your hands,' agreed Timothy. 'Come off it! What am I? Chief Suspect, or Information Bureau?'

'Yes,' said Hemingway, 'you always were about as sharp as a bagful of monkeys, sir, weren't you? I daresay it'll get you into trouble one of these days. I do want some information, but I'd like to know what you've been up to since I saw you last.'

'School – War – Cambridge – Bar,' replied Timothy succinctly.

'I'm glad to see you came through the War safe and sound, anyway. Where were you?'

'Oh, all over the place!'

'I'll bet you were. Don't tell me you weren't in that Commando gang, because I shouldn't believe you! Right down your street that must have been!'

Timothy laughed. 'I did end up with them,' he admitted.

'I knew it! In fact, if I'd found a nasty-looking knife stuck into Mr Seaton-Carew I'd have arrested you on the spot.'

'Ah, I was too clever for you, wasn't I? Beer, or whisky?'

'I'll take a glass of beer, thank you, sir. Now, joking apart, you could help me a bit on this case, if you wanted to. I don't mind telling you that I'm all at sea. Very unfamiliar décor. What I want is some kind of an angle on a few of the dramatis personae, so to speak. Well, here's your very good health, sir!'

Timothy returned the toast, and sat down on the other

side of the fireplace. 'I don't promise to answer you, but what do you want to know?'

'I want first to know what sort of a man this Seaton-Carew was, and what he did for a living.'

'Search me!' replied Timothy. 'I've often wondered. I thought the breed was dead. In fact, how anyone can live in these piping times as what used to be known as a gentleman of leisure has me beat. No visible means of support. Lives at a good address, dressed well, drove a high-powered car, generally to be seen at first-nights, Ascot, the Opera, the Ballet, and at quite a number of slightly surprising houses. Women were inclined to fall for him; men very rarely. That,' added Timothy, 'is not to be understood to include what we will politely term The Boy Friends. De mortuis nil nisi bonum, Melchizedek!'

The cat, which had sprung on to his knee, arched its back under his caressing, turned round twice, and settled down, purring loudly.

'Would you say he was a gentleman, sir?'

'I should say he was a high-class bounder,' promptly replied Timothy. 'Still, I know what you mean, and I suppose the answer is Yes. I don't know what school had the rare privilege of rearing him, but unless he was uncommon quick at picking up ways and tricks which can't possibly be described he was certainly at a decent one. I never heard him mention any relations, nor have I met anyone else of his name. You'd think anyone with a fine double-barrelled name like that would have hundreds of cousins littering the country, wouldn't you? Not so, but far otherwise! However, one must be fair, and he had no military prefix to his name. It always seemed to me the one thing lacking to complete the picture. Anything more I can tell you about him, or have I been defamatory enough to be going on with?'

'Something seems to tell me that you didn't like him,' said Hemingway, with a twinkle.

'I expect your instinct gets pretty highly developed at your job,' said Timothy. 'I didn't. Broadly speaking, I'm in sympathy with his murderer, though I can't say I'm in favour of strangling people at Bridge-parties. Breaks the evening up so.'

'If you don't mind my saying so, sir, you're a cold-blooded young devil!' said Hemingway frankly. 'Of course, if you do, I shall have to take it back, but I shall go on thinking it! My next question is what you might call delicate. Who is this Mrs Haddington?'

'Your guess is as good as mine, Chief Inspector. Widow in comfortable circumstances who gate-crashed Society about eighteen months ago. Previously unknown to Society, according to my Mamma. Said to have lived much abroad. Obvious reason for the gate-crash, one staggeringly beautiful daughter. How it was done, God knows! You wouldn't call her an attractive type, would you?'

'I would not, sir. Would money do it?'

'It would do a bit. Wouldn't get her into the houses I've seen her in. I'm told she was sponsored by Lady Nest Poulton. They appear to be bosom friends – which is another surprising thing. Lady Nest isn't exactly choosey, but she usually takes up celebrities, or very amusing types: not dull and rather off-white widows with lovely daughters. The money angle wouldn't interest her – her husband is rolling in the stuff. Nor is she the kind of woman who has a yen for launching débutantes. But she actually presented Cynthia Haddington last spring, and gave a ball for her. All very obscure.'

'Tell me a little about these Poultons, sir, will you? Lady Nest, now – would she be Lady Nest Ellerbeck that used to get her picture in all the papers when she was a girl?'

'That's right: Greystoke's daughter. Went the pace no little in the Gay Twenties. Sort of Pocket Venus. Still pretty easy on the eyes, though she must be quite as old as my Mamma. Restless, unsteady type, very Athenian – always seeking some new thing, I mean. Poulton is Big Business. I hardly know him. Seems a quiet, dull sort of a chap. Doesn't figure much at his wife's parties. I don't mean that there's anything wrong: merely that he's a man of affairs, and more often than not flying to the States, or the Continent, or somewhere on business.'

'Was Seaton-Carew a friend of the Lady Nest?'

'Yes. Nothing in that: very good man at a party, much cultivated by hostesses.'

'You wouldn't put it any higher than that, sir?'

'Lord, no! If someone's told you that she called him Dan-darling, or Dan-my-sweet, dismiss it from your mind! She calls me Timothy-my-lamb on no provocation whatsoever. It's her line. Anything more?'

'Dr Westruther?' said Hemingway.

'Pillar of Harley Street. Sort of bloke who calls female patients Dear lady, and recommends them to take a glass of champagne and a caviare sandwich at eleven every morning.'

'Now, how can you possibly know that?' expostulated Hemingway. 'Don't tell me Lady Harte told you so, because I remember her very well, and if she's taken to going to fashionable doctors all I can say is that she's changed a lot in thirteen years!'

'Oh lord, no! I had that from quite another source: one of the Old Guard – *not* at Mrs Haddington's party! Are you fancying Westruther in the rôle of Chief Suspect? What a singularly fragrant thought!'

'I'm not, but, according to the evidence, it was he who went up to the drawing-room from the library to explain how it was that the game was being held up.'

'Pausing on the way to strangle Seaton-Carew. Why?'

'I can't think,' said Hemingway calmly. 'He says he hadn't ever met him before.'

'I think the better of him. Half a shake! What price Sir Roddy? He it was who discovered the body, wasn't it? Now, there's a line for you!'

'When you kept on getting under my feet in the Kane case, sir,' said Hemingway, with some asperity, 'you may have driven me dotty, but at least you took it seriously, not as if it was a roaring farce! I don't say you haven't been helpful, because you have, up to a point, but I can see it's high time I left!'

'Oh, don't go!' Timothy begged, his very blue eyes wickedly mocking. 'If it's because you heard the doorbell, stay put. I told Kempsey to say I was out. Nobody but tradesmen would call on me at this hour, anyway. I'm one of the world's workers, I am.'

He was wrong. A halting step sounded, the door was opened, and Mr James Kane limped into the room.

'Hallo, Jim!' exclaimed Timothy, rising from his chair to the intense discomfort of Melchizedek. 'Now, this really *is* a reunion! Meet your old friend Sergeant

Hemingway, now masquerading under the guise of a Chief Inspector!'

'Then you *were* at that party!' said James Kane, casting upon the table a copy of that same periodical which had caught the Chief Inspector's eye earlier in the morning. 'You bloody little pest, Timothy! I could scrag you! For God's sake, Hemingway, clap him into a cell at Canon Row, and keep him there! How are you? I can't say, considering the circumstances, that I'm glad to meet you here, but it's nice to see you not looking a day older! Is my blasted half-brother one of the suspects?'

'Well, sir, I'm bound to say that he is!' replied Hemingway, wringing his hand.

Ten

'Y ou don't mean to tell me it's all in the papers already, Jim?' said Timothy incredulously.

'I don't know about all, but quite enough!' said Mr James Kane. 'You aren't mentioned, but you can bet your life Mother will guess you were there!'

Timothy, who had picked up the newspaper, and was interestedly reading the fatal paragraphs, retorted: 'Mamma doesn't take in a rag like this! If you hadn't such a low taste in literature –'

'Thanks very much, this is Nanny's chosen organ! How that woman knows what she does know beats me!' "Oh, Daddy, aren't these Uncle Timothy's friends? I thought you'd like to see what it says here about them!" Like hell I would! You'd better tell me the worst, and be done with it! Who is this Seaton-Carew, and are you really implicated, or not?'

'Of course I am!' said Timothy indignantly. 'I've got no alibi, I didn't like the fellow, and the Serg – I mean, the Chief Inspector, says I'm cold-blooded! So stop thinking you're the only member of the family who can be suspected of brutal murder! Such side! The only thing that stops our old friend arresting me here and now is my low cunning in using picture-wire instead of a knife. Come to think of it, I believe I've still got that lovely weapon somewhere.' He cast a look around the room. 'I don't say I could put my hand on it, but –'

'No, that I'll be bound you couldn't, sir!' said Hemingway. He turned to Jim Kane. 'I wish I could stay and have a bit of a crack with you, sir, but I can't, and in any case you'll be wanting to talk to Mr Harte, so I'll say goodbye. He hasn't changed much: I keep thinking of that burglar alarm he fixed up outside your door!'

'Wretched brat!' said Mr Kane, grinning reminiscently.

Timothy escorted the Chief Inspector to his front door, and returned to find his half-brother filling a pipe. 'What brings you up to town, Jim?' he enquired.

'Business, primarily. Also that!' Mr Kane jerked his head towards the newspaper. 'Are you really mixed up in this, Timothy?'

'I don't think so. I was present, however. Rather a mess, one way and another.'

Mr Kane grunted, and struck a match. 'I should have thought we'd had enough murders in the family, I must say.'

'Too true. Not that this one can be said to be in the family.'

Pressing the glowing tobacco down into the bowl of his pipe with his thumb, Jim Kane glanced shrewdly across at his young relative. 'Got more than a casual interest in it, haven't you?' he asked.

'Yes,' responded Timothy coolly. 'I have. The girl I propose to marry is, like myself, one of those who might have committed the murder.'

Mr James Kane was still busy with his pipe. Puffs of

143

smoke arose from it. 'So that's serious, is it? I heard something about it from Mother.'

'Did she tell you it was your duty to come and reason with me?' asked Timothy, unscrewing another bottle of beer. 'Beulah didn't go big with her at all, I'm afraid.'

Jim accepted the glass that was handed to him, and set it down on the mantelshelf behind him. 'No, she didn't. Far from it, but don't run away with the idea that I swallow all Mother says without a tablespoonful of salt, because I know Mother rather better than you do, and that isn't one of the errors I fall into! All the same, are you quite sure you aren't making a mistake, old son?'

'Quite sure,' said Timothy.

These simple words made it difficult to continue the conversation, but Jim tried his best. 'Silly question to have asked you. What I mean is, don't go and do something you'll regret for the rest of your life!'

'All right, I won't.'

Mr Kane recruited his forces with a drink. 'If you will have it in plain English, don't make a mésalliance, Timothy! God knows I don't want to barge into your affairs, but, even allowing for Mother's exaggerations, this tie-up doesn't look like the right sort of marriage for you at all! I daresay I sound damned offensive, but do think it over carefully before you do anything rash! Setting aside your own future, you ought to consider Mother, and your Father a bit!'

'I don't think Father will worry much,' said Timothy. 'He doesn't, you know. As a matter of fact, I've always thought he had more interest in you than in me. Of course, I quite see that it's disappointing for Mamma.

What with you marrying your great-aunt's companion, and me marrying Mrs Haddington's secretary – !'

'Look here!' exclaimed Jim. 'Pat may have been Aunt Emily's companion, but she comes of a good family, and she's got hordes of relations, all out of the right drawer, let me tell you!'

'That's where I score over you,' said Timothy.

'Listen, Timothy!'

'Listen, Jim!' interrupted Timothy. 'I love you very much, I love your well-born wife, I even love your extremely exhausting brats! You're the hell of a nice chap, and I wish you hadn't lost your leg, but –'

'Go to the devil!' said Jim rudely.

'You've taken the words out of my mouth, brother,' said Timothy. 'Have some more beer!'

'Blast you!' said Jim.

Timothy refilled his glass. 'What kind of an impressionable ass do you take me for, Jim? Facetiousness apart?'

'I don't. I should have said you were pretty hard-boiled, but you seem to have taken a header this time.'

'I have, but if Mamma gave you the idea that I've fallen for a cross between a film-star and an adventuress, get rid of it! So far, I've failed to get my intended to name the day; and although I happen to admire her appearance I'm well aware that she wouldn't stand an earthly in any Beauty Competition.'

'Oh!' said Jim, rather blankly. 'It's like that, is it?' He lowered himself into one of the armchairs, and leaned forward to tickle Melchizedek under one ear. 'I see.'

'I hoped you might. You fell for a lot of Lovelies before you took a similar header over Pat, who wasn't a patch on any of them as far as looks went. So, if you've finished coming the elder brother, we can go on from there. If not, we'll discuss the weather.'

'All right,' Jim said. 'Go on from there!'

'There isn't really very much to tell you,' Timothy said reflectively. 'I can set your mind at rest on one point. In spite of her often atrocious manners, she is indisputably a lady. No, blast it, she isn't! She's a gentlewoman! As far as her background goes, I only know that her mother was an Italian, and her father was an English artist. Since I've never heard of him, and since he demonstrably left his daughter without a penny, I deduce that he was a very poor artist. But since he seems to have supported a wife and a child in moderate comfort I also deduce that he had some private means – possibly an allowance from his family, which died with him. I do know that when her mother died, Beulah went to live with an uncle and aunt, on her father's side of the family. For some reason, undivulged, she broke with them; and has been earning her own living ever since.'

'Hasn't she told you why she broke with them?'

'No.' Timothy stirred the fire with one foot, and watched the flames leap up. He glanced down at his half-brother. 'I'm being very frank about this, Jim.'

'Yes, all right! Go on!'

'I'd a lot rather not, but I've a pretty good idea of what Mamma probably told you, and you'd better have the true picture presented to you. At some time or other, Beulah took a knock. I don't know what it was, but it put a crust on her. She's scared white of something, and tries to hide it under a general air of belligerence. Seems to have taken Mamma in all right. Told you Beulah was an adventuress, didn't she?'

'Well, I don't know that she actually said –'

'Cut it out! We both know Mamma! If Beulah's out to entrap me and my money and my prospective title, she's going to work in a weird way to achieve her ends! She knows damned well I'd get a special licence and marry her tomorrow, if she'd consent. All she does is to try to choke me off.'

'Any idea why?'

Timothy shrugged. 'Oh, same line of talk you've been handing out! New style in adventuresses!'

'You needn't keep on harping on that theme: she obviously isn't an adventuress. I never thought she was: you aren't nearly a big enough catch for an adventuress! But what I do think, Timothy, little though you may like it, is that she doesn't sound the girl your fond relations would wish you to marry.'

'My fond relations –'

'Yes, I know! We can all of us go to hell. I'll take that as read. You've been perfectly frank with me, and I'll be equally frank with you. I don't like the sound of this carefully shrouded background. Without wanting to hand out a lot of drip about Perfect Love and Perfect Trust, I do strongly advise you not to plunge into matrimony with a girl who conceals her past and her family from you!'

Timothy was silent for a moment; then he said abruptly: 'I'd like you to meet her. Are you going home today, or are you staying in town?'

'I've got a room at the club. So likely I'd bolt for home in the middle of this imbroglio you've got yourself into, isn't it?'

A smile of considerable affection was bestowed upon

him. 'You great fool, what do you think you can do?' asked Timothy.

'I can run down to Berkshire, and dissuade Mother from taking the first train up to town!' said Jim grimly.

'If ever I spoke of you in opprobrious terms, I take them all back!' said Timothy. 'You're a tower of strength, Jim!'

'Get out!' said his ungrateful half-brother. 'You said this Beulah of yours was implicated in the murder: were you serious?'

'She knew Seaton-Carew, she disliked him, she had the opportunity to murder him. She's implicated to that extent. Like several others, including me.'

'Could she have done it? I don't mean, *did* she: I'll accept that she didn't: but could any woman?'

'Easily,' replied Timothy. 'I know one or two neat ways of doing a man in, but I rather think this has 'em beat. I saw the body, and I saw how the trick had been worked. No strength required. Hold your arm up! I'll show you. All I need is a handkerchief, and – and – this ruler will do, for purposes of demonstration.' He cast his folded handkerchief round Jim's wrist, applied the ruler, and turned it twice.

'Hi!' exclaimed Jim.

Timothy released the tourniquet. 'Sorry! Wouldn't take many seconds, if that was round your neck, would it? In the actual murder, picture-wire was used – bought, earlier in the day, by Beulah, on Mrs Haddington's instructions, and left on a shelf in the cloakroom. No secret about that – a fact which I trust our old friend has assimilated. I should think he would have: he's got a damned intelligent face.'

'Hemingway? Got any reason to think he suspects the girl?'

'Not sure. He came here to get the low-down on what he calls the dramatis personæ. Noticeable that he asked me no questions about Beulah. That might be because he guessed I was an interested party, or it might be that your arrival interrupted him. If Beulah treated him to her talented impersonation of a clam, which is all too likely, I should imagine that he's fairly bristling with suspicion. I wanted to muscle in on that interview, just to prevent her behaving like the silly little cuckoo she is, but she wasn't having any. What happened I really don't know. I motored her home to her digs when it was over, but she wasn't communicative, and I didn't press her. I'm going round to Charles Street this afternoon, ostensibly to make kind enquiries. If I can do it, I shall get Beulah to dine with me tonight. Some quiet place – Armand's. You come and join us, Jim! Eightish, and morning dress. I'll be there anyway.'

'All right,' Jim said, hoisting himself awkwardly out of his chair. 'I've got to meet a man at the Savoy for lunch, but I don't think my business with him will take me long. If I get away in decent time, I'll nip down to Chamfreys this afternoon, administer a large soporific to Mother, and come back.'

'What a bloody pest I am to you!' said Timothy remorsefully.

'You are, and always have been. I'm punch-drunk!' said Mr Kane. 'I'll tell Mother I'm going to see Beulah for myself: that'll hold her for a bit. But she'll want to know what I made of her, so bring her along tonight! She sounds pretty alarming, but better than the blonde, if Mother's description is anything to go by!'

'Good God, did Mamma get the wind up over Cynthia Haddington? What a rare turn she is, to be sure! The mildest of flirtations! She wouldn't look at me anyway: out for big game, Cynthia Haddington!'

This lighthearted conviction was destined to be shaken. Upon his presenting himself in Charles Street that afternoon, at an hour when he judged that Mrs Haddington would still be resting, Timothy was led by Thrimby to the drawing-room, where he found Cynthia huddled in a chair beside the fire, a litter of periodicals at her feet, and an expression of the deepest discontent on her lovely face. At sight of Timothy, she sprang up, and flung herself in an embarrassingly uninhibited way upon his chest. 'Oh, Timothy, thank *God* you've come!' she cried, and burst into tears.

Young Mr Harte blenched, but he kept his head. Bracing treatment seemed to be called for, and he applied it. 'Well don't make such a song and dance about it!' he said. 'Pull yourself together, Cynthia!'

'It's all been so *awful*!' sobbed Cynthia, unresentful of this cavalier response.

'I'm sure it has,' said Timothy, detaching her clasp about his neck. 'You'd better not cry about it, though: it'll make your nose red. Sit down, and tell me what's been happening since last night!'

'*Nothing!*' she said. 'That's what makes it utterly *frightful*! Everything's *ghastly*, and Mummy wouldn't let me go to Meg's party, and she says I've got to wear this *filthy* black frock, which makes me look a hag, and Aunt Violet's here, and I can't find my powder-compact *anywhere*, and there's nothing to do, and that beastly radio's got nothing but Choral Services and Forces' Educational, and I wish I was *dead*! And on top of that I'm so *utterly* upset about Dan, but nobody understands, or cares! *He* wouldn't have wanted me not to go to any parties! It isn't as though he was a relation! Mummy ought to *want* me to go out, to take my mind off it all!'

She then dragged her reluctant visitor to the sofa by one hand, pulled him down on to it, and sobbed gustily into his shoulder. It was quite impossible to discover which item of the catalogue of disasters, so movingly recited, affected her most. Timothy did not even try, but applied his energies to the task of soothing her distress. To his intense discomfort, she acquired a limpet-like grip on the lapel of his coat; he guessed that the shoulder of his coat would shortly become impregnated with her expensive powder, and mentally registered a resolve to send the coat to the Express Cleaners without loss of time. She said that if she had to wear black until after the funeral Mummy might at least buy her some new frocks, instead of sending for that dim Miss Spennymoor to convert two frocks of her own to her daughter's use; she said that even Aunt Violet, whom she detested, thought it was ridiculous to wear mourning for anyone outside one's family; she said that in all probability Mummy's disgusting maid had stolen her favourite powder-compact; and she demanded corroboration from Timothy that she was quite too terribly sensitive, and liable to be upset by the least little thing. Whether she included the ugly murder of an old friend in this category, Timothy did not trouble himself to enquire. He assured her that no one could doubt her sensibility, and

151

tried to induce her to sit up. She said: 'Oh, Timothy, you're so *sweet*! I do love you so! I thought I was going *mad*, till you walked in, and now I feel quite different!'

Mr Harte was convinced that he felt the hair rising on his scalp. His saner self told him that it would be foolish to refine too much upon this artless speech; but his male instinct bade him fly from such a dangerous locality. He was never more glad to be interrupted in the middle of a tender passage. Interrupted he was: the door opened to admit Mrs Haddington, and her sister; and, since Cynthia relaxed her grip on his coat sufficiently to enable her to turn to see who had come into the room, he was able to free himself from her hold, and to rise from the sofa.

It was evident that both the elderly ladies had had ample opportunity to observe the touching scene, and equally evident that both regarded Timothy with approval. Mrs Haddington, trailing clouds of black chiffon, smiled, and put out her hand, saying: 'How sweet of you to have come, dear Timothy! No one could do more good to my poor little daughter, I know! The child is dreadfully upset: Dan was like an uncle to her!'

'Mummy, he was *not*!' hotly declared Cynthia.

'Nonsense! Of course he was, and if he wasn't he ought to have been!' said Miss Pickhill sharply. 'So you are Mr Harte, are you? I've heard a lot about you, and I'm very glad to meet you, very! Goodness, child, dry your face! That disgusting stuff you put on your eyelashes has made a black mark on your cheek! I'm sure I don't know what young girls are coming to! You ought to be ashamed of yourself, Lily, encouraging her to ruin the face the Almighty gave her!'

'You simply don't *understand*!' Cynthia said.

'Very likely I don't, or want to!' said her aunt, the asperity of her voice tempered by the indulgent gleam in her eyes as they rested on the lovely but woe-begone countenance before her. 'All *I* understand is that you've plunged yourself into the most disgraceful scandal, just as I always knew you would! Whatever my private feelings may be, blood is thicker than water, and I sent a message to dear Mr Broseley, excusing myself from attending the Meeting today, and came straight up to London. I sometimes think my poor father must turn in his grave!'

'Lord Guisborough!' announced Thrimby from the doorway, enacting providence.

'Lance!' shrieked Cynthia, hurling herself upon him, to the profound relief of Mr Harte. 'You *angel*!'

'Cynthia dear!' said Mrs Haddington, her smile more than ordinarily mechanical.

Miss Pickhill grasped the pince-nez which hung from a sort of button pinned to her spare bosom, pulled out a length of gold chain, and fixed the glasses on the bridge of her nose. 'Oh!' she said discouragingly. 'So this is the young man I've heard so much of, is it? Well!'

Her tone led no one to suppose that his lordship met with her approval, but, happily for his self-esteem, he was so dazed and transported by the flattering behaviour of the most beautiful girl in London that he scarcely noticed Miss Pickhill. Nor did the rapid recapitulation of Cynthia's grievances in any way shake his besotted admiration of her. He asserted, on what grounds no one could imagine, that in Russia mourning was a thing of the past, such senseless conventions belonging to an outworn bourgeoisie; and uttered a slightly involved but vehement speech, the gist of which seemed to be that the only right and proper course for Cynthia to pursue, in recognition of the hideous fate which had overtaken her old friend, was to plunge instantly into as much gaiety as London could offer, preferably in his company.

'Young man,' said Miss Pickhill, 'you are talking nonsense, and, what is more, objectionable nonsense! It is one thing to rush into exaggerated mourning, and quite another to racket about London before that unfortunate man is even buried!'

None of his advanced ideas had ever quite succeeded in quelling in Lord Guisborough an instinctive respect for the conventions of the bourgeoisie in which he had been reared. He hesitated, and then said: 'I thought you could come and dine quietly with Trixie and me, at the studio, Cynthia. Just ourselves!'

'Oh, no, Lance darling, *don't* let's!' begged Cynthia. 'Of course I adore Trixie, but she's so dim and drab, and it's no use her telling me I should love living in Russia, being called Comrade by ghastly people I don't even want to know, and being ordered about all over the place, and not having any more money than anyone else, because I should *loathe* it! And I particularly couldn't stand it tonight!'

'But it's not like that at all!' Guisborough assured her. 'You've got a wholly false idea of the Communist State, derived from prejudice, and preconceived –'

'I don't see why my idea should be any falser than yours,' argued Cynthia. 'You can't possibly know, because you haven't been there, and, anyway, I do think it's too boring and lethal to go on and on and on about some rotten foreign country that probably isn't half as nice as England, if you only knew!'

'Not half as nice as England!' echoed Guisborough, in a stunned voice.

'Of course it isn't! I daresay the Russians like it, but I never can see, and I never *shall* see why people like you and Trixie have to put on that Holy, Holy, Holy expression whenever anyone so much as *mentions* Russia, exactly as if you'd got religion! You'll have somebody thinking you *are* a Russian if you're not careful! *Too* degrading, Lance darling!'

His lordship's eyes kindled; he became very pale; and it was plain that his infatuation for Cynthia was not strong enough to induce him to swallow blasphemy without protest. Before he could give utterance to the words trembling on his lips, Timothy intervened to take leave of his hostess. Mrs Haddington bestowed her most gracious smile upon him, indicating in a subtle style that she perfectly understood that he was being driven away by Lord Guisborough's presence. She held his hand between both of hers for a pregnant moment, and said: 'You know you are always sure of a welcome here! Perhaps in a day or two – just a little *intime* party: nothing formal!'

He managed, by murmuring a few polite and unmeaning phrases, to avoid giving a definite answer to this; begged Mrs Haddington neither to ring for the butler nor to accompany him downstairs herself; and escaped, feeling much like a stag who had contrived, for a short breathing-space, to throw off the hounds.

He ran downstairs, wondering how to find Beulah. The faint clack of a typewriter led him to the library. He walked in, softly closing the door behind him, and said cheerfully: 'Hallo, ducky! How do you find yourself today?'

'Timothy!' she exclaimed. 'What are you doing here? Does Mrs Haddington know?'

'Not that I'm here, and let us hope that she won't track me down,' he replied, bending over her to drop a kiss on the top of her head. 'You look rather sweet: what are you up to?'

'Writing a rude letter to a hat-shop.'

'Enjoying yourself, in fact. Listen, my heart, are you going to be kept here till all hours, or will you dine with me?'

'No, I don't think so, but – Oh, I'd better not!'

'Well, I think you better 'ad,' said Timothy.

She smiled faintly. 'Don't be so vulgar! Timothy, I don't know what to do! This is all wrong!'

'Well, don't worry, my love: we'll thrash it out at Armand's,' he said encouragingly. 'I may as well break it to you at once that you've dam' well got to marry me, to save me from the Haddington clutches. I've just had that infernal wench weeping all over my coat, not to mention the harridan making unmistakable, if vicarious, passes at me. What they *see* in the fellow! Look, will eight o'clock suit you?'

She sat silent, staring down at the keys of the type-writer. He tickled the back of her neck with one finger. 'Well?'

Suddenly she slewed round in her chair, her face quivering, and flung up an arm round his neck. 'All right! Yes!' she jerked out. 'I don't care! I'm *going* to marry you!'

She was subjected to a breath-taking hug. 'Fine!' Timothy said. 'Champagne all round. Jim shall stand it. Oh, I didn't tell you, did I? My brother's up in town, and wants to meet you. I told him to roll along to Armand's.'

She disengaged herself. 'Oh! Has he come to stop you marrying me?'

'No, my child, he has not. Lay all those quills! He's a very nice chap, and if you're polite to him he'll very likely give us his blessing. I think I'd better push off now, in case I'm discovered philandering with you. No more visits from the police?'

'Not yet.'

'Well, if you get any, be polite to Hemingway too! He's another nice chap – and by no means a fool!' said Timothy.

A few hours later, Mr James Kane rang up his chambers. 'That you, Timothy? Well, I'm back, and it didn't go too badly, taken all round.'

'Bless you! How were they?'

'Fair. Mother seemed fit enough, but your father's had one of his bronchial attacks. Am I going to meet Beulah?'

'You are, and you meet her as my betrothed.'

'I do, do I? Well, I warned Mother it was very much on the cards.'

'What did you say to Mamma?'

'A good deal of what you said to me.'

'*What!*'

'That's all right: you ought to know Mother by now! You've only got to show her a lame dog, and she starts helping it over the nearest stile. Mind, I don't say she's in favour of this marriage, but she's willing to wait and see what I think of Beulah; and she's even gone so far as to say that if I put in a favourable report, she'd like Beulah to go down to Chamfreys to stay for a week-end, so that she can try to get to know her.'

'Jim, this is terrific! No, really, I'm hellish grateful to you! You *shan't* stand the champagne tonight: *I* will!'

Thanks largely to the easy manners of Mr James Kane, and to the conversational powers of his young half-brother, the dinner party was moderately successful. Beulah was ill-at-ease, and said very little, but she was in good looks, and if she held Jim at arm's length at least she did not treat him with hostility. He studied her without seeming to, and noted various points in her favour. His own fancy was for fair women, but he could perceive that Beulah had distinction. He liked the way her hair sprang from a peak in the centre of her forehead, approved of her slender hands, and of the nape of her neck. In repose, her face wore almost a sulky look, but if she smiled she became transformed. He thought that it had probably been her smile which had captivated Timothy. It was rare, but when it came it swept across her face, lighting the sombreness of her eyes, making her appear suddenly years younger. She had a well-modulated voice, too, and neither pinched her vowels, nor cultivated the high-pitched, nasal delivery so lamentably fashionable amongst her contemporaries. But she was sadly deficient in social graces or charm, making no attempt to keep the ball of conversation rolling, and often answering remarks addressed to her with unnecessary curtness. She was not at all the type of girl Mr Kane had imagined would attract his lively half-brother, and more than once during the course of the meal he found himself wondering what could have possessed Timothy to give his heart to so cold and brusque a woman. Then he saw her raise her eyes, and meet Timothy's across the table, and he was startled. There could be no mistaking the significance of that glowing look; the girl was head over ears in love with Timothy.

When coffee and liqueurs were on the table, Timothy perceived a party of friends seated at the other end of the room, and, in response to a wave, went across to exchange a few words with them. Beulah looked Jim squarely in the eyes, and said: 'Sorry! I'm no good at small talk. You don't want me to marry him, do you?'

This disconcerting question took Jim aback for a moment; then he laughed and said: 'What am I supposed to reply to that?'

'You have replied. Your mother disliked me very much.'

'Well, if you fired that sort of question at her, you can't be surprised, can you?'

'I didn't. I don't blame her. Or you. Only I'm going to marry him. I said I wouldn't at first. I daresay you think I'm a designing hussy, but I did try to choke him off! Only – well, I couldn't! I'm sorry I can't produce a lot of distinguished relations. My mother came of quite humble stock, and I don't suppose you'd like my Italian relations much. My father's family considered that he had married very much beneath him, which, as far as birth goes, I suppose he did. His family thought him a disgrace to their stuffy name, and were extremely glad when he went to live in Italy. I lived with two of that family for eighteen months, until I decided I'd rather starve than stay with them another day. I should add that they disliked me quite as much as I disliked them, and I don't propose ever to see them again! So now you know!'

'One way and another, you seem to have had rather a tough time,' said Jim equably.

She looked at him; something in her eyes made him uncomfortable. 'Yes,' she said. 'I have. But now – it seems as though I've been offered a chance of something I want very much. More – more than I can tell you. I'm not going to give him up. If I've got to fight to marry him – well, I shall fight! It's only fair to warn you!'

'You needn't get ready to fight me: I'm not Timothy's keeper. In fact, you won't have to fight anyone. My mother may not like the marriage, but if you and Timothy really love each other she won't try to obstruct. You've nothing to be afraid of from that quarter.'

'I'm not afraid!' she said quickly.

'Aren't you? Mind if I give you a bit of advice?'

'What is it?'

'If there's anything about you or about your family which Timothy ought to know, tell him now! Don't wait for him to find it out after you're married. For one thing, it isn't cricket, for another, a Bluebeard's chamber in the home doesn't make for happiness. Sorry if I'm insulting you, but I'm fond of Timothy, and I should hate him to be badly hit. He seems to me to be trusting you up to the hilt, and you don't seem to be trusting him any way at all. Well, that's straight from the shoulder, but you asked for it, didn't you?'

She flushed, and her lips quivered. 'Yes, I asked for it. I can't explain, only – if there wasn't any *real* reason why I shouldn't marry him – ?'

He frowned at her, a little puzzled. 'I don't think I get what you're driving at. Is there a reason – any kind of reason?'

'No! But no one would believe that! No one *could* believe it!'

'That sounds rather sinister! See if Timothy will believe it!'

'No, no, he *couldn't*!'

'Well, if that's so, you'd be well out of marriage with him, wouldn't you?' said Mr Kane calmly.

Eleven

While young Mr Harte had been pursuing his matrimonial plans, and while various interested persons wondered uneasily why the Chief Inspector had not again descended upon them, Hemingway had not been idle. Upon Inspector Grant's return from his singularly barren visit to Mr Seaton-Carew's Bank, both men had visited Mr Godfrey Poulton's mansion in Belgrave Square. Admitted by a stately butler, who regarded them with patent distaste, they were ushered into a morning-room at the back of the house a little before lunch-time, and left to kick their heels there while the butler went to ascertain his mistress's pleasure. When he reappeared, he gave Hemingway the impression of one suffering from an acute attack of nausea. 'Her ladyship will receive you,' he said, overcoming his feelings sufficiently to enable him to utter these degrading words. 'Be so good as to follow me, if you please!'

'Will you stomach the like of this?' muttered the Inspector, touched on the raw.

'That's all right, Sandy,' said Hemingway consolingly. 'You'll get used to it! It's not a bit of good thinking you can muscle into the best houses: they don't entertain the police. You come quietly, or we shall have this poor fellow bursting a blood-vessel!'

The butler's bosom swelled, but his countenance remained wooden. 'This way, if you please, gentlemen!' he said.

He led them majestically up a broad stairway to the drawing-room on the first floor, and paused outside it to demand their names. He appeared to think poorly of them, but declared them meticulously: 'Chief Inspector Hemingway and Inspector Grant, my lady!'

The two detectives passed into the room, and the door was closed behind them.

'Good-morning,' said Lady Nest, from a chair by the fire. 'Won't you sit down?'

The room smelled of Egyptian cigarettes and hot-house roses, bowls of which stood on several tables and chests. It was furnished with a mixture of careless good taste and evanescent vulgarity. Nailed to the wall above a superb example of XVIIth century cabinet-making was the coloured plaster-head of a slant-eyed female, obviously the product of a disordered imagination; cheek by jowl with a charming piece of Wedgwood stood a bowl of ornate barbola-work, filled with pot-pourri; a portrait resembling nothing so much as the jumbled pieces of a jig-saw puzzle hung beside a Girtin water-colour; and enormous photographs of persons seen through a fog stood in ranks upon several spindle-legged tables. While his chief trod across the Aubusson carpet, with its design of sprawling flowers, to the fireplace, Inspector Grant retired discreetly to a chair beside one of these tables, and surveyed with dispassionate interest the portraits standing upon it. One of them, depicting the head of a handsome man, whose excellent teeth were displayed in a flashing smile, caught and held his attention. It bore little resemblance to the distorted features the Inspector had seen in Mrs Haddington's boudoir, but it was inscribed across one corner, in dashing characters: 'Ever yours, Dan Seaton-Carew.'

Hemingway, meanwhile, had seated himself opposite Lady Nest, uttering a conventional apology for troubling her.

'Oh, not at all! I don't mind!' said Lady Nest. 'It's about poor Dan Seaton-Carew, isn't it? Do you think I can help you? I will, if I can, but I don't quite see how.'

'We have to check up, you see, Lady Nest,' Hemingway explained. 'I understand that you knew Mr Seaton-Carew very well?'

She brushed some cigarette-ash from the skirt of her exquisitely plain black frock; her thin, beautiful hands had a brittle appearance, and seemed always to be fluttering. It occurred to Hemingway that he had seldom met a more restless woman. She made him think of a butterfly, at the lag end of the season, its wings a little tattered, but still flitting aimlessly here and there. 'Oh, yes! Quite well!' she said.

'Perhaps you can tell me something about him?' Hemingway suggested. 'What, for instance, was his profession, or was he in business?'

She looked startled. 'Oh! Oh, I don't think so! I mean, I really have no idea! I suppose he was some kind of a financier. It didn't interest me: I never asked him.'

'How long had you known him, Lady Nest?'

'I don't know — some time now. I never remember dates. I'm sorry!'

'Would it be a matter of months, my lady, or years?'

She gave her light laugh. 'How persistent you are! Will anything I say be taken down and used in evidence? I shall be had up for perjury, or something dreadful. They used to say of me that I should end on the gallows, you know. Such a long time ago! You wouldn't think it — at least, I hope you wouldn't! — but I shall never see fifty again. So disheartening! The only thing is to make no secret of it. Terribly ageing to pretend to be younger than one really is!'

The Chief Inspector had called to interview Lady Nest more as a matter of routine than with any very real expectation of learning anything from her of value; but this speech made him suddenly alert. .Not only was it artificial, but he did not think it was customary for ladies in her position to talk in that strain to police officers. She had cast the butt of her cigarette into the fire, and was already fitting another into a little jewelled holder. She had twice shifted the cushions behind her back and three times crossed and uncrossed her nylon-covered legs; her face twitched from time to time; and never were her hands still: one incessantly flicked ash from her cigarette; the other either pressed the feathery curls above her ears, or fidgeted with the row of pearls round her neck, or pleated a fold of her dress.

'Well, as a matter of fact I knew you must be over fifty, my lady, because I used to look at your photos in all the shiny papers,' said Hemingway brazenly.

'No, did you? How sweet! What fun they were, those days! I sat for somebody's face-cream, once, which maddened all my family, poor darlings! They paid me the earth for it, but of course I wouldn't really have put the stuff on my *feet*!'

'I'm sure every lady bought the cream,' said Hemingway. 'Did you say it was years since you first met Mr Seaton-Carew, my lady?'

'No, I didn't say anything, and well you know it! *Must* I be accurate? I don't think I can. I never have been: accurate people are such bores, and say, let me see, was it *Wednesday*, or *Tuesday*? just as though it mattered! Years. Oh dear, how many? I don't know! Three, perhaps. Or even longer. Not a bosom friend of mine, of course: devastatingly attractive, but just the teeniest bit off-white!'

'Were you acquainted with any of his family?'

'Good heavens, no! Had he any family? I expect they are quite impossible: he never spoke of any relations. Not to me, at any rate. Why don't you ask Mrs Haddington? She knew him so much better than I did!'

'Yes, I understand they were very old friends?'

'Oh, rather more than that, I think! Don't look so shocked! I told you he was very attractive, but not, of course, a marrying man. I don't blame Lilias at all: I daresay I should have done the same in her shoes. But that's the worst of that kind of an alliance. Enchanting while it lasts, but it doesn't generally survive the first wrinkle. And then to have a raving beauty for a daughter! I'm so thankful I never had any children: I should never have survived losing a lover to my daughter. No woman could! It would make one ridiculous. I do so much admire Lilias Haddington for managing to ignore the whole thing in that wonderfully cool way. Marvellous, isn't she? She never turns a hair!'

166

'She's a great friend of yours, isn't she?' said Hemingway.

'Oh – ! Such an exaggerated term to use! One knows her socially, just as one knows so many people!'

'You presented Miss Haddington last year, I think. At least, that's what I seem to remember being told.'

'Yes. Yes, I rather took them up. Such a pretty girl, Cynthia Haddington!'

'Well, if you don't mind my saying so, Lady Nest, they must both of them feel they owe you a debt! Everyone knows that what you say goes in High Society.'

She smiled uncertainly, and put up a hand as though to shade her eyes from the light. 'How kind of you! I think someone must have asked me to call on Mrs Haddington: it's always happening. So difficult to refuse! Then one drifts into a certain degree of intimacy, really without knowing it!'

Hemingway's eyes travelled to Inspector Grant's face. The Inspector rose, and with a murmured excuse, walked out of the room. Following the intuition which he so often told his exasperated fellows never failed him, Hemingway said: 'We don't always take down what is said, and use it as evidence, my lady: particularly when we're working on a case like this, which might turn out to be a bit delicate. Now, I don't want to start something which, properly speaking, is none of my business; and I don't at all want to go asking Mr Poulton a whole lot of questions which might stir up trouble.'

'My husband! What's it got to do with him?' she said sharply. 'What questions? Is it so extraordinary that I should be friendly with Lilias Haddington?'

'Well, yes, my lady, I think it is!' replied Hemingway

frankly. 'I thought so at the outset. I don't move in High Society myself, but in my job one gets to learn a few what-you-might-call elementary facts. Why did you introduce Mrs Haddington to your friends, and what was the tie-up between you, and her, and Seaton-Carew?'

She sat up jerkily from the sofa, and moved away to the window. 'Absurd!'

'Was it Mrs Haddington who introduced Seaton-Carew to you, my lady?'

'No!'

'Other way around?' suggested Hemingway.

She put up a hand to her brow, pressing it. 'No. How can this help you? Do you mean to ask my husband these – foolish questions?'

'Not if I can help it. If ever there's any suspicion of blackmail, we're as discreet as we know how to be.'

She stared at him over her shoulder. 'You're very acute! Who told you this?'

'No one told me.'

'What makes you think – ?'

'Mrs Haddington isn't your sort, my lady. Nor, from what I can make out, was Seaton-Carew.'

She said quickly: 'Put that out of your mind! There was never any question of such a thing between Seaton-Carew and me! Just an acquaintance! A man I asked to my parties!'

'And he was pretty closely tied-up with Mrs Haddington?'

'That had nothing to do with it! I met him in the South of France – before I knew of her existence!'

'I see. And you met Mrs Haddington – ?'

Her thin chest heaved; she said breathlessly: 'I need not account to Scotland Yard for my friends, I suppose!'

'No,' replied Hemingway. 'You needn't, but it might be a good thing if you did, my lady. Of course, I don't know, but it did occur to me that you might – in a manner of speaking – have been forced to take Mrs Haddington up. Just because you didn't want any truck with Scotland Yard.' He smiled. 'I often get funny ideas into my head,' he offered. 'You'd be surprised the number of times ladies of position go and do something indiscreet, and then don't like to say anything about it to the police. Some of them would rather be bled white, in fact. Silly, but there it is!'

She burst out laughing. 'Me? No one has ever bled me for a penny, Chief Inspector!'

'You do sometimes come across blackmailers that want something other than money,' said Hemingway thoughtfully. 'Not often, of course, but I have heard of it.'

'You are quite, quite mistaken!' she said, gripping the back of a chair with both hands.

'Well, if that's so, I won't trouble you any longer, my lady,' he said, getting up.

'I'm glad to hear it! What – what do you mean to do now?'

'Pursue my investigations,' responded Hemingway promptly.

Her face twitched. 'You'd better not hint at these really rather insulting ideas of yours to my husband,' she said. 'He is old-fashioned in his outlook, and I fear he might resent it – quite violently! That's just a friendly warning!'

'I'm very grateful, my lady.'

'You're supposed to be enquiring into a case of murder,' she pointed out, still gripping the chairback. 'Neither I nor my husband had anything to do with that – indeed, how should we? I suggest you turn your attention to another household. Naturally, I don't wish to say anything against Lilias Haddington, but she is the person most closely linked with Seaton-Carew, not I! I ought perhaps to mention that my husband was barely acquainted with him.'

'Yes,' said Hemingway, 'so he told me. Still, it was quite right of you to tell me, my lady, if you thought perhaps he'd forgotten to.'

He then bade her a civil good-morning, to which she made no answer, and withdrew.

He found Inspector Grant in the hall, gravely studying a large oil painting. At a little distance, the butler stood, eyeing him austerely.

'Wester Ross,' said the Inspector. 'But forbye I know where it was done, it is not good. I would not hang it in my house.'

'Well, that's a good job!' returned Hemingway. 'You wouldn't have a chance of pinching it, not with Faithful Fido about, you wouldn't. Come on!'

Not by so much as the flicker of an eyelid did the butler betray that this shaft had gone home. He trod majestically to the door, and opened it, and stood impassively by it until the two detectives had passed out of the house. His feelings found expression only in the celerity with which he closed the door behind them.

'Almost shut my heel in it,' remarked Hemingway. 'Now then, my lad, what did you make of that little outfit?'

'I should not have known what to make of that lady, had I not seen what I did,' replied the Inspector. 'I am thinking now that we have stepped into a deal of wickedness, perhaps.'

'If by that you mean that she looked suspiciously like a drug-addict, I agree with you,' retorted Hemingway. 'I don't know that it helps us much, though.'

'When I was sitting in that room,' said Grant, 'I cast my eyes over the photographs on the table beside me. There was one with Dan Seaton-Carew signed on it. I recognised it: I had seen that face before.'

'Well, of course you had!' said Hemingway, irritated. 'You saw it last night!'

'When I saw it last night, I did *not* recognise it,' said Grant. He added apologetically: 'It would be some years before the War that I met him, and it was not Seaton-Carew he called himself, but Carew alone. And a man that has been strangled –'

'Spill it, Sandy, spill it!' Hemingway adjured him. 'What was he? An old lag?'

'He was not. There was not a thing you could charge him with. I was no more than just made a Sergeant, and set to work with Superintendent Darliston. You will mind that he was given –'

'One of these days you'll drive me nuts!' said Hemingway. 'Of course I know! Dangerous Drugs! Was that bird under suspicion?'

'I am telling you: if he was concerned in that *droch* business, we could not discover it. There was not enough evidence against him to warrant pulling him in for interrogation. He had a *sgeul* that might have been true. Since then I have never heard tell of him. Indeed, I had forgotten the man until I saw the picture of him in that house.'

Hemingway walked on beside him in silence for some fifty yards. 'Growing, isn't it?' he said at last. 'Ever add two and two together and get five for the answer? No, you wouldn't, because you've got no imagination, but it's what I can see myself doing. All the same, taking your bit of dirt with what I gathered from Lady Nest's way of carrying on, I think this'll bear looking into. When I gave you the Indian sign to clear out, I was backing a hunch. I thought there was a chance Lady Nest might talk, if there was no one but me to listen. She didn't – at least, not as much as I'd have liked; but the hunch was all right. Something Terrible Timothy said put me on to it: I believe she pushed the Haddingtons into society because Mrs Haddington had a screw on her. Plenty of indiscretions in the Lady Nest's past, I shouldn't wonder. What you tell me makes me ask myself if that mightn't have been it. If Mrs Haddington knew she was getting drugs from Seaton-Carew – ?'

'*Och, mo thruaighe!* You never asked that lady if she had had the black put on her?' Grant exclaimed.

'Well, seeing she'd been so open and friendly, I thought I'd take a chance on it,' replied Hemingway coolly. 'If you're thinking she'll lodge a complaint, you're wrong. She's scared white – particularly of her husband's getting to know anything about it.'

The Inspector thought it over for a moment. 'If that one knew that his wife was getting drugs – ach, now you have me making two and two five!'

'We won't try to add it up yet. This is a job for Cathercott and his merry men: he can go over Seaton-

Carew's flat. Sometimes I think those chaps can smell the stuff!'

'If I had recognised the man when I saw him dead, we could have had an officer posted to keep an eye on the flat!'

'Don't take on about it! If you're thinking that that curly-headed mistake we saw at the flat was in the racket, your psychology's rotten! Drug-peddling isn't a game for little play-boys. I reckon Seaton-Carew would have been caught years ago, if he'd used that kind of an assistant.'

'*Ma seadh!* But where, think you, would Mrs Haddington stand? Mind, there was nothing proved, nor found out against the man!'

'Look here, I don't mind you making two and two five, but when you start making it six you're going too far, Sandy!' expostulated Hemingway. 'I don't think Hard-faced Hannah would stand anywhere. This Seaton-Carew bird was a sight too downy to take in a female in his little games. Besides, why should he? What's more, drug-peddling wouldn't get her into all the best houses, under Lady Nest's wing. You don't take up one of the most dangerous crime-rackets just to get into Society, my lad! Yes, I know you're being very cagey about Seaton-Carew, but I've known Jim Darliston any time these past fifteen years, and if he thought Seaton-Carew was worth watching, that's enough for me! We'll get back to the Yard at once, and set Cathercott on to that flat. Meanwhile, did you get Beulah Birtley Meriden's dossier for me?'

'I did, sir. It was one of Underbarrow's cases.'

'You don't say! Yes, now I come to think of it, I remember that it was. Ran it hard, did he?'

'It is his way,' the Inspector said.

'It is, and one of these days it'll get him into trouble. Go on!'

'The jury were out above an hour,' said Grant carefully. 'You would say, looking at the evidence, that there was nothing to keep them away so long, but I have had a word with Bingham – you'll mind he was attached to that Division! – and by what he tells me, the Chairman's summing-up left the matter in a good deal of doubt. Now, in Scotland –'

'If you think I'm going to waste my time arguing with you about whether Not Proven is a good thing or not, you're mistaken!' interrupted Hemingway. 'Why did the Chairman sum up in the girl's favour?'

'That,' said Grant, 'I do not know, but from what Bingham was telling me he treated young Mr Maxstoke rough – verra rough, he treated him, when he stood in the witness-box! I should say that it was with the firm of Maxstoke's the lassie had employment. She was fresh out of one of these Commercial Colleges, and young Mr Maxstoke took her for his secretary. He is the nephew of Jasper Maxstoke, and at that time he was a partner in the firm, the old man having no sons, and –'

'At that time?'

'I am told,' said the Inspector, 'that it is a matter of three months since he left the firm. Why, I do not know.'

'Sometimes I wonder why I put up with you!' said the exasperated Hemingway. 'What was the girl charged with?'

'It was alleged,' said Grant, 'that she had forged Mr Harold Maxstoke's signature on various cheques, and cashed them; and it was proved that she had in her possession some bank-notes, of which the numbers had been taken. You would say that it was an open-and-shut case.'

'Which means, I suppose, that I shouldn't have said anything of the sort. I don't think I was in Court when this Maxstoke gave his evidence. What sort of a bloke was he?'

'I have not seen him. Sergeant Bingham tells me – but,' added the Inspector, with a touch of austerity, 'he is a vulgar man, that one! – that he would be the man to pinch and cuddle a lassie! A *droch duine*, is what he called him.'

'That I'll be bound he never did! I don't know what it means, nor I don't want to, but the idea of you putting words like that into poor old Bingham's mouth! The inference being that the whole affair was a plant? Well, I have heard of such things, but not often, and I'm bound to say I didn't take to the fair Beulah. Looked as if she'd murder her own grandmother for sixpence. *But* one of her fellow-convicts sent her to Seaton-Carew, thinking he could use her; and it looks very much to me as though he pretty soon found out he couldn't – not in the way that was meant, anyhow. Now, that's very interesting, Sandy! If you ask me, drug-peddling wasn't his only racket, not by a long chalk! He didn't want an agent for that! It wouldn't surprise me to learn that he ran a blackmailing business, by way of a side-line. That's where the tie-up between him and Hard-faced Hannah may have come in. I don't say it did, but you want to bear it in mind, as a possibility. If she didn't put the black on Lady Nest, I'll eat my hat! She's got a lot of money, too: much more than she ought to have, in these days, when honest people can't possibly have a lot of money.'

'I was not hearing from the servants anything that would bear that out,' observed Grant doubtfully.

'I don't suppose you were. What they had to say, by what I can make out, they might as well have kept to themselves, for all the good it's likely to do us. They've none of them been with her above two years, and most of 'em not half as long. She's a bad mistress, but that doesn't make her a criminal.'

'It does not. But they think she is not a lady, for all such grand people visit her house.'

'One up to you,' agreed Hemingway generously. 'If they say that, they're right: they always know!'

He ate his supper that evening in the cosy little house in Bromley in which Ex-Superintendent Darliston had retired. While this meal was in progress, and Mrs Darliston sat presiding over a teapot almost as enormous as herself, nothing was talked of but the prospects of the Ex-Superintendent's three sons, the amazing intelligence of his five grandchildren, the iniquitous behaviour of his hens, and the success he had enjoyed at the last local Show with his tomatoes; but when the Ex-Superintendent had let his belt out a hole or two, and had drawn a pipe and an aged pouch from his pocket, his spouse heaved her massive form out of her chair, piled all the crockery on a tray, and said: 'Well, I'll go and wash up. If Stanley came out here to talk to you about the new greenhouse, Herbert, I didn't marry a policeman, thirty years ago, more fool me! No, I don't want any help, Stanley, thanking you all the same! Just open that door for me, and give over doing the polite!'

So saying, this admirable woman picked up the tray, and sailed off with it to the scullery.

'You can't fool Mother,' observed Mr Darliston. He pushed his pouch across the table. 'Here, have a fill of mine! Now, what's eating you, young fellow?'

'Come to pick your brains, Super,' said Hemingway.

'Ah!' said Mr Darliston, leaning back at his ease. 'I daresay I've forgotten more than you'll ever know.'

'Well, have a shot at remembering, will you, grand-dad?' retorted Hemingway disrespectfully. 'Going on as if you were Methuselah, and me in my first pair of long trousers!'

Mr Darliston's bulk quivered slightly as he chuckled. He jerked his thumb suggestively towards the beer-jug, and invited his guest to unburden himself. He heard the Chief Inspector out in silence, remarking at the end of his discourse: 'Yes, I remember young Grant. A good lad: how's he getting on?'

'Fine, for a toddler like him!' said Hemingway. 'I'll tell him you remembered him. That'll please him a lot more than it does me. What *I* want you to remember –'

'Slow, but careful,' pursued the Ex-Superintendent. 'Of course, he owed a lot to the training he had under me. Get on with him all right?'

'I've known worse. In fact, if it wasn't for him breathing that Gaelic of his all over me, I wouldn't have a thing against him.'

'Garlic?' repeated Mr Darliston, staring. 'What's he want to eat garlic for? Tell him to stop it!'

'He doesn't eat it: he talks it. At least, that's what he says it is. He's got a shocking outbreak at the moment. They went and gave him Christmas leave, and he jumped on to the first train up to Inverness. By what I can make out, it took him the best part of twenty-four hours to get to this village of his, but he seems to think it was worth it. Never mind him! Do you remember this Seaton-Carew, alias Plain-Carew?'

'Yes, I remember the chap, and I'll tell you this, Stanley: you've got a real slippery customer in him!'

'Well, if he slips out of the mortuary, I'll know you were right. Meanwhile, I'd be glad if you'd tell me if you were playing a hunch when you tailed him, or whether you had any tabs on him?'

'Not to say tabs. Call it a lot of leads. Not one of them led me to his front-door. I could look out my old case-books, if you like, but they wouldn't tell you much.'

'No, that's all right. When you cleared up that particular gang, what became of friend Carew?'

'I don't know. He faded out, and I was under the impression that he skipped over to France.'

'Never had any enquiries about him from the Sûreté?'

'Not to my knowledge.'

'I see. Now, I've put Cathercott on to his flat, but drugs aren't my line, and I'd be grateful for a tip or two. Would he be likely to keep the stuff there?'

'He'd probably keep it there, any time he had some to dispose of – though I once met a fellow that used to dump it in a safe-deposit. That's how I caught him: seemed an unnatural sort of thing for a chap to be going two and three times a week to his safe-deposit.'

'Could he hide it in a small flat, so as his man wouldn't find it?'

'Easy. If he's been selling it to people like this Lady Nest of yours, it's white drugs he's handling – probably snow, might be heroin, might even be morphia, but that's unlikely. You don't want to go looking for a consignment of hemp, you know. The stuff's worth a blooming sight more than its weight in gold, and the amount he'd have on the premises he could hide pretty well anywhere. Take any cigarettes you find – but Cathercott knows the ropes! Probably handed it over to his customers in neat little packets of powder, anyway. One of the cleverest rogues I ever arrested used to paste chemist's labels on his packets, with Boric Acid written on 'em, and the ends sealed up with red sealing-wax. Life-like, they were.'

'That 'ud be more in this bloke's line than handing out boxes of cigarettes,' said Hemingway shrewdly. 'If that was his trade, it's my belief he'd have done his handing over at all those parties he used to go to. There were no flies on him, and, unless I find he's got a secret deposit for his papers, he's been careful to destroy every last bit of written evidence. I wouldn't be surprised if that was your fault, Super. You went and frightened the poor fellow, and a nice mess that leaves *me* with!'

'Well,' said Mr Darliston, reaching out his hand for the beer-jug, 'I don't blame you for wanting to pinch the man that murdered him, Stanley, because that's your job; but I've seen something of the horrors him and vermin like him batten on, and what I say is that whoever did him in did a good job, and ought properly to be given a medal. In fact,' he added, refilling the Chief Inspector's glass, 'it's those bastards which make me believe in hell! If I didn't think they were roasting down there, I wouldn't be able to sleep o' nights!'

Twelve

The Chief Inspector, reaching London again shortly after nine o'clock, betook himself to Scotland Yard, and found Inspector Grant awaiting him patiently in his office. He was seated at the desk, studying a dossier, but he rose when his chief came in, and closed the file. 'I thought maybe you would be looking in,' he remarked.

'I will say this for you, Sandy: you're a conscientious bloke!' said Hemingway, hanging up his hat and overcoat. 'Got anything for me?'

'Verra little, I am afraid. Cathercott was on the telephone a while back. He was wanting to know if you would have him continue searching, or if it was a mare's nest he was looking for. They found a safe, hidden in a verra unusual place, and it cost them a deal of trouble to open it. There was two or three hundred pounds in banknotes in it, and some bonds, and never a sniff of snow, nor a speck to show there had ever been any there. Och, the *truaghan*! What with the toothache he has had all day, and the pains he took to get the safe open, and then nothing to reward him, it's a fine temper he is in! There was a secret drawer in the desk, too, which Sergeant

Cringleford found, and bare as the palm of your hand when they got that open!'

Hemingway grinned, but he said: 'Did you tell him to keep on at it?'

'I did, the *duine bochd*, but it went to my heart! If he had had it, would Seaton-Carew not have kept the stuff in the hidden safe?'

'I don't know. You'd think so, but old Darliston's just been warning me he was a damned slippery customer. It would be a smart trick to install a secret safe, just to put chaps like Cathercott off the scent. Did you say there were two or three hundred pounds in it? I suppose Cathercott was so busy sniffing for drugs he never noticed a nasty smell of rat. I would have. What did the fellow want with all that amount of money in the flat? Planning a midnight flit, in case we got after him?'

'Well,' said the Inspector mildly, 'it is not an offence to keep money by you!'

'No, and if he ran a big estate, no doubt he would have a lot of cash in his safe from time to time, so as he could pay wages, and such-like. If you can tell me what he should want with a great wad of bank-notes in a small flat in town, you'll be clever! Did you check up on what the Birtley girl said about Mrs Haddington having kicked up a row because of some towel or other in that cloakroom?'

'I was not able. The girl she would have spoken to, *if* she spoke at all, is the head housemaid, and she has been ill with the influenza since two days. You would not have me push my way into the lassie's bedroom!'

'Quite right! You can't be too careful,' agreed his incorrigible superior. 'Nice thing it would be if we had members of the Department getting compromised!'

'I am susceptible to the influenza,' said Inspector Grant austerely. 'Not but what I would have taken the risk, if I had thought it proper.'

'All right, all right!' said Hemingway soothingly. 'It'll have to be checked up on, but I'm bound to say it wouldn't have been at all proper. One subject throwing a handful of mud at another isn't anything to get excited about. Not but what there's quite a lot about Mrs Haddington I could bear to have explained to me. If I could believe that a dame who looks to me to have about as much passion in her as a cod-fish would murder the boy-friend because he got off with her daughter, I think I'd pinch her.'

Inspector Grant was well-acquainted with his chief, but this made him gasp. 'There is no evidence! *Thoir ort*, you are joking!'

'It's my belief,' said Hemingway severely, 'that when you cough that nasty Gaelic of yours at me you're just handing me out a slice of damned cheek, banking on me not understanding a word of it! One of these days I'll learn the language, and then you'll precious soon find yourself reduced to the ranks, my lad! There isn't any evidence – not what you could call evidence! – against any of them: that's the trouble. You take this Haddington dame! She had a row with Seaton-Carew earlier in the evening –'

'So also did Miss Birtley.'

'That's so, and don't you run away with the idea that I've ruled her out, because I haven't! But she doesn't so far seem to have had any motive at all for strangling the chap.'

'It might be that she was afraid he would tell Mr Harte she had been in prison.'

'It might,' conceded Hemingway. 'Now tell me what that bird had to gain by telling Terrible Timothy anything at all about her!'

'That,' said Grant, 'I do not know.'

'No, nor anyone else. At this rate, there must be quite a few people she'll have to bump off. If you ask me, it was a darned sight more likely Mrs Haddington would be the one to split to Terrible Timothy. He wouldn't be a bad catch for that daughter of hers: not at all bad! As far as I remember, his father was very comfortably off, besides being a baronet. Leave the Birtley girl out of it for the moment! What have we against Hard-faced Hannah? She had a quarrel with Seaton-Carew; he was known to have been her lover; there doesn't seem to have been much doubt that he was running after her daughter; she knew he was being rung-up that evening; she knew when the call came through; she had the opportunity to commit the murder; and her account of her movements is uncorroborated. In fact, the more I think of it, the more I think I'm a fool not to pinch her at once.'

'*Seadh!* But there are others! There is young Mr Butterwick!'

'That's why I haven't pinched her,' said Hemingway brazenly. 'Did you see him this afternoon?'

'I did, and och, I don't know at all what to make of him! He is afraid for his life, that is sure; but at one moment he will be weeping like a *caileag*, and the next in such a fury that he looks fit to murder anyone! It was no more than a hint that I gave him, that, according to Mrs Haddington, he had been only twice to that house, and each time to a large party, when it is not likely he would have heard the telephone-bell ring. He went so white I thought he would have fainted; and so angry he was he could barely speak. He said he had dined with the Haddingtons once, and he had clearly heard the bell. He said I should ask myself why Mrs Haddington had told us such lies. He said we were fools to think he would have murdered his friend, speaking of that man in such terms as would have made you blush, sir! He said he would go mad, perhaps, and those may have been the only true words he spoke! It did not take him more than five minutes to prove to me it was Mrs Haddington, and Miss Birtley, and Mr Poulton, and Mr Harte that had murdered Seaton-Carew. And then, the silly creature, he would have me believe it was all wicked lies that he had quarrelled with his friend that very evening! Och, there was no dealing with him at all!'

'No, he's difficult,' agreed Hemingway, scratching his chin. 'You never know where you are with neurotics. I'm bound to say, though I don't fancy him much.'

'He has more motive than any other.'

'I'm not so sure of that. It'll depend on what Cathercott finds in that flat. Yes, come in!'

Inspector Cathercott himself walked into the room, heavily wrapped in a hairy overcoat, and with a muffler wound round the lower part of his face. He pulled this away from his mouth, and said, setting a neat package down on the desk: 'You win, Chief! Take a look at that! Two of 'em!'

'Snow?' Hemingway said. 'Good man! Where did you find it?'

'Several of the books in that glass-fronted case were hollow dummies. I might have got on to 'em quicker if it hadn't been for that safe! Clever operator, this Seaton-

Carew. I'm sorry he's dead: I'd liked to have had him here for half an hour! But,' said Cathercott, looking like a terrier on the scent of a rat, 'I think this may have given me a line on the little gang we've been after for the past four months!'

'Is that going to help me?' demanded Hemingway.

Cathercott glanced indifferently down at him. 'Help you? Oh, this murder of yours! No, sir, I shouldn't think so. With any luck this little lot may lead us to the boys who are bringing the stuff into the country. I'll be making a report on this find to Superintendent Heathcote first thing in the morning.' He rubbed his hands together. 'He'll be interested – very much interested!'

'I'm sure he will,' said Hemingway. 'You can go home to bed, and put some oil of cloves in that tooth of yours, George! You've done very nicely, and you don't want to go writing reports at this hour of night!'

'Well, if you don't want me any more, I'll be off,' Cathercott said, picking up his treasured package. 'Unless I miss my bet, it's snow all right. Enough here to keep your friend at the Ritz for months! Good-night, sir! 'Night, Sandy!'

'Talk of one-track minds!' said Hemingway, as the door shut behind Cathercott. 'Little details like murder don't mean a thing to him! Well, now, Sandy, we've got a highly significant angle on the case. We'll pay another call on Lady Nest Poulton in the morning!'

'Not on Mrs Haddington?' said the Inspector, with the glimmer of a smile.

'No, because I've *not* got a one-track mind!' retorted Hemingway.

But when he arrived at the house in Belgrave Square

next day, he was met by the intelligence that her ladyship was not at home.

'If you mean she isn't receiving callers, just take my card up to her, will you?' said Hemingway.

The butler said, in a voice carefully devoid of ignoble triumph, that her ladyship left town on the previous evening. He regretted that he was unable to give the Chief Inspector her address, or to inform him when she would return. He suggested that these questions should rather be put to Mr Poulton.

'Oh, so he's not gone out of town too?'

'No,' said the butler, raising his brows.

'Is he at home?'

'Mr Poulton is never at home during the day. You will find him at his office, Chief Inspector. Would there be anything further you would like to ask me?'

'Yes: Mr Poulton's City address!'

This was vouchsafed, and the two detectives returned to the waiting car. As it moved eastward, Grant said slowly: 'It does not seem right to me that she should have gone away from her home just now, and not a word of it said to you yesterday!'

'No reason why she should have said anything to me: she isn't under suspicion. But you're quite right, Sandy: it smells remarkably fishy! She must know that husband of hers isn't by any means in the clear. Nice moment for her to be jaunting off to the country! Well, we'll see what our poker-faced friend has got to say about it.'

Godfrey Poulton, at first declared by a competent secretary to be in conference, did not keep his visitors waiting long in the outer office. They were ushered in a few minutes into a large, turkey-carpeted room. Here, at a large knee-hole desk, sat Godfrey Poulton. He was speaking into one of the telephones on the desk, and merely nodded to his visitors, and made a slight gesture towards a couple of chairs. He did not show any signs of discomposure, but watched the detectives absently, while he listened to what was being said to him at the other end of the wire.

'Very well . . . I'm sorry: no! . . . I could give you – 'He glanced down at the open diary before him – 'twenty minutes, at 11.45 tomorrow morning. . . . Yes? I shall expect you at that hour, then. Good-bye!' He laid down the instrument, and said: 'I don't want to be disturbed until these gentlemen leave, Miss Methwold. Good-morning, Chief Inspector! What can I do for you?'

'You can, if you will be so good, sir, tell me where I can find Lady Nest Poulton,' replied Hemingway. 'I understand she has gone out of town.'

'Where you can find my wife?' said Poulton, an inflexion of surprise in his tone. 'May I know what your business is with her? So far as I am aware, she has no possible connection with your case.'

'Nevertheless, I should like her address, sir.'

'I trust you will be able to manage to get on without it.'

'Am I to understand that you refuse to disclose it, sir, or that you don't know what it is?' demanded Hemingway.

'The first,' replied Poulton calmly. 'You have already interrogated my wife once – with what object I am at a loss to know! – and she does not wish to be troubled any further about the affair.'

'No doubt, sir, but –'

'Nor do I wish it for her,' added Poulton. 'If it were

even remotely possible that she could have had something to do with the murder, the position would, of course, be very different, and I should not for a moment withhold her address from you. As it is, I rather think I am within my rights in refusing to disclose it.'

'No, sir. No one trying to obstruct an officer of the law in the pursuance of his duty is within his rights!' countered Hemingway promptly.

'Did I say that? In what way does my wife's absence from home obstruct you, Chief Inspector?'

'That's for me to judge, sir. There are certain questions I wish to put to Lady Nest.'

'That is unfortunate – but perhaps I can answer your questions?'

'Perhaps, sir, but I prefer to put them to her ladyship.'

'I regret, Chief Inspector, I cannot permit you to see her. It will save time, and, I hope, argument, if I tell you that she is extremely unwell, and in no condition to receive visitors.'

'I'm sorry to hear that, sir. Very sudden, her illness, isn't it?'

'No,' replied Poulton. 'My wife has been on the verge of a nervous breakdown for weeks. The unfortunate affair in Charles Street merely precipitated a crisis. I am surprised that you should not have seen for yourself that she was far from well yesterday.'

'I certainly got the impression that her ladyship was not herself,' said Hemingway rather grimly.

'I imagine you might,' was the imperturbable answer. 'She is a very highly-strung woman, easily upset; and she has for some time been suffering from neurasthenia.'

'That wasn't quite what I thought, sir.'

Poulton looked faintly amused. 'A medical man, Chief Inspector?'

'No, sir: merely a police-officer! There are certain symptoms we get to recognise in our job.'

'Really? I haven't the least idea what you're talking about: it sounds very mysterious! But there is no mystery about my wife's illness, or about her whereabouts. I will tell you at once that she is in a Nursing Home, and that her doctor has forbidden even me to see her for the next week or so.' He paused. 'If you doubt that, I would suggest –'

'I don't doubt it, Mr Poulton. I believe Lady Nest is in a Nursing Home, and I believe she isn't allowed to see anyone. Which forces me to speak more frankly to you than I might have liked to do if I'd been able first to see her ladyship. But what I've got to say I don't think will be a surprise to you – the way things are. When I called on her ladyship yesterday morning, it was pretty plain to me, and to Inspector Grant here, who's had a good deal of experience in that branch, that she was in the habit of taking drugs.'

'I believe,' said Poulton, unmoved, 'that she takes far more phenacetin than is at all good for her. Ah, yes, and also valerian – but that, I need hardly say, was prescribed for her.'

'No, sir, not that kind of drug. What we call the White Drugs – cocaine, heroin, morphia. In your wife's case, cocaine.'

Poulton had been playing idly with a pencil. He laid it down, saying icily: 'That, Chief Inspector, is an infamous suggestion!'

'You can take it from me, sir, that it isn't a charge I'd bring against anyone without very good reason.'

'It is a charge you may regret having brought against her ladyship!'

'If I were wrong I should regret it very much. I will tell you now, sir, that a considerable amount of cocaine has been discovered in Seaton-Carew's flat.'

The impassive countenance before him betrayed nothing either of surprise or of alarm. Poulton was still frowning. 'Indeed! I was too little acquainted with the man to know whether that was to be expected or not. I am quite sure my wife can have known nothing of it. You seem to imagine that he and she were close friends: they were not. This misapprehension, coupled with her ladyship's neurasthenic condition, has led you to assume that Seaton-Carew had been supplying her with drugs. I perceive, of course, that if that had been true I should have had an excellent motive for strangling the fellow. I may add, in view of this disclosure, that I have every sympathy for the man who did strangle him! That, however, is beside the point. You may search my house with my goodwill; and I recommend you to call on my wife's medical attendant. You have already met him: he is Dr Theodore Westruther. Pray ask him to explain to you the nature of my wife's illness! Now, since I am reasonably certain that you do not, on these fantastic grounds, hold a warrant for my arrest, I am going to request you to leave. I am a very busy man, and I have neither the leisure nor the inclination to listen to police theories which are nothing short of insulting! Good-morning, gentlemen!'

When he stood upon the pavement outside the block of offices, the Inspector wiped his brow. 'Phew!' he breathed.

'Good, wasn't he?' said Hemingway, bright-eyed and appreciative. 'Carried on from the start as if we'd come to sell him a vacuum-cleaner he didn't want. Playing it very boldly, and very coolly. He had one advantage: he knew we'd be coming to question him. Something tells me you wouldn't easily catch that chap on the wrong foot.'

'Well,' said Grant, thinking it over. 'He behaved as you would expect a decent man to behave if he was told his wife was a drug-addict, when she was no such thing.'

'Lifelike!' agreed Hemingway. 'Even down to inviting me to search his house! Though that was overdoing it a bit, perhaps.'

'He told you the name of her doctor. It's queer that one should turn up again. Will you see him?'

'I must, of course. He won't tell me a thing, beyond a string of long words I shan't understand, but it wouldn't do for me not to see him.'

'I was thinking that it is a waste of time. He will cover up for his patient.'

'I know that. And if I didn't go and see him, what would happen? – *Did you question the doctor? – No. – Why not? – Because I knew he'd only tell me a pack of lies.* You can just see me falling into that one, can't you?'

'There is that, of course,' admitted the Inspector. 'But will you tell me this? – If Mr Poulton knew that his lady was taking drugs, why is it only now that he puts her in a Home to be cured of it? You would say it was a verra bad moment to choose, for it would be bound to make us suspicious.'

'I wouldn't say anything of the sort. In her state, she'd be liable to give herself away, not to mention him. He knows very well she'd break up under close questioning. What's more, her source of supply has dried up, and that's going to send her pretty well haywire. He's running far less risk this way than if he let her traipse around on the loose. I daresay it was Seaton-Carew's death that persuaded her to consent to go and be cured, too. You can't go shoving people into hospital to be cured of the drug habit without they do consent, you know.'

'I do, of course.'

'And furthermore,' Hemingway continued, 'he may well have hoped we shouldn't search Seaton-Carew's flat, or, if we did search it, that we shouldn't find any of the stuff. I wonder if the fellow had any on him, the night he was done in? Lady Nest wasn't under the influence when we saw her: she was hungry for it. Quite possible that he was to have slipped over a little packet to her during the evening. Whoever murdered him would have had plenty of time to have slid his fingers into his breast-pocket, and taken out any little parcel he found there.'

'It is a theory,' said Grant. 'You would never prove it.'

'There's quite a few things that go to build up a case that never get proved,' replied Hemingway. 'We'd better bite off a bit of lunch now; and after that you can go and see whether you can prove Beulah Birtley was telling the truth when she said Mrs Haddington had been in that cloakroom after she left the wire there. I don't suppose Mrs H. encourages her servants to stop in bed a minute longer than they need, and if that housemaid's been having this forty-eight hour 'flu, she'll very likely be on view again by now. I don't need you in Harley Street, and I'll go back to the Yard when I'm through there. I want to have a careful look at one or two of the exhibits. Come on!'

At three o'clock, having been kicking his heels for some time in the waiting-room, he was ushered into Dr Westruther's consulting-room, a gracious apartment, decorated in shades of grey, which ranged from palest pearl-grey on the walls and in the windows, whose lights were veiled by curtains of diaphanous chiffon, to a deep elephant-grey on the floor. A few chaste Chinese prints hung on the walls; and a magnificent screen of mutton-fat jade stood in the centre of the mantelshelf, flanked by two Blanc-de-Chine Kuan-Yin figures of the Ming period. Hemingway, his feet sinking into the heavy-pile carpet, found himself wondering whether the doctor's more neurotic patients were soothed by this subdued but expensive décor. Dr Westruther enjoyed a reputation for dealing almost exclusively with wealthy, society women. He was not precisely known to the police, but once or twice the breath of ugly scandal had wafted perilously near to him. He had a controlling interest in an extremely luxurious Nursing Home, where the staff was paid with unusual generosity; he was always very well dressed, affecting the cutaway morning coat and butterfly collars of a more sartorial age; he owned, besides the house in Harley Street, a charming riverside residence at Marlow; and he generally managed to spend several weeks of the year at Biarritz, or Juan-les-Pins.

He greeted the Chief Inspector with perfect sangfroid, apologising for having kept him waiting. He had been called away to a case, he said, and had only just returned to Harley Street. As Hemingway had expected, he told him nothing that he wanted to know. Lady Nest Poulton was a woman who, in lay parlance, lived on her nerves: he would not bemuse the Chief Inspector with technical terms, but he might rest assured that the condition was one well-known to every practitioner. He agreed that certain symptoms might be mistaken by the unlearned for the after-effects of drugs. In view of what the police had discovered in Seaton-Carew's flat, he could pardon the Chief Inspector for having fallen into error, but he felt obliged to point out that such an allegation against a lady of his patient's birth and breeding was a very, very serious matter. He quite appreciated the Chief Inspector's wish to interrogate Lady Nest, and he hoped that within a week or so it would be possible for him to see her. At present he could not sanction any visits whatsoever. Rest and quiet were essential to her.

The Chief Inspector returned in due course to his headquarters, and sent down a message to the Fingerprint Department. When Inspector Grant at last joined him, he found him studying photographs through a magnifying-glass, a fair young man at his elbow. He glanced up as the door opened, and said: 'Come and take a look at this, Sandy, and see what you make of it!'

Grant trod over to the desk, nodding to the fair youth. 'I am sorry to have been away for so long,' he said. 'The lassie was sleeping, but I said I would wait. She came down to the servants' hall for her tea. In the meantime I had some talk with Mrs Haddington's personal maid – making myself agreeable. What have you there? Is it the prints on the telephone?'

'It is – by which I mean Yes! I knew I should go and catch it! Next thing I know I shall have people thinking I'm Scotch too!'

'You will not, then,' said the Inspector dryly. He bent over the desk, keenly surveying the several photographs laid out on it. 'I have looked at these before: there is no trace of Seaton-Carew's finger-prints upon the instrument.'

'Never mind about that! Anything else strike you?'

A frown creased the Inspector's brow; he picked up one of the photographs, and scanned it more closely. The fair young man coughed behind a discreet hand. 'It's very blurred,' he said apologetically. 'I wouldn't care to swear to it myself, sir.'

'No one's asking you to swear to anything. Don't try to prejudice the Inspector!'

The fair youth blushed hotly. 'I'm sorry, sir! I'm sure I didn't mean –'

'Whisht!' said Inspector Grant, casting an indulgent glance in his direction. He picked up two more photographs from the desk, and compared them with the one he still held in his right hand. 'I see what I recall I saw before: there is a clear impression of Miss Birtley's thumb, and first two fingers. It may be that all five fingers were laid upon the instrument, but there is a blur over the prints on the third and fourth finger. I observe one distinct impression of the butler's index finger – but that, I am thinking, has no bearing on the case.'

'None at all. Take a look at that blur through the glass!' said Hemingway, handing it to him.

The Inspector took it, focused it, and intently studied the photograph. He then discarded one of the photographs he held in his left hand, and subjected the other to a minute scrutiny. The Chief Inspector, observing which of the photographs had been rejected, drew a packet of cigarettes from his pocket, and offered it to the young man beside him, saying: 'There you are! Even a poor Scot can get on to what you fellows miss!'

'We didn't miss it, sir!' protested Thirsk, drawing a cigarette from the packet. 'Only it's so indistinct no one could stand up in a Court of Law and swear to it!'

The Inspector raised his eyes from the photographs, both now held fan-shaped in his hand. 'You are thinking that there is an impression of Mrs Haddington's finger, superimposed on Miss Birtley's third and fourth fingers,' he said. 'I am of Thirsk's opinion: I would not care to swear to it. The whole is verra much blurred.'

'Not so blurred but what you saw what I was after,' Hemingway pointed out.

'*Ma seadh!* But it may be that Miss Birtley never had all five fingers on the instrument, and Mrs Haddington's prints are what we would expect to find.'

'Now tell me the story that girl told was all lies, and you'll be happy!' recommended Hemingway. 'All right, Thirsk: I've done with 'em for the moment! Take 'em away!' He waited until the young finger-print expert had withdrawn, and then said: 'Let's have it, Sandy! True, was it?'

'I am of the opinion that it was true,' Grant said. 'I would not set great store by anything a lassie in her position would say, because well I know they will lie to one for no reason at all, unless it might be that they do not like the police. But I think Mrs Haddington looked into the cloakroom before any of the guests arrived, and I am verra sure that she scolded Elsie for taking the wrong towel from the linen cupboard. It is coloured towels that they use in that house, and Elsie took one of the peach ones that go in Miss Haddington's room, instead of one of the *apricot* ones that are for the cloak-room.' He smiled. 'I would not myself know the difference! Be that as it may, Elsie did not see any wire upon the shelf when she changed the towel. So she says, but that might not be true. There is no reason why she should deny that she saw it, if indeed she did, but och! *Tha eagal oirre*! – She is afraid we might charge her with the murder, the silly creature! Yet I do not think that she saw it. Now the other lass – Gwenny Mapperley – is not afraid: she is a bold one, and she would be glad to do her mistress as much harm as she can. She leaves, she tells me, at the month. She talked – och, how she talked! – of all the trouble there has been in the house, and how much to believe I will leave you to judge. There are first the servants, who will not stay with Mrs Haddington, except the butler and the chef, to whom she pays huge wages: there is then Miss Birtley, whom the servants do not like – but I think that is jealousy, for she is also in Mrs Haddington's employment, and yet above them. When Mrs Haddington is rude to her, she gives her some verra sharp back-answers. Indeed, from all I hear she has a hot temper! There was a fine quarrel between them this morning! There has also been trouble with Miss Cynthia – I caught a wee glimpse of her, Chief: she is the bonniest lassie you ever did see! – but such tantrums, and such gallivanting about the town! She was not in her bed last night until past three o'clock, but dancing at some place or other with the young lord – Guisborough, is it? It is not decent! But for all Mrs Haddington has set her heart on making a grand match for the lassie, they say she doesn't favour the lord, but it is Mr Harte she has in her eye. But the servants know as well as you or I that it is Miss Birtley and not Miss Haddington that brings that young man to the house. And I think you were maybe right when you thought that Mrs Haddington had a hold over the Lady Nest, for Gwenny Mapperley has heard Mrs Haddington speaking to her on the telephone, as though she had only to give her orders and her ladyship would obey them.'

'You *have* been having a good gossip, haven't you?' said Hemingway. 'Allowing for a bit of exaggeration, I shouldn't wonder if you'd been given a fair picture, though. Did your little pal, Gwenny, say anything about the late Seaton-Carew?'

'She did, but I think that was mostly spite against her mistress. He was paying great attention to Miss Cynthia, and I don't doubt the lass's mother would not like that; but whether she herself was his mistress or not they none of them know, whatever tales they may tell. She has not been that since she came to live in London.'

'What do they make of her reaction to his death? She struck me as pretty cool, when I saw her.'

'How can one tell with that kind? The servants will have you think she hasn't turned a hair; but the doctor went to see her today, and was with her quite a while, so maybe she is more upset than she will show.' He added: 'It was Dr Westruther. He will maybe have mentioned it to you?'

'No, he didn't, because I didn't ask him. It doesn't surprise me, though – except that I didn't somehow take him for the sort of chap who trots round to call on his patients, with a little bag in his hand. Still, I daresay he makes her pay through the nose for a visit from him: he's got a very expensive décor to keep up, I can tell you.'

'Again the doctor has turned up, Chief.'

'They do. If you're thinking that it was him twisted

that wire round the late Seaton-Carew's neck, let me tell you that he'd have a lot more classy ways of doing a chap in than that! No, the more I consider the facts, the more I think we'll go round to Charles Street, Sandy, and have a real heart-to-heart with Mrs Haddington.'

'You still think it was she?' the Inspector said curiously.

'I won't go as far as to say that: I don't know, but I think everything points to her.'

'*Seall*, Chief, with what we have learnt this day, is it still Mrs Haddington with you?' protested the Inspector. 'It was motive you wanted, and which of them has the motive but Poulton?'

'I know,' Hemingway replied. He pointed the pencil he was holding at the telephone on his desk. '*That's* what's sticking in my gullet, Sandy! Has been, from the start. It doesn't matter what we discover about anyone else: I keep on coming back to it.'

'Because you have seen prints that are verra like Mrs Haddington's, on an instrument she would naturally handle?'

'Because I've got a strong notion those prints were made after Miss Birtley had laid down the receiver, and because I never did see how the receiver came to be hanging down, unless it had been deliberately put like that. Now, don't suggest that it got knocked off the table in a struggle, because though I may look gullible, I'm not really gullible at all. Seaton-Carew might have kicked the table over, but he didn't. He never touched the receiver –'

'Could he have grasped the wire?' Grant said doubtfully.

'No, and if he had, he'd have had the whole

instrument off the table. But he wouldn't. You let me twist something round your neck, and see what your reaction is – so far as you've time to react at all, which wouldn't be very far, according to what Dr Yoxall tells me! You won't grab at telephones: you'll grab at what's round your throat, my lad.'

The Inspector was silent. Hemingway rose, and took his overcoat off the stand in one corner of the room. 'We won't waste any time,' he said. 'We'll go along to Charles Street now.'

'They will be dressing for dinner!' protested Grant.

'Yes, I don't suppose we shall be at all popular,' agreed Hemingway. 'I shan't lose any sleep over that. In fact, I'm hoping that's just what they are doing, because we shall be sure of catching them before they go – what's that word of yours? – gallivanting off round the town! Come on!'

Thirteen

The Inspector had not exaggerated the spirit of unrest brooding over the house in Charles Street. In defiance of her mother's wishes, Cynthia had spent the previous evening with Lord Guisborough, at a night-club; and, returning home in the small hours of the morning, had flung herself into bed without troubling even to remove the make-up from her face. Her mother, coming out of her own bedroom in a trailing velvet dressing-gown, met her on the landing, and exclaimed reproachfully. Cynthia, declaring with far from perfect diction that she refused to be spied upon, went into her room, and slammed the door.

She was awakened at nine o'clock by the under-housemaid who carried a breakfast-tray into her room, and thus provoked a fit of mild hysterics. 'Leave me *alone!*' she commanded. 'Take that filthy tray away! I don't want it!'

'Cynthia darling, at least drink some coffee!' said Mrs Haddington, who had followed the maid into the room. 'You'll feel better, and you know you must get up! Miss Spennymoor is coming to fit that frock on you. Put the tray down on the table, Mary! That will do!'

'Oh, *blast* Miss Spennymoor!' said Cynthia. 'And if it's that old frock of yours, I won't wear it, Mummy!'

Mrs Haddington poured out a cup of coffee, added sugar, and held it out. 'Sit up, and drink this!' she said. 'Come, childie! To please me!'

Cynthia hoisted herself up reluctantly. 'Oh, all right! Where's the milk?'

'You don't want milk,' replied Mrs Haddington, a trifle grimly. 'What did you drink last night, Cynthia?'

'Champagne, of course. Lance took me to –'

'Cynthia, I told you not to go out with him, and now I see how right I was! You had far too much to drink, my darling. That shows me what sort of a young man he is! It isn't you I blame, but you know, pet, *nothing* puts the right kind of man off more quickly than a girl who takes too much to drink! Besides, if people like the Petworths ever saw you – well, you may take it from me that you wouldn't be invited to their parties any more! I want you to drop Lance. Titles aren't everything, and even if they were –'

Cynthia hunched a shoulder. 'Good God, as though I cared two hoots about his silly title! I happen to like him! *He* isn't always trying to improve me – except about his idiotic Communism, of course, and I can always shut him up about that! He'd do simply *anything* to please me! Why, he even took me to Frinton's last night, and he isn't a member!' She giggled suddenly. 'Really, I do think it was lamb-like of him, Mummy, because he shied off it badly, when I said I wanted to go there! He carried it off with a *superbly* high hand! And those *lethal* Kenelm Guisboroughs were there, with a stuffy party, and Lance made Kenelm OK him. Kenelm *loathed* having to do it,

202

too! It was screamingly funny! Lance and I laughed for *hours*!'

This ingenuous exposition of what afforded her cherished daughter amusement appeared to daunt Mrs Haddington. She said nothing; so Cynthia added: 'If you can get Lance to forget the starving millions, and you *easily* can, he's *too* sweet for words! Of course, he isn't half as good-looking as Timothy, but Timothy wouldn't have the guts to muscle into a club he didn't belong to, and, anyway, it isn't me Timothy's after!'

Mrs Haddington was a hardheaded woman, but she had her blind spot. It was inconceivable to her that any man, beholding her daughter, could look twice at any other female. She said sharply: 'Nonsense! If he isn't after you, why does he come here? You seem to forget that I found you practically in his arms yesterday afternoon!'

'Yes, wasn't it dear and cherishing of him?' agreed Cynthia, nibbling a slice of thin toast. 'Darling Mummy, you're *too* dim! Timothy's mad cats on Beulah Birtley! I don't say I couldn't have had him, if I'd wanted him, because honestly I *do* think I could cut the Birtley girl out, don't you? – but I'm practically certain Lance is *far* more my type!'

Uncomfortable recollections chased one another through Mrs Haddington's memory. She said angrily: 'That gaol-bird! Designing little bitch! I'll soon settle *her* hash! But it's rubbish, my pet! No man would look at her while *you* were present! I've no doubt she's trying her best to catch him, but I'll soon put a stop to that!'

'Oh, hell, who cares?' said Cynthia, relaxing into her enormous, lace-edged pillows. '*I* don't want him! I'd

203

sooner have Lance! Besides, you won't stop it. She had dinner with him last night, at Armand's. Moira was there, and she saw them.'

'*Did* she?' said Mrs Haddington. Her thin lips were close-gripped for a moment. She glanced down at her daughter, hesitated, and then said lightly: 'Never mind that! I want you to get up now, my pet, and come down to my boudoir for Miss Spennymoor to fit that dress on you.'

This mildly-worded request precipitated a minor crisis. Cynthia, whose fancy had prompted her to spray herself idly with scent from a cut-glass flagon, was goaded into hurling this expensive toy into the tiled grate, where it was shattered. However, this ebullition of temper had the happy effect of inducing her to get up, because not even she could remain in an atmosphere so redolent with the perfumes of Araby as to make her head swim. In a mood of sulky tearfulness, she presently descended the stairs to the boudoir, where Miss Spennymoor was patiently awaiting her.

She allowed herself to be divested of her frock, and to have her mother's old Good Black Wool cast over her head, merely saying fretfully: 'I look hellish in black, and it doesn't fit me anywhere!'

'It's only for the funeral, my pet!' Mrs Haddington soothed her. 'Just stand still and let Miss Spennymoor see what has to be done! Darling child, *don't* stand on one leg!'

'Oh, Mummy, I haven't got to go to the funeral, have I?' wailed Cynthia. 'I simply *won't*! It's too dreary for words, and I *know* Dan would say I needn't! O God, I feel too *septic* in this frightful thing! Take it off me!'

Miss Spennymoor, clucking amiably, said: 'Oh, dear,

fancy you saying that, Miss Haddington, when I was only thinking how sweet you look! They do say a blonde always looks her best in black, don't they? Of course, it'll be very different when I've taken it in the wee-est bit. Distinguished, I should call it! Let me just slip a few pins in, and you'll be surprised! Now, I'm quite partial to a funeral myself. Well, it takes all sorts to make a world, doesn't it? Weddings, now! I don't know how it is, but if ever I want a good cry I go and watch one of those grand weddings they have at St Margaret's! But funerals are different! – Oh, quite different they are! Of course, it makes anyone think, when they lower the coffin into the ground, but you want to look on the bright side, and ten to one it was a happy release, like it was for my poor mother, when Dad died, and once the coffin's out of the house it's surprising the difference it makes. More like a beanfeast than a funeral, my Dad's funeral was. Such a jollification as we had! No one wouldn't have guessed Mother had been up half the night, boiling the ham! Not, of course, that it's the same here, you not having the coffin in the house, but I'm sure the gentleman will have a lovely funeral, all the same!'

Ignoring this well-meant consolation, Cynthia said: 'Mummy, if Lance saw me in this thing, he'd have a *fit*!'

'Dear child, if I were you I wouldn't be guided by *that* young man's ideas of what is proper!'

'Goodness, no!' said Miss Spennymoor, a trifle thickly. She removed several pins from her mouth. 'You'll excuse me, but naturally I know who you are alluding to. I knew his mother very well, as I told you, Mrs Haddington, only the other day. Oh, very well I knew poor Maudie Stratton! If ever there was a One – ! Quite set on calling her baby Lancelot, she was! She'd read a poem about some Lancelot or other, which that Hilary of hers gave her, and it quite took her fancy, though why it should of is more than I can tell you, because all the fellow could find to say when he saw the girl in the poem, all stiff and stark in a boat, was that she'd got a lovely face. Well, that's all very well, and, of course I daresay he looked ever so nice himself, in a helmet and all, and riding on a horse – because a horse *does* give a man tone, doesn't it? I always think so if ever I get the time to go into Hyde Park, which I do sometimes. Still, looks aren't everything, and I call it highly unnatural for anyone to go barmy about a fellow that went round singing Tirra-lirra, which is all this Lancelot did, by what I could made out. Laughable, I call it! But there it was! Nothing would do for Maudie but she must call her baby Lancelot! Never doubted it would be a boy, which I said to her was downright tempting providence, and so it was, because what must she do but go and have split twins! Laugh! I thought I should have died! If you'd turn round, Miss Cynthia, I could see if it's hanging straight!'

Mrs Haddington, who had listened in stony silence to these recollections, caught her eye at this point, and gave her what the little dressmaker afterwards described as A Look. Miss Spennymoor, covered in confusion, coughed, said hastily: 'But I mustn't run on, must I?' and, in her agitation, stuck a pin into Cynthia's tender flesh. By the time that sensitive damsel had been soothed into sullen quiescence, all thought of Lord Guisborough and his romantically-minded parent had been banished from Miss Spennymoor's mind, and she continued her task in chastened silence.

Miss Spennymoor had scarcely withdrawn to the seclusion of the sewing-room on the second floor when Beulah came into the boudoir, to lay before her employer the sum total of the weekly bills. Mrs Haddington's eyes narrowed; she said: 'I'll check it against the books.'

Beulah flushed. 'Certainly! I have them here!'

'Trot along, darling!' Mrs Haddington told her daughter, in quite another voice. 'I shouldn't racket about today, if I were you. Why don't you ring up Betty, and see if she'd like to go for a walk in the Park with you, and come back here to luncheon? Wouldn't that be rather nice?'

'No, hellish!' responded Cynthia frankly. 'I'm going to lie down! I feel *bloody*!'

With these elegant words, she walked out of the room neglecting to shut the door behind her.

Mrs Haddington seated herself at her desk, and held out her hand for the weekly accounts. In silence, Beulah laid a pile of books and bills before her, together with her own epitome.

'Your total appears to be correct,' Mrs Haddington said, after a pause.

'No, is it really?' retorted Beulah. 'I quite thought I was getting away with a halfpenny!'

'I advise you not to be impertinent, my good girl. You won't find that it pays in this house!' Mrs Haddington took out her cheque-book from a drawer, and dipped a pen in the silver inkpot. 'There is something else I wish to say to you. I understand that you were dining with Mr Harte last night, at Armand's?'

'Well?' Beulah shot at her.

The pen travelled slowly across the cheque-form. 'I need hardly ask, I suppose, whether Mr Harte is aware of your somewhat unusual history?' said Mrs Haddington bitingly.

The flush had faded from Beulah's cheeks, leaving them very white. 'I don't know what business that is of yours!' she said.

'It is very much my business. Mr Harte met you under my roof, and I could not reconcile it with my conscience not to drop a word of timely warning in his ear.'

Beulah put out a hand to grip the edge of the mantel-shelf. 'I see the idea, of course!' she said breathlessly. 'Recoiling in disgust from me, Timothy is to fall into your daughter's arms! I'm afraid he won't do it: his taste doesn't run to brainless blondes!' She stopped, and added quickly: 'I'm sorry! I oughtn't to have said that!'

Mrs Haddington blotted the cheque, and turned in her chair to survey Beulah from her heels to her head. 'So you actually imagine that you're going to entrap that young man into marriage, do you?' she said. 'How very amusing! But something tells me that the Hartes don't go to Holloway for their brides. We shall see!'

Beulah released the mantelshelf, and took a hasty step towards her employer. 'Whatever you do, he won't marry Cynthia!' she said.

'*Miss* Cynthia!' corrected Mrs Haddington blandly.

'Oh, don't be such a fool! My family is a damned sight better-born than yours, for what that's worth! You're trying to make me lose my temper, but, I warn you, you'd better not! I didn't cut your daughter out with Timothy Harte: he never for one moment thought of her seriously! It can't matter to you if I marry him! There are dozens of men only too anxious to marry her: why can't you let me have just *one* who prefers me? I'm going to marry him, not because he's well-off, and well-born, and heir to a baronetcy, but because I love him! If you think you can stop me, you were never more mistaken in your life! I'm not a dewy innocent any longer, so don't think it! I've put up with your foul tongue all these months because it suited me to stay in this job, but I won't put up with any interference in my private life! There's very little I won't do, if you goad me to it! If I can't have Timothy, I don't care what becomes of me! So now you know!'

From the doorway Thrimby coughed with extreme deliberation. 'I beg your pardon, madam, but I thought Miss Cynthia was here. Lord Guisborough wishes to speak to her on the telephone.'

Beulah glared at him, her full lip caught between her teeth. Mrs Haddington said coolly: 'Here is the cheque, Miss Birtley. You will pay the bills tomorrow morning, if you please, before you come to work. Kindly go down to Mrs Foston and find out from her what shopping has to be done today! Miss Cynthia is resting, Thrimby, I will speak to Lord Guisborough.'

Thrimby, recounting this interesting passage later to his colleague, the housekeeper, said impressively: 'Mark my words, Mrs Foston, there's more to that young woman than meets the eye! Well, I've always had my suspicions, right from the start!'

'Well,' said Mrs Foston, who was as goodhumoured as she was stout, 'be that as it may, I'm downright sorry for the girl, and that's a fact, Mr Thrimby! *I've* never had any words with her, but, then, Do as you would be done by, is my motto! I shall stay here till the end of the Season, because that's what I promised Mrs H., but not another moment! Well, it isn't what I've been accustomed to, and that's the truth! Only, in these days, with the best people cutting down their staffs –' She stopped, and sighed. 'Well, you know what it is, Mr Thrimby!'

'I know,' he agreed, echoing her sigh. 'Sometimes one wonders what the world is coming to!'

'All this talk about the Workers!' said Mrs Foston, shaking out a tea-cloth, subjecting it to a minute inspection, and refolding it. 'Anyone 'ud think the only people to do a job of work was in factories, or dockyards, or plate-laying! No one bothers about people like you and me, and my brother, who's doing a jobbing-gardener's work, because no one can't afford to keep a head-gardener like him, that was always used to have four under him! It makes me tired, Mr Thrimby!'

'Ah, well, it's Progress, Mrs Foston!' said the butler vaguely.

'Yes, and I suppose it's progress that makes any little chit that hasn't had any more training than that canary of mine waltz in here asking as much money as a decent housemaid that's worked her way up from between-maid!' said Mrs Foston tartly. 'Something for nothing! That's what people want nowadays. And it's what they get, too, more's the pity! I've no patience with it!'

At this point, Thrimby, well-knowing that his colleague was fairly mounted upon her favourite hobby-horse, thought it prudent to withdraw, so that Mrs Foston was left to address the rest of her pithy monologue to the ambient air.

With the exception of Mrs Foston, who stated that she

preferred to say nothing; and of M. Gaston, the chef, who professed a sublime indifference to anything that occurred beyond the confines of the realm over which he reigned, Mrs Haddington's servants were at one in declaring that murders were not what they had been accustomed to, or could put up with. The head housemaid, recruiting her strength with a cup of Bovril, informed her subordinate, who had brought this sustaining beverage up to her sick-bed, that strangled corpses were not what she would call nice; and the parlourmaid, tendering her notice to her employer, said that Mr Seaton-Carew's murder had unsettled her. The kitchenmaid, who was an orphan, said that her auntie didn't want her to stay no longer in a house where there were such unnatural goings-on; and would no doubt have followed the parlourmaid's example had she not been too much frightened of M. Gaston to give notice without his consent. This, since she was the least stupid scullion who had been allotted to him, was withheld, M. Gaston maintaining with Gallic fervour that what took place abovestairs was no concern of his or hers. Margie, a biddable girl, was quite cowed by his eloquence; and the rest of the staff, while deprecating the laxity of M. Gaston's outlook, said that anyone had to remember that he was French.

Notwithstanding the outrage to their finer feelings, it could not be denied that the servants derived no small degree of excitement, and even enjoyment, from the murder. Not only did it afford them an endless topic for discussion; but it rendered them interesting in the eyes of less experienced friends and relations, and it provided them with a series of not wholly disagreeable thrills. It even furnished the under-housemaid with an excuse for smashing Mrs Haddington's early-morning teapot, and for forgetting to draw the curtains in her bathroom. Elsie, arising shakily from her sick-bed, might declare that Inspector Grant's desire to interrogate her had materially prejudiced her chances of recovery from influenza, but his visit made her instantly important, and not for the world would she have forgone it. Thrimby, listening-in, in the pantry, to a brief conversation on the telephone between his mistress and Lord Guisborough, was able to depress these pretensions by assuming the air of an informed person, and by throwing out such doubtful phrases as Hamlet warned his friends never to utter.

Altogether, it was a rewarding day for the staff, even the visit of Dr Westruther being invested with a sinister significance. It was vain for the prosaic housekeeper to point out that the doctor's visit was not unprecedented; the fact that he was closeted with Mrs Haddington for nearly an hour was enough to give rise to speculation; for, as Miss Mapperley so sapiently observed, it stood to reason that if all the old girl wanted was a sedative for her lacerated nerves it wouldn't have taken about twenty minutes to have given her a prescription. Hard upon the heels of the doctor came the Inspector, and although his descent into the basement caused the kitchenmaid to come over ever so queer in the scullery, it afforded everyone else considerable gratification, for, while his visit conferred distinction upon the servants' hall, he was not found to be above his company, accepting cups of tea with compliments and thanks, and chatting in the easiest way with even such lowly persons as the charwoman, who came in to help the kitchenmaid with the Rough

Work. In fact, so agreeable did he make himself that even his lilting speech, at first considered peculiarly laughable, was finally adjudged to enhance his charm; and when the tea-cloth was spread in the servants' hall Mrs Foston was moved to produce from the store-cupboard a jar of honey, which she felt to be a peculiarly Scotch conserve. If anything was needed to insure the Inspector's popularity by this time, it was supplied by the tact with which he leaped into the breach caused by the under-housemaid's social lapse in reading aloud the inscription on the jar, which declared the contents to be Finest Flower Honey, the product of unequivocally English bees. Elsie, who had tottered downstairs with the firm intention of coming over faint, emerged triumphant from her interview with him, and was able to inform her fellows that she had ascertained from him that the Inquest on poor Mr Seaton-Carew would be held on the following day. No one else had quite liked to ask him this vital question, but although everyone was grateful to Elsie for discovering the date and the locality, not even the precarious state of her health saved her from being recommended by Miss Mapperley not to carry on as though she thought she was Mata Hari.

Hardly had the Inspector departed, than a mild sensation was caused by the arrival of Mr Sydney Butterwick. This, in itself, was not a matter of great moment, but piquancy was added to his visit by the fact, reported by the parlourmaid, that he had demanded speech with Mrs Haddington on the telephone, earlier in the day, and, upon being asked if he would leave a message, had replied hotly that he would not leave a message, and had rung off abruptly. Having had no instructions to exclude Mr Butterwick, Thrimby showed him upstairs into the drawing-room, where Mrs Haddington, having finished tea half an hour earlier, was attempting to convince her daughter that it would be both inadvisable and improper for her to put in an appearance at a cocktail-party that evening. Cynthia had just informed her that if the slightest restraint were placed upon her she would go mad, when Mr Butterwick stalked into the room, also in a febrile condition. Disregarding the conventions, he burst into speech even before Thrimby had announced his name, uttering in trembling accents: 'I want a word with you, Mrs Haddington!'

Never before had Thrimby longed so much for an excuse to linger! He could find none. The tea-table had been removed; on this bleak February afternoon he had drawn the curtains in all the sitting-rooms at four o'clock; the fire was burning brightly in the hearth; there did not seem even to be an ashtray that needed emptying. He was forced to withdraw to the landing, and even, two minutes later, to his own domain, because Cynthia, seizing the opportunity to escape from her mother's authority, came out of the drawing-room, and very nearly surprised him on the stairs. All he was able to report to Mrs Foston was that Mr Butterwick had demanded of Mrs Haddington what the devil she had meant by telling the police lies about him; and that when she had replied in freezing accents that she was at a loss to understand what he meant, he had exclaimed: 'You know damned well what I mean! And what I should like to know is why you're so anxious to cast suspicion on me for Dan's death!'

A quarter of an hour later, while Mr Butterwick was

still closeted with Mrs Haddington, Thrimby opened the front door to another visitor. This was Lord Guisborough, and since Thrimby had listened to his conversation on the telephone with Mrs Haddington that morning, he had been expecting him. Lord Guisborough had rung up to suggest to Cynthia that they should spend another evening together, to which Mrs Haddington had replied that she was anxious to have a little chat with him, and would be glad if he could make it convenient to call on her at some time during the course of the afternoon. An assignation had been arranged for a quarter-to-six. Mrs Foston, nodding darkly, said that Madam was going to bring his lordship to the point, and not before it was time; but Miss Mapperley maintained that the old so-and-so was more likely to tick him off for keeping Miss Cynthia out until all hours.

Since his lordship wore no hat, his black locks were tossed into more than ordinary confusion, a fact that seemed to trouble him no more than his lack of gloves or walking-stick. He refused to allow Thrimby to help him to take off his overcoat, favouring him instead with a short dissertation on the Equality of Men, which made Thrimby despise him more than ever. He was even misguided enough to say that Thrimby need not trouble to announce him to his hostess, but this revolting suggestion Thrimby was able to ignore, merely by preceding his lordship to the staircase.

At this moment, a door opened on the landing above, and Mr Butterwick's voice was heard assuring Mrs Haddington that nothing would induce him ever again to enter her house. He came charging down the stairs, and almost collided with Thrimby on the half-landing. After swearing at him, he perceived Lord Guisborough, mounting the first flight in his wake, flushed, muttered a confused greeting, and brushed past him on his way down to the hall. Thrimby, only hesitating for a moment, proceeded on his stately way, threw open the door into the drawing-room, and announced his lordship.

'Ah, Lord Guisborough! So glad you were able to spare me a few minutes!' said Mrs Haddington, rising from the sofa, and holding out her hand.

Plainly, no drama was to be looked for during this visit. Thrimby withdrew, prepared, if necessary, to assist Mr Butterwick to put on his coat. However, by the time he reached the ground-floor, there was no other sign of Mr Butterwick than his malacca walking-cane, which, in his agitation, he appeared to have left behind him. Thrimby went back to the basement, and disposed himself comfortably in his pantry to peruse the evening paper. He was startled hardly more than half an hour later by hearing the front door slammed with sufficient violence almost to shake the house. An instant later, the drawing-room bell rang insistently. Thrimby pulled himself out of his chair, straightened his hair and his tie, and climbed the stairs to the ground-floor. He did not hurry, because he was a man of portly habit and he had, besides, his dignity to consider. He was hailed from the half-landing by his employer, who demanded whether it took him all day to answer the bell. Without giving him time to reply, she said, in her most cutting tone: 'Lord Guisborough has let himself out. Kindly remember that I am not, in future, at home to his lordship! If he should ring up at any time you will say that neither I nor Miss

Cynthia can come to the telephone. Do you clearly understand me?'

Thrimby was far from understanding what could have been the cause of so sudden a change of face, but he merely bowed, and said: 'Certainly, madam.'

'And tell Miss Birtley I wish to see her before she leaves!'

'Miss Birtley, madam, left a quarter of an hour ago, at six o'clock,' said Thrimby.

'Oh! Union rules, I suppose!' said Mrs Haddington, with a disagreeable little laugh. 'Very well, never mind! You can bring cocktails up to the drawing-room now!'

Thrimby bowed again, contriving to convey the information that he had had every intention of bringing cocktails up to the drawing-room, and that if his mistress wished for drinks half an hour in advance of the usual hour she should not only have them, but he would keep his inevitable reflections to himself. 'And,' said Mrs Haddington, in the sharp tone that never failed to infuriate her servants, 'I have lost my emerald brooch!'

Thrimby stiffened. 'Indeed, madam? I am exceedingly sorry to hear it, and I can assure you –'

'I'm not accusing you of having stolen it! The safety-catch is loose, and it must have come undone. I am merely telling you that it is somewhere in the house, and must be found, when the rooms are swept in the morning.'

'Certainly, madam. I will myself inform the maids,' said Thrimby, preparing to descend again into the basement.

The drawing-room was empty when he presently brought up the cocktail-tray, but while he was still straightening cushions, and tidying the hearth, Mrs Haddington came down from the second floor. There was a frown between her brows; she said: 'Do you know if Miss Cynthia went out, Thrimby?'

'I couldn't say, madam.'

'She didn't ask you to call her a taxi, or anything?'

'No, madam. I haven't seen Miss Cynthia.'

'Oh, well, perhaps she's sitting in the boudoir!' said Mrs Haddington, with more hope than conviction. She had found abundant signs in her daughter's bedroom of a rapid change of costume, and although it was possible that Cynthia had changed into a dinner-dress suitable for an evening to be spent at home, it seemed more likely that she had sallied forth in her new and daring cocktail-frock to attend the forbidden party.

The boudoir was in darkness. Mrs Haddington closed the door, found that Thrimby had followed her down the stairs, and said: 'I think Miss Cynthia must have gone out. Tell Gaston I won't wait dinner for her, if she isn't back by eight o'clock. Oh, good God, who can this be?'

'Shall I say that you are not at home, madam?' Thrimby asked, preparing to descend to the hall, to answer the door-bell.

'Yes – no! If it should be Lady Nest, or Sir Roderick, or Mr Harte, or someone like that, I'll see them,' she replied, drawing back out of the direct line of vision from the front door.

It was none of these persons. Mrs Haddington, listening on the half-landing, heard the level voice of Godfrey Poulton requesting to be announced. She stepped forward to the head of the stairs, saying in her most social tone: 'Mr Poulton! What a pleasant surprise! I was just telling my butler to deny me, but of course *you* are always a welcome guest! But isn't dearest Nest with you?'

Poulton handed his gloves and his scarf to Thrimby, and glanced up the stairs. 'Good-evening, Mrs Haddington. No, I fear my wife is not with me. I should be most grateful if you would spare me a few moments.'

'But of course!' she said, still smiling, but with a suggestion of rigidity about her mouth. 'I hope you haven't brought bad news of Nest?'

He went up the stairs towards her. He did not answer this question, but said: 'May I see you in private? I shall not keep you long, I trust.'

She opened the door into the boudoir. 'Really, you are quite alarming me, Mr Poulton! Come into my room! We shall be quite undisturbed. Do you know, I have been feeling uneasy about Nest all day? So unlike her not to have given me a ring!'

He followed her into the room, and closed the door; Thrimby went back to the basement, where, encountering Miss Mapperley, he disclosed that Something was undoubtedly Up.

'For it is not Mr Poulton's habit to drop in at this house,' he said, 'and from the look of him he hadn't come just to pass the time of day.'

'It wouldn't surprise me,' said Miss Mapperley, pleasurably thrilled, 'if he'd come to tell Madam that he won't have her ladyship visiting here any more, not after what's happened! I saw him at the party, and he looked ever such a masterful man. A bit like Cary Grant, only older, of course, and not as handsome. I said so to Elsie, at the time. I'd give something to know what he's saying to the old hag!'

However, neither she nor Thrimby was destined to know what was said in the boudoir. The interview did not last long, the bell summoning Thrimby to show the visitor out after little more than twenty minutes.

He reached the hall to find Godfrey Poulton descending the stairs in a leisurely way. That impassive countenance betrayed no emotion whatsoever. Poulton thanked him briefly for helping him on with his coat, received his gloves and hat from him, and went out to where his car awaited him. The chauffeur sprang out to open the door for him; he got in, and as Thrimby closed the front door, the car drove away.

Miss Mapperley, eagerly awaiting Thrimby's report, was disappointed, but reflected that she would probably be able to gather from Mrs Haddington's manner, when she went up to help her change for dinner, whether or not the visit had afforded her gratification. 'You can always tell when anything's happened to annoy her,' she observed. 'I wouldn't mind betting I can't do right tonight!'

Mrs Haddington's bedroom-bell was late in ringing. No summons had reached Miss Mapperley by the time Thrimby went up to the dining-room to lay the table. He was engaged in folding a napkin into the shape of a water-lily when a soft footfall in the hall took him to the door. Beulah Birtley was just about to let herself out of the house.

'I thought you had gone home, miss!' Thrimby said.

She was startled, and turned quickly, colouring. 'Oh! I didn't know you were there! Yes, I had, but I left Mrs Haddington's cheque behind, and had to come back for it. For heaven's sake, don't tell her!'

Thrimby was aware, of course, that Miss Birtley had been granted a latch-key, for this had been bestowed upon her to save him the trouble of answering the door to her every time her employer sent her forth on an errand, but he chose to assume an air of deep disapproval, and to say: 'Madam wished to see you before you left, miss, so it is quite fortunate that you have returned. I fancy you will find her in the boudoir.'

'I haven't any desire to find her, thank you!' said Beulah. 'I went off duty at six, and I'm going home, and there's not the slightest need for you to tell her I ever came back!'

'If you will wait for a moment, miss,' said Thrimby implacably, 'I will just ascertain whether Madam has any message for you.'

He observed, not without satisfaction, that his words had brought a scowl to Miss Birtley's brow, and went in his stately way up to the boudoir.

Fourteen

It was shortly after half-past seven o'clock that the Chief Inspector arrived in Charles Street. The door was opened with unusual celerity by Thrimby, who stared at the two detectives as though he could scarcely believe the evidence of his eyes, and ejaculated: 'I didn't think you would have been here so soon!'

'So soon?' said Hemingway, his quick, frowning glance taking in certain signs of disorder in the butler's bearing. 'I want to see your mistress!'

'Yes, sir. Of course!' Thrimby said, with a gulp. 'If you'd come this way!' He waited for the two men to cast their overcoats on to a chair, and led them up to the boudoir. Without a word, he opened the door, and stood aside for the detectives to enter the room, carefully averting his gaze.

Seated in the chair beside the telephone-table, was Mrs Haddington, her eyes and tongue protruding horribly, and behind her head two strands of picture-wire projecting.

The Chief Inspector stood, as though turned to stone, on the threshold. Behind him, he heard Grant gasp: '*A Mhuire Mhathaid!*' He swung round quickly to confront the butler. 'When did this happen?'

Thrimby shook his head, moistened his lips. 'I don't know. It isn't more than ten minutes since I found her. I rang up Scotland Yard. They said you'd be along in a few minutes.'

'We must already have left the building,' Hemingway muttered. 'Any idea who could have done it?'

'Yes, sir! It can't have been anyone but Mr Poulton, or Miss Birtley: I'm sure of that! I'm holding Miss Birtley, in the library. Mr Poulton left the house nearly half an hour ago.'

'All right!' Hemingway said curtly. 'I'll have a word with you presently: you can clear off for the present!'

'Thank you, sir!' said Thrimby, with real gratitude, and effaced himself.

Hemingway shut the door of the boudoir. He laid his fingers for a brief space over Mrs Haddington's wrist, and then said in a matter-of-fact voice: 'Seem to have got on the wrong scent, don't I? A nice set-out, this is! I daresay the Department has sent the doctor off already, but you'd better ring through, Sandy, in case of accidents. I don't know how long she's been dead, but she's warm still. Tell 'em I've got a duplicate murder on my hands, and I want the usual bag of tricks sent round!'

The Inspector drew out his handkerchief, and, through its folds, picked up the telephone. While he spoke into the receiver, his superior was subjecting the body of Mrs Haddington to a close scrutiny. The chair in which she sat had been slewed a little away from the telephone-table; her head was thrown back, the nape of her neck resting against the gilded wood framing the padded back of the chair, and both her legs stuck out before her. Her arms hung limply, outside the arms of the chair, and her dress was rucked up on one side. The Chief Inspector cast a keen look round the room.

Grant replaced the telephone on its rest. 'The finger-print and photographic units are on their way, sir,' he announced. '*Mo thruaighe*, but this is a terrible thing!'

Hemingway nodded.

'Is the man a maniac, think you?'

'Can't say, I'm sure.'

'It is identical!' the Inspector said, staring at the body.

'Think so? Well, I don't! For one thing, unless I'm much mistaken, she wasn't sitting in that chair when she was murdered. Take a look at the position she's in! To have fallen back with her neck against the chair, she'd have had to have sat down on the very edge of it, and she'd have fallen forward, not backward. Take a look at those marks on the carpet too! If you ask me, she was sitting in front of the fire, and it was her heels that made those marks when she was dragged to where we see her now!'

The Inspector looked down at the carpet. The pile had been rubbed the wrong way in two diagonal lines. 'But why?' he demanded incredulously.

'You can search me! Maybe you're right, and it is a maniac. Maybe he's just got a queer sense of humour. I wouldn't know.'

'There is nothing mad about Poulton,' Grant said. 'I never saw a saner man than that one!'

'For the lord's sake, Sandy, don't go jumping to conclusions!' Hemingway said irritably. 'That 'ud land us in a packet of trouble! Not but what we're in it now. I like this fellow's nerve, bumping off a second victim while I'm still investigating the first murder! And don't tell me

224

Poulton's got nerve enough, because I know that already!'

'*Ch'an abair mi dad!*'

'If you're trying to send me haywire, my lad – ! What's that mean?'

The Inspector apologised. 'It slipped out! It means I will say nothing.'

'You stick to that and perhaps I can still pull this case out of the mud!' said Hemingway. He relented, and added: 'Sorry, Sandy! You know, I had more than half an idea I was going to make an arrest this evening.'

'I do know, of course,' Grant agreed doubtfully.

'All right, it certainly looks like being one up to you. What I'm due for is one of the bigger official kicks. See who that is!'

The Inspector opened the door to admit the police-surgeon. Dr Yoxall came briskly in, cast a dispassionate glance at the body in the chair, and set down his bag. ''Evening, Hemingway! What's all this?'

'Just another little job for you, sir. Getting monotonous, isn't it?'

The doctor bent over the body, deigning no response. After a few moments, he said: 'I can't tell you anything you aren't capable of grasping for yourself. Been dead under an hour; strangulation; method identical with the first death in this room. What have you got, Chief Inspector? A homicidal maniac?'

'Looks like it, doesn't it, sir? Did she die where you see her?'

The doctor's sharp eyes studied the position of the body. 'Hard to say. She may have slipped forward on the chair in her death-throes. I shouldn't have expected to have found her quite like that, but I'm not prepared to say she couldn't have got into that position. A ruthless man, this murderer: wish you luck, Hemingway! Have the body sent down to the mortuary when you've finished with it. Not that I shall be able to tell you anything more: I shan't. A dull case! Thought so at the start! 'Night!'

'The only case that chap thinks is interesting,' said Hemingway, when the doctor had gone, 'is the kind of messy job where you get half the medical profession into the witness-box, swearing blind that black's white just to score off the other half!'

'Och, now, whisht!' said the Inspector reasonably. 'Here is Bromley!'

Several persons came into the room. Hemingway nodded to their leader. 'Case of Here we are again, Tom! Get busy, will you? Get me a composite, taking in the body, and those marks on the carpet. I don't have to tell you what to try for, Bromley: go over all the furniture – mantelpiece – anything a man might have put his hand on! You stay, Sandy: you can let the ambulance-men take the body away as soon as these chaps have finished. Lock the room!'

He left the room as he spoke, and went down the stairs to the hall. Here, Thrimby awaited him. He said: 'Now then, let's hear what you've got to say! Come in here!'

He led the way into the dining-room. The table was laid for two persons, a circumstance which seemed to affect the butler poignantly. He shuddered, and said: 'I'd only that minute finished laying for Madam, and Miss Cynthia!'

'What minute?'

'I don't know what the time was, not for certain. It must have been soon after seven. I heard a stealthy footstep in the hall, as if someone was walking on tip-toe, and I went to the door, like this, and there was Miss Birtley, just about to let herself out of the house.'

The Chief Inspector was unimpressed. 'Any reason why she shouldn't have been letting herself out? When is she due to knock off each day?'

'At six o'clock, unless Madam wished her to stay on. And so she did, Chief Inspector, for with my own eyes I saw her leave the house then!'

'Then how did she get in again?'

'Miss Birtley has a duplicate latch-key. I was considerably astonished to see her, and it seemed to me that she was taking care not to be heard. When I spoke to her, she gave a start, and seemed much discomposed.'

'She did, did she? What had she come back for?'

'She informed me, Chief Inspector, that she had omitted to take away with her the cheque handed to her this morning by Mrs Haddington, to pay the accounts with. I need hardly say that I should be reluctant – most reluctant I should be! – to get a fellow-creature into trouble, but at the time it struck me as being Odd. I won't say suspicious, but definitely Odd. Knowing that Mrs Haddington had wished to speak with her before her departure, I requested her to wait while I ascertained whether Madam had any message for her.' He paused, and added impressively: 'Miss Birtley was very reluctant to do so. In fact, she did not wish me to go up to the boudoir. But I was Adamant! I went – and *that* was what I found! I do not know when anything has given me such a Turn, Chief Inspector!'

'And what were your own movements?' asked Hemingway.

Thrimby was not to be so easily baulked. He said: 'As soon as I realised that Mrs Haddington had been foully done to death, I commanded Miss Birtley to go into the library, and I sent immediately to request Mrs Foston, the housekeeper, to remain there with her until your arrival.'

'And what,' repeated Hemingway, 'were your own movements?'

'After the departure of Mr Poulton, which would have been at about a quarter-to-seven, as near as I can remember, I was in my pantry till I came up to lay the table.'

'Yes, well, now suppose you were to tell me just who has been here this evening?' suggested Hemingway.

'I ought, perhaps, to tell you first, Chief Inspector, that I overheard a very unpleasant scene this morning between Mrs Haddington and Miss Birtley. I'm sure I would prefer not to mention the matter, but I feel it to be my duty to inform you that Miss Birtley addressed Mrs Haddington in what I should call threatening terms. She said that she wouldn't be interfered with, and there were no lengths she wouldn't go to, if she was goaded to it. Then she said, and, I must say, I was shocked, that if she couldn't have Mr Harte – Timothy, she called him – she didn't care what became of her. At which point, I thought it proper to intervene, which, Chief Inspector, I did. Quite murderous, Miss Birtley looked: I thought so at the time!'

Hemingway listened dispassionately to this story. He was interested, but he disappointed the butler by betraying no signs of excitement whatsoever. He felt none. It was possible, in his view, that Miss Birtley had strangled her employer, but he had interrogated too many witnesses not to recognise spite when he was confronted with it. By dint of some skilful questioning, he elicited from Thrimby a fairly coherent account of the day's happenings. 'So, setting aside the doctor's visit, no one came to the house between the time he left, and the time Mr Butterwick arrived? Very well! You say that Lord Guisborough called before Mr Butterwick had left the house. Did you see Mr Butterwick out?'

'No, for I was engaged in showing his lordship up to the drawing-room. By the time I came downstairs again, Mr Butterwick had departed. I did not actually see Lord Guisborough out either, though I heard him go. His lordship, not waiting for me to show him out, slammed the door with considerable violence. Mrs Haddington seemed quite put out: in fact she spoke to me as I am not at all accustomed to be spoken to, actually coming to the head of the stairs to know what had kept me, which nothing had, Chief Inspector, but it is not my custom to go dashing upstairs! She then instructed me to say in future, if his lordship called or rang up, that she was not at home. It is my belief that Mrs Haddington did not, as one might say, fancy his lordship. Of course, it is not for me to venture an opinion, Chief Inspector, but one can't help putting two and two together. What with his lordship running after Miss Cynthia, till it is quite noticeable, and Mrs Haddington asking him to come to see her this afternoon, and then his lordship rushing out of the house, and Mrs Haddington saying what she did, one can't doubt that she had told him it was no use him thinking of

229

Miss Cynthia, for she wouldn't consent. Miss Cynthia, I should mention, is under age. Strictly between ourselves, Chief Inspector, it's common knowledge, in the Hall, that it's Mr Harte Mrs Haddington wanted for Miss Cynthia. Well, when he first visited here, I must say I thought there was something in it. But then he seemed to get sweet on Miss Birtley all at once – and there has been a certain amount of unpleasantness, Miss Birtley being a young woman with a temper, and I regret to say, not always as civil as she might be. Really, I was quite shocked at her this morning; and naturally I couldn't but recall the words she had with Mr Seaton-Carew, the night he was murdered. Almost the same they were, though I don't precisely remember them now. Threatening, is what I should call them.'

'Never mind about Miss Birtley for the moment! After Lord Guisborough left the house, what happened?'

The butler reflected. 'I went down to fetch the cocktail-tray up to the drawing-room. I fancy Mrs Haddington must have gone up to Miss Cynthia's room, for she asked me, when she came down, if I knew where Miss Cynthia was. Mapperley – that's Mrs Haddington's personal maid – thinks she went off to a party, but not having seen her go, I couldn't say. She hasn't yet returned.'

'Just as well!' muttered Hemingway. 'Then what happened?'

'Mrs Haddington went to see if Miss Cynthia was in the boudoir. It was then that Mr Poulton arrived, about 6.25, as near as I remember.'

'Did Mrs Haddington seem pleased to see him, or not?'

'Well, sir, I thought Mrs Haddington was better pleased to see him than he was to be here. I doubt if Mr Poulton has ever been in the house above twice or three times. I had the impression that he did not care for Mrs Haddington. But he is not a gentleman as shows his feelings. He asked for a private word with Mrs Haddington, and she took him into the boudoir, and that was the last time I saw her alive.'

'I see. Tell me once again exactly what happened when the boudoir bell rang!'

'When the bell rang,' said the butler carefully, 'I had of course been expecting it. I mounted the stairs from the basement, and when I reached the hall I saw Mr Poulton coming down the first flight.'

'Was he in any way agitated? Did he seem quite as usual?'

'So far as I could judge, he did. But I don't know him well, and, as I say, he doesn't give anything away. He was coming quite slowly downstairs, nor he didn't hurry over putting on his coat. His car was waiting for him, and he drove off, as I told you.'

'All right, that seems very clear,' Hemingway said. 'Did you say I would find Miss Birtley in the library?'

'Yes, sir. I could not take it upon myself to allow Miss Birtley to leave the house. Mrs Foston is with her.'

'All right, I know the way,' Hemingway said.

He found Beulah and the housekeeper seated one on either side of the electric stove in the library. Beulah had thrown off her hat, but she still wore her tweed coat, into the pockets of which she had dug her hands. She looked white, and frightened. Mrs Foston, who rose at the Chief Inspector's entrance, had been quietly knitting. She folded up the work, and said: 'If you please, sir, Miss Birtley and I have thought it best to send for Miss Cynthia's aunt, Miss Pickhill.'

'Quite right,' said Hemingway.

'I have also sent for Mr Harte!' Beulah said.

'Well, you've got a perfect right to send for anyone you like,' replied Hemingway. 'Anyone else you've rung up?'

'No.'

'That's good. It wouldn't really help any of us to have half London here. Thanks, Mrs Foston, I won't keep you any longer.'

Mrs Foston glanced at Beulah. 'That's as may be, sir, but if Miss Birtley would like me to stay with her I'm very willing. Because no one's going to make me believe a young lady would go and do such a nasty, cruel thing, whatever Thrimby may say! A piece of my mind is what he's going to get, before he's much older!'

'You go and give it to him right now!' Hemingway advised her. 'You won't do any good staying here, and whoever told you the police go around with thumbscrews in their pockets told you a lie: we aren't allowed to.'

'It's all right!' Beulah said, forcing up a smile. 'I shan't answer any questions until Mr Harte arrives.'

'Well, if you're sure, miss!' Mrs Foston said.

Hemingway opened the door, and pushed her gently over the threshold. Having shut her out of the room, he turned and looked Beulah over. 'You do get yourself into some awkward situations, don't you?' he remarked genially.

He caught her off her guard. 'This is the worst I've been in yet! You needn't think I don't know that! I suppose you've already been told that I had a row with Mrs Haddington this morning?'

'Oh, yes, I know all about that! Used threatening language, didn't you? Silly thing to do, if you meant to murder her!'

'I didn't murder her!'

'All right, let's start from there! When did you leave the house?'

'I'm not going to say any more than that! I know just where talking to the police gets you!'

'Listen!' said Hemingway patiently. 'I'm quite pre-pared to believe you had a raw deal eighteen months ago. Suppose you have a shot at believing that I'm not the Big, Bad Wolf? I'm not even Inspector Under-barrow: in fact, far from it!'

'If you mean the Inspector who dealt with my case –'

'I do, and that's all we'll say about him. He's all right in his way, but it isn't my way, and the sooner you tumble to that the better we'll get on together.'

'I expect this is the velvet glove?' said Beulah. '*I didn't murder Mrs Haddington* – and that's all!'

The door opened at that moment to admit Grant. He spoke in a low voice to his chief.

'Oh, he's turned up, has he? Yes, let him come in! I've got no objection. Just a moment: I want a word with you!' He took the Inspector by the arm, and led him out into the hall. Here he found Timothy and his brother, divesting themselves of their coats. He said: 'Now, what is all this? How many more people are going to walk in here? Anyone 'ud think it was a soirée, or something! Good-evening, Mr Kane! And who might it have been who sent for you, may I ask?'

233

'Sorry if you object,' said Jim, 'but I was with my brother when Miss Birtley rang up, and, all things considered, I thought I'd come along with him.'

'Just to take care of him, I suppose? Yes, you never know what I might take it into my head to do to him, do you? Not but what I should have thought he was very well able to take care of himself – too well! If you want to have a word with Miss Birtley, Mr Harte, you'll find her in there.' He jerked his head towards the library, adding, as Timothy passed him: 'And if you can convince her that the silliest thing she can do is to refuse to answer my questions, I shall be quite glad she sent for you!'

'I'll wait for you, Timothy,' Jim said.

'All right, but I've already told you there's not the slightest need,' Timothy replied over his shoulder.

'I take it that the extraordinary story Miss Birtley told my brother was true?' Jim said, as the library door shut behind Timothy.

'If she told him that Mrs Haddington had been murdered, it was true enough, sir. If you like to wait in the dining-room, there's a fire burning there.'

'Very well. I don't know how seriously you took my brother's lack of alibi for that other affair, but I imagine this new development lets him out, doesn't it?'

'Well, he certainly didn't commit this murder,' said Hemingway. 'If it's any comfort to you, sir, I don't propose to waste any time asking him what he was doing this afternoon. For one thing, it's a safe bet you'd swear blind you were with him all day, and I've got enough on my hands without trying to prove you're grossly deceiving me.'

Jim laughed, and limped into the dining-room. The

Chief Inspector turned to Grant. 'Go and pull Poulton in, Sandy! No charge: take him along to the Yard, to answer a few questions! I've got quite enough on him to warrant that. Treat him kindly, and let him kick his heels there till I come. That won't hurt him!'

Fifteen

In the library, Beulah, looking up defensively when the door opened, flew into young Mr Harte's arms. 'Timothy! O God, what am I going to do?'

Mr Harte, trained by circumstance to act coolly in emergency, promptly cast a damper on what he correctly diagnosed to be rising hysteria. 'Hallo, ducky!' he said, kissing his betrothed with great affection. 'Don't knock me over! Have you got any face-powder in your bag?'

'Yes, of course, but –'

'Well, put some on your nose!' begged Mr Harte. 'Begin as you mean to go on! What a heedless wench you are! Don't you know that the whole art of keeping a young husband happy is always to appear dainty in his eyes? That singularly repulsive adjective, let me inform you, embraces everything from face-powder to –'

'Thanks, I can fill in the rest for myself!' interrupted Beulah, slightly revived by this bracing treatment. 'Don't laugh at me! I've never been in such a jam in my life! I was *here*, Timothy! I had a row with her this morning, which Thrimby overheard; and I had no business to be here!'

'Clearly booked for the scaffold. Calm yourself, my love!'

She drew herself out of his hold. 'There's worse. I've never told you. I meant – but it's no use! If I don't tell you, that policeman will! You'd better hear it from me!'

'Hold all your horses!' commanded Mr Harte. 'I don't deny that I should like to know exactly what is your grim past, but if you're labouring under the delusion that Hemingway will disclose some hideous secret to me, or to any other layman, rid yourself of it! He won't.'

She opened her handbag, and took out her handkerchief. Having blown her nose with considerable violence, she said in a choked voice: 'You're so incredibly *nice*! Your brother practically told me I was a filthy cad not to confide in you, and I suppose he was right."

'The only thing that deters me from instantly bursting off to offer Jim his choice between pistols and swords is my conviction that he never said anything of the sort,' returned Timothy.

'Oh, he didn't say it in so many words, but that was what he meant! Well, here it is! – I'm a gaol-bird!'

The effect of this pronouncement was not quite what she had expected. She had been prepared to see Mr Harte make a chivalrous attempt to conceal his feelings; she had been prepared to see him recoil. What she had never visualised was that he would sink into a chair by the desk, drop his head in his hand, and utter in shaken accents: 'But what a line! No, really, darling, it's terrific!'

'It's true!' she said desperately.

'Oh, no, I can't bear it! What did they jug you for, my sweet? Manslaughter, due to furious driving?'

'Forgery and embezzlement!' she shot at him.

That made him raise his head. He looked at her for a

moment, and held out his hand. Almost without meaning to, she put one of her own hands into it. He pulled her down on to his knee. 'My poor precious! Tell me all about it, then!' he said.

Instead of obeying this injunction, Beulah subsided on to his chest, and cried and cried. Mr Harte very wisely confined his remarks to such soothing utterances as Never mind! and There, there! at the same time rubbing his cheek against her already tousled locks, and patting her in a comforting way. This very sensible treatment presently had its effect: Beulah stopped weeping, and said in an exhausted whisper: 'I didn't do it! I didn't do it, Timothy!'

'Look, ducky, don't start me off again!' begged Mr Harte. 'You don't have to tell me that! Who on earth did you have to defend you?'

'I f-forget. I applied for legal aid, and they gave me an elderly man. They said he was a soup, or something.'

'My darling, you need say no more! I have the whole picture!' Timothy said. 'This is the first time in my legal career when I've wished I'd chosen to be an Old Bailey Tub-thumper! If only I could have defended you – !'

'Oh, Timothy! Oh, Timothy!' Beulah sobbed into his shoulder. 'It wouldn't have been any use! I was such a little *fool*! No one believed me – I didn't think anyone ever would believe me! I couldn't bring forward anything to prove I hadn't done it, and that when I went to that office after hours, it was because he rang me up, and asked me to go there, and get that envelope out of the safe! He said he'd forgotten it, and he'd get into trouble with his uncle, and I was to post it to him – but it was only my word against his, and though I did think that man on the Bench half-believed me, the jury didn't, and if they didn't, why should anyone else?'

Mr Harte made no attempt to unravel this. Producing a large handkerchief, he mopped Beulah's cheeks with it, and said: 'You shall tell me all about it, my pet, once we're through with this mess. Now, you sit up, and stop soaking me to the skin! We shall have my-friend-the-Sergeant, alias Chief Inspector Hemingway, here at any moment, and you don't want him to find you in floods of tears! And don't run away with the idea that he'll arrest you for murder just because you were once convicted of embezzlement: he's far too downy a bird to do anything of the sort.'

'I haven't told you the whole of it,' Beulah said, apparently determined to make a clean breast of everything. 'Birtley isn't my name! At least, it is, but not all of it!'

'Give me a moment to steel myself!' Timothy begged. 'Because if it's Snooks, or something like that –'

She gave a shaky laugh. 'No, no! It's Meriden!'

'And what could be nicer than that? Apart from the fact that the only Meridens I ever heard of are a rather stuffy Warwickshire family, full of Good Form and inhibitions.'

'That's them,' Miss Birtley said, into his coat.

'What you mean, my girl,' said Timothy, 'is Those are They. I'm sorry, but our engagement is Off! Half your value for me lay in the fact that you weren't cluttered up with that kind of relation. Kindly get off my knee!'

The haste with which Beulah complied with this injunction was due to the reappearance on the scene of Chief Inspector Hemingway. She betook herself to the mirror that hung over the fireplace, and proceeded to repair her damaged complexion, only very occasionally giving a convulsive sob.

'Come in!' said Timothy. 'It'll probably clear the air if I tell you that I know All. So don't be shy, Chief Inspector! I've just been telling our entrancing gaol-bird that you won't arrest her merely because she got herself into a mess before she had the benefit of my acquaintance, counsel, and support.'

'No, I shan't,' replied Hemingway. 'But I give you fair warning, Miss Birtley, that if you go on treating me as if you thought I was the whole Gestapo rolled into one, I'm liable to get very nasty, and quite likely I shall set Underbarrow on to you for not having reported yourself. So now you know!'

She turned, a little flushed, and said, with an attempt at a smile: 'You can't help being prejudiced against me, and my experience of the police has not been such as to lead me to confide in them.'

'The Chief Inspector will tell you, my love, that there are good and bad policemen,' said Timothy. 'Won't you Hemingway?'

'I shan't tell her anything of the sort,' responded Hemingway. 'The most I'll say is that some of us are better than others. However, just to show you that Himmler never was what you'd call a great pal of mine, I don't mind telling you, Miss Birtley, that I think your case could stand a bit of looking-into, and I happen to know that the partnership between Mr Harold Maxstoke and his uncle has been dissolved.'

Light sprang to her sombre eyes; she exclaimed: 'Oh, do you think – ?'

'I don't think anything at all,' said Hemingway firmly. 'In fact, I'm not interested, because it wasn't my case, and the only thing that interests me is homicide. Now, you tell me this! What brought you back to this house tonight?'

She glanced uncertainly at Timothy, who said at once: 'Sit down, and answer the kind policeman truthfully, my child!'

She obeyed, but said reluctantly: 'It sounds so unlikely!'

'Most of the stories I have to listen to do,' observed Hemingway. 'And they're not always lies either!'

'Well, Mrs Haddington gave me a cheque this morning,' she said. 'She does it every week. I have to cash it, and pay all the household bills. I put it in a drawer of this desk, and forgot it. So I came back, because I'm supposed to pay the bills tomorrow morning, before I report for duty here.'

'Can I see the cheque?'

She hunted in her bag. 'Yes, it's here. I haven't got the books or the bills here: I left them at my digs. If you like to send someone to fetch them, I can tell you just where they are, though! The cheque's made out for the exact amount.'

Hemingway took it from her, glanced at it, and handed it back. 'A Bearer cheque: where do you cash it?'

'At Mrs Haddington's Branch, in Piccadilly.'

'Well, that seems all right. You've got a latch-key for this front door?'

'Yes.'

'When did you let yourself into the house again?'

'I – I don't know! I never looked at the time!'

'Let's see if we can work it out! When did you first leave the house?'

'At six o'clock,' she answered readily. 'As the clock in the hall was striking. I had finished all I had to do ages before, but Mrs Haddington won't let me go till six.'

'What did you do then?'

'I walked to Green Park Station, and caught a train to Earl's Court.'

'You live in Nevern Place, don't you? Say five to seven minutes walk each end. And then?'

She frowned in an effort of memory. 'I lit the gas-fire in my room, and took off my – no, I didn't! I put the household books, and the loose accounts, into my bureau. It was then that I looked to make sure I'd got the cheque, and found I hadn't. I carried the books back in my attaché-case, you see. It – it sounds silly, but I thought if I sneaked back here at once, Mrs Haddington would be dressing for dinner, and wouldn't know anything about it. It was the kind of thing she used to be very unpleasant about, and I should never have heard the end of it if she'd caught me here tomorrow morning collecting the cheque. Wasting my employer's time through my own thoughtlessness. That sort of thing! So I came back.'

'By tube?'

'Yes, by tube. I – I had a key, and I was able to slip in without anyone hearing, and come into this room.'

'Not too fast!' said Hemingway. 'Let's go back for a minute! Before you left the house at six o'clock, did anyone come to see Mrs Haddington?'

She hesitated. 'I didn't see anyone, but I did hear the front door bell ring once or twice.'

'Anything else?'

Her eyes sought Timothy's; he said quietly: 'Don't be silly, darling! What, if anything, *did* you hear?'

'It wasn't anything, really. I thought I recognised Mr Butterwick's voice. But I may easily have been mistaken! I wasn't paying much attention!'

Hemingway nodded. 'And after that?'

Again she hesitated. 'Well, Lord Guisborough arrived! But I knew he was expected: the servants were talking about it earlier in the day. There has been a lot of speculation amongst them about – well, about his intentions! I heard him holding forth – I mean, I heard him talking to Thrimby!'

'Do you know when Mr Butterwick left the house?' She shook her head. 'Or when Lord Guisborough left?'

'No. He was still with Mrs Haddington when I myself left: I saw his coat hanging up in the hall.'

Hemingway glanced down at his own notes. 'All right. Now let's get back to your second visit to the house. How long did you have to wait at Earl's Court for a train?'

'I didn't. I was lucky – in fact, I had to sprint to catch the train.'

'How long do you reckon the train-journey usually takes you?'

'A quarter of an hour to twenty minutes,' she replied at once. 'I usually allow half an hour from door to door.'

'Any idea how long you spent at home?'

She reflected. 'Not long. It's rather difficult – not more than ten or fifteen minutes, I should think.'

'Well, we shan't be far out if we put the time of your arrival round about ten-past-seven, shall we?' said Hemingway.

'No, I should imagine it must have been about that time,' she agreed, watching him nervously.

'Did you happen to notice whether there was still a coat in the hall?'

'No, I didn't think to look. I'm sorry. I came straight to this room. The only thing I did notice was that the light was on in the dining-room, but I didn't hear any sound of movement, and I hoped Thrimby was downstairs. He can't stand me at any price – or I him – and I knew he'd tell Mrs Haddington, if he saw me. I opened that drawer –' she pointed to the top drawer of the desk – 'took out the cheque, and – and tried to make an unobtrusive getaway. But Thrimby *was* in the dining-room, and he heard me. I expect you know the rest. Like a fool, I asked him not to give me away. I also tried to stop him going up to tell Mrs Haddington I was on the premises. I knew she'd give me some wretched errand to do – But it's no use my telling you that! Even I can hear that it sounds thoroughly phoney!' Beulah said bitterly.

'Oh, I wouldn't say that!' responded Hemingway, jotting down another note in his pocket-book.

'Why the girl wanted me to come and hold her hand I shall never know!' remarked Timothy. 'A good witness, Chief Inspector: I wouldn't have the slightest hesitation in putting her in the box.'

Beulah smiled faintly. Hemingway said: 'One more question, Miss Birtley. You might prefer me to put it to you without this legal adviser of yours standing around. He can go and talk to Mr Kane in the dining-room. You'd only have to scream, and I don't doubt he'd come bursting in to your rescue.'

'What, more hideous revelations?' said Timothy.

244

Beulah shook her head. 'No, I – I think probably I'd better not have any more secrets from Mr Harte,' she said. 'What is it?'

'What did you quarrel with Mrs Haddington about this morning?'

She blushed. 'Oh – !'

'Well, I did warn you!' Hemingway pointed out.

'Apparently you already know what I quarrelled about! I've no doubt Thrimby was listening to the whole affair. All right, I don't care! Mrs Haddington had found out that I dined with Mr Harte last night, and – she was furious.'

'Yes?' Hemingway prompted her.

She swallowed. 'She – threatened to tell him – about me.' She raised her eyes. 'Well, more than that: she said she would tell him.'

'And what did you say to that?'

'Oh, why ask me? You know exactly what I said!'

'No, he doesn't,' interposed Timothy. 'All he knows is what Thrimby says you said, so you give him your version! I'll leave the room, if you like!'

'It isn't *that*! Only you're telling me to put a rope round my own neck!'

'God bless the girl!' ejaculated Timothy. 'After that crack, my love, don't waste a moment in disclosing to the Chief Inspector exactly what you did say! It can't possibly be as damaging as the ideas you've put into his head!'

'I said I was going to marry you, and I'd go to any lengths to do it, or something like that! I don't really remember my precise words, because I was in a rage. I said I wouldn't let her stop me. I think I said there wasn't much I wouldn't do if she tried to interfere. But I didn't mean I'd kill her!'

'No?' said Hemingway. 'Suppose you were to tell me just what it was that you did mean, Miss Birtley?'

She appeared a trifle discomposed. 'Nothing! One says silly things like that – not thinking!'

'Think now!' recommended Hemingway. 'It might be important. You uttered a threat: you've admitted that. If you didn't mean violence, what did you mean? What harm could you do Mrs Haddington?'

Timothy, who had been watching him, turned his head. 'I should answer this one,' he said. 'Did you know something she didn't want disclosed?'

'I – I had certain suspicions, but – Look here, I wasn't serious! I said it to frighten her! I wouldn't really blackmail even Mrs Haddington!'

'What were your suspicions, Miss Birtley?'

'I'd rather not say. I've no proof, and – she's *dead*!'

'Yes, and I'm trying to find out who killed her,' said Hemingway.

She stared at him for a moment. 'I know you are,' she replied slowly. 'And if anything I said – caused you to discover her murderer –' She paused, and then added defiantly: 'I should be sorry!'

'Never mind that!' said Timothy. 'Your private sympathies don't come into it. I can guess what you suspected, and so, I fancy, can Hemingway. Had she any sort of a hold over Lady Nest Poulton?'

She regarded her clenched hands. 'Yes. I think so. I once overheard something that was said. I couldn't help it: they were both standing in the back drawing-room, and I came into the front half of the room. They stopped as soon as they realised I was there, of course.'

'What was said?' asked Hemingway.

She answered reluctantly: 'Lady Nest said, *I'm damned if I will!* and Mrs Haddington gave that hateful laugh of hers, and replied, *I think you'll do exactly what I ask you to do, dear Nest, because you'll certainly be damned if you don't!*'

'Thank you,' said Hemingway.

'It mightn't have meant what I thought it meant!' she said quickly.

'Never mind what it meant! That's my headache! Now, when you were sent to the late Seaton-Carew, you were sent by someone who didn't believe you'd been shopped, weren't you? Someone who thought you belonged to the criminal classes?'

'I suppose so,' she said, rather drearily. 'I thought she believed what I told her.'

'Highly unlikely. But when he saw you, Seaton-Carew found you weren't the sort of girl he was after. That's what you told me, isn't it?'

'Yes.'

'Did you get any idea of the sort of job he did want a young lady like you for?'

'Not then. Only when I thought it over afterwards, and remembered the questions he'd asked me – not that there was anything in them, taken by themselves – I began to wonder if I was to have been a sort of informant.'

Hemingway nodded. 'Any reason to think he and Mrs Haddington were in partnership?'

'I can't answer that. I honestly don't know. They were very intimate, that's all I can say.'

He shut his notebook, and restored it to his pocket. 'All right; I shan't keep you any longer tonight, Miss Birtley. I'm going to hand you over to your legal adviser, and I won't conceal from you that while he's giving you a bite of supper, I'm going to send one of my men to check up on your story. That's routine, as Mr Harte will tell you. I've got to be certain those accounts are where you say they are. I've no wish to start a lot of talk, so if you like to write a note to your landlady, authorising her to let the bearer take the books and the bills out of your bureau, he won't have to show her his card.'

She got up, and went to the desk. 'Thank you. Decent of you! I'll do that, only I can't leave this house before Miss Pickhill gets here. Cynthia Haddington might come in at any moment, and somebody ought to be here, besides the servants. Miss Pickhill has to come from Putney, you see.'

The telephone-bell sounded as she picked up a pen. She made as if to lift the receiver, and then checked herself, looking enquiringly at Hemingway.

'Don't worry about that!' he said. 'One of my chaps will deal with it.'

She began to write. She was slipping the folded note into an envelope when a man in plain clothes came quietly in, and handed the Chief Inspector a scrap of paper torn from a notebook. He read it, and said: 'All right, I'll take it in here, Snettisham. I want you to go to this address –' He handed the Sergeant Beulah's letter – 'and give this to the landlady. No need to say you're a police-officer. She's to take you into Miss Birtley's room, and allow you to bring away with you a pile of bills and household books, in Mrs Haddington's name, which you'll find in the bureau. It isn't locked, Miss Birtley?'

'No. The key is in it. He'll see the bills as soon as he opens the front. Could he – would he mind turning out the gas-fire? I left it on, and as I put a shilling in only this morning it'll still be burning.'

'And turn out the fire!' said Hemingway. 'I want you to go by the tube – Green Park station, and to come back the same way. Time it! That's all.' He nodded dismissal, and turned to Beulah, 'Do they have to switch the telephone through to this room, or can I get straight on?'

'Straight on. If Miss Pickhill arrives – can I go, or must I wait till that man gets back?'

'No, I'll trust Mr Harte to keep an eye on you,' he replied, opening the door.

She lingered for a moment. 'Thanks! I – I'm sorry I was rude to you before!'

'That's all right,' he said. 'You've been quite helpful.'

He shut both her and Timothy out, and went to sit down at the desk, picking up the telephone. 'Hallo?'

'Is it yourself, sir?' asked the voice of Inspector Grant.

'It is. Where are you speaking from?'

'From your office, sir. Mr Poulton was driven from Charles Street straight to Northolt Aerodrome, and has left for Paris.'

Sixteen

S o long a silence followed this announcement that Inspector Grant presently said: 'Are you still there, sir?'

'Yes, I'm here,' Hemingway replied. 'Where did you find this out?'

'When I left you, I went to Belgrave Square. It was the butler told me that Mr Poulton was flying to Paris for a business conference tomorrow morning. I asked him when he expected Mr Poulton to return, and he told me, tomorrow evening. As to that, I have my doubts!'

'Did you get on to Northolt?'

'*Cinnteach!* But I was too late, for the plane had taken off already. I have seen the chauffeur. He has had his orders since the day before yesterday.'

'Has he also got orders to meet some plane tomorrow?'

'*Ma seadh!* But what does that prove? He may go to Northolt, and come away without his master, it seems to me! Would you have me apply for extradition?'

'No. Not a bit of use. I haven't enough on him to have a hope of getting it.'

'*Ciod e so?* Is there another that has as much motive for these murders?'

'That's what I don't know yet. You can take it from me that Big Business interests aren't going to be annoyed on the evidence I've got. You can go round to Poulton's office first thing in the morning, and check up on this conference story. Meanwhile, I'm getting a lot of funny ideas about this case. I have to keep telling myself that first thoughts are best. I'm staying here till Mrs Haddington's sister turns up. You nip round to wherever it is Mr Sydney Butterwick hangs out – you've got the address, haven't you? Park Lane, or something – and get his story out of him. Unless you get something startling from him, you needn't show up again till tomorrow morning.'

'And where,' asked the Inspector politely, 'will you be going yourself, Chief Inspector, when you leave Charles Street?'

Hemingway grinned. 'Back to the Yard!'

'I will be seeing you there, then,' said the Inspector.

'All right, Sandy. You're several kinds of silly ass, but, barring your habit of breathing that Gaelic at me, I don't know when I've had a sub I got on with better!'

'*Moran taing!*' said the Inspector.

A click indicated that he had replaced his receiver. Hemingway followed his example, mentally registering a vow to discover the meaning of this cryptic valediction at the earliest opportunity. He went into the hall, where one of his men was sitting. To him, he issued instructions to lock and seal the doors into Mrs Haddington's bedroom and boudoir. The officer had scarcely reached the half-landing when the front-door bell rang. Forestalling Thrimby, who had retired to his underground fastness, Hemingway opened the door, and admitted into the house Miss Violet Pickhill, who bore all the appearance of one who had snatched up the first hat and coat that chanced to meet her eyes. Fumbling within the folds of the coat, she drew forth her pince-nez, on the end of a thin chain, and jabbed them on to her nose. Through them she subjected the Chief Inspector to a suspicious scrutiny. 'Who may you be?' she demanded.

Hemingway announced himself, and was annoyed to detect a note of apology in his own voice.

'Disgusting!' said Miss Pickhill. She removed the pince-nez from her nose, and added in a milder tone: 'I don't mean you, but to think it should have come to this! Well, I always knew Lily was heading for trouble! Time and again I've told her that her behaviour was enough to make my poor father turn in his grave, and now we see how right I was! Where's my niece?'

'Miss Haddington hasn't come in yet,' said Hemingway. 'The servants seem to think she went off to some party or other, but she's expected to come home for her dinner. Miss Birtley – Mrs Haddington's secretary –'

'I know very well who Miss Birtley is!' interrupted Miss Pickhill. 'She rang me up, and I thought the better of her for having done so! It showed a very proper spirit, whatever my sister may say! Not, of course,' she corrected herself punctiliously, 'that my sister can say anything now, for I will tell you at once that I am not a believer in this Spiritualism, and never shall be!'

At this point, and considerably to the Chief Inspector's relief, the taxi-driver created a diversion by appearing on the scene for the purpose of dumping a suitcase inside the hall, and of collecting his just dues. Miss Pickhill groped in her capacious handbag, and handed these to him, forestalling criticism by informing him that if he wanted to receive a more handsome gratuity he should not have put his fares up. She clinched the matter by adding that if he had anything to say he might address his remarks to Hemingway, whom she introduced to him under the title of 'this policeman.' The taxi-driver wisely decided to withdraw without uttering the expostulation trembling on his tongue, and Miss Pickhill, shutting the door on him, turned to Hemingway, and demanded to be put in possession of the facts of her sister's murder.

He took her into the library, and told her briefly that her sister had been strangled in her own boudoir. She ejaculated first that it was a judgment on her, and then commanded Hemingway to tell her who had perpetrated the deed. Rather to his surprise, she accepted without comment his reply, that he was unable to enlighten her. She said: 'Well, I was saying only yesterday to Mr Broseley – he is our Vicar, and a most enlightened man! – that a woman without religion is like a ship without a rudder. I may say that he *entirely* agreed with me! We were not, of course, discussing my poor sister. Whatever I may have thought, I hope I am too loyal to discuss *any* of my family, even with dear Mr Broseley! But it all goes to show! From the moment she married Hubert Haddington – right against her father's wishes, I may say! – Lily (for call her Lilias I never would!) took a turn for the worse! My father always said – he had a very unconventional way of expressing himself, though a *thorough* Churchman! – that Hubert was a bad hat. Of course, Lily took after the *Whalleys*: there's no getting round that! My mother's people – not that I wish to say a word against them, but there's no denying that they were not Pickhills! My mother, naturally, was different, but I well recall hearing my dear father saying that her relations were some of them most uncongenial people. Quite irreligious, I fear, and with what my father used to call an eye to the main-chance. It was the same with Lily. As hard as nails! The only person she ever cared twopence for was my niece, and, as is always the way, she spoiled her atrociously! Often and often I've told her so, but you might as well have talked to a brick wall! And what has been the result? The child spends her whole life making up her face, and going to cocktail-parties, and my poor sister has been murdered! Of course, if he weren't dead already, I should have said that Mr Seaton-Carew had done it!'

'Would you, madam?' said Hemingway, in a conversational tone which would not have deceived Inspector Grant for even the fraction of a second. 'Now, I wonder what makes you say that?'

'I always trust my instinct,' said Miss Pickhill darkly. 'It's never at fault – never! The instant I clapped eyes on him I *knew*! A friend of Hubert Haddington's, I need hardly say! Pray do not ask me what his relationship with my unhappy sister was! That is something I prefer not to think about! *Hear* no evil, *speak* no evil, *see* no evil!'

'Very proper, madam!' approved Hemingway. 'What, if I may ask, was the late Mr Haddington's profession?'

'If you can discover *that*,' said Miss Pickhill, 'you will have discovered more than my father ever did! It was his belief that Hubert was an adventurer. Those were the very words he used. One moment they were driving about in Rolls-Royces; the next they hadn't a penny to bless themselves with! Never shall I forget the day we discovered that Lily was being sued in the County Court for a bill to a dressmaker! That was too much! As my father said at the time, one can put up with a great deal, but *not* with being County-Courted! However, the next time we saw her she was in her own car, with a chauffeur, so naturally my father had to allow her to enter the house, which at one time he said he never would again. That was many years ago, of course, when Cynthia was a baby. After Hubert died, she chose to gad about all over Europe, instead of coming to live at home with me, which I naturally begged her to do, because whatever my feelings may have been I've always held that blood is thicker than water, and Cynthia could have attended the High School, which, if you were to ask me, would have been far better for her than that ridiculous Swiss school Lily sent her to! But that wasn't good enough for Lily! Cynthia had to have the very best of everything! Why, when she was a toddler even, nothing would do for Lily but all her little dresses had to be hand-embroidered! Goodness only knows what she squandered on the child, from first to last! Of course, I don't deny that she's a very pretty girl, but for my sister to be setting her heart on making some grand match for her was just tempting Providence! "You'll have her running off with the chauffeur!" I said to Lily once; and never shall I forget my dear old Aunt Maud asking me if Lily meant to get the Prince of Wales for her daughter! That was a figure of speech, of course, because we hadn't got a Prince of Wales at that time, and Aunt Maud knew that just as well as anyone else, for it was only on certain subjects that her mind wandered, and then only quite at the end.'

255

She paused for breath, and Hemingway, who, while not unappreciative of her discourse, had reached the conclusion that she knew nothing about her sister's more private affairs, seized the opportunity to ask if she could furnish him with the name of Mrs Haddington's solicitor.

'Well, if Lily took her affairs out of our dear Mr Eddleston's hands, it's news to me!' replied Miss Pickhill. 'Of course, I daresay it's *young* Mr Eddleston who looks after things now, but that her Will is deposited with them I *do* know, for Lily told me she was making me one of poor little Cynthia's trustees, just in case anything should happen to her, which she didn't for a moment expect, or I either, if it comes to that, and Mr Eddleston the other. For I said to her at the time, *Don't* name Mr Lowick, because if you do, I said, I shall refuse to act. Mr Lowick is the junior partner, and when I tell you that the day I went up to see him about the ground-rent he not only kept me waiting for ten whole minutes, but received me with a pipe in his hand, you will understand why I said what I did. There are limits!'

Jotting the name down in his book, Hemingway said: 'Well, madam, I think that's all at present. I shall be getting into touch with Mr Eddleston at once. You'll understand that I shall have to go through Mrs Haddington's papers, and her solicitor will of course be present. Until then, I have had the boudoir and her bedroom locked up.'

Miss Pickhill plainly took this amiss, for she bridled, and said in a stiff voice: 'Well, really, I can't see what you want with my poor sister's private papers, and as for locking her bedroom, I call it most officious!'

'Just a matter of routine!' Hemingway said.

'I've no doubt!' interrupted Miss Pickhill. 'It's exactly what Mr Broseley was saying to me only the other day! Encroachment! Ever since the War, officials seem to think they can do exactly as they like, and I daresay the police are just as bad as the Ministry of Food, interfering right and left, and telling people how to cook cabbages, which we all knew long before they were ever born or thought of!'

'I wouldn't think of telling you how to cook cabbages, madam!' Hemingway assured her. 'For one thing, I don't know, and for another –'

'I should hope not indeed! It would be a great deal more to the point if you drilled some of your new policemen, let me tell you! In *my* young days the police were fine, upstanding men, but whenever I come to London now all I see is a lot of young constables, standing about with their chests in and their stomachs out, and their mouths hanging open. I wouldn't even ask one of them for the time! Enough to make my father turn in his grave!'

Reflecting that Mr Pickhill's ghost must be the most restless one ever to disturb a cemetery, Hemingway said meekly: 'It's a scandal, madam: I've often thought so. But I daresay you wouldn't want to stop me finding out who murdered Mrs Haddington!'

'Certainly not! Quite apart from my personal feelings I trust I am a good citizen! Good Citizenship was the subject of the last lecture we had at the Women's Conservative Institute, and *most* interesting! But why prying into my sister's letters, and things, should help you to find out who murdered her is more than I can fathom! In fact,' said Miss Pickhill, obscurely but terrifyingly, 'it is all on a *par*!'

Fortunately, the Chief Inspector was rescued from these deep waters by the entrance of Detective-officer Bagby, who informed him that Miss Haddington had that instant let herself into the house, and was being held in check by Miss Birtley.

Miss Pickhill shuddered, and got up from her chair, saying: 'I will come at once! Poor child, she little knows! In the midst of life we are in death! I don't suppose she has ever heard those very true words, for, having been educated in a foreign country, how should she?'

Cynthia Haddington, exquisitely clothed in primrose yellow under a coat of dark mink, and with a close hat of shaded brown and yellow wing-feathers on the back of her shining head, had been coaxed into the dining-room, and was interestedly surveying Mr James Kane. She held a cigarette between the fingers of one hand, and dangled a handbag and a pair of long gloves from the other. Only a purist would have described her as drunk. Not even the exaggeratedly high heels of her cutaway shoes caused her to stumble in her walk; and if her eyes seemed slightly blurred, and her inconsequent laugh a little too ready, her speech was perfectly clear. 'Oh, are you Timothy's brother?' she said. 'How marvellous! Oh, darling-Timothy, why weren't you at June's party? You could have taken me on to dinner somewhere! I got stuck with Philip Arnecliffe, and he was *so* drunk he let that ghastly Terrington woman tack herself on to us, *with* the latest boy friend! *Too* dim, so I said, *Definitely* not! and came home! Is Mummy livid with me? Honestly, I couldn't face spending the *whole* evening at home! June's got some marvellous new cocktail you make with absinthe: it makes you feel simply terrific! O God, is that you, Aunt Violet? . . . Who on *earth* are you?'

Hemingway, to whom the last question was addressed, preserved a tactful silence. He was a trifle stunned by this, his first, sight of Mrs Haddington's beautiful daughter, for although he had been told that she was a very pretty girl he had not been prepared for quite so much empty loveliness.

Miss Pickhill, managing to soften the sharpness of her habitual tone, said that there was bad news for Cynthia to hear, and suggested that she should accompany her upstairs to her bedroom.

Cynthia stared at her in the blankest incomprehension. 'Oh, hell, no, I don't want to trail all the way up to my room!' she protested. 'Besides, why should I? No one's coming to dinner! I shall stay as I am.' She blinked, as though to clear her vision, and suddenly demanded: 'What are you all doing in here, anyway? You haven't *had* dinner, have you? Where's Mummy?'

Miss Pickhill cleared her throat. 'Your dear mother has – has met with an accident, Cynthia!' she said.

'An accident? What's happened?' Cynthia asked, pitching the stub of her cigarette into the grate.

'Oh, dear, I don't know how to tell her!' said Miss Pickhill, sitting down suddenly, and, in the agitation of the moment, sniffing into one of her serviceable gloves, which she held in one hand.

'You tell her, Timothy!' Beulah said, in a low voice. 'You'll do it best.'

Timothy, who, with Mr James Kane, had been attempting in an unobtrusive way, to slide out of the room, cast his betrothed a glance of reproach, but

259

responded to her appeal. He went to Cynthia, and took one of her hands, saying: 'There isn't a best way of telling her. You've got to prepare yourself for a shock, Cynthia.'

'Gosh, Mummy isn't dead, is she?'

'Yes,' replied Timothy. 'She is dead.'

Cynthia stared at him, and then at his silent companions. She gave an uncertain laugh. 'Oh, don't be so silly! *Quite* unfunny, darling!'

'Quite,' said Timothy steadily.

'But how *can* she be dead? There was nothing the matter with her at tea-time! You don't mean she's been run over, or anything, do you?'

'Not run over. She's been murdered, Cynthia.'

It seemed as though for a moment she scarcely took in what he said. She repeated stupidly: 'Murdered? Murdered, like Dan was?'

'Yes, like that.'

'But she can't be! She can't be!' Cynthia cried shrilly. 'What'll happen to *me*?'

This exclamation not unnaturally shook her auditors. Miss Pickhill cast her a horrified glance, and then plucked at Mr Kane's sleeve, saying in an urgent whisper: 'It's the *shock*! Perhaps a little drop of brandy – just to pull her together! I am an opponent of all forms of intoxicating liquor, but in a case like this – !'

'No, I don't think so,' replied Jim.

'I don't believe you!' Cynthia said, pulling her hand out of Timothy's. 'You're simply trying to have me on!' He said nothing. She caught her breath, and clutched the lapels of his coat, trying to shake him. 'Say it isn't true! You don't *understand*! I shall have to go and live in Putney, or something ghastly, and I couldn't *bear* it! Is that why Aunt Violet's here? I won't go with her, I won't, I won't!'

'God, this is too awful!' muttered Beulah.

'Bit tight,' Jim said, under his breath. 'Good job. Better get her up to bed as soon as you can!'

There seemed, however, to be no immediate prospect of being able to follow out this advice. Cynthia, apparently convinced by now that her mother was indeed dead, was engaged in working herself into a state of alarming hysteria. A spate of words jostled one another on her lips and for a few moments stunned the assembled company into appalled silence. 'It's all because I broke my mirror!' she said. 'I *knew* something frightful would happen! Mummy said it was just a superstition, and now you see! *Everything's* gone wrong, every single thing! First I lost my powder-compact, and Dan said he'd give me another one, but he never did because he was murdered, and then everything was ghastly, and Mummy made me wear black, and was beastly about Lance, and now *she's* been murdered, and nobody cares about me, or what becomes of me! I wish I'd married that dreary Bill Uffington! I wish I'd married *anybody*! It's all Mummy's fault I'm not even engaged, because *dozens* of men have asked me, only she kept on saying I was too young, and could do better if I waited, and now look what's happened!'

'Cynthia!' uttered Miss Pickhill, finding her voice at last. 'Be quiet, child! You don't know what you're saying!'

'Go away!' shrieked Cynthia, hurling her handbag at her aunt with more passion than accuracy. 'I know what you mean to do! You mean to drag me off to that foul

261

house of yours, and cover me up with antimacassars, and make me go to Church, and I'd rather *die*! And nothing will ever make me believe it wasn't *you* who stole my precious compact!' she added, rounding suddenly on Beulah. 'It *must* have been either you or Mapperley, and it was you who said it was the prettiest one you'd ever seen! Mapperley said she didn't like it as well as my *gold* one, so that shows! Oh, what am I going to do, with only Aunt Violet left? Oh, Mummy! Oh, Dan!' She burst into a fit of wild sobbing, which turned into a succession of screams, when her aunt moved towards her. Neither her aunt's appeals, nor Timothy's stern command to her to Shut up! had the smallest effect; it was left to Mr Kane to put a summary end to a scene the echoes of which could probably be heard in Berkeley Square. This he did by limping to the sideboard, pouring out a tumbler of water, and casting it full in Cynthia's face. The shock startled her out of her hysteria; she gave a gasp, stood for a moment in complete silence, and then began to cry in good earnest.

'Take her up to bed!' Jim said imperatively.

Between them, Beulah and Miss Pickhill managed to get her out of the room, and up the stairs. Hemingway said: 'Poor young lady! What you might call a highly-strung type. If you'll excuse me, there's a call I want to put through.'

He then withdrew to the library, to discover Mr Eddleston's home address; and the half-brothers were left alone in the dining-room.

'Well, my God – !' said Mr Kane. 'The company you do keep, Timothy!'

'You *would* come!' Timothy retorted savagely. 'I told you not to!'

'Yes, but I've got to face Mother!' said Jim. 'You know perfectly well she thinks that if I wasn't holding your hand at every critical stage in your career I ought to have been! Look here, Timothy, the whole of this affair's fantastic! Who murdered the woman? Have you any idea?'

'Only what I've gathered from the questions Hemingway asked Beulah. If you rule out Beulah, and the servants, everything seems to point to Godfrey Poulton. Apparently, he was the last person to see her alive. Butterwick – you don't know him: Seaton-Carew's boy-friend – Guisborough, and Poulton all came to see her this afternoon, in that order. I don't know why, or what happened. And I can't see the ghost of a reason for either Butterwick or Guisborough to have murdered her. If, as I've rather suspected, Mrs Haddington had been blackmailing Lady Nest, that gives Poulton a motive – but, good God, he must be mad to do it bang on top of the first murder! And I'm damned if I see why he murdered Seaton-Carew, unless Seaton-Carew was joined with Mrs Haddington in the blackmailing business. Even then – ! Well, it doesn't make sense! He's one of those who *could* have murdered Seaton-Carew; so's young Butterwick – who, incidentally, is just the sort of neurotic who *might* have done it, in a fit of jealousy! Guisborough couldn't possibly have had anything to do with the first murder, and why he should suddenly burst in and strangle Mrs Haddington, in exact imitation of the first death, is more than I can fathom! The only motive he's got, as far as I know, is that Mrs Haddington didn't favour his suit, and if you think this is a good way of promoting it, all I can say is, it's too far-fetched for me!

He's an overbalanced, tiresome sort of a chap, frothing over with half-baked political ideas, but he's not by any means mad.'

'Well, Poulton is most certainly not mad!' said Jim. 'I don't know him well, but his reputation in the City is for long-headedness. Unexcitable chap, too. Don't bite my head off! – I'm not trying to be offensive! – but just where does Beulah stand in this imbroglio?'

'You can take it from me she didn't do it. Unless I miss my bet, she all unwittingly provided herself with an alibi. That's being checked up on at this moment. I don't think she quite grasped what Hemingway was after, but I did. If the man he's sent off to her digs finds there what she says he will – and he will! – I think the time factor will let her out. She couldn't possibly have got here from Earl's Court a minute before she says she did. And, I ask you, Jim, is it likely that she'd go all the way to Earl's Court, if she meant to slip back into the house and murder her employer? How was she to know in which room Mrs Haddington would be, too? The likeliest bet, at that hour, would be her bedroom, with her maid in attendance! Would even a lunatic go looking into all the possible rooms in a house teeming with servants? It doesn't make sense!'

'No,' Jim agreed. 'But unless there's a homicidal maniac sculling about, none of it makes sense! I can just swallow Poulton's murdering someone who was blackmailing his wife – though I find that difficult, because from what I know of him he'd be far more likely to settle a blackmailer's hash in some equally ruthless but strictly legal fashion – but I can't swallow his murdering the blackmailer's partner two days later! I don't know your pal Guisborough, but I suppose, if he's crazy about that afflictive girl, and Mrs Haddington was an effective bar to matrimony – the kid's only nineteen, isn't she? – he might have thought it would be a clever thing to murder the woman in exactly the same way the first chap was murdered, banking on Hemingway thinking that the same man must have done both deeds.'

'You know, Jim, that's definitely good!' Timothy said thoughtfully. 'The only snag is that it requires a cold-blooded type to think of it, let alone carry it out, and Guisborough isn't that type. Far more down Poulton's street, but of course the theory doesn't fit him, because he's already a suspect for the first murder. Guisborough's an impulsive chap, and, to do him justice, I don't think he'd murder a woman with the object of marrying her daughter! He might commit a murder in the heat of the moment, but I honestly don't see him coolly plotting a crime like this.'

'All right, what's your theory?'

Timothy was frowning. 'I haven't really got one. The whole thing seems to hinge on the first murder, and I haven't a clue who did that. There were five people who could have killed Seaton-Carew: Mrs Haddington, Poulton, Butterwick, Beulah, and me. You can rule Beulah and me out, and you can also rule out Mrs Haddington. I thought at one moment that things were pointing her way. No real reason, but what Beulah told me about that wretched coil of wire made it look slightly fishy. Well, that theory seems to have ended in a pretty nasty blind alley. We're left with Poulton and Butterwick – and, of the two, Butterwick's my fancy for the first murder, and Poulton for the second. And that combination doesn't add up, look at it how you may!'

'Hold on a minute! Didn't you tell me that the doctor's movements weren't entirely accounted for that evening?'

'No, hang it all, Jim, you must draw the line somewhere! *Do* you see a fashionable physician strangling a man in the middle of a Bridge-party?'

'Why not? What if Seaton-Carew was a danger to him?'

'Blackmailing him, do you mean? More likely to have slipped something lethal into his drink, if he wanted to get rid of him!'

'Not at all,' said Jim. 'Poison would have made him instantly suspect!'

'You win that point,' admitted Timothy. 'Now tell me why he murdered Mrs Haddington!'

'I haven't yet worked that one out,' confessed Jim.

'And while you are working it out, work out how he got into the house without anyone's knowing it!'

'I can't.'

'Of course you can't! And don't ask me to consider poor old Roddy Vickerstown, because it's a sheer waste of time. He's not above lending the light of his countenance to hopeless outsiders, who feed and wine him in the style to which he's accustomed, but he does draw the line somewhere! He's tottering round the town saying that the fellah can't be a gentleman, because strangling is the lowest form of murder, and no one with any breeding at all would dream of killing a man in somebody else's house. Damn' bad form, my boy!'

Jim grinned. 'All right, wash him out too! Where do you go from there?'

'I think the first murder was premeditated, and the second wasn't. And, working from that point, it looks as if the same man did both. Quite obviously, things were desperate, and Mrs Haddington had to be silenced. Supposing she knew who committed the first murder?'

'Then why didn't she clear herself by telling the police what she knew?'

'That's just the point: if she'd been in danger of taking the rap, she undoubtedly would have told the police. But you weren't privileged to know the lady! She was one of the most coldblooded, calculating females I've encountered. My guess – and I admit it is only a guess – is that she was planning the biggest blackmailing coup of her career, and that was why she had to be eliminated.'

'Yes, but wait a bit, Timothy! What was to stop the guilty party paying up until all the smoke had cleared away, and then disposing of Mrs Haddington, when the police were *not* haunting the house?'

'The fact that Mrs Haddington was herself a suspect!' said Timothy instantly. 'He dared not chance it. If she got charged with the murder, she'd spill the beans at once: she'd have to!'

'I expect there's a flaw in it somewhere,' said Jim, 'but I'm bound to say it's quite ingenious, if you can clear the first hurdle. Would she really cash in on the death of an old friend?'

'I should say that the only thing she wouldn't cash in on would be Cynthia,' replied Timothy. 'She was a remarkably repellent piece of work, but I'll hand her this! – she was utterly devoted to that very unrewarding girl! Praise be to God, here's my intended at last! How are things, darling?'

'Nightmareish!' Beulah said, shuddering. 'We've got her to bed, and Mrs Foston's going to sit with her till she

267

goes to sleep. I don't think it'll be long. I'm sorry for Miss Pickhill, having to take on the job of looking after her. I know she's a bit drunk, and, of course, shock *does* make people react queerly, but when I left she seemed to be deriving consolation from the thought that she would now be frightfully well-off, and could do anything she liked. For God's sake, take me out, and give me something to eat! With the slightest encouragement, I shall pass out, which is probably because I've had nothing but a cup of tea and a biscuit since luncheon.'

'You will get no encouragement from either of us,' said Timothy, taking her arm in a sustaining way, and propelling her towards the door. 'Come on, Jim! Dinner!'

Seventeen

It was some little time later that Sergeant Snettisham returned to Charles Street, and laid before his chief Mrs Haddington's household bills. He explained that it had taken him rather a long time to complete the journey, because in each instance he had just missed a train. His timing added ten minutes to Beulah's estimate of the double journey; he gave it as his opinion that to allow only half an hour from door to door was running it very fine.

'That seems to let her out, then,' Hemingway said. 'Not that I ever fancied her much, I'm bound to say.' He glanced at his watch, and once more turned to the stand which held the telephone directories, and drew out one of the volumes. As he flicked over the pages, he said: 'I don't think there's anything more you can do tonight: you can get off home.'

'Thank you, sir. What's going to happen about the Inquest tomorrow?'

'We shall ask for an adjournment. I'm meeting Mrs Haddington's solicitor here later in the morning. You've sealed up those two rooms? All right: tell your chaps they can clear off now!'

He himself, when he left the house, was driven to the street in Chelsea where Lord Guisborough shared a maisonette with his sister. It was by this time after nine o'clock, and it was apparent to Hemingway, as he alighted from the police-car, that someone in the house was entertaining a party. One or two small cars were parked outside; and from the lower floor issued a muffled roar of sound, strongly reminiscent of the lion-house at the Zoo, but indicated to the initiated that a number of persons, being gathered together, were all talking together. The noise was obviously too great to allow of anyone's hearing the front-door bell, so, after keeping his finger on it for nearly a minute, Hemingway resorted to the knocker. At the third assault on the door, it was opened to him by a dark young woman in a crumpled skirt, and an orange knitted jumper, who held a large jug in one hand, and had a half-smoked cigarette between her lips. She blinked at Hemingway, and said: 'Hallo! Who are you? Not that it matters: come right in! The gin ran out twenty minutes ago, but there's plenty of beer. Have some!'

She raised the jug, and seemed to be about to pour some beer into a non-existent glass. Hemingway thoughtfully straightened the perilously poised jug, saying: 'No, thank you, miss. Are you the Honourable Beatrice Guisborough?'

'No, I'm bloody well not! Don't you go saddling me with outworn titles! I'm Trix Guisborough! Neither more nor less! Try the title-stuff on my brother: he'll lap it up! Give him time, and he'll be one of the pillars of the Tory party, poor little sap! Are you one of his nice new respectable pals? Strictly speaking, this is my party, but make yourself at home! You'll find Lance in that mob.' She jerked her head towards the door into the studio, which stood open, and revealed a glimpse of many people seen through a thick haze of tobacco-smoke.

Hemingway produced his card, and handed it to her. It took her a moment or two to get it into focus, and he wondered how many more slightly inebriated young women he was destined to meet that evening. When she had succeeded in deciphering it, she gave a laugh, and exclaimed: 'God, I shall dine out on this one! A whole, live Chief Inspector at one of my parties!'

'And very nice too, I've no doubt,' said Hemingway. 'But I haven't come to the party, miss, thanking you all the same. What I want is a few words with your brother.'

'I shouldn't think they'd do you much good: he's well away!' she replied. 'If you want to call me anything, call me Comrade, not miss! What do you want with Lance?'

'I'll tell him, if you'll be so good as to fetch him along,' said Hemingway.

'But why?' she argued. 'If it's about the murder the other night, Lance can't tell you anything! The man you want is Butterwick. If you don't recognise the description, I mean a God-awful little pansy-boy, with curly hair and long eyelashes! You take a look at him, and you'll know why the privileged classes are doomed! And I don't want any dirty cracks about Lance!' she added fiercely. 'He's got himself into a rotten set, that's all that's the matter with him! He's got a bourgeois streak which makes him think it's the hell of a thing to be a peer of the realm, but he'll get over it! Trust me!'

'Listen, Comrade!' said Hemingway. 'If you were to carry on like this in Russia, keeping the police hanging about instead of hopping to it double-quick, you'd wake up to find yourself in a salt-mine, and not such a bad thing either! You go and tell this bourgeois brother of yours I want to speak to him, and don't waste your time blasting the privileged classes to me, because, for one thing, I don't belong to them, and, for another, I don't like corny stories! That one was stale before the War!'

'Damn your eyes, how dare you speak to me like that?' demanded Miss Guisborough furiously.

'Yes, I thought it wouldn't be long before we stopped being comrades,' said Hemingway. 'When I was a lot younger than what I am now, it was one of my jobs to move your sort along, and try to stop you spoiling everyone's fun by chucking yourselves in front of leading horses, and a lot of other silly tricks of the same nature. Now, I've had a long day, and I'm not in the mood to listen to what they call stump-oratory. You go and fetch that brother of yours, and while I'm talking to him you can tell that crowd in there how to suck eggs! My old grandmother showed me the proper way before you were born!'

Fortunately for the peace of the evening's entertainment one of Miss Guisborough's guests came out of the studio at that moment. He had a pleasant face, but was otherwise distinguished only by his evident predilection for good tailors and barbers. He slid an arm round Miss Guisborough's waist, and demanded to be told what was eating her.

The Chief Inspector answered him. 'It's just this, sir! I want a word with Lord Guisborough! I'm Chief Inspector Hemingway, of the Criminal Investigation Department, and I shan't, I hope, keep his lordship many minutes from his party!'

The newcomer regarded him curiously, but said: 'Fair enough! I'll get him for you. Come on, Trixie! you walked off with the beer, you mindless wench!'

He then swept his hostess back into the studio; and in a few moments Lord Guisborough came into the lobby, rocking a little on his heels, but with his eyes bright and intelligent still. 'Hallo!' he said. 'Want me, Ch-chief Inspector?'

'If you please, my lord!'

Guisborough flung open the door into a small parlour. 'All right, come in here! M'sister doesn't like people to call me my lord. I don't mind it m'self. Funny! Wouldn't mind living at Guisborough, really. Can't, of course. Let it to old Letty Guisborough. Cousin, or something. Stinks of money! Kenelm's one of her pets. That shows you! Daresay she makes him an allowance, but she can't give him the title! Dam' funny, that!' He stopped, seemed to make an effort to collect his slightly scattered wits, and said: 'What do you want with me?'

'I think you called on Mrs Haddington this afternoon, didn't you, my lord?'

'That's right. What of it?' said his lordship, rather belligerently.

'I should like to know, my lord, what was the purpose of your visit.' Hemingway saw Guisborough's eyes fixed on his face, at once wary and suspicious, and added: 'And what passed between you.'

'What the hell's it got to do with you?'

'Your lordship may take it that it has a lot to do with me.'

'Bloody cheek! Mrs Haddington didn't like me taking her daughter out to dance last night, that's all. Silly old trout!'

'Was there any sort of a quarrel between you, my lord?'

'Like hell there was! If you want to know, did I slam out of the house? Yes, I did! And if that's a crime, it's the first I've heard of it!'

'At what time would that have been, my lord?'

The wary look was deepening. 'No idea! Why?'

'Perhaps you can tell me, my lord, when it was that you entered the house?'

A frown of intense concentration descended on Guisborough's brow. After a moment for consideration, he replied: 'About a quarter-to-six, I think.'

'Was anyone else present when you arrived?'

'Butterwick. Passed me on the stairs.'

'Thank you, my lord. And how long do you think you may have been with Mrs Haddington?'

'You don't think I kept my eye on the clock, do you? I don't know.'

'Where did you go when you left Charles Street, my lord?' said Hemingway.

'Came home.'

'And when did you reach this house?'

'Look here!' demanded Guisborough. 'What's all this leading up to?'

'If you'll answer my question, my lord, perhaps I'll answer yours.'

'Damned if I will! I know you policemen! You're trying to catch me out or something! Minions of aristocratic power, that's what you are, the whole bloody lot of you! Upholding one law for the rich, and another –'

'You've got that wrong, my lord,' interrupted Hemingway tartly. 'It was a Turncock, not the police, and not *aristocratic* power either!'

'What the hell are you talking about?' said Guisborough, staring at him.

'Dickens. He happens to be my favourite writer, that's all!'

'Dickens!' exclaimed Guisborough, in accents of repulsion. 'What do you suppose I care for him?'

'I'm sure I don't know, my lord, but that's no reason to go about misquoting him!' retorted Hemingway. 'What's more, there's a time and a place for everything, and this isn't either the one or the other for Dickens! What I asked you was, when did you get back to this house after you left Charles Street today?'

Guisborough glared at him, but after a few moments he said sullenly: 'God knows!'

'I don't doubt that, my lord. If you can't remember perhaps Miss Guisborough can help me.'

'Well, I shouldn't think I was much more than half an hour with Mrs Haddington.'

'Thank you. And when you left the house?'

Guisborough passed a hand across his brow, sweeping back the loose lock of black hair that drooped over one eye. 'What a moment to choose to come and ask me conundrums!' he said fretfully. 'Do you want me to remember the names of all the streets between here and Charles Street? Because I don't!'

'No, my lord, I don't want that at all. Did you take a taxi, or had you your own car, perhaps?'

'I suppose you think that just because I've got a title I'm one of the idle rich?' said Guisborough jeeringly. 'Well, you're wrong! I walked!'

'All the way?'

'Yes, all the way! And if I didn't happen to like walking

I should have taken a 'bus! If my – if anyone's been telling you that the title makes any difference to me, it's a damned lie!'

At this moment the door opened to admit Trix Guisborough, who stood leaning against it, and demanded how much longer the Chief Inspector meant to keep her brother away from the party.

'Just as little time as I need, miss – Comrade, I should say!'

Guisborough jumped up from his chair. 'Oh, do, for God's sake drop that!' he shouted. 'You only do it to annoy me!'

Correctly divining that this remark was addressed not to him, but to Miss Guisborough, Hemingway preserved a discreet silence.

'Before you allowed yourself to be seduced by visions of power, and rank, it didn't annoy you!' Miss Guisborough retorted. 'You're a rotten renegade, Lance!'

'Begging your pardon,' intervened Hemingway, 'can you help us, Miss Guisborough, to fix the time when your brother got back to this house this evening?'

'This evening?' She stared at him. 'About half-past seven, more or less. Why?'

Hemingway raised his brows at Guisborough. 'Well, my lord?'

'I daresay. I don't know. I stopped to have one at a pub on the way.'

'Which pub would that be, my lord?'

'Hell, how should I know? Some place in the King's Road!'

'Fancy! What had the Ritz done to offend you?' mocked his sister.

'Oh, shut up!'

Feeling that there was little to be gained by prolonging the interview, Hemingway closed his notebook, and picked up his hat. Guisborough's fiery, dark eyes searched his face. 'Why did you want to know? What's happened?' He paused. 'Or is it a police mystery?'

'Oh, no, my lord, there's no mystery! You'll very likely read all about it in tomorrow's papers, so I've no objection to telling you that Mrs Haddington has been murdered.'

Whatever Lord Guisborough's reply to this may have been it was lost in the sudden crack of laughter that burst from his sister. She gasped: 'Oh, go on! That's too ripe! And who had the nerve to do in that old battle-axe? He has my vote!'

Lord Guisborough grasped her by the shoulders, and gave her a vicious shake. 'Stop it!' he commanded. 'Stop it, I say! It's not funny! You're tight, Trix!'

She choked, but her laughter ceased. 'Well, you needn't look so utter about it! You didn't do it, did you?'

'Of course I didn't do it! Why the hell should I? Pull yourself together, for God's sake!'

She looked at Hemingway. 'Is that why you came here? Because Lance – oh, it's too fat-headed! You might as well suspect me! Who really did it?'

'Can't you see he doesn't know?' said Guisborough savagely. 'Probably the same man who killed Seaton-Carew!'

'What makes you say that, my lord?' asked Hemingway.

'I don't know. Association of ideas, I suppose. Two murders in the same house.'

'I didn't say Mrs Haddington was murdered in the house,' said Hemingway mildly.

Guisborough scowled at him. 'You may not have said it, but you asked me when I left the house, so the inference is fairly obvious! I'm not half-witted!'

'True enough,' Hemingway agreed. 'She was murdered in the house. In her boudoir, just like Mr Seaton-Carew.'

'Ugh!' exclaimed Miss Guisborough, shuddering. 'What a cold-blooded beast! Damn it, I loathed the woman, and everything she stood for, but I didn't wish her as much harm as that! I'm sorry I laughed. What about that kid? Is she all alone there, except for those up-stage servants? Look here, Lance, ought we to do something? I mean, I don't mind, if you'd like me to bring her back here, or stay there with her.'

Lord Guisborough had apparently no faith in his sister's ability to comfort and support the stricken, for he replied: 'Very decent of you, but I don't think I should. There's the secretary, you know – and Cynthia hardly knows you! Besides, she – Well, I don't think it would work!'

'You mean she doesn't like me. Oh, all right! But if you want to go and hold her hand, you go! I can look after this mob.'

'No,' he said. 'No, I'm not going. Not this evening, anyway. She probably knows I lost my temper with her mother, and she might not want to see me, as things are.'

'That's all right, my lord,' Hemingway said. 'Miss Haddington had gone to bed before I left, and she has her aunt with her in any case.'

Guisborough looked relieved. 'Oh, I'm glad of that!

She'll look after her. Much better if I call on her tomorrow. Leave a message of sympathy, even if she doesn't feel up to seeing me.'

'Much better,' agreed Hemingway, and took his leave of them both.

When he reached Scotland Yard, he found that Inspector Grant had not yet arrived there. He went up to his room and sent down a message to have certain exhibits brought to him. While he was waiting for them, the buzzer sounded on his desk, and he lifted one of his telephones. The voice of his friend and superior officer, Superintendent Hinckley, assailed his ears.

'Chief Inspector Hemingway?'

'Sir?' said Hemingway.

The voice altered. 'Stanley? How's it going?'

'Fine!' said Hemingway. 'I've only got two murders on my hands so far. Of course, it's early days yet. I dare say there'll be some more by tomorrow. Who's my successor?'

'Not named. Keep at it! Between you and me and the gatepost, a Certain Person is still backing you. Thought you might like to know. Said he'd bank on you bringing home the bacon, and the worse the mess got the less he wanted to give it to anyone else. That's all!'

'Thanks, Bob! You're a trump!' said Hemingway flushing slightly.

A decisive click informed him that Superintendent Hinckley had cut short his gratitude. He grinned, and hung up the receiver. When Inspector Grant entered the room some twenty minutes later, he found him frowning at two looped lengths of picture-wire, lying side by side on his desk. He glanced up as the Inspector came in, and a certain intent look in his eyes caused that officer to exclaim: 'Och, you have discovered something! *Ciod e?*'

'I'm not sure,' Hemingway said slowly. 'What about you? Have you seen young Butterwick?'

'I have, then, and I questioned him, though it is my belief I had no need to, for it was at the Opera House I found him, and him in his evening clothes. But it is not opera, but ballet they are having there, and for all he swore he was there at the start, he may have been telling me a lie. He was alone.'

'The people sitting on either side of him ought to be able to tell you!' Hemingway said.

'*Ma seadh!* But there were no people sitting beside him, sir. Mrs Butterwick has a box for the whole season, and there is not one of the attendants can say for sure when he arrived this evening. Whether it was before –' He produced his notebook, and painstakingly read from it – '*Les Présages*, or *Petrouchka*. It was while *Petrouchka* was on that I reached Covent Garden, sir, and it seemed as though these ballet folk think a great deal of that, for when I asked to have Mr Butterwick brought out to me, they kept saying, In the middle of *Petrouchka*? as though I had asked to have him fetched out of Kirk. Which,' added the Inspector, 'I would not do! Indeed, such a stramash was there, with them telling me this *Petrouchka* would not last above a quarter of an hour more, and would I not wait for the interval, that I said, *Gle mhath!* and I waited.'

'Well, if that's what you said, it's a wonder to me they didn't call in the chap on point-duty!' said Hemingway. 'They probably thought you were an Undesirable Alien, and I don't blame them. How did you know Butterwick was at the ballet?'

'Och, that was the worst part of the whole business!' replied the Inspector. 'I went to that address in Park Lane when I left you, and at first I could discover nothing, because I found only the servants – just a man and wife, for the housemaid is a daily girl, and had gone home – and neither of them knew where the young man might be, or whether he had been in the flat since he took his tea there, with his mother. And that, I think, was true, for they have the kitchen and the servants' quarters a wee bit apart from the living-rooms of the family, and you get to them through a door, and along a bit passage. Young Mr Butterwick has his latch-key, I need not tell you, and there is no valet. However, while I was talking with the manservant, Mrs Butterwick came in.' He smiled. 'I can tell you, it was not long before I was thinking I would give you *moran taing* for that assignment, sir!'

Hemingway sat up with a jerk. 'Oh, it wasn't? Now, you just tell me what that means, my lad, because, it isn't the first time you've said it to me tonight, and it's my belief that –'

'Och, it means only Many thanks!' said the Inspector meekly.

His superior regarded him with blatant suspicion. 'I'll have to take your word for it at the moment, but the first chance I get I'll ask young Fraser! Well, what next?'

'Whisht, would I lie to you? I am telling you, Chief Inspector, I would sooner face a tigress than that woman! From the moment she knew I was a police-officer, I was in terror of having the eyes torn from my head! Och, it is a baby she had made of that *truaghan*! But she is afraid for him – verra much she is afraid for him!,

Hemingway grinned. 'Came up against mother-love,

did you? Poor old Sandy! I've had some! What's she afraid of?'

'The first murder,' Grant replied instantly. 'She thought I had come to question her son about that, and such a *sgeul* as she told me about that is no matter at all, for she was not present, and she knows nothing. Coming to it verra doucely, I asked her where Mr Sydney Butterwick would be just then, and she told me there was some man with a name I don't call to mind dancing *Petrouchka* for the first time, and her son would never miss such a sight. So I got from her the number of her box, and away I went.' He paused. 'Well, they brought young Butterwick to me in a wee office, when this *Petrouchka* was finished, and in he came, with his shirt no whiter than his face. You'll remember, sir, the way he carried on when you interrogated him: then it was a great deal of nonsense he talked about psychology, to make you think he was quite at his ease. Tonight it was Dalcroze Eurhythmics, and – now, wait while I get this right! – Cecchetti's Method, and Choreography, till I begged the silly *gille* to whisht!'

Hemingway nodded. 'Just like you do me! What did you make of him?'

'It is hard to say. There is verra little doubt in my mind he thought I had come to question him about the first murder, for it was of that he talked, until I asked him to tell me what time it was when he reached the Opera House. I am bound to say that he looked scared for his life when I put that to him, and when, later on, I told him what it was I was enquiring about, he gave a *sgiamh*, and fainted away!'

'Good God!' ejaculated Hemingway.

'You may well say so!' agreed Grant. 'When he came round, och, I thought he was going to weep! But a wee dram pulled him together, and he swore to me that all he went to Charles Street for was to ask Mrs Haddington why she had told lies about him to us. Forbye, he remembered that he went past Lord Guisborough on the stairs. He rushed from the house, leaving his walking-stick behind him. There were all sorts of times he gave me, but the truth is he does not know when he left Charles Street. According to his tale, he went home to Park Lane, and changed into his evening-dress, and came in a taxi to Covent Garden just in time to get to his box before the curtain rose on the first ballet. And whether he was speaking the truth to me or not I cannot tell. For there is no knowing how to take him! For all he fainted under my eyes, no sooner did he hear the bell ringing for the end of the interval than he was in a fret to get back to his box for fear he would miss the last ballet!'

'Might have been in a fret to get away from you,' Hemingway said. 'However, it doesn't seem to me as though he had any reason for killing Mrs Haddington, so we'll give him the benefit of the doubt for the moment.'

'It might be that she was killed – though I will not say it was by Butterwick, mind! – because she knew too much about the first murder,' Grant pointed out.

'It might,' Hemingway agreed. 'Always a possibility.'

'You do not think it?' Grant said, eyeing him shrewdly.

'Who said I don't think it?' Hemingway retorted. 'What you want to do, Sandy, is to keep an open mind! Now, you take a look at Exhibits 1 and 2, and tell me if anything strikes you about them!'

The Inspector frowned down at the lengths of wire on the desk. 'Picture-wire, both,' he said. 'But one is older than the other, for it is tarnished. They got no distinguishable prints from the second one?'

'None at all.' Hemingway picked up a short length of twine, and held it out. 'Just take this, Sandy!' He set his elbow on the table, holding his forearm vertically. 'I want you to imitate our interesting murders round my wrist. You can use that ruler for your tourniquet, and there's no need to go to extremes! Just show me how you'd set about the job, if you were going to bump anyone off like that!'

The Inspector looked faintly surprised, but he obediently slipped the twine round Hemingway's arm, held the two ends in his left hand, and with his right inserted the ruler above his grip, and gave it a couple of twists. He paused then, glancing enquiringly down at his chief. Hemingway nodded. 'That's enough. Let go! Now do it again!'

The Inspector's brow creased. He said nothing, however, but faithfully repeated his performance.

'So that's the way you'd do it every time, is it?' said Hemingway. 'So would Carnforth. Young Thirsk, on the other hand, does it my way!'

'Your way?'

'We use our right hands for the grip, and our left for the tourniquet. Thus, my lad, we get the twist from left to right, and you get it from right to left – same like Operator Number One.'

The Inspector uttered an exclamation, and looked quickly down at the wires on the desk. '*Mo thruaighe!* I never noticed it! Is one a left-handed man, then?'

'No, not necessarily. None of us four's left-handed. It's all according to taste. Some find it natural to do it one way, some prefer the other. Try doing it my way!'

The Inspector obeyed, but slowly. He said: 'It is not just natural to me – but I could do it!'

'Could, but wouldn't. Well, I think that's about enough for today – and not so bad, either! You get off home now. I don't want you at the Inquest tomorrow: once we're through with Sir Roderick Vickerstown and the doctor, I shall ask for an adjournment. You go to Poulton's offices, and see what you can discover there! I'll see you here, after the Inquest: I'm not meeting this Eddleston chap till twelve o'clock, in Charles Street.'

The Inspector picked up his hat, saying with his fugitive smile: 'You always say, do you not, that when a case becomes so tangled there is no solving it something will break?'

'I daresay, because it's perfectly true! Why I wasn't made a Superintendent years ago I shall never know! These two bits of wire, Sandy, show how the best laid plans of mice and men can gang agley!'

'*Ma seadh!*' said the Inspector, his hand on the door-knob. 'But where you learned that Lowland accent I know not!' Upon which Parthian shot he circumspectly withdrew, closing the door softly behind him.

Eighteen

They met on the following morning. The Inspector made a little gesture of incomprehension. 'It becomes more and more *duilich*!' he said. 'Unless they lied to me at Poulton's office, or he to them, they expect him to return this afternoon. I had the particulars of this conference he has gone to attend from his head clerk. Och, I suspected there was no conference, but it is true enough!'

'Well, that doesn't surprise me,' replied Hemingway. 'Somehow it never seemed likely that a bird like Poulton would have skipped the country for good. Too hard a head, for one thing; and too much at stake for another. Not counting that wife of his. If, as seems the safest bet at the moment, he committed the second murder, I don't doubt he's got an unshakeable alibi up his sleeve.'

'Now, that he cannot have,' the Inspector said reasonably. 'For well we know he was the last man to see the poor lady alive!'

'The murderer was the last man to see her alive, my lad, and don't you lose sight of that fact! If the murderer is Poulton, I shall find myself up against something, because he hasn't got where he is without being a very cool customer! Now we'll get along to Charles Street!'

They reached Charles Street barely five minutes before the younger Mr Eddleston was also set down at the house, and were received by Miss Pickhill. She informed them that her niece was closeted with the dressmaker, who had arrived that morning with the altered black frock, and was making some final adjustments to it. She said, in rather a grudging way, that she had been agreeably surprised in Miss Birtley, who had not only come to the house at the correct hour, but had been helpful in drafting the notice for *The Times*, and ordering mourning-cards. Of her niece's activities she said nothing, but from the prim look round her withered mouth it was to be inferred that these had not met with her approval. The sealing of the two rooms seemed still to rankle in her mind; and she said with a good deal of asperity that she would insist upon being present when the Chief Inspector searched her sister's bedroom.

Young Mr Eddleston was discovered to be a middle-aged man with the long upper-lip that was so often to be found amongst the members of his profession. He had been bred in a firm whose chief livelihood derived from Conveyancing; he was always opposed to any form of litigation, invariably advising his clients to keep out of the Law Courts; and, as he informed Hemingway at the outset, he had never before found himself involved in criminal proceedings. He said that he had very little knowledge of his late client's affairs: he had drafted her Will; he had conducted the negotiations for the leasing of her house; but he had rarely been called upon to advise her in affairs of more moment.

'I may say,' he remarked, as the seals on the door of the boudoir were broken, and they entered this apartment, 'that I was very much shocked by the intelligence you conveyed to me on the telephone last night, Chief Inspector. I was never at all intimate with Mrs Haddington, but, as I told you, I think, it so happens that I had had a telephone conversation with her that very day. Nothing of importance: just a slight question about the repairs to this house; but I had quite a little chat with her, and she seemed to be in good spirits – quite herself! How little did I think that before nightfall she would be dead!'

'Did she say anything to you about the murder of Mr Seaton-Carew?' asked Hemingway, moving towards the desk.

'A few words! Just a few words! She was not a woman who ever wore her heart on her sleeve, as the saying is, and naturally I forbore to question her closely.'

'Naturally,' Hemingway agreed. 'I daresay she was a good deal upset? An old friend, I understand?'

'So I believe,' said Mr Eddleston, gravely nodding his head. 'She was disinclined to discuss the matter, but I should not have described her as upset, precisely. A very unpleasant thing to happen in one's house!'

'Was that all Mrs Haddington felt about it?' Hemingway asked.

'No doubt,' said Mr Eddleston, 'Mrs Haddington was distressed to have lost a friend under such tragic circumstances; but I am quite sure there was no reason for her to feel – um – any stronger emotion! Indeed, I can confidently assert that she did *not* feel such an emotion. We conversed together perfectly cheerfully for several minutes, first about her landlord's liabilities; then about possible marriage settlements for Miss Cynthia – poor child, this will have come as a crushing blow to her! Then Mrs Haddington desired me to furnish her with certain information about the Marriage and Legitimacy Acts, for a friend of hers; and I think that was all – no, not quite! Mrs Haddington wished to know what her legal position was in regard to her servants' wages, two of whom, as I understood, had threatened to leave without the customary notice given.'

As he spoke, he seated himself at the desk; but before he opened it, he cast a glance round the room, and said, with a cough: 'This, I believe, is the actual room where . . .?'

'That chair,' said Hemingway, indicating it.

Mr Eddleston set his pince-nez on his nose the better to survey the fatal chair. He then said: 'Terrible! Terrible!' and turned his attention to the desk.

There was nothing amongst the papers discovered in it to give the slightest indication of who might have killed Mrs Haddington, or from what source she had derived the greater part of her income. She had never consulted her solicitors on the disposal of her property; Mr Eddleston only knew that she was a woman of considerable substance. Pressed, he admitted that he had had reason, during the past years, to assume that her investments had been fortunate; but he was ignorant of the sum bequeathed to her by her husband, a gentleman whose affairs he had not handled. He disclosed to Hemingway that her Will was a very simple document: she had left everything of which she died possessed to her daughter. Until the Will was proved, her trustees, of whom he was one, could not know the size of her estate.

The desk contained such oddments as a ball of string, a pair of large scissors in a leather case, paper clips, visiting-cards, and wrapping-paper. The only documents of possible interest were some Bank Pass-sheets, and an investment book. A cursory glance at this yielded little information, beyond the bare fact that Mrs Haddington's investments had been many, and, apparently, sound. The Pass-sheets showed a small over-draft: it was plain that Mrs Haddington had been living for some time rather beyond her very large income.

This was shown to be much too large in an epoch when not the largest fortune was permitted to yield its owner more than five thousand pounds yearly, nor did the entries on the credit side bear any relation to certain outgoing sums made payable to the Commissioners of Inland Revenue. This discrepancy was accounted for by the frequent occurrence of the word Cash against some of the sums received. Mr Eddleston, peering at these, looked faintly revolted, but said, removing his pince-nez from his nose and polishing the lenses with his handkerchief: 'It is regrettable, Chief Inspector, but, I fear, inevitable under our present system of taxation, that more and more people are being forced to evade excessive taxation by employing shifts they would not, I venture to state, have stooped even to contemplate ten years ago.'

'It might be that, of course,' Hemingway said, shutting the leather folder which contained the Pass-sheets. 'I shall want this, sir.'

'Certainly,' said Mr Eddleston. 'You are, of course, entitled to retain whatever you wish.'

'There's nothing else I want here, thank you, sir. She doesn't seem to have kept many papers. We may find some more in her bedroom.'

When they left the boudoir, they found Miss Pickhill hovering outside the drawing-room, on the landing above. She eyed them with some hostility, and informed young Mr Eddleston that she was bound to say she was surprised at his conduct. He very unwisely tried to explain the difficulties of his position to her. Before he had in any way convinced her either that he was powerless to prevent the police from searching her sister's house or that his father would have acted otherwise, a further interruption occurred. Thrimby came up the stairs, bearing, on a silver salver, a large, square-cut emerald, set in diamond claws on a platinum bar. This he presented to Hemingway, saying: 'Madam's brooch, Chief Inspector, which she lost yesterday afternoon, and asked to have carefully looked-for. I fancy the safety-catch is defective, for it was found slipped down the side of one of the armchairs in the drawing-room. I thought it best, sir,' he added, staring over Miss Pickhill's head, 'to give it into your charge.'

As Hemingway picked the brooch up, and looked at its catch, which was indeed loose, Cynthia appeared at the head of the stairs, with Miss Spennymoor behind her. Cynthia was clad in the altered black frock. She looked ethereally fair, but her beauty was spoilt by a sullen pout. She exclaimed, on catching sight of the brooch: 'That's Mummy's! What are you doing with it?'

She came running down the stairs, and almost snatched it from Hemingway's hand. Miss Pickhill, clucking her displeasure, explained the circumstances to her, whereupon she said: 'I know the catch is loose. It came undone at tea-time, and Mummy said she must take it to be mended.' She began to pin it to the bosom of her frock, adding: 'Has the chemist sent yet, Thrimby?'

'No, miss.'

'Well, Miss Birtley can dam' well go and collect the stuff! It's no use giving me marvellous medicines if they're not even *sent* for me to take!'

'Cynthia, I beg you will take that brooch off at once!' Miss Pickhill said, her cheeks showing a heightened colour. 'It isn't *decent*! Besides, emeralds for a girl of your age – ! Let alone that you are in deep mourning!'

'All that sort of thing is *hopelessly* out-of-date!' Cynthia declared. 'I don't mind wearing this ghastly rag just at first, but I'm not going to stay in mourning for a year! I'd rather die! What's more, *all* Mummy's things are mine now, and I have a perfect right to do what I like with them! *Haven't* I?' she demanded, turning to Mr Eddleston.

This gentleman, finding himself much in sympathy with Miss Pickhill, coughed, and suggested that perhaps it would be more proper if the brooch were put amongst Mrs Haddington's other jewels, until the Will had at least been read. Cynthia at once displayed a lamentable desire to argue the point, but her aunt, of whom she secretly stood rather in awe, clinched the matter by wresting the trinket from her, and announcing her intention of bestowing it in her sister's jewel-case with her own hands. Cynthia then complained of the total lack of sympathy she met with on all sides, and added that Mummy always kept her jewel-box locked, anyway, and as nobody knew where her keys were it would puzzle her aunt to put the brooch with the other jewels.

'I have Mrs Haddington's keys, miss,' Hemingway interposed. 'They were in her handbag – some of them, that is. Perhaps you can tell me what they belong to?'

'I call it pretty good cheek of you to take my mother's keys without asking me first!' said Cynthia. '*That's* the one to her jewel-box, and the other's the little desk in her room. And that's her latch-key. And if you're going to unlock her room now, I'm coming too!'

'Cynthia, dear child!' said Miss Pickhill, repressing, as a Christian, her strong desire to box her niece's ears, 'there is no need for you to do that. *I* will accompany these Persons. You do not want, I am sure, to go into your poor mother's room today.'

'Yes, I do,' asserted Cynthia obstinately. 'Of course it'll practically *kill* me, but I've got to face it sometime, haven't I? And if I *have* to wear this dingy frock, I don't see why I shouldn't have that marvellous black-and-silver scarf of Mummy's, to go with it. She'd *like* me to: I know she would!'

Miss Pickhill found this speech so daunting that she was unable to think of a reply to it that would not violate her own canons of behaviour towards the bereaved. Inspector Grant, averting his grave eyes from the pretty, spoilt face of the orphan, encountered a glance from Hemingway, and went up the stairs, carrying the key to Mrs Haddington's bedroom in his hand. With the exceptions of Miss Spennymoor and Thrimby, the party followed him.

The room was in darkness, the heavy curtains of brocaded silk still being drawn across the windows.

When these had been pulled back, it was seen that Mrs Haddington's dinner-gown of black velvet had been laid out on the bed, her opulent dressing-gown disposed across a chair, and a pair of paper-thin stockings placed ready for her to put on. Miss Pickhill drew in her breath with a hissing sound, and Cynthia burst into tears. However, when it was suggested to her that she should withdraw from a scene so painfully reminiscent of her loss, she stopped crying, very nobly announcing her determination to face facts, and went to powder her face at the dressing-table between the two windows.

The furniture in the room, besides the bed and the dressing-table, included an enormous wardrobe of Victorian design, the central division of which contained shelves and drawers; an upholstered day-bed, several chairs, and a small walnut bureau on cabriole legs, which stood on one side of the fireplace. The top of this contained nothing of more interest than two cheque-books; an engagement diary; a bundle of letters tied up with faded ribbon, which a cursory glance informed Hemingway were the letters Cynthia had written to her mother from school; and a quantity of writing-paper and envelopes. There were three drawers to the bureau, the two small top ones containing such oddments as sealing-wax, a supply of postcards, stamps and telegraph-forms; the long drawer beneath them was, unlike them, locked. In it lay a piece of petit-point, with the needle still stuck in it, a sewing-bag, and, lying beneath the unfinished embroidery, a large black lace fan, mounted on ebony sticks.

The sight of it most vividly conjured up the picture of Mrs Haddington, as he had first seen her, to

Hemingway's memory. She had been holding the fan between her ringed hands, gripping it rather tightly when some question he had asked her annoyed, or perhaps alarmed her. Hemingway lifted it out of the drawer, staring at it. Across the polished guards several deep scratches were visible, and where the lace-leaf protruded beyond them he saw that it had been slightly torn. Standing with his back to the room, he carefully opened the fan, observing as he did so that it had suffered some kind of a wrench which had thrown the sticks out of the straight. The tear in the lace cut irregularly across the leaf, small holes occurring here and there only, but always in the same diagonal line. He shut it, found Grant at his elbow, and gave it to him, muttering: 'Take that, and keep your mouth shut!'

'You won't find anything in there,' Cynthia said, over her shoulder. 'That's only where Mummy keeps her work!'

Hemingway shut the drawer. 'So I see, miss. Now, if you'll be so good, I should like just to look inside the wardrobe.'

'I find it most objectionable to have my poor sister's clothing pawed about by Men!' announced Miss Pickhill, her eyes snapping.

'I shan't disturb anything more than I need, madam. Yes, I see: dresses in the side-wings: I don't want to touch anything there, thank you. If I may see inside the central division?'

As he had expected, shelves, with drawers below them, were concealed by the double doors in the middle of the wardrobe. On one of the shelves a large jewel-box stood, beside a glove-box, and a quilted handkerchief sachet.

Miss Pickhill, perceiving this, instantly called upon Mr Eddleston to open it, and to place in it the emerald brooch, which she was still holding. 'And for the present,' she said, 'I consider the case ought to be in safe custody! Perhaps you will take charge of it! My sister possessed some very valuable jewels.'

Cynthia at once protested, pointing out that it had nothing to do with her aunt. Miss Pickhill retorted that as her niece's guardian it had everything to do with her, a pronouncement which caused Cynthia to express an impassioned wish that she too were dead. Meanwhile Mr Eddleston, carefully avoiding the Chief Inspector's speaking eye, lifted the box out of the wardrobe, and asked for its key. Hemingway handed it to him, and he unlocked the box, disclosing a collection of ornaments of a fashionable rather than a valuable nature, tumbled into a velvet-lined tray.

'That isn't where Mummy puts her good stuff!' Cynthia said scornfully. 'Oh, couldn't I just have those paste-clips to wear now? I don't see why I shouldn't! They aren't real, but they'd look rather marvellous on this frock. Mummy used to wear them with it. They *go* with it!'

'Jewellery is not worn with deep mourning!' said Miss Pickhill. 'Can you think of *nothing* but personal adornment, child?'

'I think you're most unfair!' Cynthia cried, tears once more starting to her eyes. 'You *know* I'm absolutely *shattered*, and you *begged* me to try not to think about it, and the instant I manage to take my mind off it you're beastly to me!'

Mr Eddleston, who was beginning to look harassed, lifted out the tray of the jewel-box, and laid it aside. A number of leather cases were stacked under the tray.

'If you *must* put the brooch away, just as if you thought I meant to steal it,' said Cynthia, 'this blue case is where it lives.' She lifted the case out as she spoke, and gave an involuntary exclamation. 'My compact!'

Under the blue-leather case lay a powder-compact, its lid covered in petit-point.

Cynthia dropped the blue case on the floor, and eagerly snatched the compact from the box. Her cheeks were suddenly flushed, and her eyes sparkling. She cast a quick look at Hemingway, and said: 'It's the one I lost. My *favourite* one! Mummy must have found it, and – and put it here to be safe!'

'Nonsense, child!' said Miss Pickhill. 'Why should your mother have done any such thing? Put it back, for goodness' sake!'

'It's *mine*, I tell you! It's mine!' Cynthia declared clasping it tightly to her bosom. 'It's the one Dan gave me! No one but me has any *right* to it!'

'May I see it, miss?' said Hemingway, holding out his hand.

She backed away from him, frightened, staring at him. 'No! Why should you? It isn't my mother's! Send for Miss Birtley! *She'll* tell you it's truly mine!'

'I'm not doubting that, miss, but I should like to see it.'

Rather unexpectedly, Miss Pickhill took her niece's part. 'There is no need to be hysterical, Cynthia, but I'm bound to say I can see no reason why you should want to look at a powder-compact, Chief Inspector!'

'No, madam, very likely not. Come, miss! Mr Eddleston here will tell you that you mustn't try to obstruct me in the performance of my duty.'

'But it has nothing to do with you! Look, I'll put it back in Mummy's box, and Mr Eddleston can keep it! I don't mind doing that!'

'Miss Haddington,' said Hemingway, 'I don't want to make things any more unpleasant for you than what they are already, but if you don't give me that compact I shall have to. You see, I'm going to inspect it, whether you want me to or not, and it will be very much better for you to give it to me without any more fuss.'

She began to cry again, but when Hemingway unclasped her fingers from about the compact she only feebly resisted.

Inspector Grant said: 'Will you give it to me, if you please, sir?'

He took it from Hemingway, and walked over to the window with it, standing there with his back to the room, his head a little bent. After a moment, he glanced over his shoulder. Hemingway went to him, while Miss Pickhill and Mr Eddleston stared at him. Cynthia had collapsed on the day-bed, and was sobbing into one of its opulent cushions. The Inspector said nothing at all, but showed Hemingway the compact, lying in the palm of his hand. He had opened it, but no little powder-puff and mirror were disclosed. A very small quantity of white powder was all that met Hemingway's gaze. He looked up questioningly, and the Inspector nodded, shut the case, and opened it again, this time revealing mirror, puff, and powder-filter. Hemingway turned from him.

'Miss Haddington,' he said, 'I want to have a word with you. Now, I think it would be best if I saw you privately, but if you wish it you may have your aunt or Mr Eddleston with you.'

She raised her head, gazing up at him out of terrified, tear-drowned eyes. 'What are you going to do to me?'

'I'm going to ask you one or two questions, miss, and you may take it from me that if you answer me truthfully you've got nothing to be afraid of.'

She seemed to be undecided; Miss Pickhill exclaimed: 'I demand to be told what all this means!'

'No, no, don't!' shrieked Cynthia. 'Please don't!'

'No, miss, I've no wish to do so. Suppose we were to go down to the drawing-room – just you and me, and Inspector Grant?'

'I think,' said Mr Eddleston, clearing his throat, 'that I ought to be present, Chief Inspector, if you wish to question Miss Haddington on any serious matter.'

'I have no objection to your presence, sir.'

'No, no, I don't want him!' Cynthia said. 'I'll go with you, if you *swear* you aren't going to do anything to me!'

'No, miss, I'm not going to do anything to you at all.'

'Well!' said Miss Pickhill. 'I'm sure I don't know what the world is coming to! I consider this most extraordinary!'

Nobody paid any attention to this, Hemingway merely opening the door for Cynthia to pass out of the room, and Mr Eddleston looking as though he were uncertain what to do.

A fire was burning in the drawing-room, and Hemingway suggested to Cynthia that she should sit down beside it. She seemed relieved by this humane invitation, but poised herself on the very edge of one of the deep armchairs, and, for once in her life, sat bolt upright. Her eyes watched the two detectives warily, with something in them of a child caught out in wrongdoing.

Hemingway said: 'Now, miss, we won't beat about the bush. I know just what you've been up to and very wrong of you it was, which I'll be bound you know already, for I think Mr Seaton-Carew warned you that there would be bad trouble if anyone found out you had cocaine in your possession, didn't he?'

She gave a frightened nod, catching her breath on a sob.

'When did he start giving you the stuff?'

'I don't know. I only tried it for f-fun, at first! Only I felt so marvellous afterwards – It's my *nerves*!'

'It precious soon would be, if you went on at that game!' said Hemingway dryly. 'What made Mr Seaton-Carew give it to you at all?'

'Oh, I don't know! It was the night of the Gem Ball, and I felt so *bloody*, and I looked haggish, and my head was splitting, and Dan was utterly *divine* to me! Actually, he always rather bored me before – I mean, *definitely* old, and uncle-ish, besides being Mummy's boy-friend, which made me choke him off, on account of its being so *dim* to get a Thing about one's Mother's boy-friend! Of course, I just didn't *know* him properly, because really he *utterly* understood about my nerves, and always being tired to death, and he was *too* cherishing!' Her eyes filled. 'It's awful now he's dead! I can't bear it! Mummy never understood a bit, but Dan did!'

'When did he give you that powder-compact?'

'Oh, it was a Christmas present! He made me promise not to use it unless I felt absolutely *finished*, and he swore he wouldn't refill it till Easter, but I expect he would have, if I'd been nice to him, because, if you want to know, he had a complete yen for me!'

'I don't doubt it,' Hemingway said, more dryly still. 'When did your mother discover that you were taking drugs, Miss Haddington?'

'Mummy never knew a thing about it!' she exclaimed. 'She *couldn't* have known!'

He gave her an appraising look. 'No! Well, when did you lose the compact, miss?'

'It was the day of that ghastly Bridge-party. I don't know when Mummy found it, because she hadn't the *least* idea – really she hadn't! I can't think *why* she locked it up in her jewel-box! Unless she wanted to get back on me for going out with Lance Guisborough, when she said I wasn't to, which is quite likely, because she simply *loathed* him, God knows why!'

'I see. Now, I understand that Dr Westruther called here yesterday, at lunch-time, miss. Did you see him?'

'Yes, he gave me a prescription for my nerves.'

'Wasn't what he gave you a prescription for someone who'd been taking dangerous drugs?'

She looked startled. 'No!'

'Are you quite sure of that, miss? Didn't Dr Westruther ask you certain questions about the length of time you'd been –'

'No, no, no! I swear he didn't! He just went over me like they do, and said I had been overdoing things, and he was going to give me some dope or other which would make me feel utterly different, and Mummy said we'd go to some marvellous place he knew of, where I could ride, and get absolutely fit before the Season starts – and he never said one single word about – about *that*! I *promise* you he didn't!'

'Very well, miss. Don't get all worked-up! You take the doctor's medicine, and I daresay you'll find, after a bit, that you don't hanker after that filthy drug any more. I don't know if Mr Seaton-Carew told you this, but in case he didn't, I will! It's an offence against the law to have that kind of drug in your possession. You could get into very serious trouble, let alone ending up as a hopeless addict – and if you'd ever seen anyone in that state, believe you me, you'd take good care never to let the habit get a hold on you! I'm not going to take any steps, because I can see you're only a kid that didn't know any better, and I've got a pretty good idea that now Mr Seaton-Carew's dead, you don't know how to get hold of the stuff. What I *am* going to do, and I know you won't like it, is to tell your aunt.' Cynthia uttered a shriek of dismay. 'No, don't start to carry on, miss! It's my belief Miss Pickhill's very fond of you: I wouldn't mind betting she'll do everything she can to help you – and it's that or worse! You wouldn't want to be prosecuted, would you?'

'You promised!' panted Cynthia.

'Yes, I know I did, and I'll keep it, if I can. But you've got to pull up, and maybe it won't be easy, not at first. And if you didn't pull up – well, then, it wouldn't rest with me any longer, but you'd wake up to find yourself in a Home, undergoing the sort of treatment you wouldn't like at all, with a prosecution looming on top of that!'

The warning frightened Cynthia so much that she only cowered in her chair. Hemingway then left her, and, encountering Miss Pickhill on the landing, took her into the boudoir, and embarked on an extremely trying half-hour with her. However, after running the gamut of shock, horror, revulsion and condemnation, the good lady dissolved into tears, saying into a large linen handkerchief: 'I blame my sister! Anyone could have

302

seen with half an eye the child was never robust, and what did she do but drag her from party to party? Over and over again did I tell her that she was heading for trouble, and now we see how right I was! If I have to devote the rest of my life to her, I shall cure her! No principles, of course! Brought up in that Godless way! It doesn't bear thinking of!'

'Och, I am sorry for the lassie!' said Grant, as they passed out of the house.

'Well, I'm not!' said Hemingway. 'A proper little detrimental, that's what she is, and she's getting off lightly! Sandy, what we've discovered this morning is nobody's business! Haven't I told you, time and again, that when a case gets properly gummed up something'll break?'

'You have,' agreed the Inspector gravely. 'Now, I have not had the opportunity to look at that fan you gave me. What is it you have in your head?'

'You'll see!' Hemingway said. 'We're going to do a little experiment with that fan and a bit of wire, my lad!'

'Ah!' said the Inspector. 'I thought it would be that, maybe.' He added, with a half-smile: 'You have always believed it was Mrs Haddington murdered Seaton-Carew, have you not?'

'I never believe anything until I get proof,' replied Hemingway. 'But what I've got is *flair*!'

'I have heard you say so,' meekly responded his subordinate.

The experiment, conducted in the Chief Inspector's room, with a length of wire and Mrs Haddington's fan, caused the cautious Gael to say: '*Gle mhath!* I do not doubt it was the fan she used for her tourniquet. *That –*' he pointed to where Cynthia's compact lay – 'gives us the motive, which before we never had. But what possessed that man to give snow to a bit lassie like yon?'

Hemingway shrugged. 'I daresay we shall never know. My guess is that he fell heavily for her, and she wasn't having any. He didn't give her much of the stuff – just enough to make her dependent on him. May have meant to break her of it, once he had her where he wanted her; may not have cared, as long as he did have her. You ought to know what effect the stuff would be likely to have! Only he reckoned without her mother. Now, you may think Miss Pickhill's nothing more than a pain in the neck, but that's because you haven't got *flair*! I got a lot of very valuable information out of Miss Pickhill, and the most important was that the late Mrs Haddington pretty well doted on that daughter of hers. All right! Nobody knew better, if you were to ask me, than Mrs Haddington what becomes of people who get the drug habit. Don't you run away with the idea that she was a plaster-saint! She wasn't! She knew what Seaton-Carew's little racket was, *and* cashed in on it! She knew the signs all right, and I'd be willing to stake a month's pay she spotted them in the fair Cynthia! It wouldn't surprise me if I had proof given me – which I shan't have, the way things are – that she'd made up her mind to eliminate the boy-friend long before that party of hers.' He paused. 'No, I'm wrong there. Didn't that silly girl say she only lost the compact on the day of the party? All the same, Mrs Haddington may have had her suspicions before that. Why else did she pinch the compact? For what we can't doubt she did! She found what she was looking for, and she knew there was only one thing to be done: wipe out Seaton-Carew!

And she was longheaded enough to see that she couldn't have a better opportunity than at her own Bridge-party! I daresay she got the idea as soon as he told her he was expecting a 'phone-call. She was clever enough to have staged that, I daresay, but maybe she didn't. Lots of other ways of getting him away from the rest of the party. As for the wire, I always did think it must have been she who took it out of the cloakroom. Whether she did that only to tidy the place, which seems likely; or whether she did it with the murder in her mind is another of the things we shall never know. Bit of both, perhaps.'

'It is possible,' Grant said. 'But if it was she who killed Seaton-Carew, *who was it who killed her?* And why?'

Nineteen

'There,' said the Chief Inspector frankly, 'you have me, Sandy! Nice set-out, isn't it? First we get Mrs Haddington planning as neat a murder as you could wish for; and then we have someone unknown taking careful note of her methods, and coolly copying them to do her in! Banking on us thinking the same person was responsible for both deaths, which we might have if I hadn't found that fan, and you hadn't known the trick of that compact. We got motive and means in one fell swoop, as you might say, which is a piece of bad luck for Murderer No. 2. On the face of it, it looks a bit as if this bird was fitted out with a water-tight alibi for the first murder.'

'That would rule out Poulton,' said Grant.

'It would, of course, and we haven't reached the stage of ruling him out, not by a long chalk. What we've got to discover was what possible motive he can have had for wanting to dispose of Mrs Haddington good and quick. If he thought it was she who was giving his wife cocaine, I suppose he might have done it. You'd think, though, that a level-headed chap like him would have wanted some solid proof before committing a pretty nasty murder, let alone the foolhardiness of it!'

'They say in the City that he is verra canny. It might be that he would bank on us believing he would not be so silly as to have done it.'

'Yes, I always heard you Highlanders were an imaginative lot,' commented Hemingway. 'I'm bound to say I've never seen any signs of it in you before, and, if that's a sample, I hope I never will again! If Poulton committed the second murder, he wasn't banking on me getting any cockeyed ideas into my head, you can bet your life on that! What's more, he must have had a damned good reason for doing it. It might be the one I've already suggested, and the more I think about that the less it appeals to me; it might be that Mrs Haddington knew of Lady Nest's habits – which I don't doubt – and was threatening exposure. If so, why?'

'Not exposure: blackmail!'

'Yes, that's a possibility. He's a very wealthy man: she may have over-reached herself. I shouldn't think he'd part readily with any substantial sum. On the other hand, supposing she did demand a young fortune from him, and he'd come to us? What would we have done?'

'We would have kept his name out, as far as was possible, but these things sometimes leak out, sir, and well you know it!'

Hemingway nodded, but pursed his lips rather dubiously. 'You may be right. All the same – Well, we'll see! Meanwhile, as soon as we've had a bit of lunch, we'll pay Dr Westruther another call. He's got some explaining to do. He wasn't looking altogether happy at the Inquest this morning, and I'm sure I don't blame him. Sailing very near the wind, is Dr Westruther.'

When they met again, it was nearly three o'clock, and

the Inspector was able to report that his enquiries had elicited the fact that Mr Godfrey Poulton was a passenger on the aeroplane due at Northolt at about four o'clock.

'Good!' said Hemingway. 'This time, perhaps I can get him to be a little more open with me than he was before.'

'You saw the doctor, sir?'

'I did. From his face, I should say he'd just as soon a polecat had walked in as me. Luckily I've never been one to set much store by popularity, otherwise my feelings might have been hurt. As it was, I was rather glad to see I wasn't a welcome guest. It encouraged me to be a bit unconventional with him. He's a slippery customer, but he doesn't like this case. Talked the usual stuff about his duty to his patients, but when I pointed out to him that when we'd had two murders he was carrying that a bit far, he turned a very nasty colour. What he says, and, I don't doubt, would swear to, is that he never connected Seaton-Carew's death with the drug-traffic. Says he wasn't told who'd given snow to the Haddington girl. Well, that's quite likely, but I think he put two and two together. What's shaken him is Mrs Haddington's death. It's in the cheaper papers, but he says he only sees *The Times*. Came as a shock to him. Sat there goggling at me like a hake. He hadn't a clue, that I'm sure of. She did call him in to prescribe for the girl, and she told him the plain truth. You'll probably like to know that he doesn't think there's been any irremediable harm done. As regards Lady Nest, he was a good deal less forthcoming, but I didn't press him too hard on that. If Poulton goes on stone-walling, I've got enough evidence now to force him to disclose the address of the Home he's put his wife in. Did I tell you I'd had a crack with Heathcote? He and Cathercott are hot on their trail, and just about as pleased as punch with themselves. Heathcote even spared me a pat on the back, but two chaps less interested in a brace of murders you'd never find! I'm going to have a talk with the AC now. You nip down to Northolt, and catch Poulton as he steps out of the 'plane! Bring him here – all nice, and civil: wanted for further enquiries. Tell him there have been developments which make it necessary for me to ask him a few more questions, and watch his reactions. There won't be any, so that won't take you long!'

It was nearly five o'clock when Inspector Grant ushered Godfrey Poulton into the Chief Inspector's room. Mr Poulton appeared to be quite unperturbed, merely saying: 'Good afternoon! I understand you want to ask me some more questions, Chief Inspector? I have no wish, of course, to impede the course of justice, but I should be glad if you would come to the point as quickly as possible! I'm expected at my office.'

'Good afternoon, sir. I shan't keep you longer than I need. It really depends on you,' said Hemingway. 'Will you sit down?'

Mr Poulton seated himself without hesitation in a deep, leather-covered armchair. He did not seem to be in any way embarrassed by the necessity, thus imposed on him, of being obliged to look up to meet the Chief Inspector's eyes. He merely glanced at his wrist-watch, and said: 'Well, what is it?'

'I think, sir, that you visited Mrs Haddington yesterday afternoon?'

'I did, yes.'

309

'Rather less than half an hour after your departure, sir,' said Hemingway unemotionally, 'Mrs Haddington was discovered dead in her boudoir. Strangled with a piece of wire,' he added.

'*What?*' ejaculated Poulton, stiffening suddenly, in a way which made Inspector Grant think that the news came as a shock to him, but which only caused his superior, one of the pillars of an Amateur Dramatic Society, to consider that the exclamation had been well-rehearsed.

'Yes, sir,' he said phlegmatically.

'Good God!' Poulton paused. His eyes, under their level brows, lifted to the Chief Inspector's face. 'I see. I can only tell you that when I left Mrs Haddington she was alive, standing before the electric fire in her boudoir. She had just rung the bell, to summon her butler to show me out.'

'Did you wait for the butler to appear, sir?'

'No. I took my leave of Mrs Haddington, and left the room. The butler reached the hall as I was coming down the half-flight of stairs from Mrs Haddington's sitting-room.'

'And what, sir, was your reason for paying this call?'

Silence followed this question. Poulton was frowningly studying his finger-tips. After a moment he again looked up. 'Yes, I see. You are bound to ask me that. I shall make no secret of the fact that my call was not of a friendly nature. Mrs Haddington had been ringing up my house to ask for news of my wife: I went to Charles Street to inform her that my wife was unwell, and that it was my fixed intention to put an end to the intimacy that had hitherto flourished between them.'

'Yes, sir? And why was that your fixed intention?'

'I did not care for the connaissance.'

'That, sir, is not quite a good enough answer.'

Poulton smiled faintly. 'I suppose not. Very well, Chief Inspector! I see that I must rely upon your discretion. Before she married me, my wife was one of the more prominent members of a set which prided itself on its total disregard for accepted conventions. I do not propose to divulge any of her indiscretions to you, but I will say, between these walls, that there had been indiscretions. By some means, unknown to me, Mrs Haddington had been put in possession of the details of perhaps the most serious of these. The price of her silence was not money, but sponsorship into the class of Society to which my wife holds the key.'

'And when, sir, did you discover this?'

'Not, unfortunately, at the time.'

'No, sir. Only after Seaton-Carew's murder, in fact?'

'Recently,' amended Poulton.

'Mr Poulton, I hope you mean to stop fencing with me. I know a lot more than I did two days ago, and you may believe me when I say that I know beyond doubt that Lady Nest is now in a Home, being cured of the drug-habit. I also know that it was Seaton-Carew who supplied her with cocaine.'

He encountered a glance as keen and as searching as a surgeon's scalpel. 'Have you proof of that?'

'I have proof that cocaine was found in Seaton-Carew's flat; I have proof that Lady Nest was not his only victim.'

'I see.' Poulton was silent for a moment. 'I was never sure, myself. I suspected him, but no more.'

Hemingway waited. After a pause, he said: 'Was this the hold Mrs Haddington had over your wife, sir?'

'No.'

'When did you discover that Lady Nest was an – was taking the stuff, sir?'

'After Seaton-Carew's murder, and your visit to my house. How much of what I say to you do you propose to make public property?'

'That will depend on circumstances, sir.'

Poulton smiled faintly. 'I understand you. I did not murder Mrs Haddington, so I must hope that "circumstance" will not arise. Seaton-Carew's death came as an appalling shock to my wife. Under the stress of – considerable emotion – she was induced to confide in me. I should add that her nerves have never been robust, and that I did not suspect what you have discovered until an old friend of mine, who is an eminent physician, met her in my house, and – confided to me his suspicion. When the source of her supply was murdered and it seemed probable that you would discover what that source was, I was able to persuade her to go into a Home.'

'You knew it was Seaton-Carew?'

'Only on Tuesday night, after his death.'

'Did Lady Nest also divulge to you that she had been blackmailed by Mrs Haddington?'

'She did.' Poulton looked steadily at Hemingway. 'I visited Mrs Haddington yesterday to inform her that I was in full possession of all the facts of that old scandal, and that I should have no hesitation, in certain eventualities, in placing the matter in the hands of the police. There was no conceivable reason why I should

312

have murdered her, nor did I do so. I have no more to say than that.'

'At what hour did you leave Charles Street, sir?'

'At a quarter-to-seven. I was keeping my eye on the time, for I had a 'plane to catch.'

'So far as you know, there was no other visitor on the premises?'

'I saw no one. Mrs Haddington led me into the room she calls her boudoir. No one was present but ourselves.'

'Thank you, sir. I won't keep you any longer now,' said Hemingway.

The Inspector, having shown Poulton out, said: 'Och, you have let him go, but he is a canny one!'

'I can pick him up any time I want to,' Hemingway replied shortly. 'I want those two lengths of wire, Sandy! Send down for them!'

But the gleaming brass wire which had been twisted round Seaton-Carew's neck occupied him for only a minute. Over the other, older, length, he pored for an appreciable space of time, his magnifying-glass steadily focused on its ends. He said suddenly: 'Come here, Sandy, and take a look! Would you say this wire has been used to hang a picture with?'

The Inspector studied it intently. 'You are right!' he said. 'The ends have been straightened, but you can see where the kink was, for the strands are untwisted just there. What might that mean?'

Hemingway leaned back in his chair, his eyes narrowed. 'That's what I'm wondering. That it was taken off a picture seems certain. Where was the picture?'

'*Mo chreach!* It might be anywhere!'

313

'Yes, it might be anywhere, if the second murder was premeditated. If it wasn't, then I say that picture was in all probability hanging in Mrs Haddington's house.' He paused. 'And, putting two and two together, most likely in that sitting-room of hers! We can but try! Get me through to Bromley, Sandy! I shall want him.'

When the two police-cars drew up in Charles Street, their drivers were unable to park them in front of Mrs Haddington's house, since a raking sports-model was already occupying most of the available space there. 'Terrible Timothy!' surmised Hemingway.

They were admitted, not by Thrimby, but by the parlourmaid, who showed no disposition to linger in their vicinity. Informed by Hemingway that he wished merely to go up to the boudoir, she shuddered in a marked way, and said that anyone could say what they liked, but go into the boudoir she would not. She added that she had always been sensitive, right from a child, producing in corroboration of this statement Mother's apparently oft-repeated remark that she was too sensitive to live. She then withdrew to the nether regions, there to regale her companions with a graphic description of her symptoms on opening the door to the police.

The Chief Inspector, followed by his various assistants, proceeded up the stairs. He had been aware of a shadowy figure hovering on the half-landing, and when he reached the head of the flight he found Miss Spennymoor, shrinking nervously back against the wall, a black garment over one arm, and in her other hand an incongruous bouquet of Parma violets. He paused, recalling that he had seen her earlier in the day. Miss Spennymoor, prefixing her words with a gasp, hurried into speech.

'I hope you'll pardon me! Reely, I didn't hardly know what to do, for I was just coming downstairs, only, of course, when I saw you in the hall I stepped back, for one doesn't like to intrude at such a time, does one? But I should be very upset if you was to think I was hanging about for no reason! No, I was coming downstairs to ask Miss Birtley what I could be getting on with, because Miss Pickhill asked me if I would run her up something to wear at once, and got the material and all, so naturally I said I should be pleased to, but it ought to be fitted on her, and reely I don't like to set another stitch till I'm *sure*! Such a kind lady – well, reely, no one could be more considerate, and I should like to have her mourning-dress made *nice*. Quite overcome I was, when she said I might work in the dining-room, with a nice fire, and one of the maids to bring me a cup of tea. Well, anyone appreciates things like that, don't they? So I just popped up to fit the dress, and I said to the maid, I'll carry the flowers up to Miss Cynthia, I said, not knowing that Miss Pickhill had taken her off to the dentist not twenty minutes ago. They say it never rains but it pours, don't they? It came on after lunch, and oil of cloves didn't do a bit of good, nor anything else, poor young lady! Not that it's anything to wonder at, for with all the upset, and getting the police in on top of it – not that I mean anything personal, but there it is! Well, it's bound to create a lot of talk, isn't it? And then the butler going off duty, like he has, without so much as a by your leave – ! Enough to give anyone the toothache, as I said to Mrs Foston, for reely one hardly knows what the world is coming to, what with the maids creating, and that Frenchman walking out of the house with not so much as a moment's warning!'

Hemingway managed to stem the tide of this eloquence by saying: 'Chronic, isn't it! I think I saw you here this morning, didn't I, Miss . . . ?'

'Spennymoor is the name,' disclosed Miss Spennymoor, blushing faintly. She added: 'Court Dressmaker! You are looking at this lovely bunch of violets. They're not mine, of course. Oh dear me, no! They're for poor Miss Cynthia. Lord Guisborough left them with his own hands, just after Miss Cynthia had gone off to the dentist, it must have been, though I never heard her go, the door being shut. I was just about to go upstairs to find Miss Pickhill when he called, and as soon as I heard his voice, of course I slipped back into the dining-room at once, for although I don't suppose for a moment he'd recognise me, not after all these years, you can't be too careful, can you? And, though I'm sure I never meant to say anything, perhaps I was the wee-est bit indiscreet, talking to Mrs Haddington the other day. Well, I knew his poor mother. Oh, ever so well I knew her! And when I got to remembering old times – well, anyone's tongue will run away with them, won't it?'

'Easily!' responded Hemingway, in his friendliest tone. 'And what was it you were telling Mrs Haddington about Lord Guisborough?'

'*Nothing* against him!' Miss Spennymoor assured him. 'Only knowing Maisie like I did – that was his mother, you know, and if ever there was a Lad – ! I couldn't hardly fail to know the ins and outs of it all. Because I was dresser to all the girls when she first took up with Hilary Guisborough, and I don't know how it was, but I always had a fancy for Maisie, and she for me, and I often used to visit her.'

'After he married her?' suggested Hemingway.

'Oh, and before he did! They used to live in a little flat, Pimlico way, because at that time he'd got some kind of a job. He lost it later, of course, but that was Hilary all over! Well, as the girls used to say, what could you expect of a man with a soppy name like that? Still, I never heard Maisie complain, never once, and, give him his due, he married her within a month of her twins being born, which made it all right, only naturally it isn't a thing anyone would want talked about. Well, is it? Maisie used to feel it a lot, because, say what you like, legitimated isn't the same as being born in wedlock, not however you look at it! Maisie used to say to me that if there was one thing she couldn't bear it was having Hilary's grand relations look down on her twins, which is why I'm sorry I ever mentioned the matter, because they none of them knew anything about Maisie, not till Hilary wrote and told his people he'd been married for years, and got a couple of kids. They behaved very properly, by all accounts, having Maisie and the twins down to stay, and all, but it was a great strain, and she told me wild horses wouldn't drag her there again, and nor they ever did, because she died before they invited her again. Well, they always say there's a silver lining to every cloud, don't they? But I never ought to have mentioned it to anyone, and I hope you won't repeat it, because it wouldn't be a very nice thing for Lance, and him a lord, to have people saying he'd had to be legitimated!'

This anecdote, though of human interest, was not felt to have contributed anything of marked value to the problem confronting the Chief Inspector. 'Though, mind you, Sandy,' he said, as, having parted from Miss

Spennymoor, he entered the boudoir, 'I've always thought it was a bit unfair, the way they just stamp Legitimated on birth certificates. Doing a thing by halves, is what I call it. I daresay Lord Guisborough doesn't like it much, but try as I will I can't fancy that as a motive for murdering Mrs Haddington. What's more, from what I saw of that sister of his, she'd fair revel in having been born on the wrong side of the blanket, and she seemed to me to be the master-mind of that little party.' He glanced round the walls of the boudoir, which were hung with a few dubious water-colours, mounted and framed in gilt. None of them was of sufficient size or weight to have made it necessary to hang them on hooks from the picture-rail. Hemingway pulled on a pair of wash-leather gloves, and began to make a systematic tour, lifting each picture away from, the wall, and peering to see how it was hung. At the third masterpiece – The Isles of the West, from which Inspector Grant had averted his revolted gaze – he paused. He cast one triumphant glance at his assistant, and lifted the picture down, and held it with its back to the assembled company. A piece of string had been knotted to the rings screwed into it: virgin string, as everyone saw at a glance, with not a speck of dust upon it.

'*A Chruitheir!*' uttered Grant, under his breath.

'Very likely!' said Hemingway. 'You can get busy on this one, Tom!' He bent to examine the string, and suddenly raised his head. 'String!' He turned, and jabbed a finger at the desk. 'Top right-hand drawer, Sandy! Also a pair of large scissors in a leather holder!'

'I remember.' The Inspector pulled open the drawer, handed the ball of string to his superior, and, more circumspectly, using his handkerchief, picked up the scissors, in their case, and stood waiting for Sergeant Bromley to take them from him.

'Same string – and that means nothing!' said Hemingway, comparing the ball with the string attached to the picture. 'Ordinary string, used for tying up parcels.' He drew forth a length of tarnished picture-wire from his pocket, uncoiled it, slid the ends through the rings on the back of the frame, lightly twisted them where the strands were already a little unravelled, and observed the result with a critical eye. 'As near the same length as the string as makes no odds!' he remarked. 'That seems to settle that! Got anything, Tom?'

'Yes, but I can't tell you yet if the prints are the same as any we took on Tuesday, sir. I'll have to take 'em back to the Department.'

Hemingway nodded. 'Do that now. Rush it!' He rehung the picture on the wall, and turned, holding out a gloved hand for the scissors. Inspector Grant gave them to him, and he drew them gently out of their coloured leather sheath. 'Of course, you can't say with any certainty how a pair of large scissors comes by its scratches,' he remarked. He handed the scissors to Bromley. 'Go over them carefully, Tom!'

'I will, of course, sir,' said the Sergeant, receiving them tenderly. 'But if you can see your way through this case – well!'

The Chief Inspector, his gaze travelling slowly round the room, vouchsafed no response to this. His mind was plainly elsewhere; and it was not until a few moments after the Finger-print unit had departed that Grant ventured to address him.

319

'If the murder was committed with the wire from that picture, it was not Poulton that did it!' he said.

Hemingway's eyes came to rest on his face. 'Oh, wasn't it?' he said. 'Why not?'

'Och, would he take down the picture and remove the wire from it under the poor lady's very eyes?' demanded the Inspector.

'Certainly not. What makes you so sure she was in this room with him the whole time he was here?'

The Inspector stared at him. 'But – !' He was silent, suddenly, frowning over it.

'Going a bit too fast, Sandy. All we know is what Thrimby and Poulton himself told us. According to Thrimby, he arrived here at about 6.25; according to both of them, he left at a quarter-to-seven. That gave him twenty minutes, during which time only he and Mrs Haddington knew what happened. We have only his word for it they were together in the boudoir throughout. I admit, it doesn't seem likely she'd have left the room, but she might have: we don't know.'

'Well,' said the Inspector slowly, 'supposing she left him to fetch something – it would not have given him much time, would it?'

'No, it wouldn't, and one would say he'd have wanted a bit of time to find that string – if it was that string and those scissors which were used! I don't say I think it was Poulton, but I do say it's still a possibility, and one we won't lose sight of. Setting him aside for the moment, who are we left with? I don't think it was Miss Birtley: I've considered her case carefully, and I don't see how she could have got to Earl's Court and back in the time. There's young Butterwick, who dashed out of the house, leaving his stick behind him; and there's Lord Guisborough, who also went off in a rage, slamming the door behind him. Neither was actually seen to leave the premises; either, I suppose, could have concealed himself somewhere – in the cloakroom, say – until the coast was clear, and then slipped up to this room, and waited for Mrs Haddington to come in. Look at those windows! They're both in slight embrasures, and you see how the thick curtains would shut off the whole embrasure. Plenty of room for a man to stand behind them, and I'll bet they were drawn by tea-time. Now tell me what possible reason either of those two can have for murdering Mrs Haddington, and we shall both be happy! And don't say Guisborough did it because she flung his birth in his teeth, and he was touchy, because I don't like tall stories, and never did!'

'It could not have been the doctor?' Inspector Grant said doubtfully.

'You've got him on the brain!'

'It's the way he keeps on turning up!' apologised Grant. 'If you mean he was here in the middle of the day, there's no dispute about that: he admitted he was. Are you asking me to believe he lurked in the house till nearly seven o'clock at night? Talk sense! I saw him myself this afternoon!'

'Ach, I did not think it was he! I have wondered if Butterwick too was in this drug-racket, and yet I do not think it. That he is an addict himself is possible, but I saw none of the signs. Moreover, he was wearing his evening-dress when I found him, and he would not have had time to have gone home, let alone have changed his clothes – if he was in the Opera House for the first ballet.'

'Well, unless he's a better actor than what I take him for, I should say he was there in time for the first ballet. I know that type! So that leaves us with Lord Guisborough, who either murdered Mrs Haddington because she didn't want her daughter to marry him – funny thing, that! I should have thought a chap with a handle to his name was just what she was after! – or because Miss What's-her-name had told her his parents' wedding was just a trifle late.'

The Inspector shook his head. 'It will not do. He is a foolish, and maybe a violent young man, but he would not murder anybody for such silly reasons as those. Besides, it was known that he was coming to see Mrs Haddington! Do you tell me he came with murder in his head?'

'At the moment, I'm not telling you anything. He wouldn't have had to have had it in his head, though. We do know they had a row, for she told Thrimby not to let him into the house again. If he did it, it was something that happened at that interview which made him decide to bump her off. In which case, he dashed downstairs, grabbed his coat, slammed the door, and nipped up to the boudoir again, which he knew was empty, and –'

'He had no time!' the Inspector ejaculated. 'Mrs Haddington rang to have him shown out, and she herself came to the head of the first flight of stairs!'

'Yes, because his High and Mightiness took such a time to answer the bell! Plenty of time for anyone who knew the house! And then she went up to the girl's room, and Thrimby went down to the basement, and while they were both nicely out of the way, his lordship got to work on the picture. There's only one thing wrong with that reconstruction: there's no motive! Pity! The more I think about it the more I like it! I mean, it would have been quite neat, wouldn't it? We were bound to think the same man committed both murders, and there he was alibi'd up to the ears for the first one, never even under suspicion! Of course, my trouble is I don't know enough about the fun and games they get up to in this precious Russia of his. If I was to discover that they go around murdering their mothers-in-law before ever they get engaged –'

'*Nach ist thu!*' interrupted the Inspector severely. 'Will you not whisht now? You have only the butler's word for it she did not favour the young lord!'

'No, I haven't! The Blonde Bombshell told me so this very day, let alone the row he had with Mrs Haddington, and her telling Thrimby never to let him in again!'

'That is true,' admitted the Inspector. 'I would not have thought it of the *cailleach*! Was it a Duke she meant to get for her daughter?'

'According to what I've managed to gather it was Terrible Timothy she had her eye on, if "the calyack" means Mrs Haddington, which I take it it does! It gives me a better idea of her than I had before, but I agree with you it isn't what you'd have expected of her. What I can't make out is why she kept on inviting Lord Guisborough to the house, if she didn't like his politics. You can't suppose he ever made any secret of them! Perhaps she suddenly found out that he hadn't got any money to speak of or –' He stopped, reminding his subordinate irresistibly of a terrier winding a rat. 'Good God, Sandy!' he exclaimed. 'Don't tell me I've missed something!'

'I will not, then,' said the Inspector soothingly.

'You keep quiet, and whatever you do don't start spouting Gaelic at me! You're putting me off!' said Hemingway. 'What did that lawyer-chap say? She rang him up about repairs and they had a little chat after that about the Marriage and Legitimacy Acts. Then she tells Lord Guisborough she'd like to see him, and he comes, and – Here, the man I want is Terrible Timothy!'

'Och, what will you be wanting him for?' demanded the Inspector protestingly.

'I want him because he's the handiest lawyer I can think of!' replied Hemingway.

Mr Harte was discovered in the library, arguing with his betrothed on the propriety of her accepting his mother's urgent invitation to her to seek asylum in Berkshire. Miss Birtley was moved by the news that Lady Harte, hearing her story, had been seized with a crusading fervour, and was not only determined to spread the mantle of her approval over her but was already formulating stern, and rather alarming, plans to bring her late employer to belated justice; but she maintained that until such time as Miss Pickhill had coerced or persuaded her niece to retire with her to Putney, her duty chained her to Charles Street.

'Hallo, here's Hemingway!' said Timothy as the Chief Inspector walked in. 'Let's put it up to him!'

Appealed to by both parties, the Chief Inspector firmly refused to become embroiled in matters beyond his ken.

'Cowardly, very cowardly!' said Timothy. 'All right, my girl, you'll have my Mamma descending upon you, that's all! What brings you back again, Hemingway?'

'Never you mind what brings me back, sir! Just you tell me what you know about the Legitimacy Act!'

'The questions the police ask one!' marvelled Timothy. Behind the amusement in them, his eyes were keen, and speculative. Keeping them on Hemingway's face, he said: 'It is an Act, Chief Inspector, passed in 1926, legalising the position of children who were born out of wedlock, but whose parents afterwards married one another.'

'That's what I thought,' said Hemingway. 'What it means is, that as long as you *do* get married, your children are legitimate, doesn't it?'

'Yes, within certain limits,' agreed Timothy.

'What limits, sir?'

'Well, neither parent must have been married to someone else at the time of the child's birth, for instance; and legitimated offspring are debarred from inheriting titles, or the estates that go with them. Otherwise –' He broke off. 'I seem to have uttered something momentous!'

'Yes, sir,' said Hemingway. 'You have!'

Twenty

'**W**ell,' said Mrs James Kane, replenishing her
husband's cup, 'I'm thankful to have you
back again, anyway!'

Mr James Kane, luxuriously ensconced by his own
fireside once more, bit into his third crumpet, and said
somewhat thickly: 'Cuckoo!'

'*Not*,' said Mrs Kane, with dignity, 'because I was in
the least anxious about you, but I thought I should either
have to come to town myself, or go mad, if it went on
much longer! All I had to go on were those lurid reports
in the papers, and a letter from your mother which I
couldn't make head or tail of!'

'I rang you up every night!' said Mr Kane indignantly.

'Yes, darling, and every time I asked you anything,
you said you couldn't talk over the telephone!' retorted
the wife of his bosom, with some asperity.

'Well, I couldn't. I did tell you there wasn't anything
for you to worry about!'

'That was when I looked out the trains to London,'
said Mrs Kane grimly. 'And if it hadn't been for Cook
having to go home to nurse her mother, I should have
come up, let me tell you!'

'Oh, my God, has the Cook left?'

'She's coming back. At least, that's what she *says*. Anyway, Nanny and I can manage! Never mind about that! What actually happened? Tell me all about it!'

'I don't think there's anything much to tell, really,' said the maddening male reflectively. 'It was easy to see Hemingway never suspected young Timothy for as much as a split second, which is what mattered, as far as we're concerned. I only stood by because of Beulah. At one time it did look a bit as though she might have had a hand in the affair, and I thought, if that was so, Timothy would need a bit of support.'

'Yes, dear,' said Mrs Kane, schooled into patience by thirteen years of marriage.

'Of course, he couldn't possibly have had anything to do with Mrs Haddington's murder,' pursued Mr Kane, licking his buttery fingers in a very vulgar way. ''Matter of fact, Hemingway did a pretty neat bit of detection, taken all round. I should think, myself, that Guisborough must have been a bit unhinged. I mean, from what Timothy told me about the way he nattered about the Equality of Man, you wouldn't have expected him to have cared two hoots whether he had a title or not! What's more, if he'd stopped to think, he must have realised that the whole thing might have come out at any moment! I mean, you never know when you may have to produce your birth-certificate, do you? He might have wanted to apply for a passport, or something – though, I suppose, as a matter of fact, that wouldn't have mattered much, because the authorities wouldn't have been worrying about whether he was legitimate or only legitimated! Still – ! Young Timothy put Hemingway on to that, all unbeknownst. Then Hemingway got Guisborough's finger-prints, as soon as he heard the prints on the picture-frame didn't belong to any of the suspects for the first murder, and after that it was all U.P.! Silly young fool seems to have come badly unstuck when he was arrested. Nasty business, whichever way you look at it! Main spring of both murders, one nit-witted blonde!'

'What has happened to her?'

'Whisked off by formidable maiden-aunt. She'll probably marry a wealthy stockbroker within the year – if there are any wealthy stockbrokers left!'

Mrs Kane shivered. 'However nit-witted she may be, it's pretty ghastly for her, knowing that her mother was a murderess.'

'Won't know it,' said Jim, drawing out his pouch, and beginning to fill a pipe. 'Hemingway will put in a report, and it'll be Murder by Persons Unknown.'

'Did he tell you so?'

'More or less. After Guisborough's arrest, Timothy got hold of him, and he came round to Paper Buildings, to have a drink, and talk over old times. Lord, do you realise how many years it is since –'

'Yes,' said Mrs Kane. 'I expect you had a lovely evening, but I don't want to remember those particular old times, thank you, dear! Isn't the girl bound to wonder about that first murder, and perhaps guess?'

'I shouldn't think so. As far as I could see, she isn't given either to speculation or to the process of reasoned thought. What's more, it stood out a mile that she didn't care two hoots for her mother. According to what the aunt poured into my ears yesterday, Mrs Haddington's obsession about her took the form of sending her to expensive boarding-schools, arranging for her to spend her holidays winter-sporting, or sun-bathing, lavishing money on her, but rarely having her with her, until she brought her out.'

'But why?'

'Not disclosed. Timothy thinks Mrs Haddington and Seaton-Carew were hand-in-glove in various shady undertakings. Doesn't seem to be much doubt they lived together, so I daresay that was why Cynthia was kept away.'

'It's all quite horrible!' Mrs Kane said. 'What will happen to Lord Guisborough?'

'He'll stand his trial, of course. I daresay he'll get a few trick-cyclists to go into the witness-box, and tell the court he'd got some kind of a fixation, or whatever they call it, due to seeing his mother taking her false teeth out, when he was five years old, which makes it all right and above-board for him to go about murdering people who get in his way. In fact,' said Mr Kane gloomily, 'it wouldn't in the least surprise me if we find ourselves helping to keep him at Broadmoor! Except,' he added, on a more hopeful note, 'that Timothy says juries have got a lot more common-sense than you'd think, to look at them.'

Having packed his pipe to his satisfaction, he struck a match, and became partially enveloped in a smoke-cloud. Mrs Kane at last reached the nub of the matter. 'And what about the adventuress?' she asked. 'The line was so bad last night I couldn't hear you properly at all. I *thought* you said she was going down to Chamfreys!'

Mr Kane grinned. 'I did. All due to my well-known tact and diplomacy, too! I passed on to Mother what

Timothy told me, which wasn't a lot, but quite enough for Mother. I don't know the rights of it, but it does seem as though Beulah was made a sort of catspaw of by some nasty piece of work she was employed by in the City. Anyway, Timothy said she'd had the rawest of raw deals, the which I faithfully reported. You know Mother! All up in arms in defence of her sex before you could say knife! As a matter of fact, I think she and Beulah will get on all right. I didn't take to the girl at first, but when you get to know her she isn't a bad kid at all. Madly in love with Timothy!'

'She is?' Mrs Kane said quickly.

'Oh, thinks he's the bee's roller-skates!'

'Then your Mother *will* like her! Are they actually engaged?'

'Yes, but nobody knows it yet.'

The door opened to admit Miss Susan Kane and Master William Kane, washed, brushed, and escorted by their amiable tyrant. 'Are Mummy and Daddy ready for us?' enquired this lady winningly. 'May we play in here while Nanny pops the casserole in the oven? Ever so excited we are to have Daddy back again, and to hear all about the new Auntie we're going to have, aren't we, my ducks?'

So saying, the despot surrendered Master William Kane to his mother, smiled kindly upon Mr Kane, and withdrew, bearing the tea-tray with her.

'Pat!' said Mr Kane thunderously. 'This is the End! Either you get rid of –'

'Yes, dear, but *not* in front of the children!' said Mrs Kane hastily.